# FITZWILLIAM DARCY, MAN OF FORTUNE

## A PRIDE & PREJUDICE VARIATION

JENNIFER JOY

D1712700

"Fitzwilliam Darcy, Man of Fortune: A Pride & Prejudice Variation
Dimensions of Darcy, Book 5"

This is a work of fiction. The characters, locations, and events portrayed in this book are fictitious or are used fictitiously. Any similarity to real persons, living or dead, is purely coincidental and not intended by the author.

Published by Jennifer Joy

Email: contact@jenniferjoywrites.com

ISBN-13: 978-1-944795-42-9

Chapter 30                          261
Chapter 31                          271
Chapter 32                          280
Chapter 33                          287
Chapter 34                          294
Chapter 35                          301
Chapter 36                          313
Chapter 37                          324
Chapter 38                          334
Chapter 39                          344
Chapter 40                          352
Chapter 41                          363
Chapter 42                          371
Chapter 43                          378
Chapter 44                          388
Chapter 45                          397
Chapter 46                          409
Chapter 47                          415
Chapter 48                          425
Chapter 49                          432
Chapter 50                          444
Epilogue                            454

*Thank You!*                        465
*About the Author*                  467
*Other Books by Jennifer Joy*       469

# CONTENTS

*Free Book*                          v

Chapter 1                            1
Chapter 2                            11
Chapter 3                            20
Chapter 4                            30
Chapter 5                            38
Chapter 6                            48
Chapter 7                            56
Chapter 8                            67
Chapter 9                            76
Chapter 10                           85
Chapter 11                           93
Chapter 12                           100
Chapter 13                           111
Chapter 14                           120
Chapter 15                           127
Chapter 16                           135
Chapter 17                           144
Chapter 18                           154
Chapter 19                           160
Chapter 20                           171
Chapter 21                           183
Chapter 22                           193
Chapter 23                           205
Chapter 24                           215
Chapter 25                           222
Chapter 26                           230
Chapter 27                           239
Chapter 28                           246
Chapter 29                           254

FREE BOOK

**Want a free novelette?**
**Join Jennifer Joy's Newsletter!**

# CHAPTER 1

LONDON

AUGUST 30, 1812

Spilled ale and urine assaulted Fitzwilliam Darcy's senses. The soles of his boots squished against the floor of The Devil's Tavern. Adding insult to injury, the putrid water of the Thames lurked a stone's throw away.

Wishing he could breathe without smelling, Darcy squinted at Wickham in the dim, smoky room and wondered how his old friend had fallen so low. To think he had once considered Wickham as close as a brother.

Darcy never would have found this place had he not

coerced Mrs. Younge to reveal Wickham's where-abouts. How could the profligate bring Miss Lydia to a place like this? Darcy would never expose a young lady he claimed to love to this thieves' den near the water-ways—a tavern inn in the worst part of the east end of town where a man's coat was valued more than his life.

Darcy had dressed accordingly, careful not to draw attention to himself. He could neither afford to be mistaken as wealthy (a tempting target for thieves), or a seafaring man (a target for the press gangs desperate to fill the Navy's demand for able-bodied men). Even so, Darcy could not bring himself to sit or touch anything in the establishment. Already, his skin crawled.

In contrast, Wickham lounged against the soot-smeared wall, the rough bench creaking under his weight. Even in his red regimental coat and polished boots, he gave the air of a gentleman on the rocks. Pickpockets would not bother with him.

Leaning forward, Wickham clasped his hands together on top of the turned barrel that served as a table between them. "I have no intention of marrying Lydia when I have an heiress ripe for the taking under my influence. Nothing you can say shall change my mind. I would rather attach myself to a rich, toothless harpy than saddle myself with Lydia Bennet."

Darcy clenched his fingers into a fist, feeling every muscle in his body tense. Wickham did not have a sixpence to scratch with; nevertheless, he presumed to negotiate. Not for the first time, Darcy was tempted to bash the smirk from his face.

But he was a Darcy. Darcys did not give in to their base desires or impulses.

He controlled his rage and continued with his plan. He would not leave that vile room until the Bennets' reputation was salvaged.

It was the least he could do for Elizabeth, though she must never know of his interference. She would think he was attempting to buy her affection. He could not bear for her to think worse of him than she already did. Or worse still, to prove her right.

No, he would right his wrongs and live alone with the consequences of his infernal pride that had built a haughty, reticent image of him in Elizabeth's mind.

Even from afar—in distance and time, even after her impassioned refusal—Darcy loved her. He had thought perhaps there might be hope.

Until Wickham.

Darcy had believed himself free of him, and now Darcy would pay for his error in judgment the rest of his days. He had tried to protect the Bennets from Wickham, but his warning had been too weak, too late. He had failed Elizabeth.

And now he would spare her.

One irrevocable act to appease his conscience. One final interference to ensure she would have a chance of being as happy as he wished her to be.

His one path to redemption was right now, in this

moment, and he would not let it slip. For Elizabeth, Darcy would bribe a man he despised and yet to whom he would make himself a brother. "I shall make it worth your while to marry Lydia Bennet on the morrow."

Wickham chuckled and leaned back, stretching his legs in front of him.

Darcy was not joking, nor would he negotiate his terms. The marriage license was secured, as was the clergyman in Wickham's parish who, with a few extra coins, was willing to perform the service at such short notice. Darcy would give Wickham no time to think or renege once he agreed. He would accept now or get nothing.

Pulling a thick parchment out of his pocket, Darcy pushed it across the barrel to Wickham.

Wickham jolted forward, grabbing the paper greedily. "A commission in the regulars. How did you secure this?"

"That is of no concern to you." His cousin Colonel Richard Fitzwilliam had called in several favors, and Darcy had paid a premium to obtain the commission as quickly as they could arrange it. The parchment in Wickham's grubby hands offered not only a reliable living with room to advance, but it also represented the prestige he so craved.

Not giving Wickham time to consider, Darcy pulled a stash of receipts out of his other pocket. He retained every bill he had covered for the leech over the years for protection should Wickham attempt to blackmail him or Georgiana. Never could he have dreamed that his caution would benefit Elizabeth. Dropping the receipts, he let them smack against the table and spread. "Your debts, paid in full."

Wickham thumbed through the pile, the sum of which was over one thousand pounds.

"Is that all of them?" Darcy demanded.

Struggling to maintain his nonchalance when he knew he had been bought, Wickham sneered, "Your man is thorough."

As he should be. Darcy remunerated Hastings well for his exertions.

Darcy moved on to the next enticement. "In addition to the commission and paid debts, I shall settle one thousand pounds on Lydia to be paid once you sign the wedding register on the morrow, witnessed by myself and Mr. Gardiner, who shall act as Miss Lydia's guardian in lieu of Mr. Bennet."

Mr. Gardiner was as eager as Darcy to see his niece married. He had agreed to hide Darcy's role from Mr. Bennet, who should not be greatly inconvenienced with the paltry one hundred pounds per annum plus the settlement of Wickham's debts in Meryton. Darcy would have been happy to spare Elizabeth's father that expense as well, but he had to lend some credibility to Wickham's sudden marriage to the gentleman's most undesirable daughter. Mr. Bennet was too clever by half, as was Elizabeth. They would suspect another's involvement if it was too easy.

While Wickham considered the offer, Darcy pressed his advantage. "Hastings will ensure your travel costs to Newcastle are covered. Additionally, he will secure suitable accommodations for you and Mrs. Wickham that shall be ready after you have been seen as a properly wed couple and have allowed your wife to bid her adieus to her family. I think a fortnight should suffice."

Wickham scoffed but held onto the commission firmly, obviously aware that it promised instant relief. "You have thought of everything, as you always do. However, I could really use that thousand pounds tonight. I owe some unsavory men—"

Darcy shook his head firmly. He would not budge. "Once I witness your signature in the register—and only then—shall I pay. That is my final word on the subject."

And now, the ultimate incentive. Collecting the pile of receipts, Darcy tucked them inside his pocket. "If you do not accept my conditions, I shall call in your debts."

That had Wickham's full attention.

"The commission does you no good if you are in debtor's prison." If looks could kill, Wickham would have impaled Darcy with his eyes. "Marry Miss Lydia, and you may leave for your new commission free of debts, reclaim your dignity, and be a thousand pounds richer."

Wickham clenched his jaw and slammed his fist against the barrel. Darcy had won, and Wickham knew it. "Devil take you, Darcy. I am not in a position to refuse," he hissed through gritted teeth.

"Do we have an agreement?" Darcy folded his arms over his chest and glared down at Wickham.

Bowing his head, Wickham snarled, "You have my word. I shall marry Lydia."

Darcy turned toward the door. Breaking glass, bawdy laughter, and angry, drunken shouts awaited him on the other side of the street. It was only a matter of time before shots were fired. Uncrossing his arms, he said, "Meet me at St. Clement's at ten o'clock on the morrow."

Without further leave, he departed, shoving his way through the odorous bodies, trays of rancid beef, and raised tankards. As wretched as the Thames smelled, it was a relief to breathe the night air outside the tavern.

He would order a bath the moment he returned to Darcy House. A couple of glasses of his finest brandy ought to dispel the remnants of the tavern.

Glancing cautiously about, Darcy walked swiftly to the corner, his gaze roving for a hackney to convey him far away from this unsavory neighborhood. He wished he could have brought his own carriage, but a gang of ruffians would have harmed his men and stolen his conveyance.

He rounded a corner, raising his hand when a hackney came into view, his voice catching in his throat when he heard a scuffle behind him.

Nerves on point, he turned. There was a blur of motion, then his hat flew off his head. At the same time, he heard glass shatter and felt his head part. Blurry and unbalanced, he flung out, catching his assailant with his fist.

"Pretendin' to be a gent. Almost didn't recognize him," he heard in a strange man's voice.

He felt another hand—a rough one that scratched against Darcy's shaved cheeks—pressing something against his mouth and nose, smothering him. "Don't forget how dangerous he be. Stay alert 'til he sleeps."

"Busted yer nose proper, didn't he," chuckled the other.

Two men. Darcy struggled, but the cloth smelled sweet, and his limbs grew heavy. He felt himself fading into the night.

"Elizabeth," he whispered before he succumbed to the black void.

DARCY WOKE HOURS LATER—DAYS later. He did not know.

His head swam and throbbed. Careful not to make any abrupt movements, he tested the strength of his limbs, discouraged when his body did not react as he needed it to.

Unable to do much more, he observed his surroundings. Curtains billowed at the small, round windows. Ruffles and frills adorning bright silks and shimmery fabrics were draped over the open door of a closet. A woman's room.

The ground swayed beneath him, and Darcy groaned. If this was a dream, he wished he would wake.

He thought back, remembering his assault. There had been two men. They had rough accents—Devonshire men. Seafaring men, no doubt. Press gangers? No, Darcy thought as he recalled bits of their conversation. They had spoken like they knew him. But how could that be? He had few friends in Devonshire, and certainly nobody of their sort. Where had they brought him? And why did it look like the inside of a mantua maker's shop?

They had claimed he was dangerous, pretending to be a gentleman. Clearly, they had mistaken him for someone else, but for whom? This was a horrible misunderstanding. He had to get out of there so he could make it to the church on time.

Had he already missed the wedding? Would Wickham marry Lydia if Darcy was not there to make him? Bile rose in his throat, and his stomach churned.

Darcy tried to sit up. He needed to find someone and tell them of their mistake.

From the shadows, a woman appeared. "Ye always

had a hard head." She reached down her side and pulled a dagger from her boot. "I'm not ready for ye yet," she sneered, her voice full of venom as she flung the dagger at him.

He tried to move, but she was faster. He heard the crack of the blunt end of the weapon against his skull before he felt it. Once again, Darcy slipped into oblivion.

## CHAPTER 2

Colonel Richard Fitzwilliam paced outside St. Clement Church, stopping only to glance at his pocket watch, then up and down the lengths of the street at increasingly frequent intervals. Still no Darcy.

Wickham had been unwilling to begin the ceremony until Darcy's arrival, and Richard could not remain under the same roof with the man without doing him bodily harm. The scoundrel was more interested in the thousand pounds promised to him than in salvaging the foolish girl's reputation he had so thoughtlessly ruined. The vicar had allowed an extra quarter of an hour, but more than that he could not spare.

Richard glanced at his pocket watch again. One minute remained.

It was not like Darcy to be late.

Counting the seconds down in his mind, Richard continued watching, peering inside every passing carriage and observing every passerby and rider. *Three, two, one.* He peeked at his watch to confirm. Time had run out.

Darcy was not here.

There would be no wedding today.

Heaving a sigh, Richard returned inside to see what he could salvage from the wreckage.

Mr. and Mrs. Gardiner stood on either side of their niece. Miss Lydia's bottom lip pouted and quivered, and she crossed her arms tightly in front of her as if she could not decide whether she would rather burst into tears or throw a spectacular tantrum.

He shook his head at Mr. Gardiner, then at the vicar. But though Darcy had failed to make an appearance, he had charged Richard to be there, and Richard would see his cousin's plans through in his absence. As insistent as Darcy had been, Richard feared something dreadful had happened. Why had he not called at Darcy House the night before? He should have called. What could have happened to Darcy—and when? Last night? This morning?

Darcy had been out of sorts lately, staying up all hours, sleeping at his club, and riding before daybreak. Richard had never seen him so restless. He had stayed with his agitated cousin as much as he could, but a soldier took advantage of rest when he had the opportunity. Now Richard felt guilty for sleeping soundly when he might have helped his cousin.

Shaking the worry that churned in his mind, Richard marched until he stood toe-to-toe with Wickham. In the same tone he used with the men under his command, Richard said, "I will witness the signature with Mr. Gardiner. We may proceed."

Wickham held up a hand, taking a step away from Richard. "Darcy was clear. I will not get a penny from him unless he personally witnesses my signature. Therefore, I will not marry if he is not here to witness it."

Gritting his teeth, Richard reminded himself that he was inside a church. Taking a deep breath, he forced his shoulders down and his fists to relax. When he found himself in a boxer's stance, he crossed his arms over his chest and, once again, reminded himself where he stood. His father would understand his predicament —he despised Wickham as much as Darcy and Richard —but his mother would not excuse him for a lapse of control. Not even when Wickham was on the receiving end of his knuckles.

Miss Lydia let out a wail that echoed off the walls and pierced his eardrums. Mrs. Gardiner shushed her with the help of the vicar, but Miss Lydia would make her displeasure known (albeit at a more respectable volume). Glaring at her betrothed, she whimpered, "He said he loved me."

If any good was to come of this situation, Richard

JENNIFER JOY

needed to act. And fast. He asked the vicar, "May we return on the morrow?"

"I have no additional time to spare until Friday. I am sorry. However, should my obligations allow for an earlier time, I promise to inform you of it."

Richard groaned. "That is well enough. Thank you for your patience." That did not suit at all, but it would have to do. Addressing the rest, he said, "I will consult immediately with Hastings to see what arrangement might be made. If the settlement was to be paid in ready money, then there is no reason why I cannot act as a witness in Darcy's stead."

Perhaps Hastings would know where Darcy might be. It was unlike Darcy to disappear without a word. Over the past week, he had been like a man possessed, working night and day to arrange this patched-over affair in order to give the Bennets some semblance of respectability after their youngest daughter's reckless behavior.

Richard knew Darcy would want him to see the wedding through. To help the Bennets. To save Elizabeth. He had been adamant. Richard would not give up.

His own conscience would not be at ease until he had done his part to put things right, especially since he had been the one to drive a wedge between his cousin and the lady he loved. Not that Darcy had not done a sufficiently thorough job of offending the lady on his own, but Richard owned that *he* certainly had not helped when he had let it slip that Darcy had "saved

14

Mr. Bingley from the inconvenience of a most imprudent marriage." Merely recalling the words made him wince. How was he to know that the lady about whom Darcy had expressed strong objections—to a man of deep passions like Darcy, nothing would be worse than his lady's indifference—was none other than Miss Elizabeth's sister?

Darcy held little hope of a reconciliation, but Richard hoped where his cousin dared not.

Which made Darcy's disappearance dashed inconvenient … and suspicious.

Richard watched Wickham. Did he benefit more from Darcy's disappearance than he stood to gain by marrying Miss Lydia? Richard had never known Wickham to be truly evil, merely opportunistic (which was bad enough). Still…

He steeled his voice and dropped his chin to his chest. "Do not leave town. Stay at the inn where I can find you."

Wickham's eyes widened. *Be afraid, you no-good blackguard. Be very afraid.*

Richard continued, his voice low, threatening, "If I find out you had anything to do with Darcy's delay, I shall not be as lenient as I have been in the past. You shall pay. Dearly. Nobody will hold me back." Not like last time.

Wickham swallowed hard, holding his hands in front of him. *Squirming coward.* "I had nothing to do with Darcy's failure to appear today. It is blasted—"

The vicar cleared his throat noisily, his displeasure plain.

Another hard swallow. "The delay is a grave inconvenience to me. My circumstances demand immediate payment. I am quite destitute."

Richard had no pity left for the likes of Wickham.

Miss Lydia emitted another wail, which softened from a scream to a harsh but level tone. "You promised me a fashionable apartment on Bond Street!" She turned to her aunt and uncle, pointing her finger crudely at her betrothed. "I do not want to marry him. He has deceived me, and I will not marry him." She jutted out her chin and huffed.

If ever there existed two individuals who stood to benefit from a good thrashing, it was this unwillingly pair. Richard tightened his arms over his chest.

Mrs. Gardiner raised her eyes heavenward, no doubt supplicating for forbearance.

Mr. Gardiner spoke firmly. "If you wanted our sympathy, you ought to have acted in a way befitting our compassion. As it is, I cannot pity you. What is more, I shall not permit your sisters to suffer the burden of your foolishness. Your selfishness would ruin them. Do you not see that you have already made your choice? You must marry Mr. Wickham."

Her face burned red, but she shed no tear. Tantrum it was, then.

"We will have no more outbursts, Lydia." Mrs. Gardiner patted her niece's shoulder, but her words were as firm as her husband's. "Every action has a consequence, and you shall reap what you have sown. This is the only way for you to save your reputation and that of your sisters. Surely you do not wish to drag them down with you?"

With each passing minute, Richard admired the Gardiners more. A firm hand was needed at this moment. They would ensure Miss Lydia's compliance. As for him, Richard would drag Wickham back to the church by the ear if need be, but he would see the louse hold up his end of Darcy's bargain. "I will seek out Hastings immediately," he said, bowing to take his leave.

He hoped Wickham was as desperate as he claimed, or the reprobate would surely ditch Miss Lydia and run. The sooner Richard fixed this mess, the better.

The Gardiners had little choice but to take their niece home with them, where she would likely remain until she wed.

Mr. Gardiner fell in beside him. He asked softly, "Do you really believe Wickham responsible for Mr. Darcy's delay? I see the necessity of Lydia marrying the man, but I will not attach her to a monster capable of harming another."

Richard pulled him aside, away from Wickham and the ladies. "Wickham is an irresponsible epicurean, but I have never known him to be cruel or violent. Darcy never would have arranged for your niece to wed him otherwise."

Mr. Gardiner nodded, his sigh audible. "Thank you, Colonel. I hold no delusion that theirs shall be a happy union. However, it is my hope they will at least learn to endure each other's company and make the most of it, as I know Lydia has been taught to do." Standing taller, he added, "We had better let you go. I, too, have an urgent message to send to my brother-in-law." He bunched his cheeks, the pained look in his eye revealing how little he looked forward to writing that letter. Richard could hardly blame the man.

They ushered Miss Lydia out of the church and into their carriage.

With one final reassurance of further communication with the vicar, Richard once again turned to leave, keeping Wickham in his sight and out of arm's reach. A man could only endure so much temptation.

Wickham turned to him with a sneer, but Richard cut him off before he could speak. "Stay where I can easily find you, or, I assure you, you shall have the Devil to pay." He turned, walking away at a brisk pace.

The sooner he could arrange to have the man shadowed, the better. He could not do it himself. The temptation to bend that perfect, straight nose or run the scoundrel through with his saber was too great, and that simply would not do … at least not until after the wedding.

Richard's murderous thoughts perversely lightened his heart. He was not so stupid as to ruin a brilliant military career over a ne'er-do-well like Wickham, but he took comfort in the possibility of the vile Don Juan vanishing.

As Darcy had vanished.

Richard hurried to the mews, his footsteps echoing in rhythm to his thoughts, his purpose: *Save Miss Elizabeth. Find Darcy.*

# CHAPTER 3

*E*lizabeth Bennet watched her sister Mary sit down at the pianoforte, knowing nothing good would come of it. Nothing could repair the day. Not the fine summer afternoon. Not the scent of roses wafting inside from the garden. And certainly not Mary's musical attempts.

Lydia was to marry—had doubtlessly already exchanged vows by now—that scoundrel Wickham. Uncle's message had reached them the evening prior, and nobody besides their mother spoke openly about it.

Mary played a dirge. Of the four Bennet daughters remaining at Longbourn, Lydia's sin fell heaviest on Mary, who seemed to think the other members of her family ought to atone for her errant sister's poor choices by afflicting their ears with mournful hymns.

Mama groaned. "Please, Mary, could you not play a

happier tune? It is, after all, the day of Lydia's wedding. Oh, how I wish they could have delayed a day or two so we could join them in London for the festivities."

Elizabeth exchanged a look with Jane, her eldest sister. While she was relieved to have their reputations spared, Elizabeth could not celebrate Lydia's union to such a man.

Mary obliged Mama with a heavy sigh, making it plain that she did so against her better judgment and only to appease the mother she was Scripture-bound to respect.

By now, Lydia was Mrs. Wickham. There would be no wedding feast. No cause for rejoicing, contrary to what Mama thought. And although Lydia was too foolish to know it, her happiness was certain to be short-lived.

Kitty pouted on the settee she usually sat on with Lydia, whose empty space Jane attempted to fill with her soft encouragement and gentle attentiveness. "Papa will not let me do anything or go anywhere," Kitty complained.

Jane smoothed Kitty's hair away from her face. "You can hardly blame him after what has happened. He loves you a great deal and seeks to protect you."

"But it is not fair! Lydia got to do everything, and now I am stuck here."

Mary stopped playing and turned to Kitty, showing more emotion than usual. "How do you not see how close Lydia came to ruining us all? She shall reap what she has sown, and the fruit shall be bitter. Do not wish the same for yourself, Kitty, when it is only thanks to Uncle's generosity that we have the chance, no matter how slight, of marrying men less self-serving than Mr. Wickham."

Mama snapped her fan open. "Mary! I will not have you speaking so poorly of your brother; such a fine, dashing soldier! You would do well to make such a catch."

Elizabeth could not think of a more depressing prospect, and she could not excuse her mother's willful blindness no matter how well-meant her motive. Mama did not see—or she refused to acknowledge— how the connection to such a man, as well as the circumstances forcing his union to Lydia, would affect her unmarried daughters.

Mama resumed her speech, extolling Lydia's good fortune. Before she could expound on Mr. Wickham's merits, Elizabeth stood to leave. She could hear no more.

Mary resumed her dirge, and Elizabeth did her best to ignore her surroundings until she closed herself behind the solid oak door of her father's book room. It was quieter in there—the quietest room in the house due to its location behind the stairs.

She sat on her usual perch by the window over-looking the rose garden, doing her best to be quiet lest she disturb her father's reading. She did her best to ignore Mary's playing, Mama's voice, and Kitty's complaining, but the soft rustle of her father turning pages could hardly compete.

Eventually, her mind did wander, and she was back at Hunsford Cottage. Mr. Darcy stood before her, his heart exposed. In these dreams, she always answered more kindly. She would not have accepted him—she could not accept the offer of a man who had interfered with the happiness of her most beloved sister—but she might have asked for an explanation. He might have recognized his error and made amends. Understanding his character as she did now, she suspected he would own to his misunderstanding and make the necessary reparations. Mr. Darcy was everything dutiful and responsible.

And Elizabeth loved him for it.

Leaning her forehead against the cool glass, she squeezed her burning eyes shut. Not only had she spitefully refused the only man she could ever love, thus severing all hope of reconciliation, but her sister was now married to Mr. Wickham. Mr. Darcy would never agree to attach himself to the vile man who had abused his friendship and that of his innocent sister.

Elizabeth would not receive another offer from him.

She did not know how long she had been woolgathering, but she noticed when the papers at her father's desk ceased to rustle. He watched her, a pensive look on his face.

"What is it, Papa?" she asked.

He bunched his lips as though he had something unpleasant to say. "You were right, Lizzy. I would have been wise to heed your warning."

She shook her head. "I take no pleasure in it when I would rather have Lydia home with us, protected from the likes of Mr. Wickham."

"As would I," he mumbled, clasping his hands together on top of his desk and leaning against his forearms. "I hate to think how much your uncle must have laid on that wretch. I shall never be able to repay him, nor do I consider myself worthy of his kindness." His voice trembled with shame.

"Mama and Kitty do not understand how fortunate we are that Uncle found them and arranged for them to marry." Elizabeth watched her father's reaction, praying he would continue to withstand their complaints when they threatened his cherished peace and time dimmed his regret.

He took off his spectacles, wiping them slowly and meticulously with his handkerchief. "Your mother is of a mind that marriage rights all wrongs—a view I might have helped dispel had I not been too indolent to correct her. Kitty knows no better." Settling his spectacles on his nose, he tucked the handkerchief into his pocket. "I shall not fail my other daughters as I failed Lydia. Do not fear that their demands will be met, no matter how tiring they become."

Elizabeth hoped with all of her heart that he meant it.

Galloping hooves and flying gravel interrupted their conversation, followed shortly by a knock on the door. Mary ceased playing, and even Mama went quiet. Mr. Hill's heavy footsteps grew louder as he traveled from the entrance to the book room door. Holding out an envelope, he said, "Brought by messenger."

Papa stood. "I shall see to him immediately."

Mr. Hill shook his head. "He has already gone."

Elizabeth glanced at the envelope as it passed between Mr. Hill and her father. It was Uncle's handwriting. Furthermore, Uncle had seen to the expense of sending a message. This was not good news. Had the wedding not taken place after all his trouble?

Panic whipped her heartbeat into a frantic pace, echoing in her ears. *Ruin ruin ruin.*

Papa opened the letter, his eyes fixed on the page as he groped for his chair. Pale, he fell into it.

It was true, then. Their worst fear. They were ruined.

The door behind them creaked open, and Elizabeth looked to see Jane standing in the doorway, her features etched with concern.

The page slipped from Papa's fingers to his desk. With teary eyes, he pushed the letter to Elizabeth and dropped his head into his hands. "I am so sorry. Oh, my poor, dear girls." His voice cracked. "The fault is mine to bear, and yet you shall be the ones to pay."

Elizabeth took the letter, her eyes catching on the last name she had expected to see her uncle pen.

Mr. Darcy.

Mr. Darcy? She devoured the contents of the page, her heart plummeting and her stomach churning as she read how *Mr. Darcy* had been the one to find Mr. Wickham and Lydia, how *he* had arranged for the wedding, paying for Wickham's commission and settling an additional enticement of one thousand pounds on Lydia. All of it had been arranged, not by Uncle, but by Mr. Darcy.

And now, Mr. Darcy had gone missing and Wickham would not marry Lydia without promise of full payment.

The next paragraph was devoted to Uncle's concern at this sudden turn of events. Never a steadier gentleman had he known than Mr. Darcy. He had managed the affair with a thoroughness and expediency Uncle praised enthusiastically. Mr. Darcy had even seen to the detail of Lydia's trousseau, small though it must be, thus adding to the image of a planned union rather than the forced one it was. That he should fail to appear at the wedding was inconceivable.

Uncle ended with some assurance, though it did little to minimize the disaster such a delay created. Colonel Richard Fitzwilliam was doing everything he could to step into his cousin's place, but Lydia was inconsolable and swore she would rather die than marry a man who had to be paid to marry her. Uncle did not say as much directly, but Elizabeth knew Lydia was too much for him and Aunt Gardiner to manage when they had their own children and obligations. He begged Father's immediate presence in London, whereupon he hoped Papa might persuade Lydia beyond her histrionics to see reason.

Elizabeth's throat was too tight to read aloud or give a summary to Jane. She handed the letter to her sister.

Papa raised his head. "I trust both of you to keep the details to yourself. Mr. Darcy has shown me more consideration and respect than I deserve, and I shall not be the one to make known what he took great pains to conceal. Your uncle's concern must be grave, indeed, for him to write as he did."

*Why did Mr. Darcy do it?* A small part of Elizabeth dearly wanted to believe he had done it for her, but that was a vain delusion. She had made her opinion of him clear—painfully and articulately clear. Not even the pleasant time she had briefly spent in his company at Pemberley with her aunt and uncle could erase that.

Jane handed the letter back to Papa, her eyes wide, one hand covering her mouth. Tucking it inside his pocket, he said, "I shall have to tell your mother that the wedding did not occur. Otherwise, she shall spread the news all over Meryton."

Elizabeth groaned. It had taken all of her ingenuity and Jane's persuasion to keep their mother from calling on Lady Lucas that same day so that she might brag of her success. If Papa left so suddenly for London, Mama would not understand why they could not accompany him in the hope of seeing the newly wed couple.

Uncle and Aunt had already done much more than any relative should be asked to do. They did not need another fitful female given to vexation and nerves to add to their burden.

Elizabeth caught her sister's eye, and she saw her own concerns mirrored in her gaze. Jane held her look for a moment, then nodded. Good. They were in agreement.

Taking a deep breath, Jane smoothed her skirts and clasped her hands together. "I shall stay with Mama."

Elizabeth added for their father's benefit, "And I shall go with you to London."

He nodded.

They departed from Longbourn one hour later, leaving Kitty stunned, Mary more self-righteous than ever, and Mama wailing. Jane and Mrs. Hill had their hands full, and Elizabeth knew her turn was soon to come with Lydia.

However, the farther away they drove from Longbourn, the less Elizabeth dwelt on her family's concerns and the more her worry for Mr. Darcy grew. A man like him would not disappear without finishing what he had started.

Where had he gone?

She held on to the expectation that he would resurface by the time they arrived at Gracechurch Street, and that all would be settled before she and her father reached the outskirts of London. Wickham and Lydia would marry on the morrow, and Elizabeth would properly express her gratitude to Mr. Darcy for salvaging her family's reputation.

They arrived at nightfall. And still, Mr. Darcy was gone.

# CHAPTER 4

*D*arcy opened his eyes and waited for his vision to clear. It was dark. He lay on a soft surface. It swayed. Everything swayed.

He did not know where he was, nor did he know the day or the hour. He knew, however, with a certainty that made his stomach knot, that he had missed Wickham's wedding. Would the ingrate go through with it if Darcy was not there to give him the promised bribe? What kind of a man sold himself for a thousand pounds and a commission?

Darcy's disgust turned again to frustration. Why had he insisted on being the one to witness the signatures? He could easily have included Richard. The fact of the matter was that the idea had not even occurred to Darcy until that moment. Was he so proud that he believed others incapable? Even Richard—a man who had repeatedly proven his strength of character and proficiency? Darcy shook his head, and instantly regretted it when the throbbing there increased.

Gritting his teeth and holding his head still, he tried to find solace in Richard's reliability. Richard was competent. He would lose no time making the needed adjustments with Hastings. Richard knew how important this was; he would not fail.

Slowly, gingerly touching the bump on the back of his skull and the swollen protuberance on his forehead, Darcy sat upright.

Moonlight shone into the room through a round window—a porthole. His stomach bottomed out at the implication. He was on a boat, on the water, sailing away to Lord-knew-where.

Spinning around so that his feet touched the smooth wooden planks, he found his boots by the bunk, wiggled his feet inside, and then looked for the door. His examination of his surroundings came to an abrupt halt when he saw a shadow.

He was not alone in the cabin.

A large man with skin the color of the night blocked Darcy's escape. The ship dipped, casting moon's rays over the stranger. A leather vest covered his muscled chest. Canvas trousers frayed above his ankles. The curved scimitar at his side discouraged Darcy from attempting to wrestle his way through. Besides, there was a good chance that more men like him were on the other side of the door. Darcy would not get far.

The man uncrossed his arms, dropping his chin to his chest. "You, stay." With that, he left the room, securing the door behind him.

Darcy listened for footsteps. Were there guards outside the door? Where was he? What kind of ship was this?

He stood, trying to gain his balance, and looked about the cabin for clues: the gowns draped over closet doors, the ruffles on the curtains, the faint smell of perfume. A woman's quarters.

Strange. Sailors were a suspicious lot, and most would agree that a female aboard a ship was asking for trouble. Naval ships did not allow women on board. Most pirate ships avoided them, although every Englishman knew the stories of Lady Killigrew, Anne Bonny, and Mary Read. It could not be Ching Shih, could it? Darcy swallowed hard. The fearsome Queen of the South China Sea had been granted amnesty two years before, but with a fleet numbering into the thousands, she had many who would be willing to expand her floating empire in her stead. Or had she joined forces with the Navy?

A penknife on a desk built against the opposite wall offered a small but effective weapon. Darcy grabbed it, losing his balance on the way and knocking his shins against a chest.

Before he could see if the chest contained a better weapon—what he would give for a sword! —the door opened.

Concealing the penknife in his palm, Darcy fingered the weapon up his sleeve as the big guard crossed the room and patted him down.

He tried to hide the knife, but the man found it. Pulling it out from its hiding place, he held it in front of Darcy's face. "If you lay a finger on her, I shall cut you from navel to nose."

Darcy did not doubt he could do it, but he risked the guard's ire. He needed information. "Who is she? Why am I here? Where are we?"

The man ignored him, shoving Darcy in front of him and jabbing the knife against his back, reminding Darcy of his disadvantage. Up a set of stairs he prodded Darcy, who bounced against the railings like the landlubber he was, until they reached the helm.

A woman stood at the wheel, her long, black hair braided down her back. She wore a loose shirt spilling with lace frills down the front tucked into dark breeches, high boots, and a bejeweled dagger gleaming at her thigh. She did not appear to be Chinese.

She shouted an order—she did not sound Chinese either—and two men immediately scrambled up the masts like monkeys to tie up the sails, shouting, "Aye, aye, Cap'n."

Captain?

She turned to him, stance wide, chin high—a woman confident of her command.

Darcy felt his chest puff, and he drew himself to his full height. She might be the captain of this ship, but he would not allow her to command him.

The goon behind him pushed him forward, sending Darcy sprawling toward her as the boat underneath him rolled. He righted himself, doing his best to appear dignified when his legs were as steady on the water as a newborn foal's. Knowing full well that the strength of his intimidation was in his glare, he leveled his eyes at her and communicated the depth of his displeasure with a firm stare.

Freckles dotted her nose—darker and more plentiful than the light spattering over Elizabeth's nose and cheeks. Blue-gray eyes, harsh and steely like the edge of a blade, inspected him in turn. Like Elizabeth, this woman was not easily intimidated.

The scimitar-wielding man slipped by Darcy and whispered into her ear, then took his place between them, his hand poised over his curved sword.

"Jaffa says me men must've knocked out yer senses, Nicholas," she said.

Darcy bunched his forehead, trying to perceive her meaning. "Why do you call me Nicholas?"

She nodded at Jaffa. "I see what ye mean. He's even talkin' funny."

Darcy did not know what she was talking about,

34

but if she had mistaken him for another man, then there was no reason for her to hold him on her ship. "My name is Fitzwilliam Darcy of Derbyshire."

Her eyes narrowed, her gaze raking over him from head to toe.

He was grateful he had dressed in more simple attire. Glancing at the cutthroats crowding the lower decks, any one of them would have killed him for the diamond he usually wore in his cravat. He would prefer to leave the ship alive and in one piece, thus his omission of Pemberley. He would only use his wealth if he could use it to purchase his freedom.

The woman captain swaggered up to him, her finger tracing up his arm and over his chest. "Ye sound like Nicholas. Ye always was good with accents." She trailed her finger up the center of his neck, her nail scratching a thin line up to his chin.

Darcy sensed her danger to him, but it was not in his nature to back down. He met her gaze boldly, planting his feet wide and steady. "I assure you, I am not whom you claim me to be."

"Yer glare tells me otherwise."

"I do not lie."

She crossed her arms, and watched him warily. "Every man lies. I'll get the truth from ye … one way or 'nother."

Darcy gritted his teeth. Blast, she was stubborn.

Slowly, her look boring through him, she asked,

"Does the name Alexandra Lafitte mean anything to ye?"

Darcy breathed in slowly, restraining every part of his body to hide his alarm. He had read the stories, heard her incredible adventures read at the broadsides and shouted in the streets. A female pirate so fierce, she was claimed to have ripped the hearts of her victims out of their chests while they yet breathed. Not to mention her brothers, Jean and Pierre Lafitte, the plagues of the southern colonies. A pirate dynasty.

And Darcy was on La Femme Lafitte's ship, where her word was law and his life was dispensable. He felt the blood drain from his face, and he praised the heavens for the darkness concealing his discomposure. "La Femme Lafitte," he repeated the name given to her in the papers and pamphlets.

Her eyes hardened. "Call me Alex. Unless ye make yerself difficult, then ye'll call me Cap'n." She walked around him, continuing her inspection. "I don't believe ye're not Nicholas. I know yer voice. Yer face." She twirled around him, trailing her finger around his shoulders. "Yer body."

Darcy struggled to keep his limbs loose when every nerve stretched taut.

She tilted her head. "Do ye have family? A brother?"

"No. It is only me." Whatever the lady pirate's plan was, he would not involve his family. He would rather die than put Georgiana in danger.

She tsked, her raised eyebrows settling into a smirk. "No secret, twin brother?"

"No."

"Too bad. I wouldn't mind havin' two of ye at me beck and call." Her breathy voice turned sharp, and she jabbed her nail into his chest. "There's only one way to settle this. Take off yer shirt."

# CHAPTER 5

*D*arcy leaned down, forcing the impertinent captain to focus solely on him so that she would not mistake his meaning. Nothing she could say or do would make him change his mind. "No," he said resolutely.

Quicker than a flash of lightning, Alex reached to her side, her eyes never wavering from his.

Darcy held his breath, determined to face the consequences with his eyes wide open. Before he could so much as flinch, he heard a thunk at his foot. He looked down to see a blade, six inches long, vibrating at the tip of his boot. He bet that if he looked, there would be a neat nick on the sole.

"Next time ye refuse a direct order, I'll aim higher." She pulled her dagger out of the deck, rubbing her fingers lovingly over the sharp tip.

Darcy untied his cravat and worked on his

buttons, hating how easily she had made him yield. Worse than the discomfort of disrobing in the cold, the humiliation of standing half-naked in front of hundreds of men led by this unscrupulous woman irked Darcy.

She watched him with a self-satisfied smile, replacing her dagger in its sheath only when he untucked his shirt. How he hated her. Pulling the soft linen over his head, he let the shirt dangle from his hand. It could work as effectively as a rope should she step closer.

As though Jaffa could read his thoughts, he took the shirt from Darcy, arching an eyebrow in warning.

Alex grinned, satisfied to be the cause of his shame, and drew closer. Her smile faded when she did not see what she had expected. She rubbed her fingers against his shoulder, poking and prodding. "It's not here."

Darcy was curious, but he had no desire to engage Alex in conversation.

She jabbed again. "Nick has a jagged scar here."

"How do you know that?" he asked, despite himself.

She looked up at him, challenge in her eyes. "I was the one who put it there."

He should have kept silent. He could practically feel her anticipating all the scars she could leave on his person.

She tapped his side where his breeches covered his skin.

Darcy jumped away from her.

Arching a brow, she pointed at the puckered skin at his side. "How'd ye get that?"

He was so relieved she did not order him to remove his breeches, he replied, "I jumped off a rock into a lake. There was a fallen tree under the water that had not been there the summer before. One of the branches cut me."

"Never leap before ye look, Mr. Darcy."

Did she now believe he was not Nicholas? Her use of his real name was promising.

A gust of frigid air puckered his skin, and he shivered. "It is a mistake I have not repeated since." He reached out to Jaffa. "I would like to put my shirt back on."

"Where's the fun in that?" Alex said, letting him stand exposed in the cold for longer than necessary, milking every advantage she gained from his cold humiliation. Finally, she nodded her assent to Jaffa.

Darcy slipped on his shirt and rubbed his arms. It was either the last of August or the first of September —he did not know how long they had kept him under. A day? Two? A week? Nor did he know where they were. Had the breeze been warmer, he would suspect they had sailed south to the warmer currents. But it was too cold for them to be anywhere but in the northern Atlantic. So much for attempting to swim to shore. He would freeze before he made it.

He would have to use his wits. "Now that we have established that I am not this Nicholas, when can you return me to London? I presume we are not far from shore?"

She tapped her ragged nails against her chin, keeping her eyes on him and revealing nothing of their location. Not so much as a glance in the direction from whence they had come. "Ye're the mirror image of him, but ye're not Nick." Her nostrils flared. "And ye've made me lose precious time, exposin' me and me crew to capture in these Navy-infested waters. Bauer! Cotton! Come here, ye scurvy good-for-nothins! I gave ye one job. One."

The crew quieted, the only sound that of the flapping sails overhead and the feet of the two men Alex had called scrambling to the helm. One was as large as an ox—the muscle. The other was lanky and wore an eye patch—the brain? Darcy's abductors.

They stood in front of her, their heads bowed, hands clasped in front. The large one was missing the tip of his little finger on his right hand. Looking at the pair, Darcy tried not to be overly disappointed in himself for allowing them to overpower him outside the tavern.

Eye patch opened his mouth to speak, but Alex shut him up with a hiss and the point of her dagger. "Not a word from ye, Bauer." Flicking the pointy end of the blade between the two, she added, "I ought to cast both of ye over the side. Ye've endangered me and yer shipmates—yer brothers—our entire livelihood, and, most unforgivable, the *Fancy*. Have ye anything to say in yer defense?"

Only the worst fool would try to defend himself when Alex had already passed judgment.

Cotton mumbled, "Ye said it yerself, Cap'n: He and The Blade, they's identical."

Bauer, to whom Darcy had credited with more mental faculties than the man deserved, added, "Ye had a hard time knowin' 'tweren't him, Cap'n. Ye can't punish us fer makin' the same mistake."

Darcy cringed. How had he fallen prey to *these two*?

Alex shot them a look as sharp as her preferred weapon. Her words were clipped, acute. "When I ask me crew to get a job done, they'd better get it done right. Or would ye have me take a ship with a bunch of buffoons blundering at the cannons, cuttin' their fingers on their own cutlasses, and blastin' each other to pieces with misfiring pistols? Out here, failure to follow orders leads to early death. Stupidity is unforgivable." She turned to a man standing behind her. "Keelhaul 'em. Side to side. Once over." To Cotton and Bauer, she said, "May God have mercy on yer souls, for I cannot."

The two men trembled in place, their eyes wide, and their knees buckling as they were jostled down to the lower deck—two men who had been asked to fulfill a task beyond their capabilities.

Like a slap across the face, the irony of Darcy's situation struck him. Far be it for him to defend his kidnappers, but the injustice of them paying for their mistake so harshly burned in his bones. He could not remain silent. In his most authoritative voice, Darcy commanded, "No. Do not do this. It is inhumane."

Silence. Darcy's skin prickled as hundreds of eyes turned to him. Even Cotton and Bauer gawked open-mouthed at him.

Slowly, very slowly, Alex spun around to face him. Stepping closer, she said, "Ye dare to defy me? The cap'n of this ship? My word is law here. To defy me is to die." She now stood toe-to-toe with him. She barely reached his shoulder, but her commanding presence more than made up for her lack of height.

Darcy stood his ground, grateful the boat did not sway so much lest he budge from his intimidating pose. Looking down at her with all the imperiousness in his possession, he said, "It is cruel. You are renowned as a fierce pirate, but before me, I see a lady capable of commanding the respect and obedience of her crew without making herself a bloodthirsty, unredeemable monster."

"I already have their obedience."

He pierced her with his sternest stare. Tougher men had wilted under it, but Alex did not even flinch. Steeling his voice, Darcy said, "Tell me, do your men serve under you out of fear, or have you won their respect, thereby earning their loyalty and making each of them an invaluable member of your crew—men who would die before they would even consider betraying you?"

The men milled about, whispering and grunting.

He had struck a nerve.

Alex noticed, too. She was not a fool. When her gaze returned to him, he saw as much fury as there was frustration, and Darcy knew she would make him pay. Dearly. But then, she winked—twice, in quick succession—confounding Darcy fully.

Spinning away, she shouted to the lower decks, "Cotton, Bauer, ye owe this man yer miserable lives. Since Mr. Darcy is so eager to save ye, then he'll take yer place. Side to side, two times, one for each of yer sorry carcasses."

At her nod, Jaffa gripped Darcy's arms and pushed him to the main deck. At the bottom of the steps, Jaffa whispered, "Hold your breath. Protect your head. You will live." He pushed Darcy forward.

Another sailor looped a rope around Darcy, and in one fluid motion pulled it snug and shoved him over the side.

Freezing water stabbed Darcy like thousands of glass shards scraping his skin. He gasped just before he was pulled under the surface. The rope tugged him deeper, jostling his memory to recall Jaffa's instructions. *Hold your breath.* If only he had thought to take another breath sooner.

The rope heaved, and Darcy struck against the keel of the ship, knocking the precious breath from his lungs. *Protect your head.* Darcy wrapped his arms over his head, curling into a ball as he slammed against the bottom of the ship.

Barnacles slashed into his arms and legs. He opened his eyes, desperate to see the surface, desperate for air. The salt water burned, but he kept them open, watching for the surface, for hope. *You will live.* Darcy prayed Jaffa was right.

A slight shift in the weight of his body told him that he was surfacing. Darcy counted seconds, convincing himself that he would make it. He had to make it. *Ten. Nine. Eight. Seven. Six. Five. Four. Three. Two. One. Come on! Three. Two. One. Almost there. You have to live! Three.*

Darcy could not tell the night sky from the water, but he felt the breeze cuff his face. Quickly, he gulped in the blessed air just as he was plunged back under.

Again, he smacked against the keel, but he was prepared this time. He did not lose all of his breath. Dragged across the bottom, his arms and legs took a beating. He tried to hold himself into a tight ball, his arms crossed over his head, but the shock to his body and the lack of air in his lungs made Darcy weak.

He drifted through the water, his limbs unfolding. He fought it; he tried to pull himself back. He attempted to count, but no sooner had he thought of a number than he forgot it. He needed air.

Fear gripped Darcy, and try as he might not to lose consciousness, he could not deny the very real possibility that this was his end.

*You will live.* He had to live. He had to see Elizabeth again. He saw her—hair wild and billowing around her, cheeks in high color—and a calm warmed his chest. She was as real as if she stood in front of him at the Meryton Assembly, then at Lucas Lodge, where she had refused to dance with him. Darcy smiled as the images flickered through his mind like portraits lining a gallery: Elizabeth tramping through the muddy fields, reading at Netherfield, playing the pianoforte at Rosings, the fire in her eyes at Hunsford Cottage, her smile at Pemberley. That was the memory Darcy cherished the most. He had made her smile. He had pleased her when he had thought such a worthwhile aim impossible.

Darcy needed Elizabeth like he needed air. *Elizabeth. Elizabeth,* he repeated over and over, seeing her smile and letting her pull him to her side.

With a violent jerk, he broke the surface of his watery grave. He coughed and gasped. Cold needles stabbed his skin, and he shook uncontrollably. It occurred to him that he might have survived; misery made him doubt.

He hit the deck with a smack. Rolling on to his side, he coughed and sputtered more, every breath an agony and a relief. Darcy felt like a cat that had used up one of its nine lives, but Jaffa had been right. He was alive. Wrapping his arms around his knees, he dreamed of Elizabeth, her dark eyes warm and vivacious.

There is nothing like a near-death experience to

give a man clarity. Darcy was alive, but he did not want to live without Elizabeth … if he could convince her to have him.

He would get off this infernal ship. He would gallop his fastest horse to Hertfordshire. He would grovel on his knees. And he would beg her to end his misery and become his wife.

# CHAPTER 6

"Come, Mr. Darcy. Up with ye," a rough voice said at his side. Two firm hands pulled him into a sitting position. A dry blanket dropped around his shoulders, and Darcy clung to it as well as he could with icy fingers that would not bend.

From his other side, a flask appeared, tipping toward his mouth. "Drink. This'll warm yer insides."

Darcy did as he was bid, gin burning a deliciously warm trail down his throat.

He heard Alex's commanding voice. "Jaffa, see Mr. Darcy to me cabin."

Shoving the flask away and rising on his wobbly feet, Darcy barked a haggard but profound, "No!"

She tilted her chin. "Ye dare defy me again?"

He would rather embrace a viper than spend a night in the same room with her. Steadying himself against the mast before he toppled over, Darcy straightened his shoulders under the blanket. "You may comport yourself as you wish, but I am a gentleman, and I shall continue to act like one."

She scoffed. "A gent used to comfort and luxury, no doubt. Are ye prepared to sleep in a hammock below decks with one hundred and fifty men who've not bathed since the last port? Men who'd sooner slit yer throat than have another body crowd 'em more than they already are?"

He looked around at the men. A few nodded agreement, but the majority shifted their weight uncomfortably. Darcy would take his chances. "You cannot convince me that I am any safer with you."

Cotton and Bauer stepped forward. "We'll keep ye safe, Mr. Darcy." A few others joined them, lending their support.

Alex looked like she might burst into flames. Deliberately defying her was stupid, but Darcy was too miserable to care.

"Take him below," she snapped, marching away from him as quickly as he had done from Wickham.

How long ago had that been? What day was it? The wedding! Was Elizabeth safe? Would that he could get off this accursed vessel. He kept an eye out, peeking inside the quarters they passed, looking for maps or compasses—anything that might tell him where they were.

They went down narrow walkways, winding around to another set of stairs, then around again until

Darcy lost all sense of direction. Some navigator he was.

By the time he puzzled through the maze, deciding they must be at the stern of the ship, Bauer ducked inside a doorway.

Hammocks stretched from beam to beam down the width of the space, some bearing up to four hammocks, one on top of another. It smelled of mold and unwashed bodies.

Cotton noted Darcy's reaction to the odor. "Ye'll get used to it."

Bauer shoved a change of clothes at him with a grunt, and Darcy thanked him. Even Pemberley's servants were dressed finer, but at least these garments were dry.

Another sailor dumped a pair of boots at his feet. "Reckon' these'll fit well enough."

Before Darcy could even thank him or ask where his own boots had gone, a fourth sailor came out of the shadows with a blanket large enough to wrap himself in.

Carefully peeling off his wet shirt, Darcy inspected the gashes along his arms and back. One still oozed, while the others were angry, red welts.

The man who had handed Darcy the blanket tipped a flask onto a handkerchief and dabbed at his wounds. "I'm Affonso da Silva, ship surgeon," he said, splashing more liquid over the linen and pressing it against

Darcy's broken skin. The spirits stung like a dozen bees.

Darcy winced, but he turned to allow the man better access to the injuries on his other side, asking, "Portuguese?"

"*Sim, senhor.* We are from all over the world," he answered, his English accented with a pleasant lilt. "Our foreign status discourages the British from impressing us into service. It is a protection, like the black sails we often use and the letters of apprenticeship we carry on our person from the captain." He tucked the flask into his pocket and pulled out a jar.

"The captain gave you letters?" Darcy prompted, more in disbelief than in a pursuit of more information. Unless Alex had someone else pen the letters for her, she might know how to read and write.

"Aye, she did. Every one of us. Penned them herself."

Drat. The she-devil was more cunning than Darcy had hoped. However, she obviously cared for her crew to give them means by which to protect themselves should a naval ship seeking new recruits seize them. It did not guarantee their freedom during this time of war, but it certainly could help. Darcy would do well not to underestimate her.

Dabbing his fingers inside the jar, da Silva smeared a vile-smelling ointment over Darcy's stinging flesh. "It does not smell good, but it will keep infection away."

The pungent odor diminished in strength as it

JENNIFER JOY

dried. Or, more likely, Darcy grew accustomed to the smell. The nose, as his recent experiences were teaching him, was a forgiving organ. The balm was soothing.

Injuries treated, dry clothes donned, and feet encased in worn, soft leather, exhaustion overpowered Darcy. The men showed him to a hammock. It was inches off the floor, at the bottom of a stack of four.

"'Til we know if ye get seasick or not," Bauer explained.

A young man joined them, carrying a tin plate. "Eat while ye can. Once we're farther from port, ye'll get nothin' but salt pork and hardtack."

"London port?" Darcy asked, senses sharpening. So, they were not too far.

The men closest to the young man smacked him on the back of the head. Those too far shot sharp glares at him.

Da Silva spoke for the group. "Aye, but do not get any notions of jumping ship. The currents are too strong and the shore is too far."

Darcy knew better than to trust the word of a pirate —even a well-spoken, educated surgeon like da Silva, but he wasn't fool enough to test the man, either.

The surgeon poked the bruises on Darcy's head. "With the beating you have taken, you would not survive the swim. You should be grateful the men pulled the ropes quicker than usual." His eyes met Darcy's. "Captain is firm, but she is not heartless."

Darcy doubted that, and he would not waste his

breath arguing with the man. Taking a bite of the stale bread and finding a deliciously seasoned slab of beef inside, Darcy devoured the meal, washing down every bite with a hot, spiced tea laced with rum. It was perhaps the best meal he had ever eaten.

So engrossed was he in his meal, he did not notice Bauer, Cotton, da Silva, and the others depart until he looked up and saw they were gone.

Only one man remained behind, watching him and listening. He had strong, wiry limbs and a square jaw grizzled with gray whiskers.

"What day is it?" Darcy asked, voice slurred. He shook his head. He had to know where he was if he had any chance of returning to London.

"Last day of August," the grizzled man replied, his voice clipped and stern.

One day? Darcy reeled. It seemed like an eternity since he had been at the seedy tavern by the shoreline. He had missed Wickham's wedding. The ingrate would give Richard difficulty, but Darcy trusted his cousin to manage him.

The man crossed his arms and leaned against a beam. "Name's Beckett. I'm Cap'n's first mate."

The next in command. Darcy would do well to keep Beckett's favor. He bowed his head, his frustration growing when he had to stifle a yawn. "I am pleased to make your acquaintance, Mr. Beckett," he responded with a thick tongue.

"Ye're as slick as Cap'n Nick."

Darcy caught himself before he laughed. Only months ago, he had snubbed most of a village and delivered the most offensive proposal known to man, and now he was being accused of having smooth manners.

Perhaps he was slick ... for a pirate. Elizabeth would appreciate that. He wondered if he would ever be able to tell her. She would laugh.

Beckett watched Darcy woolgather, seeming to understand when he once again had the attention of his audience before continuing, "The cap'n be a woman scorned. She's a hot temper, and she be fierce in battle. Ye betray her, and any one of her crew'll take pleasure slittin' yer throat."

Darcy nodded. He had felt her fury and was in no hurry to draw her ire until he had gained more strength. Lord, he was tired. He blinked several times, trying to focus on Beckett.

"That said, she'll keep yer hide alive if ye prove to be a worthy sailor and a trustworthy man."

The first mate did not trust him—not yet—but Darcy knew his own strengths, and inspiring trust and respect were foremost among them. He would prove himself, and he would see how he could leverage the crew to help him. At the very least, he would live long enough to get back to Elizabeth. "I shall learn whatever you are willing to teach me," Darcy enunciated. His lips had gone numb.

Beckett nodded. "That's good to hear, Mr. Darcy."

He slipped away, his footsteps creaking up the steps to the gangway.

Darcy stretched out as much as he could in his hammock, the canvas curling around him like a cocoon that rocked back and forth, back and forth, lulling him to sleep with the image of two fine, bright eyes.

# CHAPTER 7

"Covent Garden. No. 4 Bow Street," Colonel Fitzwilliam barked to the hackney driver. "There shall be extra if you get me there in under twenty minutes."

The carriage lurched forward, and though there was no time to relax, Richard's body melted against the cushions. He had not been so bone-tired since his last campaign on the continent—riding for months through sleet and rain, too exhausted to care how hard the ground was at night, too hungry to mind the meager, tasteless rations. How he wished he were back in Portugal. It was better than this.

After all night searching for Darcy, all night facing dead trails, the dawn forced them to face new, worse realities. Either Darcy had been kidnapped or impressed into service, or he was dead.

Richard hoped he was early enough to catch Phil

Rouncewell at the Bow Street Runners' office. Father had agreed that involving Richard's former colonel was the wisest step.

Rouncewell took satisfaction in helping people, seeing justice done, and making England a safer place for his children and grandchildren to live. He did not chase after the prize money most of the runners pursued when their criminals were convicted and punished. His duties seemed to satisfy his need for purpose while ensuring he returned to his comfortable bed, dinner table, and loving family every night.

Richard envied him.

Fifteen minutes later, the carriage jerked to a halt. Richard settled with the driver, adding a few extra coins in appreciation for his haste.

The Bow Street office was a hive of activity—runners with their blue tailcoats and top hats darting to and fro amidst a sea of victims and defendants clamoring for their attention.

Rouncewell stood out with his gray whiskers and stiff posture—the vestiges of his military days.

He spotted Richard, dismissing himself from the companion with whom he was speaking, and clapping Richard enthusiastically on the shoulder. "Colonel! It has been many moons since I have had the honor of seeing you. What brings you here? You are looking well."

Richard returned his friend's warm greeting. "How is your family?"

"My youngest married last year and recently blessed us with another strapping grandson." His chest puffed with pride. Elbowing Richard, he asked, "When will it be your turn, lad? Only those who marry young have the energy to play with their grandchildren."

Richard brushed off his question with a vague, "Soon enough." Nonchalant as he pretended to be, the question always pinched his heart.

Rouncewell kindly let the matter drop. "I trust your excellent father is in good health?" He had the utmost respect for Richard's father, Lord Matlock. One word from the earl had secured Rouncewell's paid position on the Bow Street force.

"Fit as a man half his age. He wished for me to convey his regards. It is, however, another family member who brings me to you."

Rouncewell's smile faded into a marked frown. "And here I had hoped your call was of a social nature. How can I be of assistance?" He clasped his hands in front of him, his gaze intent, head tilted so that his ear leaned toward Richard—a stance of attentive concentration.

"Do you remember my cousin Fitzwilliam Darcy?"

Rouncewell nodded. "Tall, dark, proud-looking gentleman."

"He has gone missing."

His gaze snapped up to Richard's. "How long?"

"Since Sunday night, about nine o'clock."

Rouncewell tugged his whiskers. "There has been

trouble in town of late, especially at the east end. War has made the press gangs desperate."

"It is a possibility." That had been Father and Richard's primary concern. The Devil's Tavern was an unsavory place, not just for the hardened folks who frequented such an establishment, but for its location near the Thames. Even if Darcy had identified himself as a landowner, they might not have believed him. Gentry had no reason to enter that part of town.

Why had Darcy not told him he was meeting with Wickham? Richard would have accompanied him, wearing his uniform to offer a degree of protection for them both.

He had argued as much to Father the night before, and his father's retort rang in his ear then, too. "What about Georgiana?" And he was right.

Darcy would have reasoned that, should something befall him, she would not be left without a guardian so long as she had Richard. And so his stubborn cousin had gone to the enemy's camp, determined to bend Wickham to his will, risking his own neck to save the standing of a family with whom Darcy held no hope of uniting himself.

Richard spent most of the night and a fair portion of the early hours that morning cursing Darcy's heightened sense of responsibility and honor. His cousin did not take his life lightly, but if someone he loved was in danger, he would not hesitate to stand between them and peril.

Richard hissed a slow exhale. How could he condemn his protective cousin when he would do the same for his family? For the lady he would one day love?

Rouncewell interrupted his thoughts. "Do you wish for me to put a word in 'The Quarterly Pursuit'? Get the public to assist in finding him?" The weekly newspaper provided the public with descriptions of criminals, information on stolen goods, and other activities of the underworld. While the journal kept people informed, it had also proved to be a valuable resource for the runners when readers came forward with helpful testimony.

But Richard's father had been adamant. It was too soon to expose their family to the public eye. The paper was helpful, but there were people who preyed on anxious families. Sorting false testimony and dealing with fake ransom notes would only slow them down. "My father believes it best to keep Darcy's disappearance quiet for now. We are prepared to devote all of our time to his recovery."

"Very good. Has there been a ransom note? Any known threats?"

"Nothing. One moment, he was in town, and the next, he was gone. He was last seen by the waterfront." Richard gave the specific location of the inn where Wickham stayed.

Rouncewell stewed on that, eyes staring unfixed, fingers tugging his side whiskers.

Richard's thoughts turned to the potential dangers. Aside from the press gangs and thieves, there were the Resurrection Men. Those unscrupulous monsters, tired of grave robbing, had begun killing able-bodied men so that they could sell the fresh cadavers to eager surgeons.

Finally, Rouncewell spoke. "It is not as bad there as St. Giles, but that is no place for a gentleman. What was he doing in that area?"

Richard told him about Wickham, keeping certain details about the lady silent to protect the Bennets' reputation.

"What about this Wickham? Could he be involved?" Rouncewell asked.

"I have three reliable youths posted near the inn. If Wickham attempts to escape or if he meets with anyone suspicious, they are to report to me immediately. His involvement is unlikely, but until we find Darcy, I must acknowledge the possibility."

Rouncewell nodded. "Good. You cannot afford to overlook anyone. Too many times, the originator of the worst, most brutal crimes are members of one's own family. Or a close friend."

"A sad testament to our times."

"It is at that, but I see too much of it to ignore the reality."

The entrance door opened, and they stepped aside to allow the young lady and her maid a wider path. Richard only caught a glimpse of her face before her bonnet blocked his view. She left a soft trail of jasmine in her wake, an improvement over the pressed bodies in the office.

"She is a persistent one," Rouncewell muttered.

Richard noticed the determination in the young lady's rigid posture and the confidence with which she approached one of the senior runners. Whatever she was after, she would not give up easily.

She spun around, and Richard sucked in a breath. The quality of her gown, the elegance of her bonnet, and the perfection of her auburn ringlets around alabaster skin suggested she was of a privileged class that did not belong in a place such as this. And yet, she did not seem in the least bit uncomfortable.

"What is her story?" Richard did not have the time to ask, but he was intrigued.

"Poor lass," Rouncewell said, dropping his hand from his whiskers. "I feel for her predicament, but she will never get her sort to admit to what she fears they have done. They are above the law. And unless she finds the persons involved in a crime committed over twenty years ago—a crime for which she has no proof —she is unlikely to get them to admit to any wrongdoing."

"What does she suspect?"

Rouncewell's voice was low and cold. "Baby snatching."

Revulsion twisted Richard's stomach. It pained him

to know there existed such an evil in the world. "Who is she?" he asked.

"The only child and heiress of Mr. and Mrs. Rothschild. They recently died in a carriage accident."

"Foul play?"

"Worse. Miss Rothschild suspects she was not their child at all."

Richard gasped. "She suspects *she* was snatched? By them?"

"Unlikely. Mrs. Rothschild was well known for her philanthropic work. Mr. Rothschild was generous and supported her every cause."

"Guilty consciences?"

"Perhaps. If Miss Rothschild was, indeed, snatched as a babe. About a year ago, she met a family from Kympton—"

"Kympton? That is near Pemberley, Darcy's estate." Richard's heart leapt into his throat at the connection. It hardly seemed like more than a coincidence, but with the little Richard had to go on, every lead was worth pursuing.

Rouncewell rubbed his whiskers again. "Perhaps you know the family. Hale is their surname."

A sharp inhale. "Mr. Hale is the rector there. My cousin gave him the living when it became available some five years ago. The rectory is suitable for their large family."

"And far away from Kent, where their infant was stolen from their home all those years ago,"

Rouncewell said gravely. "Miss Rothschild is of a similar age to their lost child, and she bears a striking resemblance to Mrs. Hale. As tempting as it is for me to probe further into the matter, I fear it would only be a waste of time and cause her more hurt. Grief does not settle well with anyone, but some take it harder than others." He sighed. "I suspect that Miss Rothschild is a lonely young woman so desperate to have someone in her life, she has imagined herself a new family."

Richard tried to remember the Hales—the parents and their children. They all had various shades of ruddy hair, from bright red to the darker auburn Miss Rothschild possessed. Richard could not say if there were additional similarities. He looked at the young lady, searching for something familiar he could link to the Hales.

She spoke to her maid, her gaze roving over the people in the room until she locked eyes with him. The noisy room silenced and, for the briefest moment, time stopped as she peered at him with piercing emerald eyes. Something inside him softened. He instantly knew that, should she ask him for help, he could not refuse her.

However, he could not abandon Darcy to chase after a whim.

Richard looked away. He would write to his aunt Catherine as soon as he returned to his apartment. If a baby had been stolen in Kent, she would know about it. Nothing else about Miss Rothschild's case seemed to have anything to do with Darcy, and Richard did not have time to help lonely heiresses. He had to find Darcy and make sure Wickham married Miss Lydia.

Turning to Rouncewell, he said, "I mean to go to the River Police next. Is there any officer in particular I should speak to?" With a force of over eighty men on their payroll and an additional thousand on reserve, the River Police had gained a foothold against the thieves and looters preying on anchored ships. They might know something.

"I have several contacts there, and I suggest you allow me to speak with them. They are more willing to help one of their own than an outsider."

That would save a great deal of time. Richard thanked him.

Before he could take his leave, Rouncewell gripped his elbow. In a low tone, he said, "The waterman brought in three new bodies. I was on my way to see if they belong to anyone I know when you arrived. I hate to ask, but should you accompany me?"

A shiver gripped Richard. He could not bear to think of Darcy—his cousin and closest friend— drowned or otherwise dead, but he had to know. He nodded.

They made their way to the banks of the Thames where a morgue housed the unfortunate souls washed up onto the shores, caught in dragnets, dredged from the bottom, or fished off the surface by the watermen who made their living rowing people from one side of the river to the other. It was a damp, dreary place.

Richard closed his eyes and said a silent prayer, overwhelmed at the task before him. He uttered another when he discovered that Darcy was not one of the three corpses.

Seizing onto hope, Richard hailed another hackney. "Gracechurch Street," he instructed the driver.

CHAPTER 8

*E*lizabeth closed the door softly behind her and tiptoed down the hall to the stairs. It had been a long night full of tantrums and tears, and her head felt like the drum her younger cousins beat, but Elizabeth longed to know if her uncle had received any news. She was disappointed in herself for falling asleep as long as she had.

The parlor was fuller than she had anticipated. Aunt and Uncle sat on the settee in front of the window, looking more rested than they had the day before when she and her father had arrived at Gracechurch Street. Papa and Colonel Fitzwilliam occupied the chairs opposite.

Her uncle greeted her. "Lizzy, I had hoped you would join us soon." He nodded as the colonel rose from his seat to bow, and added, "I believe you know Colonel Fitzwilliam?"

Elizabeth smiled at the colonel. He looked as tired as she felt. She had always liked his company, but this proof of his devotion to his cousin raised him all the more in her esteem. "We met in Kent last spring. It is a pleasure to see you, Colonel, though I wish it were under more agreeable circumstances."

"I do as well, Miss Bennet." His smile did not reach his eyes, and she knew that whatever news he had come to share was not good.

"How is Lydia?" Papa asked.

Taking a seat in the empty chair beside the colonel, Elizabeth gratefully accepted the tea Aunt poured while she pondered how best to adjust her reply to suit their hopeful expressions. "Lydia's hysterics cannot last much longer. Either she shall wear herself out or she shall tire of being so much in her room, and calm herself enough to venture out."

She heard multiple sighs. It was not what they would have preferred to hear, but it was the truth, gently delivered.

Uncle set his cup and saucer on the table. "Colonel Fitzwilliam has been kind enough to keep us informed of his progress regarding Lydia's impending nuptials and Mr. Darcy's whereabouts. Both your father and I intend to assist as much as we can."

Aunt touched his hand. "My dear, might I suggest that you allow the colonel to communicate what has transpired to Lizzy while you begin making arrangements? You have many business contacts in town, as well as Bennet's university chums, to alert."

"Yes, we shall be writing and sending messages for most of the day." Uncle patted her hand in turn. "There is no time to lose. Brother, shall you join me in my study?"

Without protest, Elizabeth's father departed from the room with Uncle. Papa's indolence had caused a great deal of suffering to their family, and while he had vowed to take a more active role as the head of their household, it pleased Elizabeth to see proof of his determination.

Aunt motioned to her sewing basket at the table and chair behind the settee, facing the window to allow Elizabeth and the colonel a degree of privacy. "I shall be right here if you need me."

Elizabeth clutched her hands together. "Have you received any word of Mr. Darcy?"

The colonel's smile disappeared completely.

"I see." She spared him from having to say the dreadful words. "What has been done to recover him?"

"I have been to Bow Street and to the morgue, a trusted friend is making inquiries with the River Police, and my father has hired several men to assist us." Colonel Fitzwilliam spoke quickly and precisely, like a military commander. "It is only a matter of time."

*Before he is found alive ... or otherwise*, Elizabeth completed his sentence in her mind. She swallowed hard, a notable tremor in her voice when she spoke.

"Do you have any reason to believe he has come to harm?"

"I do not know. Thus far, I have seen no evidence to indicate Darcy is in imminent danger."

She appreciated his delicacy, but she needed the truth. "Nor have you evidence to imply he is safe."

The colonel nodded.

Elizabeth chewed on her lips. "Does Mr. Darcy have any enemies?"

"Gentlemen such as Darcy always have enemies—people who resent their privilege."

"Such as Mr. Wickham?"

"If you are asking if Wickham is responsible, I do not think so. To believe him capable of elaborating such an extravagant plan would be to give him more credit than he deserves. He has always been one to exploit opportunities that fall into his lap, but I have never known him to exert himself to create those opportunities."

As tempting as it was to peg a crime on a man whom she held in contempt, Elizabeth had to agree. "What of the press gangs? We often hear shouts of protest coming from the market or down by Uncle's warehouses. All of his apprentices carry letters on their person."

"My father met with the First Lord of the Admiralty, who has agreed to send dispatches to his commanders. Such a measure takes time, but if a captain is disinclined to believe Darcy is a landowner, Melville shall sooner convince him than Darcy shall."

Lord Matlock must be a powerful man, indeed, to have the freedom to gain an audience with the viscount on such short notice. And to think, she had refused his nephew…

Refusing to dwell on a past she could not alter, Elizabeth asked, "What about a kidnapper? Or the Resurrection Men?" She swallowed hard, her heart beating in her throat.

"There has been no ransom note, and I have yet to receive word from the men I sent to the Royal College of Surgeons with a miniature of Darcy's likeness." He dropped his voice and leaned toward her. "Does this concern for my cousin's welfare signify that he has redeemed himself in your estimation?"

Elizabeth's exhale quivered. "He never deserved my poor opinion to begin with. For several months I have considered Mr. Darcy with nothing but the most profound respect." She looked down at her hands and blinked and blinked.

"I am glad to hear it. Especially after that fine speech he made at Hunsford Cottage."

Her gaze whipped up to his. "He told you of that?" Oh, what she would give to erase that scene from her memory. She prayed Mr. Darcy did not dwell on it as much as she did.

"His remorse was great."

Elizabeth groaned. If it had been possible to defend

her family's shameful conduct, her indignation at the time would have at least been righteous. "He said nothing which was not true."

"But his manner speaking of it was unfortunate. It is no wonder you called him out."

Her face burned with shame. She did not deserve the colonel's understanding when there was no excuse for her cruelty. "I lashed out in anger. Not a day goes by that I do not wish my spiteful words unsaid."

"A sentiment Darcy has also voiced. I do not mean to chastise, Miss Elizabeth, but rather to reassure. I hope Bingley's return to Hertfordshire shall appease your mind."

Mr. Bingley was to return to Netherfield? Any other day, such news would fill Elizabeth with boundless joy, but the timing was terrible. "Jane will not feel herself in a position to accept him should he make an offer. Lydia's scandal—"

"If Bingley's resolve is not firm enough to withstand this trial, then he does not deserve to marry her. From what Darcy has told me, she has everything to recommend her. As for the potential for scandal … Bingley can afford to weather society's scorn when he stands to win a wife who shall rise above it."

Elizabeth hoped so. Jane had suffered more than enough senseless heartbreak lately. This reminded her of another lady who would be devastated to learn Mr. Darcy had vanished. "Have you told Miss Darcy?"

Colonel Fitzwilliam shifted in his chair. "She is

coming to stay with my mother and sisters at Matlock House. We felt the news would be best delivered in person."

Elizabeth nodded, her throat too tight to speak.

"It is possible we will find Darcy before she arrives." The tenderness in the colonel's tone made her look up. He continued, "Between our efforts and the further assistance your father and uncle are willing to provide, we *will* find him."

Elizabeth could not blink fast enough to contain her tears, which spilled over her cheeks. When she had learned he had arranged for Lydia to marry—thus saving her and her sisters from certain ruin—the small spark of hope in her heart had kindled into a flame that burned for Mr. Darcy. She loved him more than she had dreamed possible for her to love anyone.

And now, she must face the grim reality that she might never see him again.

The colonel cleared his throat and handed her his handkerchief. "How fares Miss Lydia?"

Dabbing her eyes and taking a sip of tea, Elizabeth was grateful for the change of topic. "I do not suppose the vicar has had a cancellation and the wedding could take place sooner?"

Aunt had told her all the details, relating that the colonel looked perilously close to piercing Wickham through when he refused to wed Lydia immediately. Elizabeth almost wished he had, for all the trouble the rake had caused her family and the Darcys.

"I fear we must wait until Friday."

Three days hence. Elizabeth sighed. As long as the previous night had been, three days sounded like an eternity.

Colonel Fitzwilliam continued, surprising Elizabeth by describing the adjustments he had made with Mr. Darcy's man of business—matters gentlemen did not usually discuss with a lady, much less a lady who was not family. In conclusion, he stated, "There is nothing for Wickham to object to. They shall wed, and any talk of ruin shall be squelched before it can begin."

*If only it were so simple.* Elizabeth said bitterly, "It is only Lydia who needs convincing now."

The colonel sat forward in his chair. "What is this?"

"She threatened to swallow poison rather than marry Mr. Wickham. My aunt, her maid, and I must keep watch over her constantly."

He leaned back in his chair, shaking his head. "Hardly a promising beginning." When he looked up again, his eyes were intense, his voice deep and sincere. "Would that we could turn back time—undo the senseless damage which separates two people who would otherwise be happy. I spoke out of turn that day at Rosings, and caused you and Darcy pain. I beg your forgiveness."

Not a moment had passed since reading Mr. Darcy's letter that Elizabeth did not wish the same. She could no sooner fault the colonel for his honesty and openness than excuse the real villain for his false charm. She had been completely taken in, and while Elizabeth could easily forgive Colonel Fitzwilliam's loose tongue and Mr. Darcy's interference, she could not forgive herself for her ignorant prejudice and stubborn pride.

"You have it. Only, find him. Please."

If she ever saw Mr. Darcy again, she would seize the chance to make amends.

# CHAPTER 9

*I*t was daytime when Darcy woke. The clothing he had left to dry at the end of his hammock was gone.

Rising, careful not to entangle himself in the hammocks above or hit his head on the low ceiling, he stretched, enjoying the effortless movement all the more because he knew it would not last. Beckett would make certain he worked, and Alexandra would love to see him suffer in as many ways as her first mate could imagine.

He had planned to wake during the night, when there were sure to be fewer sailors to catch him snooping for clues of their location. If only he knew where the charts were kept.

Smoothing the wrinkles from the lawn shirt and rough trousers, he made his way to the upper deck, peeking inside every cabin he passed along the way.

Jaffa found him.

Darcy looked around for listeners. Lowering his voice, he said, "Thank you. If not for your advice, I would have perished last night."

Jaffa shook his head firmly. "Cap'n Alex knew you would survive."

Darcy frowned. "How can you say that? She tried to kill me."

A string of pearly white teeth widened. "If she wanted to kill you, we would not be speaking right now."

"Pardon me, but I remain unconvinced."

Jaffa pointed at his eye and winked twice. "That is what this means."

There was nothing Jaffa could tell Darcy which would alter his opinion of Alex.

But Jaffa was loyal. He must have sensed Darcy's disbelief, for he continued, "You told her you could swim. And the ship was careened and cleaned of barnacles recently. She knew you would survive. Just like Cap'n Nick would."

"Who is he?" Darcy was sick of hearing how similar they were in appearance, but he was curious.

"That is for the cap'n to tell you. Not me." With no further word, Jaffa turned and motioned for Darcy to follow.

The breeze felt different. Where it had been at his back the night before, it was now blowing against his face. "Have we altered course?" he asked.

Jaffa did not answer. He walked in silence until he stopped at the door next to Alex's cabin. "The cap'n expects you."

Darcy peeked inside. Aside from Alex, there was another man sitting at the table, which was nailed to the floor in the middle of the room.

She saw him and motioned with her knife for him to join them. "Mr. Darcy, ye're up early. I had da Silva slip some of his sleepin' medicine in yer cider. Knocks most men out for a full day."

So she was responsible for his deep slumber. Why was he not surprised? The woman was a plague.

She motioned with her knife for Darcy to join them, but he had no desire to share a meal with her, so he stood at the foot of the table.

If his superior position bothered her, she gave no indication of it. She continued, "Mr. Darcy, this is Quartermaster Boone. He's the *Fancy's* Civil Magistrate, trustee, record keeper, and accountant. When we take a prize, he's the one who counts up and divides the spoils."

The quartermaster was tall and solid with a shock of blonde hair tied in a queue. "The right-hand man," Darcy surmised, addressing Boone. He could not bring himself to speak to *that* woman.

Boone's chest puffed out, and his appraising look turned to one of approval. "That I be, Mr. Darcy. 'Tis a pleasure having ye aboard, though I daresay the pleasure's all ours."

Darcy liked Boone's honesty. "You are not wrong."

Alexandra stabbed a chunk of meat, tearing a piece off with her teeth, her cheek bulging as she chewed and spoke. "I hear ye have a young lady on land."

Darcy's blood ran cold. He would allow himself to be dragged over the hull of the ship a hundred times before he spoke of Elizabeth to the she-devil with a wad of masticated cow lodged in her cheek. "Should that be true, I would not share my confidences with you."

She shoved the ball of meat to her other cheek. "Then ye'd better learn not to speak her name in yer sleep."

He felt his heartbeat all over his body.

Taking several gulps from her wine glass, she added, "Elizabeth. It's a fine, strong name. Is she a fine, strong woman?"

The disdain in her tone made Darcy snap. "You do not deserve to utter her name."

Alex stabbed her knife into the table, looking at Boone and gesturing at Darcy. "That! What's a woman gotta do for that?"

Boone held his peace, an impossibility for Alex, who did not know the meaning of the word. "If Nick loved me like Mr. Darcy loves his Elizabeth, he never would've—" she cut her sentence off with a fiery scowl. Whoever Nick was, Alex would make him pay for whatever it was he had done.

Taking another gulp of wine and wiping her chin

against the back of her hand, Alex asked, "What'd she do to make ye love her?"

"Nothing. I gave her my heart willingly, not under duress." Something he doubted the woman sitting beside him could comprehend.

She mulled that over for a bit, then asked, "How long did that take?"

"From the moment I first saw her until now, ten months."

She twisted her lips. "I've loved Nick these ten years."

Boone offered, "He couldn't do anything with yer brothers nearby. But, now that ye're away, ye have a clean slate. A fresh start."

"But ten months? I'm not that patient. Is there a way to hurry things along?" She looked at Darcy expectantly.

A pushy pirate asking him for romantic advice? Elizabeth would appreciate the humor in that. There had to be a way he could gain the upper hand here. Some way to convince Alex to let him go. Maybe if he played along…

Swallowing down his reservations, Darcy spoke before he could take back the offer. "I could teach you how to act like a lady if you will let me go. One week should suffice." A lifetime would not be enough for a woman such as Alex to transform into the crudest lady. She made Elizabeth's younger sisters look saintly.

Alex laughed. "I'm not that naïve, Mr. Darcy. I'll

need much longer than a week. I'll take yer week and up ye three more. If I'm happy with me lessons, I'll leave ye at the nearest port after the fourth week."

"London port."

"And here I was thinkin' of droppin' ye at A Coruña or Amsterdam. Ye ever been to Boston?" She wiggled her eyebrows.

Darcy was not amused. "Four weeks," he mumbled, weighing his options (of which, in reality, he had none). His family would tear England apart, searching for him. They would leave no stone unturned. His uncle had friends in high places, and his cousin had many sources who would be eager to return a favor. They might find him before the passing of a month.

Then again, they might not. In which case, Darcy could guarantee his own release in four weeks. It beat being stuck on this godforsaken ship or left marooned on some uncharted island.

Still, Alex enjoyed all the leverage. Darcy needed more. His lack of knowledge was his greatest disadvantage. If he only knew the workings of a ship, he could better formulate a plan for escape. To do so now would be the height of stupidity. He could not even find the chart room. "Teach me the skills I need to be a worthy sailor during the twenty-eight days starting from my abduction, and I shall teach you how to be a lady." He held out his hand.

"Hey, ye's tryin' to cheat me. One month."

"Twenty-eight days from the time Bauer and

Cotton struck me over the head outside the tavern. That leaves you twenty-five days."

"Not countin' today."

"Counting today." He pushed his hand closer to her.

With a marked scowl, Alex tugged her dagger free of the table, slicing her palm and handing him the knife. Blood dripped from her palm onto the edge of her plate. "Ye've a deal."

Darcy stared at the knife, the edge still wet with her blood.

"It's a blood oath, Darcy. When I give me word, I keep it. This is yer guarantee." She shoved the dagger toward him.

Taking the weapon, he wiped it with a clean-looking linen napkin and pulled it over his hand.

Alex gave him a funny look, but they shook.

Twenty-five days. Twenty-five days to freedom.

Boone handed Darcy a flask and a length of cloth, and Darcy pondered how best to begin their lessons as he cleaned and wrapped his wound. Handing the flask back to Boone, he saw Alex stab another chunk of meat, and Darcy decided what the theme of their first lesson would be. "A lady cuts her meat into small bites, which she eats with a fork." He sat on the bench across from her and showed her on the plate of food that had been set out for him there.

"Does it have to be so small?"

"Yes."

She ate her first bite in one swallow.

Darcy exhaled. "You must chew"—he adjusted the number to one more manageable for a complete savage —"thirty times."

Her eyes widened. She sliced another small piece and began chewing. "With all these little bites and all this chewin', how long does it take to eat a meal?"

Darcy raised a finger. "A lady never speaks with her mouth full."

She opened her mouth and pointed at the tiny blob on her tongue. "Ye call this a full mouth?"

To call her savage was to insult the word. Darcy had always considered himself a patient man, but Alex required the forbearance of a martyr. "You are the one who requested lessons."

"How long?" she insisted, swigging down the contents of her glass.

"Sip. Do not gulp."

She slammed the glass down on the table. "How long fer a meal, blast ye!"

"Three hours."

"Three hours! D'ye think I've nothin' to do with me time? I've charts to study, sails to mend, lines to splice, decks to have swabbed, men to order, attacks to plan, and treasure to plunder. Some nights, I don't sleep a wink, and ye're tellin' me that a lady spends three hours of her day eatin' dinner?"

Darcy had no pity for her. "You really must learn to be more patient."

She scowled. "I'd sooner stab me eyes out with a fork than endure that slow torture."

They finished their meal in silence, Darcy clearing his throat every time Alex took too large of a bite or swallowed without chewing, and taking diabolical delight in her every glare in return.

Boone stood, a grin on his face. "Really, 'tis a pleasure, Darcy." He took his leave, the stiff breeze carrying his chuckle back to the table from the walkway.

Alex tapped her knife against her chin, and Darcy considered it prudent not to correct her just then.

Slowly, her lips curled up, and a calculating gleam spread up to her eyes that troubled Darcy a great deal more than the dagger she held so deftly in her hand. "Ye're quite the hoity-toity gent, aren't ye, Darcy? Ye must think ye're mighty clever. Mighty proud. Well, I can cure a man of pride."

That gleam in her eye bode ill for Darcy.

# CHAPTER 10

*D*arcy's discomfort increased the greater Alex's satisfaction grew. She was like a wolf that smelled fear, a shark smelling fresh blood.

"Ye want to learn the ways of a sailor? Ye'll start as the ship's boy, and ye'll start where all the ship boys do, helpin' Cook in the galley."

Darcy tried to contain his relief. Alex could gloat all she liked. He did not care. Any skill he could learn might mean his life—his freedom. No task was too low for him if it meant he could return to shore. To Elizabeth.

He left, finding Bauer swabbing the deck by the dining hall.

"Good day, Bauer. I trust you slept well?"

Bauer looked at him with a blank expression. Clearly, social niceties were lost on this lot. "Perhaps you would direct me to the galley?"

Laying his mop down at the edge of the walkway, Bauer grunted, "This be the way." He took Darcy to the back of the ship, and down several steps, where there were fewer sailors. "Careful with the cap'n. She be a clever one."

Darcy understood the warning. Alex had not tried to kill him yet that day, and he supposed he ought to count it as a blessing. It seemed out of character, though. Was she merely moody, or was she scheming something more than using him to secure Nick's affection? Darcy did not know if Bauer knew, but it was worth asking. "Why is she being more agreeable?"

Bauer scratched his head. "The way I see it, she found a use for ye. Or she saw how quickly ye won over the crew and she be playin' nice."

"What does it matter if her crew sympathizes with her prisoner?"

Shaking his head, Bauer said, "Ye don't know much about our kind, do ye? We may not abide by the laws of the land, but every pirate adheres to our code. Cap'ns be elected."

"Rule by crew? A democracy?" Darcy could not believe it.

Bauer shrugged. "How else? On a ship full of murderers, bandits, and thieves, we'd never agree on anything. So, we vote. The sailor with the most wins the post."

Darcy's plan to gain the favor of the crew now had a

solid motive. If he could turn them against Alexandra…
But what hold did she have over them? "How did she
come to be captain?"

"Cap'n be a good commander, quick to decide a
course and confident to carry it out."

She was controlling. Bossy.

Continuing, Bauer added, "She be a first-rate navigator, and she be mighty handy with a knife, sword,
and pistol."

Darcy was well aware of that.

"She keeps her head in battle. Many a skirmish she's
gained the upper hand. Nerves of steel, she has.
Stronger than most men. Has to be." Bauer shrugged.
"Can't expect anything less from a Lafitte. The sea be
all she's ever known." He stepped aside to allow Darcy
through a narrow space that opened into the galley.

Barrels and crates lined the walls. An oven hovered
over the tin-covered floor, swinging from chains
attached to large hooks in the ceiling. "Plus, she keeps
us in good food." Nodding at the man cracking eggs
into a large bowl, Bauer said in a low tone, "Jean-
Christophe used to cook fer the royal family. Or so
they say."

"Then what is he doing on the *Fancy*? Is he another
one of your captain's prisoners?"

Bauer leaned closer. "Word be he poisoned a Lord
of Parliament. He never goes ashore. Best stay on his
good side … just to be safe."

Darcy nodded his thanks and Bauer departed, leaving him alone with the deadly chef.

"Who are you, and what are you doing in my galley?" The cook had an accent the years had faded.

Swallowing his pride, Darcy presented himself. "I am the new ship boy."

The man guffawed. "You are very tall to be a ship boy, but I will forgive you this if you can peel those potatoes." He pointed at a mound of dirty potatoes in a crate that reached Darcy's knees. He prayed there was straw on the bottom. There were so many, and Darcy had never peeled a potato in his life.

But how hard could it be?

Jean-Christophe sharpened a knife and handed it to him. "Keep the peel thin, or I will make you cut the onions."

Taking a seat on the wooden stool, Darcy grabbed a potato, holding the knife in his other hand. Slowly, he cut into the potato and dragged the knife across the bulk of the vegetable until a chunk fell at his feet with a thud.

The chef glowered at him. "Much too thick." Grabbing the knife and potato from Darcy's hands, Jean-Christophe turned the blade to face him, pulling it toward his thumb. Raising the thin ribbon of peel, he waved it in front of Darcy's eyes. "You see? Like this? Thin."

Feeling like he was back in the schoolroom, Darcy

set his jaw and held the knife as the Frenchman had shown him. Carefully, he drew the blade toward his thumb. It was just like carving. His father's valet had taught him how to cut figurines into soft wood. He raised the peel for the chef to approve, proud of his quick improvement.

Jean-Christophe tsked. "Thinner!" he demanded.

It took several more potatoes before Darcy mastered the technique. By the bottom of the crate (which did not have straw at the bottom), the peels at his feet were paper thin.

Knuckle-sore, back aching, Darcy stood from the stool, too tired to celebrate his triumph. When he made it back to shore, he would raise the wages of his kitchen staff. And he would remove potatoes from the menu for the foreseeable future.

"You waste too much. Chop the onions," Jean-Christophe said, still cross.

One onion later, and with a dozen more to go, tears ran down Darcy's cheeks. This was a whole new kind of torture. The pungent odor burned his eyes, soaking through the cloth tied over his palm with a vicious sting. He did not know which was worse: keelhauling, chopping onions, or the horrors awaiting him over the next twenty-five days.

THE FOLLOWING day brought no relief to the Gardiner household.

Still full of nervous energy, Elizabeth was grateful when Aunt suggested they leave Lydia under the maid's charge to take the children for a stroll in the park.

They walked along the nearby paths while the nurse supervised the children. They ran and skipped as though they had no care in the world.

Elizabeth searched the pavements for signs of Mr. Darcy. It was a vain search, she knew. With so many people unable to find him, he was unlikely to be discovered strolling leisurely through a park.

Aunt took her hand. "You are not as averse to Mr. Darcy as you led us to believe, are you, dear?" It was more a statement of fact than a question.

"No." Elizabeth would not deny it. Aunt could not have helped but overhear her conversation with Colonel Fitzwilliam the day prior. Elizabeth's throat swelled and she could say nothing more.

Aunt tucked her hand against her side and resumed walking slowly. "I suspected as much while we were at Pemberley."

Elizabeth heated at the memory. "I was mortified to see him. H-he offered for me last spring," she admitted.

"And?"

"And I refused him—most resolutely."

Aunt raised her eyebrows, her lips curling. "Did you, now? Mr. Darcy certainly knows how to inspire strong feelings in you."

"I was very passionate," Elizabeth mumbled.

"A quality most men desire in a wife, dear. It seemed to me that Colonel Fitzwilliam gave you reason to hope."

"He did. But all the reassurances in the world mean nothing if Mr. Darcy is—" She could not say it. Could not think it. "I would give anything to know he is alive. And well." And willing to give her another chance.

Aunt squeezed Elizabeth's hand and bunched her lips. She would not make a promise she could not keep, no matter how badly Elizabeth wanted to hear it.

That night, Elizabeth dreamed of walking London's streets. Swarms of tall gentlemen with silk hats whisked past her, their faces blurred.

One man looked over his shoulder. It was him! She ran, calling out, but Mr. Darcy could not hear her. Or maybe he chose to ignore her.

It did not matter. He needed her help. She ran and ran. Someone pulled her from behind, and she twisted free.

Then a rough hand covered her eyes, blinding her. She flailed out, trying to break free, but stronger hands pulled her back, lifting her off the ground.

She screamed, kicked, and lashed, startling herself awake. Sitting in bed, her chest heaving, Elizabeth looked about the dark room and sensed Lydia's figure curled up beside her. It was only a bad dream.

Pulling the covers down where she held them over her head, Lydia whined, "Oy! I know you are cross with me, Lizzy, but pummeling me in my sleep is beneath you!" She took a pillow (one of Elizabeth's) and made a show of placing it between them. Within minutes, her breathing fell into the soft rhythm of sleep.

Elizabeth tried to rest. If only she knew Mr. Darcy was alive.

## CHAPTER 11

*N*icholas Blackburne was in a foul mood. It had begun at Barataria Bay and had festered all the way across the Atlantic over the past month. The colder the water under him became, the more heated his temper.

He should have known the Lafittes would betray him. All that talk of brotherhood, family ties…. Lies. The lot of it.

Feeling downright ferocious in the back of the barred carriage, Nick ground his teeth with every jolt and bump digging into the irons binding his hands to his feet with a ridiculously short chain. Connell was taking no chances with him.

Not that Nick could blame him. He made daily attempts to escape, and nearly met with success jumping over the side of the ship and splashing into

93

London's harbor. Even with his hands bound, Nick was an excellent swimmer. Every sailor worth his salt ought to be, though few enough were.

But Nick was too valuable a prize. Connell had not spent five years chasing the currents running along Africa and the Americas in pursuit of his prey to let Nick escape now. The man was dogged in his purpose.

The promise of coin had been enough to secure the help of a nearby waterman bobbing like a cork on the Thames. The traitor had hauled Nick over the side of his boat by the hair.

Now, Nick was wet and wreaking of filthy water, his feet and wrists rubbed raw from weeks of wearing shackles, and the back of his head throbbing where the waterman had smacked him with his oar.

He shivered, unable to rub his arms against the cold. He'd sworn he would never set foot on British soil again. It was too cold. Too damp. Too foggy. Too crowded with folks who didn't give a jot about him. He had no family. No friends. He had nobody.

The carriage came to a stop, and masses of people poked their noses through the bars holding him inside. Protecting them from him. Like a caged animal.

He heard Connell's voice, boasting, "That is Nicholas Blackburne. You have read stories about him, sung ballads extolling his conquests as The Blade." Connell was determined to make certain he got the credit (and the reward) for his capture.

"The Blade," they whispered. It was hard to tell if

they dropped their voices in awe or fear. Dozens of eyes inspected Nick, making him feel like a lion in an exhibition. He roared for good measure, causing several to leap away from the bars and others to laugh.

The opening in the crowd allowed him a view of what was beyond—the gallows—and he shivered again, this time from something other than cold. Already, he could feel the rope chafing against the skin at his neck.

The mob's exclamations and gasps grew. "The Blade," they repeated.

Nick tried not to hear them. He'd been stuck with the appellation since he overtook a slave ship with that she-devil, and a handful of those scoundrels got away. He despised slavers. Men who wrenched folks away from their loved ones deserved to be gutted. They were how the stories were created and spread by men so grateful to be alive that they spun yarns about their narrow escape with death. They always glorified the details.

Nick hated the stories circulating about him. Most of them weren't true.

"Is it true you've never lost a sword fight?" a boy barely taller than the floor of the carriage asked.

That was true, but Nick gave no reply. Feeding that report would set all the young blades out to test their skill against him … if he managed to escape before he was hanged. If a pirate was good at anything, it was getting himself out of trouble.

Another man asked, "Did you really fight off twenty men with a single sword?"

True, but they were untrained imbeciles. That hardly counted.

A woman asked, "Do you feed off the hearts of your captives?"

*Only the contents of their coffers*, Nick thought. What did they think he was, a savage barbarian?

A girl sitting on top of a man's shoulders shouted, "Are you really the most skilled man on earth with a blade?"

Nick scowled. He hadn't set foot in England for nearly two decades, but he already had a reputation that would send him to an early grave. While he prided himself on his skills, he'd never claim to be the best. And no matter how much he had practiced over the years, he could not equal Alex's artistry with a knife. His shoulder throbbed at the memory.

Looking up at the girl, he said, "Give me a knife, and I'll show ye."

The crowd guffawed, but he didn't care. He had to try, to seize every opportunity, or it would be the gallows for him.

Connell threatened the crowd. "The Blade is a dangerous man, a ruthless, bloodthirsty pirate. Nobody is safe until he drops from the gallows."

One man in the audience jeered, "You're no better than that filthy pirate, you thief-taker."

Nick might have been offended, but one sniff confirmed that the man merely spoke the truth. Nick had smelled better.

Most thief-takers, the honest ones, hated that term, preferring to be called something more elegant. Like "enquiry agent" or some such. Connell was no different. To a degree, Nick sympathized. He would rather be called a privateer than a pirate. Privateers—the honest ones—did not hang. Pirates did.

Connell's voice was stiff, his laugh hard. "Call me what you want. I am the one who will collect the bounty when The Blade is convicted of his crimes against humanity."

Which was precisely the fate Nick was determined to avoid.

Another voice from the crowd said, "Too bad it's not Monday."

Nick swallowed hard. Monday was hanging day at Newgate. Every pirate in the world knew that.

The hairs on his arms stood on end. Someone in the crowd was watching him in that way that piqued the senses and alerted one to danger. Nick had learned not to ignore those warning signals. He scanned over the people pressed against the carriage until he met eyes with a man with gray whiskers wearing a high-collared, blue coat with brass buttons and a tall, black hat. He spoke, but Nick couldn't hear him clearly. "Darcy," he seemed to say.

Darcy. What was a Darcy? A surname? A place? An insult he hadn't yet heard?

The carriage jolted forward, and daylight faded in the shadows of Newgate's high walls. They looked sturdy. Sturdier than the rotten, crumbling walls of Marshalsea Prison where pirates were normally housed until their conviction. Connell wasn't taking any chances.

Nick tried to keep his bearings as he was shoved down damp corridors, around curving, dark halls, and up a floor of stairs until he was shoved into a cell. The door slammed behind him before he caught his balance.

Alone in a stone cell, without even a chair to sit on, Nick inspected his new abode—only some straw in a corner and one barred window too high and too small to be of any use.

Shadows passed over the light seeping under his door. The jingling of keys and the groan of a chair being sat on. So, he had his own guard outside his cell. It was blasted inconvenient to have the reputation he did.

At least his chains were off. Nick hunkered down on the bed of straw and tried to sleep. But without the lull of the ship, he couldn't relax.

He rubbed the ragged scar at his shoulder and saw the blue eyes and raven black hair of the termagant who'd put it there. Fool woman. When he got out of this place, he'd find her, and he'd strangle her ... or kiss her senseless. He still couldn't decide which, and his indecision blackened his mood once more.

Alexandra had betrayed him. Her name should fill him with hate.

But he missed her.

# CHAPTER 12

*Make haste to Newgate Prison.*

*Ask to see Nicholas Blackburne. Do not take no for an answer.*

*Be very cautious.*

*Rouncewell*

Richard followed the guard along Newgate's corridors. Around one turn, a section stretched several feet in front of them, lit only by one sconce on the wall. At the end of the hall was a bolted metal barrier with hinges as thick as clubs. A guard sat in front of the door, a pistol in his lap.

"Colonel Richard Fitzwilliam to visit the prisoner," the other guard informed him.

"This prisoner's not allowed any visitors," the gruff man replied.

Assuming his stiffest posture, Richard stepped forward, addressing the man as though he were giving orders. "Then I shall return with my father, Lord Matlock, so that he may insist you allow us passage." He did not like using his father's position as a peer, but it did come in handy in moments like these.

The man squinted his eyes and moved aside. Unlocking the door, he asked, "You have any weapons on you?"

Richard had a knife in his boot, but he was not about to give that up. Rouncewell had said to be cautious. Instead, Richard handed over the knife he carried in his coat. And when the guard motioned at his fob chain, he handed that over as well.

Both of the guards moved in front of him, pistols ready should their prisoner rush them at the door. He must be as dangerous as Rouncewell had implied.

They motioned him forward, and Richard heard the doors close behind him as soon as he set foot inside the room. His skin crawled at the sound. He was as much of a prisoner as the man Blackburne—at the mercy of the guards to allow him out. Not a pleasant realization.

The prisoner stood in the corner, as still as a statue. His features were obscured in the dim light of dusk, away from the only window in his cell.

"Nicholas Blackburne?" Richard asked, stepping forward when the man still did not move.

No reply.

Cautiously, Richard took another step forward, now standing in the middle of the small space. "Are you

Nicholas Blackburne?" he repeated. He blinked several times, his eyes adjusting to the dark.

Still no answer. Was the man still alive? His hair fell over his face, long, dark, and curly. There was no puff of breath where his mouth would be. But he was upright. Richard looked for a cord above the man's head. He had heard too many stories of men hanging themselves before their trial.

He took another step forward, reaching his hand out to feel for a pulse, eyes searching, pulse racing, sensing a trap and choosing to spring it and be done with it rather than wait.

With a shout, the man lunged at him, whipping around Richard and wrapping his arm around his neck.

Immediately, Richard dropped his chin to his chest, preventing the man from choking him.

And then, he felt the cold edge of a knife pressing into his neck. From the corner of his eye, he saw the silver tip on the handle. His knife. "How?" Richard grunted, not expecting an answer. He had not even felt Blackburne slip the shiv from his boot.

The next seconds would mean the difference between life and death. The man behind him was taller than he was—Darcy's height. He was strong. Perhaps stronger than Richard. It was safer to assume his opponent was stronger and more skilled than he was. To underestimate him again would be a fatal mistake.

Irritated at himself for losing possession of his

weapon to the prisoner when he knew better, Richard jerked his right shoulder upward while his hands pulled the prisoner's knife-wielding hand down.

Slipping his head through the narrow gap, keeping the sharp end of the knife away from his face, he twisted Blackburne's arm behind his back. Richard could have stabbed him in the side, but Rouncewell had sent him here for a reason, and he would find out why.

Blackburne grunted, but he held fast to the knife. Lord, he was strong.

Richard thrust his arm upward, the prisoner's shoulder snapping. Only then did he drop the knife.

Holding up his free hand, Blackburne said, "Are ye going to finish me off, or what?"

His voice sounded so much like Darcy, Richard released his hold.

Slowly, Blackburne stood, rubbing his shoulder and wincing. "Ye're a bold fighter. I could've sliced yer jugular."

"And allow a prisoner to escape using my own knife? I think not."

Turning to face him, Blackburne brushed his hair away from his face, and Richard felt his jaw go slack.

The man standing in front of him was the spitting image of his missing cousin. It could not be, but the words crossed his lips anyway. "Darcy? Is that you?"

"There's that name again. Second time I've heard it today." He frowned, inspecting Richard as thoroughly as Richard looked at him. From the top of his head to his hairy toes, he was Darcy's identical twin.

Richard asked, "What is your name?"

"Nicholas Blackburne."

"Where are you from?"

"Devonshire."

"Who were your parents?"

Blackburne shrugged.

"Who raised you?" Richard asked.

"An old fisherman and his wife saw I was fed, let me use their surname, helped me find work on me first ship."

"You have been at sea most of your life?"

"Aye."

"How did you become a pirate?"

"The Lafittes took me ship." He spat on the floor.

"And they let you live?"

"I was just a lad, light on me feet and good at climbing. When they saw me crawl up the ropes like a monkey, they decided they'd keep me. T'weren't much of a choice."

He did not think much of his mentors, then. Encouraged to hear evidence of a conscience, Richard pressed on. "Does the name Darcy mean anything to you? Anything at all?"

"Should it?"

"Have you no family?"

"Who'd claim the likes o' me?"

"What do you know of your history? Were your parents from Devonshire?"

Another shrug. "I suppose."

"Did the fisherman tell you anything about them?" Lack of information was frustrating. Richard could not imagine how awful it would be to grow up completely alone, with no place, nobody.

"He said a fish vomited me onto the shore. Found me wailing on the beach. I always thought he made it up to keep me from asking 'til I heard the vicar talk about Jonah." He looked down, adding softly, "The vicar's wife taught me to read with that story."

Blackburne was literate, then, and intelligent. He had learned to adapt, skilled at survival under what Richard imagined as the most adverse circumstances.

"Where can I find the fisherman?" he asked.

"I don't suppose ye can. He was old when I left, and that was fifteen years ago."

Fifteen years away, at sea. "How old are you?"

"Eight and twenty, as far as I know. I know the year, but not the day."

Richard needed more than that. "What of his wife? Might she still be alive?"

"Doubtful."

Tugging his hand through his hair, Richard pressed, "Did they have children? Or friends they trusted?"

Blackburne folded his arms over his chest and scowled, looking so much like Darcy in appearance and manner, Richard was struck anew with awe. "Why all these blasted questions? I've no family here. No friends on land." He scoffed. "Right now, ye're me closest acquaintance, and I don't even know yer name, only that ye're skilled at fighting and therefore deserving of me respect."

Richard took a deep breath. "I apologize. Your resemblance to my cousin is so striking, I forgot my manners."

"Darcy? Is that why I keep hearing that name?"

With a nod, Richard bowed. "Colonel Richard Fitzwilliam, at your service."

Blackburne looked at him askance. "Why're ye here, Colonel?"

Richard shook his head, trying to find a starting place when nothing made any sense. "I do not know how it happened, how a secret of this magnitude could be kept this long, but there is no other logical explanation. You are the mirror image of my cousin Fitzwilliam Darcy of Pemberley in Derbyshire." He watched Blackburne for a reaction, not expecting his laughter.

"Ye can see that through this filth and all this hair?"

"You have the same height, same build. You even sound like him."

Pulling his shirt down to expose his shoulder and chest, Blackburne asked, "Does he have this scar, too?" His tone was mocking.

"No, but he has a similar one lower on his ribs. If you are a Darcy, you have family—a powerful family who shall offer you their protection." Pirate or not, Richard could not let Blackburne hang until he knew why he had been taken away from Pemberley.

How he wished his aunt Lady Anne were still alive. Or Uncle George. But neither of them could have known there had been two Darcys born that day. They would have hired every enquiry agent and investigator in the country, searched every house, and talked to every family until they found their missing son. With their influence and wealth, their search would have met with success.

But they had not known. Nobody had known.

Blackburne glowered at him. "What're ye about, Colonel? I've yet to meet a man who'd not rather betray me for a profit." Under his breath, he mumbled, "Blast that infernal female."

Richard ignored his comment. "Clearly, you have not met your brother."

"I have no brother. And if I did, where's he been all these years?"

"He is as ignorant of your existence as you were of his. Darcy will want to meet you."

Blackburne looked like a dog backed into a corner. He did not trust easily.

Richard reassured him. "Darcy is the most honorable man I know. He will want to know what happened. He shall track down the person or persons responsible for your exile, and he shall ensure matters are dealt with justly." Richard could do no less either.

Was it a coincidence Darcy should disappear days before his identical likeness showed up at Newgate? The two events did not seem related, but the timing was too close.

He needed to talk to his father. The family needed to know. Father could use his influence to convince the magistrate to let Blackburne free under his charge.

Richard eyed the man. As easily as he had snatched the knife from his boot, Blackburne would find a way to escape unless Richard made haste.

He knocked on the door to let the guards know he was ready to leave. "I shall be back," he told Blackburne.

"I'll be here … probably."

"See that you are." Richard stared at him, conveying his severity to the charge.

"It's me nature to escape. It's how I stay alive."

"Fair enough, but you shall always be escaping, always on the run and never free. I can offer you my family's—your family's—protection."

"Sorry, Colonel, but I've a hard time believing that. Nobody does anything unless there's something in it for them. What do ye want from me?"

Something more immediate, then. Pirates sought pleasure, luxury. Richard knew just the thing. "I can promise you a bath and a shave."

Blackburne stilled. "A change of clean rags?"

Richard's gaze flickered down to Blackburne's bare feet. "And a pair of boots." He had the advantage, and he pressed it. "If you agree not to disappear until after I find Darcy."

"Ye mean ye lost him?"

"He was kidnapped … I think." Richard gritted his teeth. How could he find Darcy and discover why his brother had been separated from him at the same time? He sensed many long days and nights ahead of him. "Do I have your word?" he asked instead, eager to get somewhere he could discover some answers.

"Ye'd believe the word of a wanted pirate?"

"I shall believe your word until you prove yourself untrustworthy."

"Innocent 'til proven guilty? That's not the way yer laws work."

"It is the way I work." Blackburne was as skeptical as Darcy—another trait they had in common.

After some seconds' consideration, Blackburne nodded. "I'll meet yer Darcy, if ye find him. But the second ye cross me, I'll leave, and ye'll not be able to find me." He held out his hand.

They shook, and Richard raced away from the river to Mayfair.

A carriage waited outside his father's residence. It was too dark to see who it belonged to. Richard dismounted in front of the house, tossing his horse's reins to the first man to run down the steps to him.

Mr. Gardiner and Mr. Bennet stepped out from the conveyance, calling out, "Colonel! We must speak with you without delay!"

As hurried as he was, there was something in their manner that brought Richard to a halt.

"It is Elizabeth," Mr. Gardiner said.

Mr. Bennet's hands shook as he raised them in supplication. "Please help her, Colonel. One minute she was with me. And the next, she was gone. Vanished."

CHAPTER 13

*E*lizabeth stretched out her legs, muscles sore, bones aching.

She tried to remember, but the past hours—days?—had been a blur. There had been a lot of jolting and bouncing. Now, gentle swaying.

"Miss Elizabeth," a man's voice called. He was not her father, but his tone was gentle, musical. "Miss Elizabeth, you must sit up and drink."

Tilting her head to the side, Elizabeth opened her eyes, blinking as her vision cleared. A wall of black and gold and vivid hues met her gaze. She sat up, trying not to look at the bare chest under the brightly colored vest, and focusing, instead, on the beautiful tray loaded with plates and platters which he balanced on one arm. The smell was divine, and her empty stomach groaned in anticipation. In his other hand, he handed her a glass of water.

As tempting as it was to dwell on the food, she had not come here of her own volition. "Who are you?" she asked.

He bowed. "Your servant, Jaffa. Cap'n Alexandra sends her deepest apologies for the inconvenience to you."

"Inconvenience is putting it lightly. I was kidnapped."

"She hopes you will be comfortable aboard the *Fancy*."

A female captain. Interesting. Still, Elizabeth was cautious. Women were as capable as men of committing the worst crimes. She could not let her guard down, nor could she give in to hunger before she had learned who her captor was. "Captain Alexandra?" she prompted.

Jaffa set the tray down gently on her legs, and pulled the lids off of the plates. Freshly baked bread, scrambled eggs, sausages, a thick slab of butter, a small bowl of strawberry jam, and an entire pot of coffee with her own bowl of sugar and cream.

The aroma did its best to break her defenses, but Elizabeth held Jaffa's steady gaze. "Who is Captain Alexandra?" she repeated.

"She is the cap'n of this ship and my master. Her welfare is my responsibility, as is yours."

"I am her prisoner?"

"You are her guest."

Looking down at the feast spread over her legs, Elizabeth found it hard to debate the point.

"Please, Miss Elizabeth, you must eat."

Who was she to argue? He poured her coffee while she tucked into her meal. Every bite made her hungry for more; each morsel tasting better than the last as her hunger abated enough for her to savor the tastes crossing her tongue. Longbourn's cook had never prepared a breakfast this delicious. She did not know Captain Alexandra, but Elizabeth would pay her compliments to her chef.

Pausing to sip her sweet coffee and cream, she looked up at Jaffa, who stood over her like a guard ready to pounce should her cup get too low or an unwanted guest arrive. "Do you treat all of your prisoners"—he shot her a look—"I mean, guests, this well?"

He did not reply but promptly poured more coffee into her cup once she set it down.

The man wore a curved sword at his side, and despite her success averting her eyes, she could not help but notice how strong he was. And yet, she did not feel threatened by him. In fact, she was quite at ease. Remnants of whatever she had been drugged with?

She had many questions, and Elizabeth knew she would get more answers if she was polite to her captor. Thanking him, she asked, "Where are you from, Mr. Jaffa?"

"It is only Jaffa, Miss. I am from the North of Africa, where the Nile floods the delta."

A place she would love to know more about … later. "Why am I here?" Her heart leapt into her throat, and the tray rattled as she shifted. "What day is it?"

"It is Friday, Miss."

Lydia's wedding! Had she missed it? Had Lydia married Wickham? Or had Elizabeth's disappearance thrown her family into another panic? They would be frantic with worry. Poor Papa! Poor Aunt and Uncle!

Elizabeth had no way of knowing if it was that same Friday or a week after. She looked through the window as though that might supply an answer but saw only a spot of blue. She clutched her fingers into a fist. How would she find Mr. Darcy out here? She did not know where *here* was.

She had been standing by her father reading the broadsides, hoping to find information about Mr. Darcy, and the next thing she knew, she was being dragged into a carriage. The memory brought back the sweet smell of whatever had been on the handkerchief held over her mouth and nose. And then, the bitter taste of laudanum.

Elizabeth reached for her coffee, the strong liquid burning the recollection away. Her captors could not have drugged her for an entire week. Which meant that they had either gone East or South to get to the ocean.

"It is mid-afternoon. You have been resting after an arduous journey and must be greatly fatigued," Jaffa explained, nodding at the small, round window.

The door opened, and Jaffa moved to the side, closer to Elizabeth.

A beautiful woman with raven black hair and striking blue eyes smiled at her. She wore a silk shirt with more ruffles and lace than even Mama or Lydia would wear and trousers that fit her like a second skin tucked into boots that reached her knees.

"Ye're awake. I've been impatient to meet ye." Her voice was firm and not unwelcoming. Elizabeth could not place her accent. It sounded like a combination of every accent Elizabeth had ever heard, which were, admittedly, few enough.

"How do you know me? Where am I?" she asked.

"Ye're aboard me ship, the *Fancy*. Don't let me presence keep ye from eatin'. Ye'll need yer strength out here."

"How did I get here?"

The woman shrugged. "The usual way. Startin' at The Swan with Two Necks on Lad Lane to Bagshot, nearly thirty miles. Another change of horses at Alton, again at Alresford. Then, finally, Southampton. Seventy-eight miles overland, then a small fishing vessel that brought ye right to the *Fancy*."

Off the coast of Southampton? While Elizabeth would never wish to repeat the trip, she did wish she might have seen some of the scenery. "What kind of ship is this?"

Alexandra smirked. "Today, we're ambitious merchants with a hold full of cotton. Tomorrow, we might be privateers representin' whichever country is most convenient. I've several letters of Marque from which to choose. Perhaps we'll be corsairs returnin' to the Mediterranean or buccaneers lookin' for a Spanish ship to take. One must be adaptable with the British Navy lurkin' about."

Elizabeth shivered. "You are a pirate."

Longbourn was far away from the threat of pirates, but she had read stories. She recalled the tales she had heard and wondered if they could be true. Most of them were terrifying.

The lady pirate sat at the foot of Elizabeth's bed. Reaching forward, she plucked a piece of sausage from Elizabeth's plate and tossed it into her mouth. The woman who counted as she chewed did not look like the sort of person who had carved the beating heart out of a victim's chest.

As though she had read Elizabeth's thoughts, Alexandra locked eyes with her and, shoving the wad of half-chewed sausage into her cheek, she asked, "Are ye frightened? Ye don't look afraid."

Elizabeth was grateful for that when, in truth, she was more afraid than she had ever been in her life. Calmly, she replied, "Ladies feel many things they train themselves not to show." She considered how she would fare defending herself with the dull butter knife and fork … until she saw a second dagger hiding under one of the folds of lace at her captor's side.

Alexandra smiled at Jaffa. "I knew I was right to

bring her here." She covered her hand over her mouth and cast a look so repentant, Elizabeth had to stifle the urge to laugh. "I know I'm not supposed to speak with me mouth full of food, but I can't quite figure out how I'm supposed to carry on a conversation during a meal. If I chew like I'm told a lady does, I've forgotten what I meant to say by the time I can finally swallow."

"It helps to take smaller bites."

"That's what he tells me, but I'd die of hunger before I could complete a sentence, what with all that chewin'. I don't know how ye do it, Elizabeth."

Elizabeth had not given Alexandra leave to use her Christian name or to eat from her plate, but she trusted her instincts enough to know not to insist on propriety. The woman wore two daggers that Elizabeth could see and who knew what else that she could not see. She was not about to criticize Alexandra's manners when she was the prisoner-guest. "What am I to call you?" she asked.

"Me friends call me Alex, but ye can call me what ye like. I know the circumstances which brought ye here are suspect, but it's me hope that we'll become fast friends. Ye're me guest while ye're aboard the *Fancy*, and I mean to help ye feel comfortable. How's yer stomach? Lots of folks get bilious out at sea. I had Jaffa put a bucket by ye, in case."

The food on Elizabeth's platter lost its appeal. She pushed it away and pulled her knees up to her chest under the blankets.

"Ye're not feelin' ill right now, are ye?" Alex asked, pointing at the bucket for Jaffa to push closer.

Elizabeth took a deep breath. "I am well enough." She had been out on a fishing boat once and, until Alex had mentioned nausea, she had been perfectly fit. Now she was not so certain.

Jaffa placed the bucket closer, saying to Alexandra, "Perhaps the mention of bile would put most ladies off their food."

Twisting her face, balling her hands into fists, Alexandra said heatedly, "I can calculate a cannon's trajectory at a glance, throw me knife within a hair-breadth of me target, and creep up on a ship before the lookout calls a warnin', but this lady business'll be the death of me." She pounded her fist against her thighs. "I'll learn how to act like a lady. Darcy said ye're the finest lady he knows, and I trust ye can teach me."

A shiver shot from Elizabeth's head down to her toes. Had she heard correctly? "*Who* told you about me?"

A mouth full of sausage, bread, and egg along with her newly acquired table manners prevented Alexandra from answering. And then, when she had counted her chews and swallowed, a scuffle from the other side of the door interrupted her further.

*Bang bang bang!* A fist hammered against the door.

Alexandra rolled her eyes. "That'll be him. That lout, Cotton, must've told him. Nothin' but fluff in his head."

*Bang bang bang!*

"Open the door 'fore he breaks it down!" she ordered.

Jaffa opened the door.

And Elizabeth's breath caught in her throat. "Mr. Darcy!" she whispered.

He stood in the breeze, five days of stubble covering his face, his shirt open at the collar. Never had Elizabeth seen him so handsome. So rugged. So angry.

# CHAPTER 14

*D*arcy had never known such fury and horror! Yet Elizabeth looked as composed as a lady receiving guests at a ball. He had always wondered how long her hair was when it was not smoothed and pinned into submission. The sight of her untamed curls cascading over her shoulders to her waist made him want to bury his fingers in her tresses to test their silkiness.

The corners of her lips pulled into a smile, and Darcy felt her brave humor like a stab to the gut. Were it not for him, Elizabeth would not be on this God-forsaken ship. She would not be in danger. As if his faults to the one woman whose good opinion he craved were not enough, he could never forgive himself for exposing her to the likes of Alex and her crew.

Alex. Darcy leveled a glare at her.

She rolled her eyes and stood. "Stop scowlin', Mr.

Darcy. Ye ought to be happy to have yer young lady aboard. She's as handsome as ye said, and intelligent."

Darcy felt his frown deepen. He must have said a great deal more than just her name while he slept. Voice hard, his irate stare fixed on Alexandra, he said, "Ladies do not kidnap people at their will."

She shrugged. "Ye never told me not to. How was I supposed to know?"

He had thought it obvious.

Alex continued, the satisfaction in her expression deepening Darcy's ire, "Now that yer Elizabeth is here, she'll take over me lady lessons while ye carry on with yer ship duties." She used Elizabeth's fork to stab a piece of sausage from the plate. "Very good," she commented around her mouthful. Tearing a piece of bread and popping it into her mouth, she said, "The bread is tougher than I like, though. Have Jean-Christophe show ye how to make it softer."

Elizabeth looked down at her tray and up at Darcy, and he tried to control the burn rising to his cheeks. For her to know he had been reduced to the role of a cook's helper, a servant, was more than he could bear. He turned his palms, hiding them against his trousers. Where he did not have cuts and burns from the kitchen, he had blisters and raw flesh from the ropes aloft.

Oblivious to the consequences of her blabbering, Alex said, "When ye're done with that, ye can race

Cotton up the riggin'. How're yer hands?" She motioned for him to hold them out for her to inspect.

He crossed his arms over his chest. A man could only take so much humiliation. "Strong enough to strangle you unless you return Miss Elizabeth to her family immediately." His tone was murderous.

Darcy was not given to violence. Wickham's continued existence was proof enough of that. Before this moment, Darcy never would have believed himself capable of threatening a woman. But Alex was his foremost enemy. The rage she inspired surpassed all that Wickham had ever provoked within him—all the anger and fear of a lifetime eclipsed in the blink of an eye the moment Darcy saw Elizabeth aboard the *Fancy*.

He had to protect her. He had to get her off this cursed ship. "We cannot be far from the shore. Return her."

"Or what?" Alexandra purred, watching him like a cat with a bird in its paw.

"Or you shall regret it." Darcy did not say the words lightly. He always meant what he said; he always kept his word.

She rolled her eyes. "Ye're too honorable to do me any harm. I'm not afraid of ye, Darcy."

"I am wealthy. I will pay."

She huffed as if he had offended her. "I'm not interested in yer money. I need lady lessons from a real lady so Nick'll love me like ye love her."

Darcy's heart seized in his chest, and his shame

burned everywhere. What would Elizabeth think of him now? He wanted to know more than anything, but he dared not look at her or risk losing his composure completely. Was he so desperate, so obvious, that his feelings were an open book for anyone to read?

Taking a deep breath, he widened his stance, the ground feeling unsteady where it had been firm a moment before. "What kind of pirate is not interested in a fortune?" he asked.

Elizabeth gasped. "This is a pirate ship?" Her gaze roamed over him, seeing his wrapped hands, the bindings his clothing did not cover. Color rose to her cheeks and, tossing the blankets off her legs, she stood. She would have presented an irate figure had she not stumbled about with the swaying of the ship just as Darcy had done his first day.

But Elizabeth was not discouraged. Her courage rose as it always did. He loved that about her.

Bracing herself against the wall behind her, she glared at Alex. "How could you hurt a gentleman who would never raise his hand against a woman? What have you done to him?"

Alex grinned. "I like her. She has some fire."

Jaffa, who had been quietly watching until now, warned her under his breath, "Take care not to get scorched, Cap'n."

Elizabeth lifted her chin. "I do not care for your good opinion. Answer my question. What have you done to Mr. Darcy?"

With a shrug, Alex motioned to his wrapped hands. "Those're from climbin' ropes and burnin' his fingers on the galley stove." She pointed to his leg. "And I'm guessin' that's from the keelhaulin'."

"You dragged him under your ship? You might have killed him!" Elizabeth looked at him, the tender concern in her eyes making Darcy's heart swell so much it hurt.

Alex waved off her concerns. "He told me himself that he knew how to swim, and only last month, the *Fancy* was careened and cleaned of barnacles. Me men knew I wanted him alive, so they pulled the ropes right quick." She shrugged. "I knew he'd survive. Just like Nick would."

Elizabeth heaved a breath. "Why make him suffer? What kind of monster are you?"

"I ain't no monster." Alex said uncertainly, showing the first glimpse of a conscience Darcy had seen in her. "I was upset. He was supposed to be my Nick. And he challenged me authority in front of me crew. What else was I supposed to do?"

"You could have rebuked him in the hearing of your crew. That would have been enough."

Alex's brows furrowed.

Elizabeth softened her tone. "Would your crew not appreciate knowing their captain is capable of mercy?"

Throwing her hands upward, Alex retorted, "I was bein' merciful. I didn't shoot him."

Darcy supposed he ought to be grateful. Watching

Elizabeth take on Alex in his defense curtailed his anger to a more manageable degree. It did not, however, dampen his determination. "A lady always controls her temper, a fact I could have taught you without dragging Miss Elizabeth away from her family."

Crossing her arms defensively, Alex mumbled, "I'm the captain of this ship. I'm the one in control, and I say I can learn more about bein' a lady from her than I can from you. She stays." Jutting out her chin, she added, "And that's final."

Gracious, she was stubborn. "Over my dead body," Darcy seethed between his teeth.

"No. Not that, please," shouted Elizabeth, moving to stand between them and adding more quietly, "Never that, I beg you."

Hope fluttered in Darcy's chest.

Alex looked contentedly between the two, her gaze finally landing on Darcy. "Ye'd give yer life to keep her safe."

He nodded. He would.

Squinting her eyes, Alex examined him, looking as though she were attempting to read his thoughts. Darcy would stir up a mutiny if it got Elizabeth to shore—to her family. He would not rest until she was secure and far away from this wretched place. Far away from Alex.

Finally, she spoke. "I see I'll have to secure yer word—a promise on yer honor that'll bind ye to accept me decision. Ye'd sooner stir up a mutiny than give up."

Darcy would not deny it.

"Then there's only one thing to do. How 'bout a bit of sport?"

Darcy was listening. Until Alex wink-winked at him, just as she had before she had him thrown over the side of her ship.

## CHAPTER 15

*D*arcy's blood froze in his veins. Whatever scheme Alex devised boded ill for him. They always did.

Plopping her hands on her hips, raising her chin and her voice, Alex said, "I challenge ye to a sword fight. First to draw blood—"

He cast her a look.

She raised her fingers, pinching them. "Just a little nick, a bit of pink—"

Darcy stopped her there. "No blood." He would insist on some degree of propriety while she did not hesitate to put his life in peril. The irony was not lost on him.

She pouted. "That's no fun."

"I will not fight a woman."

"I've been fightin' men me whole life. I'm just as capable than ye."

"I do not doubt you are more capable than I am."

"Then why won't ye fight? I'm not goin' to kill ye." She motioned to Elizabeth, who still stood between them. "Not with her here. Although ye're blasted stubborn enough to tempt me. Ye know, I ought to have me men string ye up by yer thumbs—see how bullheaded ye be then." She looked behind her, shouting, "Jaffa, get—"

"The first to disarm the other," Elizabeth raised her hands, pushing Darcy away, her fingers spaying over his chest. Her touch sent a jolt through him that was capable of convincing him of anything. Such fine bones and narrow fingers, and yet, so powerful. One touch, and he was under her spell. Their eyes met, and Darcy mourned when she moved her hand.

Looking pointedly away from him, Elizabeth addressed Alex. "The first to deprive the other of their weapon, you understand? There will be no cutting off of limbs or stringing up by thumbs."

"I know what disarmin' means," Alex grumbled. "So blasted honorable. Must run in yer blood…"

Her sentence trailed off, and Darcy knew she was thinking about her Nick—the man for whom she had mistaken him. Darcy was curious to learn more about Nick. Perhaps they were related somehow.

With a blink, her eyes focused and sharpened. "If I win, Elizabeth stays, and ye stop schemin' yer escape. If ye win, I'll have me two best oarsmen see her safely to shore with enough blunt to send a message to her family and pay for a room at a decent inn until they can fetch her. Ye'll stay for the remainder of the time we shook on. I need lady lessons."

Darcy considered. He had seen Alex's skill with a knife. She would be a formidable opponent. It would be dangerous for him to underestimate her, but he was not without skill. He had trained with the masters—had bested many of them.

Therein, however, lay her advantage. He was accustomed to level floors and spacious arenas in clubs that enforced certain rules. He needed to even out his deficiency. "Proper fencing rules. No kicking, hitting, or attacks outside the boundaries accepted by any fencing club. I take it you are familiar—"

She twisted her mouth. "Of course I know the rules. I'm not a complete savage, ye know." She fiddled with the top of the shiv hidden in her boot. "Very well, I accept. Let the game begin."

Elizabeth stumbled forward. "Mr. Darcy, you do not have to do this! I know what I said, but what about your freedom?" Darcy and Jaffa reached out to steady her.

Darcy softened his harsh focus, trying to reassure her with a smile that felt pinched. "I have to try. I know how much you prize your freedom." His smile relaxed, feeling more genuine.

"But I do not want it at the price of yours."

Her tender words caressed Darcy. She cared for

him, perhaps not as much as he loved her, but it was more than he had dared to hope for.

Alex stepped toward the door, ruining the touching moment, but Darcy blocked her path. Holding out his palm, he said, "Your knives, please."

With a huff, she removed the knife from her boot, the other strapped to her side, and another one Darcy had not noticed in her hair. These, she handed, with a pointed look at Darcy, to Jaffa.

Jaffa nodded, doing his best not to smile.

She breezed past him, and Darcy followed past the aftercastle and down the stairs to the main deck where Jaffa handed her two sabers.

Elizabeth gripped the railing on the deck above them, her emotions playing out in her eyes. She was worried about him. Darcy supposed she would be distressed for any man in his position, but he gloried in her concern all the same.

A glint at his side alerted him just in time. A saber flew through the air at his face. He caught it, his heart galloping in his chest and hammering in his ears. That had been too close. He could not afford any distraction.

Alex laughed and urged on her crew's bawdy cheers. Coins clinked and bets were cast.

Darcy balanced the saber in his hand, testing its weight and fit. Sailors scrambled to the edges of the deck or up the rigging, eager to see the action up close and shouting taunts from the lines above Darcy's head.

The crowded deck was nothing like the fencing

salons he knew. It was cramped, close quarters. Not only would Darcy have to focus on Alex, but he would have to pay attention to his surroundings lest he hurt a sailor or stumble over a rope. There was a hatch in the middle of the deck. The main mast provided another obstacle. Boons and ropes.... He continued taking note of the details while he waited for Alex to signal the start of their fight.

She signaled with a charge.

Darcy warded off her blows, studying her over the next several minutes, letting her tire. Fencing was a skill which required as much thought as it did strength and endurance. She was skilled—of that there was no doubt. She held her weapon confidently and delivered her blows soundly. But it did not take long for Darcy to see his advantage. Alex fought as he had imagined she might—as he had hoped she would—all fury and bluster.

If he could make her angry or frustrate her, he could make his move.

She feigned left, trying to provoke a reaction.

Darcy smiled at himself. He could do this all day. His strength had always been in keeping his head when under pressure. He did not react.

The crew shouted and roared when her bluff was exposed as the empty threat it was.

Nostrils flared, Alex twirled, lunged, and thrust with greater force. Sweat poured down Darcy's face and back as he parried, bided his time, and waited for her frustration to reach its peak.

Her breath came in quick heaves and her cheeks were red from exertion, but she was strong. She advanced.

Darcy retreated, seeing his opportunity the closer he got to the mainmast. When one more step would have pinned him against the unforgiving surface, he pivoted around the mast to the other side, shuffling his feet as quickly as they could move.

He heard her frustrated screech.

Now! Darcy attacked, advancing relentlessly, thrust and lunge, again and again. Metal clanging against metal; blades flying; sweat stinging his eyes.

Her parries got sloppy, and Darcy surged forward, knowing that her wrists were weakening. He almost had her against the foresail, and she knew it. Her eyes widened.

Still, he continued, thrust-parry-block-lunge-thrust-thrust. He had her now. One more blow, and her saber would fly from her hands. He raised his arm, putting all of his weight in the movement because he would not fail Elizabeth now.

Alex dodged down to the deck, one hand gripping a rope. Before Darcy could change his stance, she whipped it around his feet and pulled.

He toppled to the deck like a felled tree, the breath knocked out of him, his saber still in his hand.

Elizabeth shouted, but he could not hear her over the louder crew.

Vision filled with blue sky, ropes, and sails, Alex's shadow fell over him, and he felt the sole of her boot, then her weight on his wrist.

He gripped the saber harder.

She stepped down harder, twisting her foot.

Darcy's bones shifted and cracked, his fingers had gone numb, but he did not loosen his grip.

Alex reached down and pried the saber from his hands with her fingernails, holding the weapon up triumphantly.

Darcy rolled to his side, trying to catch his breath and recover the feeling in his arm.

Elizabeth now stood at his head. "You did not win. You did not play by the rules."

Alex laughed. "Me ship, me rules."

"You gave your word."

"I lied."

"You cheated."

"What'd ye expect, lovey? Can a tiger change its stripes? I am what I am—a wily pirate."

Darcy pressed his eyes closed, feeling foolish. You could not hold a scorpion in your hand and expect it not to sting you. What had he been thinking, making a deal with Alex? He rose to his feet, but he felt low.

Alex turned to her crew, waving her arms in victory. "We have a new crew member. Miss Elizabeth is a lady, and I expect ye miserable lot to treat her with respect and yer best manners." She pointed the tips of her sabers at them. "If any of ye make any unwanted advances on our lady guest, ye'll answer to me, to Jaffa, and to Mr. Darcy, who's proved himself today, d'ye not agree?"

Cotton and Bauer cheered his name. Da Silva, Beckett, and Boone clapped, nodding in deference. Even Jean-Christophe applauded.

Alex twirled to face Darcy, lowering her voice. "That was a good fight, Darcy. Ye're not The Blade, but ye should be proud of yer performance."

Darcy was not flattered.

"If yer lady had any doubts about ye before, ye can bet she doesn't now. Ye can thank me later."

A sick feeling clenched Darcy's stomach. Once again, Alex had manipulated him for her own purpose. He searched the crowd, finding Elizabeth standing with Jaffa. "I failed," he mumbled under his breath.

"Ah, but now ye're somethin' ye weren't before," said Alex.

Darcy glared at her with open disdain.

She continued, looking entirely too satisfied with herself. "Ye're her hero. I may not know how to make Nick love me, but I know how a woman thinks. And I've made ye irresistible."

CHAPTER 16

*N*icholas woke up in his dank, dreary cell the following morning, cold and stiff. Either the colonel was full of drivel or he'd come to his senses and changed his mind. After all, who was Nick to this Darcy and his family? He was a complete stranger—a reformed pirate. The law would never allow Nick to prove himself a changed man. Why should the colonel?

Sitting in a ball, he waited for the chill to seep out of his chest while he inspected the bars. He was too weak to attempt to bend them. He hadn't had a proper meal in.... Nick's stomach growled. He would trade his soul for a loaf of Jean-Christophe's bread. A bite of his beef stew. Perhaps it was best not to remember.

Nick kicked the straw at his feet and stood. He and Alex had drawn straws over the chef—lengths of twine, but close enough—and Alex had won. Nick had known

135

she'd cheat; she always did. He hoped she choked on a chicken bone.

Keys clanged against the metal door, and a guard stepped inside, fumbling through more keys on a ring. "You have friends in high places," he grumbled as he crossed the room and grabbed Nick's bound hands and unlocked them.

Nick dared not say anything lest his good fortune shift like the tide. Colonel Fitzwilliam seemed like a good man. Nick was inclined to like him, though it remained to be seen if he could be trusted.

Trust was everything. If a man had nobody to trust, he had nothing. And if a so-called friend betrayed his trust, that person was dead to him. He accepted his resentful nature; it had kept him alive this long.

He followed the guard down the long hall and down the stairs to the open yard where the less offensive criminals meandered, past the guardhouse. They did not stop him, so Nick kept walking. But the sight of the gallows in the courtyard drew him up short. The sturdy beams and trap doors invoked as much fear within him as they did in his nightmares.

"Blackburne," a voice to his left called out.

Colonel Fitzwilliam walked away from the carriage he must have been waiting in, freshly shaved, coat brushed, and boots gleaming—a stark contrast to the mucky streets and the stench of the prison.

He looked down at his own frayed trousers and

stained shirt. "I'm sorry I didn't dress for the occasion. Are we going to have tea with Prinny?"

The colonel chuckled. "Not the Prince Regent. My father."

Nick swallowed down his shock. Who were these people?

"My father is the Earl of Matlock, and as a peer of the realm—"

"He can do whatever he wants," Nick supplied, wary. He had known too many peers—so-called princes—who abused their status and got away with crimes men like Nick hanged for.

"That is one way to put it."

"I'm on bail, then? He paid off the warden?"

"He secured your release, Nick, on the condition that you are under our care. Anyone who challenges it shall have His Lordship to deal with."

"Connell won't like it."

"Connell shall have to accustom himself to disappointment." The devilish glint in the colonel's eye reassured Nick. This man wasn't a fool. Nor did he seem scheming. Still, Nick would be cautious.

A servant in fancy livery held the carriage door open. Colonel Fitzwilliam motioned for Nick to follow him. "My father is eager to meet you," he said.

For a flicker of a heartbeat, Nick was tempted to return back inside the prison rather than face this new world full of rules and contradictions he did not understand. A world he could never belong to.

But freedom was a heady sensation, and not one to take lightly.

He followed the colonel, trying to ease his misgivings with conversation. He despised idle chatter, was no good at it, but if His Lordship had gone to so much trouble to get him out of Newgate, Nick figured he could make a worthwhile effort to be polite. "Ye've had a busy morning, I take it?"

"I apologize I could not come earlier. There was an urgent matter I had to attend to—a wedding."

"Yers?"

"No." If the colonel meant to elaborate, him stepping inside the carriage prevented it.

"I wish the couple happy," Nick said, sitting gingerly against the cushions, doing his best to make himself small and therefore minimize the damage he was certain the interior of the fine conveyance would suffer.

The colonel bunched his chin, then spoke. "I would rather they be happy, too; however, I doubt they shall be."

Nick held his raw wrists, meaning to comment but getting distracted when the carriage jolted forward. Gripping the sides of the padded bench, he watched the streets through the windows. He was unaccustomed to being a passenger.

He didn't like how close the sides of the carriage got to other passing vehicles, but his uneasiness inside the confined box paled compared to his anxiety in meeting His Lordship.

What if Lord Matlock took one look at Nick and sent him packing? So long as he did not send Nick back to prison, he would manage. But Connell would be a problem.

Nick would have to keep his head low until he could get aboard a ship—a nice frigate would do—and… He shook his head at himself. Old habits were hard to break. That was the *old* him. The one he had left behind in Louisiana. Nick was an honest man now. Or as close as he could be to it, he chuckled facetiously.

The colonel raised his eyebrows.

Nick explained, "You know, when I lived as a pirate, I was prosperous and at peace. And ever since I decided to leave that life behind, I've been properly damned. Me ship was seized, I've been in prison, and I've been threatened with the noose."

"Why did you leave?"

A question Nick had spent weeks pondering of late. He shrugged. "Me conscience got too loud. It was time for a change."

"A pirate with a conscience. You are a rarity. How did you get captured?"

A flash of black hair and steel-blue eyes crossed his mind. Nick shoved the memory of her away with a scowl. "I was stabbed in the back by me own kind. She didn't want me to go, and when I went anyway, she turned on me." That was the only explanation for it. Connell had been waiting for him. It had been an ambush. And *she* had been the only one who had known Nick's route.

"She?" the colonel asked.

"Alexandra Lafitte," Nick spat her name—a name which had once been sweet across his lips but now filled him with bitterness. "Ye might know her as La Femme Lafitte. Blasted proud of that name, she is, too."

"Is she any relation to the Lafittes operating at the Louisiana Purchase?"

Nick nodded. "Their little sister." He rubbed his chest. Why had she not come with him? Why the betrayal? Nick hated the void her absence created in him. It hurt. He'd rather be angry. "If I ever see her…" he seethed, cutting short his threat. He could never hurt her, no matter how tempting the prospect. "She'd better pray I never see her again."

The colonel left him to woolgather, so Nick stewed over that blasted woman until the lanes widened and he saw houses as clean as his ship, *The Revenge*, on the other side of the carriage window. That was where the familiar ended and the new began.

Parks with velvety green lawns and trees in full bloom lined the pavements. Flowers bordered pointy iron fences. Nick hadn't seen flowers in weeks, and there'd been a time during his youth when he'd gone years without seeing their vivid colors or smelling their exotic perfume. Roses were his favorite.

He let out his breath and turned to the colonel. "I forgot how pleasant being on land can be."

"You shall like Matlock House. That is where I am taking you. Under the circumstances, it was what my father and I considered best."

Nick nodded. He would not argue with the man who had freed him from Newgate. He'd bide his time and slip away quietly.

They rolled to a stop in front of a tall, wide house. Nick tried not to look impressed when he alighted the carriage and stood on the pavement.

Two rose bushes flanked either side of the entrance, and had the butler not opened the door before they reached the threshold, Nick would've paused to sniff their aroma.

Nick stood tall, trying to give a semblance of dignity in his unfortunate state.

To his credit, the butler did not look shocked or in the least bit shaken by Nick's appearance. He merely informed the colonel that the guest room was ready, as was a bath—a glorious, blessed bath. He wondered if he'd get a meal out of the deal soon. A bath was already more than he'd dared to dream.

In a lower voice, which only made Nick more determined to listen, the butler added, "Miss Darcy and Mrs. Annesley arrived while you were away."

The colonel's jaw clenched, and Nick imagined that the army man was swearing in his head. He certainly looked like that was what he was doing.

He did not give Nick time to ponder more on the subject. He spirited him up carpeted steps and down a wide hall so long, there were chairs placed partway down the length, which Nick supposed were for guests to rest on their quest to their room.

The colonel opened a door, and the first thing Nick saw was a large, four-poster bed piled with blankets and pillows. He didn't need to lay on it to know it'd feel as soft as clouds. It was a beautiful sight ... but not as beautiful as the copper tub filled to the brim with steaming water. It was enough to make a man weep.

He started unbuttoning his shirt when a stiff man wielding a towel over his arm like a shield joined them. The colonel introduced him as Mr. Darcy's valet, Hopkins.

Hopkins' jaw dropped, but he closed it quickly enough. "He is the spitting image, sir, just as you said. I apologize for doubting you." He bowed to the colonel.

Nick guffawed. He'd expected criticism, not comparisons to this mysterious Darcy. "When I shave this beard off and ye get a better look, ye'll change yer mind."

Snapping the towel off his arm, Hopkins said, "I shall shave you, sir." His tone was offended.

Holding up his hands, for Nick really meant no offense, he said, "Nobody touches a blade to my neck besides me."

The valet looked to the colonel.

The colonel nodded. "Hopkins shall see to your hair. Is that acceptable?"

Nick reluctantly agreed, and the colonel departed to speak to his father, who'd attend to Nick once he was more presentable. Nick didn't blame the man. He was sure the inside of the carriage had smelled rather ripe by the time they arrived.

Hopkins reached forward to help Nick undress.

Nick smacked his hand away. "Make yerself scarce for five minutes, will ye?" he said, seeing to his own buttons.

With a dignified bow and a forbearing sigh, Hopkins said, "I shall brush your coat, sir."

"I've no coat to brush."

"I brought several changes of clothes from Mr. Darcy's closet."

Waving him off because the water beckoned, Nick stepped out of his tattered breeches and into the tub. With a groan, he lowered himself, letting the water soothe his aches. Shouting, he said, "Hopkins! Make that ten minutes!"

# CHAPTER 17

*A*fter a lifetime of salty brine, not to mention the past few weeks of filthy bilge water and bug-infested cells, Nick reveled in the soft, fresh, steaming water. He dunked himself under, letting his body relax before he grabbed the razor and nice-smelling shaving cream on the table beside the tub. The razor was sharp, just like it should be.

He didn't know when Hopkins had slipped inside the bathing room, but Nick appreciated the tray of food sitting on top of the table where the shaving implements had been.

Washing off his face and shaking his hands mostly dry, Nick grabbed a biscuit, tapping it against the platter out of habit. No weevils or worms crawled out. Had he died and gone to heaven? Nick crammed the whole biscuit in his mouth. It went down his throat like melted butter. He reached for another. He hadn't tasted this kind of cooking since—.

Nick stopped his treacherous thoughts. Jean-Christophe had been *his* find. It'd serve Alexandra right if Nick stole him away from her.

He'd polished every crumb and piece of meat and cheese from the platter clean by the time Hopkins came in to cut his hair. Being full and in a more amiable mood, Nick let him snip and comb away. He even donned the stiff collars and breeches without complaint. They'd fit perfectly once he got a few more meals in his belly. The boots fit his feet like kid gloves.

But when it came time to tie the noose Hopkins called a cravat around his neck, Nick put his foot down. "I've spent my whole seafaring life avoiding a noose. Why would I agree to have ye tie one around my neck? It's unnatural," he argued. No sailor worth his salt would agree to that torture.

"A proper gentleman wears a cravat."

"What makes ye think I'm a gentleman? It's bad enough I've got to wear these collars up to me ears."

Hopkins did not yield. He was made of tougher stuff than Nick had initially credited him with. "A simple knot, tied loosely, should suffice, but you must wear a cravat."

This altercation was leading nowhere. "Loose," Nick repeated, pointing his finger at Hopkins' face, holding him to it.

He still broke into a cold sweat as the valet tied the

fabric, and it was all Nick could do not to pull the dreaded thing off. But he resisted the impulse.

When the deed was done, Nick stepped back. Opening his arms and turning to the side, he asked, "What d'ye say now, Hopkins? Am I still the spitting image of this Darcy fellow?" He lifted his chin, certain of the valet's reply.

"It is striking, sir. An exact replica."

Nick dropped his arms. That was not at all the reply he had expected.

The colonel tapped on the door and entered along with an older gentleman—a portlier version of the colonel. He introduced him as his father, the Earl of Matlock.

The earl wore a gold signet ring on his finger and walked in a bold manner which communicated that, wherever he went, he was in charge. He also wore a smile.

Nick bowed. "Thank ye for getting me out of Newgate, Me Lord." Now, down to business. "What do ye want from me?"

The earl eyed him for several moments. Nick stood his tallest. Finally, the gentleman spoke. "I sense you are a man without a place in the world. We might be able to help you with that."

"That's fine, Me Lord, but ye didn't answer me question. What's this generosity going to cost me?"

"Must assistance have a price?"

"I've always known it to."

Again, that assessing stare. "I see you will not accept my help until you are convinced it shall not be too dear—"

"If I accept." Only after he'd interrupted did Nick realize that probably wasn't something you did to an earl.

His Lordship tilted his head, repeating, "If you accept. However, young man, by all appearances, you are my nephew, and I shall act toward you as I would to Darcy or any of my other nieces and nephews."

Nick deflated. Changes in fortune were earned with the sweat of a man's brow, not handed to him on a silver platter. As much as he wanted to believe he had a place with these kindly people who had already done him more favors than he could ever repay, he also expected for reality to come crashing over his head at any moment. "I can't…" He looked up at Lord Matlock, over at the colonel, unable to complete his sentence.

"Then, you shall have to trust that whatever I ask of you shall be reasonable and within your power to provide," Lord Matlock said.

He had Nick there. He was already too far in debt; there was nothing for him to offer but a degree of trust.

"You do not understand the gravity of your discovery to this family, do you?" The earl motioned and began charging down the long hall. "Follow me."

Down the stairs to the main level, he entered the third door to the right. Portraits lined the walls, portraits of men and women Nick did not know—faces as strange to him as he was to them.

Until he saw himself.

Nick was too stunned to breathe. He pointed at the picture, the only explanation answering his unspoken question before it crossed his lips. Two dark eyes with thick eyebrows regarded him sternly—his own eyes. Nick reached his hand up to his dark, curly hair, cut in the same style as the man in the portrait. Rubbing his fingers over his chin, he felt the same small dimple the artist had captured in the painting. Even their build was the same. Taller than most men, lean, and strong. It was him. But it wasn't.

Until that moment, Nick had thought Darcy's family half-mad. He'd planned to get a few more meals, at least one more delicious bath, and then make his escape.

But now...

He was curious enough to stick around.

"William! You are here!" a girl squealed seconds before a young lady jumped at Nick and wrapped her arms around his chest, squeezing him to her and rubbing her cheek against his shoulder. She smelled perfect, like heaven.

Nick did not know what to do with his hands. He patted her on the back, looking at the earl and the colonel for help.

Their frowns were deep. "Georgiana, I thought you were resting in your rooms." The earl glared at his son.

She stepped away, her brow furrowed. "William, what is wrong? You do not seem yourself." She looked between Nick and her relatives.

Nick was tongue-tied. The young lady, Georgiana, was a rose-scented angel. He recoiled, lest he tarnish her with an ill-spoken word or impolite gesture. He wasn't worthy of her company.

The earl wrapped his hand around her elbow, steering her closer to them. Away from Nick. Gently, he said, "Georgiana, this is Mr. Nicholas Blackburne. Mr. Blackburne, this is Miss Georgiana Darcy." He took a deep breath. "Your little sister."

Georgiana's neck snapped back and forth between them. "Uncle, why do you call William by another name? I am not blind."

The poor girl was so confused. Nick was too, but it pained him to see the bewilderment etched on her innocent face. He stuck out his hand. Then, thinking better of the gesture, he bowed. He felt like a fool not knowing how to greet a proper young lady, but he did his best. "Name's Nick, Miss. Yer uncle and cousin think we might be related." After seeing the portrait, he was more inclined to agree with them, but he was still managing his own shock.

"A twin?" she whispered. She was quick, Nick thought proudly.

The earl nodded. "That is what we aim to discover."

Georgiana looked up at Nick in awe, as though she were seeing flowers for the first time in ages. She gave him a shy smile that did funny things to his heart. "I have another brother!"

Nick felt the honor of her comment and the surge of panic. He would have to be on his best behavior around her. She was a *real* young lady, the sort respectable folks kept away from the likes of him. He was rough and ill-mannered, a rogue of the sea. Shame filled him. He said to the gentlemen, "She shouldn't be in me company. I'm not … I don't talk right, and I'll forget me manners."

The earl eyed him again, taking his time and adding to Nick's discomfort. "I think you shall do. The bonds of blood run deeper than you are aware."

Nick was not so certain. Tigers couldn't change their stripes.

"Besides," the earl continued in a lighter tone, "Richard shall stick to your side and make sure you stay out of trouble."

The colonel bowed his head, a twinkle in his eye. "I have never chaperoned a … shall we call you a *privateer* captain? … before."

Their levity appeased Nick.

The butler appeared like a ghost in the doorway, startling Nick when he spoke. "Mr. Jonathan Connell demands to see you, sir."

"Demands?" boomed the earl. To the colonel, he asked, "He is the thief-taker?"

Richard nodded.

Nick tugged at his cravat, his back slick with sweat.

Connell would be a problem. Thief-takers gained rewards for the criminals they arrested only after their prey was convicted and sentenced. From the moment they landed, Connell would have been gathering enough evidence with which to bury Nick before a jury. After tracking him across the Atlantic, Connell would stop at nothing until Nick dangled from a short rope.

Georgiana clasped her uncle's arm. "He cannot take my brother away when we have only just found him! You cannot allow it, Uncle!"

The earl said in a firm tone to the butler, "I am not taking calls today. Until Mr. Connell learns a measure of respect, he shall not get an audience with me … or anyone else in my household." He looked pointedly at Nick.

Never in his life had anyone protected him like these folks. Nick's throat swelled, and he reached up to pull the blasted cravat away again.

The butler disappeared as quietly as he had come.

In a low voice, the earl said, "It was no small feat to have you released into my custody. You have quite a reputation."

Nick blushed. He hoped Georgiana hadn't read any of his stories or heard any of the songs. He didn't want her to be scared of him.

"Richard tells me you have already taken measures to leave your previous profession. Is this true?"

Nick clasped his hands in front of him and bowed

his head, feeling as though he was on trial. "Aye, Me Lord, I have," he answered honestly.

"Do I have your word of honor that you will do nothing to make me regret my decision to offer you my protection?"

While a part of Nick rebelled at the unsolicited assistance, he was a rational man. He knew when he needed help. Were it not for Lord Matlock, he'd still be in prison.

And his curiosity was growing. If he had a family, he'd like to know them. He'd like them to be like the people standing with him in the portrait gallery.

And, since Nick was being completely honest with himself, he knew better than to turn down baths and food when prison was his alternative.

Georgiana watched him, her eyes full of expectation, of hope ... and something else he didn't recognize because nobody had ever looked at him like she did right then. Whatever it was, he couldn't disappoint her.

Placing a hand over his heart, Nick said, "I swear on the stars, I'll not betray yer trust."

Richard crossed his arms over his chest, tucking his chin down. "And we shall not delay getting to the bottom of this matter. Have you had any success locating the midwife?" he asked his father.

"Mrs. Finchley's last known residence was near Cambridge. She cannot be far. We shall find her."

Georgiana's gaze remained fixed on Nick. Releasing

her hold on her uncle, she stepped toward Nick. "You will help us find William? Please ... Brother?"

That dashed cravat did its best to choke Nick, but he got the words out. "I'll do everything in my power to bring him to ye," he swore. How easily the promise came to him. He, a man who was beholden to nobody, was now indebted to this family. His family, in all likelihood.

If he could find Mr. Darcy—his twin—he would do it. Nick always paid his debts.

# CHAPTER 18

*D*arcy dunked his mop in the bucket, one eye on his chosen chore and the other on the captain's quarters where Elizabeth stayed as a forced guest.

By the time he finished swabbing the quarterdeck, he considered that enough salt had landed on the surface to justify cleaning it again.

All the while, he watched the door.

Beckett was at the helm and kindly kept his thoughts to himself. Boone softly chuckled but spoke not a word. When Alex took over, however, she pointed to a knot in the plank. "Ye missed a spot, Darcy." But she did not send him away, so he scrubbed the clean spot and began polishing the copper and brass, coiling and re-coiling ropes. All this time, his senses fixed on the cabin.

Jaffa nodded at him occasionally, as though to reassure him that Elizabeth was safe. That no harm would come to her so long as he was on guard. And Jaffa, Darcy knew, was always on guard. He had yet to see the man sleep, and somehow he was always alert. Always at his best.

Darcy did not feel his best at that moment. He was sweaty and unshaven and had not enjoyed a proper bath in days. The canvas hose that pumped frigid ocean water over them every morning hardly counted. It left Darcy sticky and itchy.

He stretched his back, rubbing his hand over his face. Five days of stubble prickled his fingers. Alex did not trust him with a razor, and, truth be told, he did not trust his own hand with the constant movement of the ship.

Rapid steps made him turn in time to see a flurry of black hair and ruffles. Alex snatched the polish rag out of his hand. "I didn't have yer lady brought here to watch ye avoid her." She pointed at her cabin. "Go! Woo her!"

As if he could when he was the reason for her capture. "It is not so simple."

Alex plunked her fists on her hips. "Why not? Yer a man; she's a woman. An idiot can see ye like each other. There are many dark corners on the *Fancy*. Why don't ye find one? Whisper in her ear; sneak a kiss; do something!"

Darcy stood erect, towering over her. "I am a

gentleman. I could never treat a lady as you describe, much less Elizabeth."

Alex looked befuddled. "No honeyed words?"

He nodded his head.

"Not even a little peck?"

He nodded again, more sternly.

"How're ye supposed to woo her if ye don't talk or kiss?" she asked, flailing her arms in the air.

"We may dance at social occasions. It is understood that a gentleman who wishes to express his particular regard may call the following day during calling hours." A far cry from kissing and whispering in dark corners … though the image that provoked in Darcy's mind was not unpleasant—not in the least.

Alex smiled. "Nick and I used to talk for hours. Lord, I miss that."

Darcy imagined the luxury of conversing at length with Elizabeth. They would have little difficulty filling the hours. But that simply was not how it was done. "Calls last fifteen minutes. To stay longer than half an hour is impolite."

Alex gasped. "That's a pittance! I suppose ye get right to business if yer time together's so short."

"It is difficult to discuss much of importance when others are present. One cannot ignore the lady's family if they are in attendance."

Her eyes bulged. "Ye mean ye're not alone?"

"Never. To be alone would be to compromise the lady's reputation."

"How do ye know if ye're a good fit if ye hardly get to talk to each other or spend any time together?"

If she were not the reason he and Elizabeth were floating on the Atlantic, causing their loved ones no end of concern, Darcy might have laughed at Alex's bewilderment. He tried to imagine her in the gaudy parlor at Rosings. Aunt Catherine would chew Alex up one side and down the other with her tongue, and Alex would silence the lady with her dagger. He imagined the pirate's shiv flying through the air, getting caught in his aunt's old-fashioned pompadour.

Alex jabbed him. "I'm waitin', Darcy."

He had forgotten the question.

She rolled her eyes, tapping her toes impatiently. "How do ye know if ye're a fit?"

"By watching and observing."

She made a face. "Sounds borin'. I prefer to act."

"You would do well to contemplate the consequences of your actions before you carry them out."

"I'm not patient enough for that."

"A fact of which I am well aware."

She tilted her chin to the side, regarding him. "Tell me about yer courtship."

Darcy heaved a sigh. She was like a barnacle. She would stick to him until he told her enough to satisfy her curiosity, but that was a story she would not pry from his lips. "A gentleman never tells."

"Blast ye and yer gentlemanly manners! If ye won't tell me, then show me. Go and tell her ye love her."

Alex pushed Darcy down the deck until they stood in front of her cabin. *Knock-knock-knock.* She rapped the door with her knuckles before Darcy could stop her.

He glared at her, wondering if there was anyone more infuriating on the whole earth than Alexandra Lafitte.

She nodded at him encouragingly, watching and grinning like the interfering pest she was before she spun away and disappeared.

He could not look at her without feeling his blood boil. Turning away at the same time the door opened, Darcy stood like an oaf, too breathless, too shocked to utter an intelligent word. Or even an unintelligent one.

Elizabeth wore trousers. They hugged her curves all the way down to the bare skin where the fabric fell short of her half-boots. Darcy swallowed hard. She was shapelier than he had dreamed.

He forced his gaze upward, away from her exposed ankles. She wore a simple linen shirt with one ruffle down the front, tucked in at her waist. Such a small waist, he bet his spread fingers could span her circumference.

Darcy knew he had been looking too long, and he felt his face blossom with heat. But he simply was incapable of looking away.

Elizabeth clasped her hands in front of her, shuffling her feet. "There are too many ladders on the ship to continue in skirts," she explained.

He had to say something. Clearing his throat, he

choked out, "Very sensible. Practical." More than that, he could not say, but it seemed to be enough. Encouraged, he opened his mouth to offer further reassurance.

She met his eyes then, and whatever he had been about to utter blew away with the wind. His senses were so full of her, he had no room to spare for himself. Thoughtlessly, without regard for the consequences, he held out his arm. "Would you care to take a turn about the deck?"

# CHAPTER 19

*E*lizabeth was mortified. She crossed her arms over her chest, wishing she had a blanket with which to cover herself, not knowing what to say or how to say it. Not one clever remark surfaced to save her. Mr. Darcy already thought her family scandalous, and after Lydia's elopement—which Elizabeth prayed had ended in a respectable, if not ideal, wedding —he had every right to think so.

And now, for him to see her dressed so indecently….

Alex's trousers and blouse were made to fit *her*, not Elizabeth's taller, rounder figure.

She did not, however, intend to spend all day, every day, inside the cabin. Nor was Elizabeth willing to allow any of the sailors a peek up her skirts every time she took the stairs. She really had no other option. Trousers were more sensible.

Mr. Darcy sucked in a breath. Had he been holding it? Head bowed, he lowered his arm. "It is my fault you are here." He peeked up at her, his expression so full of remorse, so adorably guilty, Elizabeth could not but forgive him.

"I do not blame you." She reached out to the nearest furniture to steady herself when the ship rolled and blushed when her hand gripped the foot of the bed.

"I pray you might someday forgive me." He met her eyes. They were so profoundly dark, so troubled, so meltingly pleading.

Elizabeth's skin prickled and burned, aware that she ought to look away but too captivated to do so. Several days of stubble covered Mr. Darcy's chin. Rather than appearing unkempt, it made him look … rugged … dangerous. Sweat and salt curled the hair falling over his forehead, and it was with every ounce of self-possession that Elizabeth clasped her fidgeting fingers together to keep from brushing them through his curls. She had known his body was strong, but seeing the lines and angles of his form through the thin linen of his open-collared shirt made her throat go dry. She licked her lips and tried to swallow.

What had he been saying? She tried to focus, but the cabin was small, and getting smaller with every passing second.

This was ridiculous! Forcing her gaze away, she took a deep, shaky breath and summoned what clarity she yet possessed.

An apology. Before his letter, Elizabeth would have basked in the satisfaction of Mr. Darcy's plea, her prejudices indulged and her own vanity vindicated. And she had accused *him* of pride!

Rolling her eyes at her own folly, her humor was at last restored. "Forgive you, Mr. Darcy? Pray tell, for what? For finding Wickham and Lydia? For covering up their foolhardy behavior with a layer of respectability, thereby raising my family out of the clutches of scandal and absolute ruin?" He raised his hand to stop her, but she was not finished. "Or perhaps you refer to Jane and Mr. Bingley, who I am told has resumed his residence at Netherfield Park? You placed my sister's happiness above your own pride and placed my family's reputation above the small fortune you must have settled on that wicked wretch Wickham and my spoiled sister. How could I deny you forgiveness? Do you believe me so unjust?"

A sardonic half-smirk, which she found entirely too attractive, lightened his features. "I see you are still determined to misunderstand me."

She shot back, "And you are determined to think the worst of yourself."

His smile deepened, then faded. "It is my fault you are here."

"How exhausting it must be to assume responsibility for everyone and everything."

"Only for the causes—and people—I care a great deal about."

Elizabeth could not poke fun at that. He cared for her still. She had hoped as much, seen evidence of it. But to hear him say it ... it was perfect.

He looked everywhere but at her, as though searching for the right words.

She took a deep breath and held her impatient foot still, allowing Mr. Darcy time to think.

He cared for her. She dared not dream that he would propose again, but he might ask to court her. Or was she jumping to conclusions again? Did he care for her in the same manner he cared for Mr. Bingley? Was Mr. Darcy trying to tell her that his ardor had cooled into friendship? Elizabeth tried not to be disappointed, but she felt the blow deeply. Mr. Darcy did not love her anymore. She tried to take comfort in the certainty that they could still be friends. Friends were nice. Friends were good.

Mr. Darcy's chest heaved a frustrated sigh, and Elizabeth knew that his inspection of the ceiling, floors, and walls had not revealed what he sought. Determined to prove herself a worthy friend, Elizabeth opened her mouth to voice something flippant and sure to make him laugh.

But with rushed urgency, in a manner so unusual to Mr. Darcy as to be shocking, he blurted, "I was overheard saying your name ... while I slept. In my dreams."

Elizabeth's heart soared. "Oh!" She bit her tongue to contain her laughter. What a fool she was! Convincing herself she was nothing more than a friend to Mr.

Darcy—Fitzwilliam—when she could not have been more wrong. It was heady stuff for a maiden to know she occupied a special place in the dreams of the man she loved and had thought was forever lost. It made her bold. "You think of me, then?" She cringed. She was bold, but not that bold. "Sometimes?" she added, as though the qualifier made her any less impertinent.

"As often as I blink." His voice cracked.

Did there exist a greater happiness than what she felt at that moment? Elizabeth's heart swelled and swayed. She reached out to steady herself, her thoughts swirling around one, singular, wonderful thought— Fitzwilliam loved her still.

He stepped forward, extending his arm to her once again, ever the gentleman. "It gets better."

Elizabeth looked up at him questioningly.

"The rocking," he explained. "Learning to move with the ship."

Oh, that! Elizabeth was happy to blame her lack of balance on the ship … and not on her own wobbling knees. "That is reassuring." She smiled. If he wished to move on to lighter topics, she would oblige. For now.

"Would you like to stroll along the walkway? The sunset is striking … and … we have a great deal to discuss."

Elizabeth delighted in the firmness of his arm under her hand. She knew she ought to be afraid—she had been kidnapped by pirates, for heaven's sake!—but she was not. Not with Fitzwilliam at her side.

The walkway opened up to the deck, allowing a splendid view of the sunset. Red accented with hints of purple, orange, and gold streaks dotted with small, puffy clouds. The sky was on fire. "It is spectacular," she whispered in awe.

"It is humbling to feel our own insignificance in the vastness of the heavens, the power of the water." Fitzwilliam turned to her, eyes pensive, mouth open to speak.

"Red sky at night, sailors' delight," remarked a rough voice behind them. He wore an eye patch. "We be blessed with fair weather and smooth seas."

Fitzwilliam nodded at the man. "Thank you, Bauer." Elizabeth heard the impatience in his tone.

Another man walked behind them. "Ye and yer lady be blessed with strong stomachs. Maybe the sea be in yer blood? Most folks hang over the rails retching their first week."

Bauer punched the man in the shoulder. "Like yer first week, Cotton."

"And yer first two," Cotton retorted, hanging behind to continue insulting his crew mate.

Fitzwilliam cast her such an apologetic look, Elizabeth sucked in her cheeks to stifle a giggle. She could not fail to appreciate how these rough men treated him, with a sense of camaraderie and respect.

Another man joined them on the upper deck, an opened bottle in his hand. Fitzwilliam introduced the wine-wielding man as the ship's cook, Jean-Christophe.

"You two, shoo! Adieu!" he barked at the sailors. Gesturing openly at the endless sky, he said, "There are few clouds; the sea is as smooth as glass. Can you not see it is a night for lovers?"

Bauer scurried down the steps to the main deck, but Cotton stayed where he was.

Turning to Elizabeth, Jean-Christophe added, "Mr. Darcy is not so bad in the kitchen, is he, mademoiselle? I will say this in his favor: he learns very fast."

She smiled at the Frenchman. "Thanks, without a doubt, to his teacher, I should think."

Fitzwilliam looked as though he wished the sea would swallow him whole. While Elizabeth wished to spare him embarrassment, his inability to hide his vulnerability made him ever more dear to her.

Jean-Christophe laughed heartily, nudging Fitzwilliam with his elbow. "I like this one. You do too, eh?" Wiggling his eyebrows, he then turned to Elizabeth. Taking her hand, he bowed over it. "Good food makes the heart happy, but the love of a good woman … ah … now, that makes for a happy life."

"Females be trouble. Ye can keep 'em so long as ye keep the weevils out of me biscuits," Cotton grumbled.

Jean-Christophe waved his bottle at Cotton's head, and the two of them continued arguing while Mr. Darcy steered her away.

Looking up at the tall pole, Mr. Darcy examined the ladder stretching up to a platform at the top.

Elizabeth knew what he was thinking, and she delighted in his surprise when she placed her hands on the wooden rungs and began to climb. It was no worse than the trees she had climbed as a child at Longbourn, only much easier without her skirts wrapping around her feet. Or so she thought until she was part-way to the platform and made the mistake of looking down. The trees she had climbed were half this pole's height, and they did not swing about.

Clinging to the rungs, bolstering her resolve to gain the platform, she yelped when a sliver pierced through her palm.

Fitzwilliam climbed behind her faster than she could turn her palm for a look, then replaced it when she decided her grip on the rung was more important than removing the wooden fragment. His body was warm and solid and had they not been hanging perilously high, she would have been more tempted than she presently was to lean against him.

"Are you hurt?" he asked, pressing against her, lending her his strength and addling her thoroughly.

"It is only a sliver." Her voice sounded breathy in her own ears.

"Let us get to the foretop, and we shall have a look."

Slowly, quietly, they inched their way upward, every shift of her weight brushing against Fitzwilliam and sending tingles bursting through her limbs.

The pole they climbed was called the foremast, Fitzwilliam explained to her, pointing out and naming the different parts of the ship and its sails until they reached the platform and Elizabeth forgot her brief bout of fear. She had almost forgotten her sliver, too, until he reached for her hand and plucked it out. It amazed Elizabeth that Fitzwilliam's large, calloused hands could turn her palm so gently. And when he tenderly blew against her skin, her heart flipped in her chest. "Is that better?" he asked.

She nodded. So much better.

He tucked her hand into the crook of his arm. There was much to say, but neither of them were in a hurry to speak. They watched the golden red sun dip into the ocean's horizon and observed the first stars twinkle.

A sailor played the flute below, and several others shuffled, stomped, and clapped. The more agile of the motley bunch did all three. It was getting darker, and Elizabeth only saw the outlines of their forms. "Why do they not light candles?" she asked.

"Candles are not allowed after dark. It is one way they avoid discovery, and it prevents the men from setting the ship on fire when they are in their cups."

She tilted her chin to see him better. "Jean-Christophe was right. You have learned a great deal in the short time you have been aboard this ship."

"Elizabeth," he whispered her name softly, his

breath caressing her cheek. "I am sorry I expressed myself so poorly at Hunsford."

She had been prepared to relay every detail she could remember of his and her family's efforts to find him, of the colonel's exertions on his behalf to see Lydia and Wickham married, to tell him that his sister would soon arrive at London. She had not expected another apology. This must be the night for them, and she would rather get them out of the way. "I spoke in ignorance."

"I insulted your family."

"I insulted your character."

"I said I loved you despite my better judgment."

She could do better than that. "And I professed that you were the last man in the world I could ever be prevailed upon to marry."

"I called you barely tolerable in your hearing when I found you very attractive, indeed. It was a boldfaced lie."

Elizabeth's humor stopped her tongue before she attempted to best Fitzwilliam's offenses against her. "Are we really willing to waste such a perfect night competing over who insulted whom the worst?"

His lips twitched. "We can both agree I deserve that prize."

She laughed. "I shall not admit defeat so easily."

"I deserved everything you said to me. I was haughty and condescending and so certain of a favorable reply, I gave no consideration to how my words must have made you feel. For that, I am truly sorry. Not a day goes by that I do not regret it."

"As do I. We are even."

"You forgive me?"

"Fully. Can you forgive me?"

His shoulders relaxed. "I already did. Months ago."

The remorse Elizabeth had been clinging on to for months lifted from her, a wonderful, welcome release.

Their silence did not last long. They had too much to discuss. Elizabeth told him everything she knew had transpired since his disappearance. In turn, Fitzwilliam regaled her with an entertaining account of his time aboard the ship. She teasingly accused him of embellishing certain details, which they both knew he would never do. He asked what it was like to grow up with so many sisters, and he rewarded her with stories of him and his cousins making mischief at Pemberley.

They talked and laughed like trusted friends for hours, enveloped with a blanket of stars sparkling off the glassy ocean surface.

CHAPTER 20

*R*ichard rode carefully through Bloomsbury. One never knew what to expect in this part of town. Like a gentleman fallen on hard times, Bloomsbury kept up appearances until you noticed its frayed collar and threadbare coat. Grand houses with broken windows stuffed with paper, flagstones grimy with age or neglect. Even the residences scrubbed clean gave a shabby appearance.

Foundling hospitals where displaced and deserted children alike were given an education and a bed, boarding houses run by (mostly) respectable women, and parks dotted both sides of the lane. Richard rode past doctors and lawyers, men who worked too much to spend their spare time making their residences more comfortable.

He reached Bedford Square, the current residence of Mrs. Finchley his father's network of informants had discovered. Richard had been delighted that his interview with her would not require him to travel more than a few miles east.

Leaving his horse with his groom, he walked up to the terraced house of black brick. The glass in the fanlight above the painted door was still intact, the cast iron railing above it polished to a dull sheen.

An elderly servant saw him into the drawing room on the second floor, the one most people reserved for family and close friends. A warm fire crackled in the fireplace, and an old woman stood between the flames and a worn, velvet chair. Her hand shook on top of her cane. Had she stood erect, Richard measured she would nearly reach his height. Her face was round, her hair tidy, and her eyes alert. This was a woman who inspired comfort and confidence, and who never overlooked a detail. She would have been a formidable employer in her prime.

"Colonel Fitzwilliam," she greeted, nodding to the chair opposite hers. "I received your card and message earlier this morning, and I must say that I am intrigued. Please, have a seat. The tea shall be here shortly. I hope you brought an appetite. I do not often have occasion to entertain guests, so I must take advantage of the opportunities that fall into my lap." Her voice was soft, melodic. He could imagine her singing lullabies to sleepy babies.

He crossed over to her side, holding her elbow and easing her down into her chair. "I thank you for receiving me so kindly and on such short notice, Mrs. Finchley."

She smiled up at him. "You are hardly a stranger. Lady Anne and Lady Catherine trusted me in their most delicate moments, and if there is anything I can do to be of assistance to their relations, I am glad to help."

The tea tray came in then and, true to her word, it was stacked with sandwiches, cold cuts, cheese, and several pastries. He must have looked surprised, for she explained, "I am always prepared for company. What I am unable to eat normally goes to the children at the foundling hospital."

Urged on by her encouraging looks and brimming generosity, Richard piled his plate, making certain to leave plenty for the orphans.

Mrs. Finchley poured a second round of tea. "I am eager to hear the reason for your call, Colonel. I recall the Darcys with fondness, but I have not seen nor heard of the family in close to thirty years."

Finishing off his tea, Richard leaned forward in his chair. "What can you tell me about the night my cousin Darcy was born? Twenty-eight years ago at Pemberley?"

She balked. "A most irregular question, indeed!"

Richard nodded. "I am aware of the awkwardness of my inquiry, Mrs. Finchley. Childbirth is not a subject of which a lady speaks freely to anyone, much less to an unmarried gentleman. However, I assure you it is necessary."

"I shall not divulge Lady Anne's confidence. Her Ladyship trusted me."

Holding up his palms, Richard assured her, "I would never ask that of you. What I must know is how many children were born that night."

"H-how many *what?*" She jiggled her left ear. "Pardon me, Colonel, but my hearing is not what it used to be. I do not think I heard you correctly."

He smiled reassuringly at her. "You heard me perfectly well. How many children did you help bring into the world?"

She sank against the back of her chair, and Richard was not certain if it was in shock or a desire to distance herself from her mad guest. "I am afraid I do not understand why you should ask such a question. There was one baby born that night. One Darcy, a boy, the heir."

"That was what I thought, but recent events have made me doubt."

She huffed. "I might appear frail, but my mind is sound. There was one child born that night. One. A boy. It was a difficult birth, and Lady Anne fell unconscious by the end. She was not well, but my nurse and I saw her through. We cared for the babe and nursed Her Ladyship back to the living." She looked into the fire, lost in her memories, her voice softening into a whisper. "I urged her not to have more children. I warned her of the danger."

Richard waited until her attention returned to the present. "I do not doubt your word, Mrs. Finchley, however, I am sure you understand how having another eyewitness to confirm your account would go a long way in establishing veracity. Where might I find the nurse who was with you?"

She sighed. "Her name was Catherine Currey—a lovely woman, very capable. From Gloucestershire, if I recall correctly."

"How might I find her?"

Mrs. Finchley pinched her lips into a frown, speaking slowly. "I am dreadfully sorry to inform you she died some time ago."

A dead end. Richard rubbed his hand over his face. "When?"

"I can never forget. Mrs. Currey disappeared without a word. She gave no indication she was in trouble or that she would be away. She just left. I waited and waited for her to return, and I recall the day clearly because I had put in an advertisement to hire her replacement when I saw a notice about her in the paper. She had suffered a horrible carriage accident."

"Where did this happen?"

"It was just outside Devonshire."

Devonshire. Richard sat on the edge of his seat. "What was she doing there?"

"I cannot account for it. She had no family, none that I am aware of. The vicar of the parish had put the

JENNIFER JOY

notice in the paper in the hope that someone might claim her, give her a proper burial. I was happy to oblige. More than that, I do not know." She looked blindly into the fireplace, tears dimming her eyes.

Richard gave her time to compose herself. She dabbed at her cheeks, and when she had tucked her handkerchief into her sleeve and poured the last of the tea out of the pot, he asked softly, "Do you remember the name of the village?"

Her hand trembled, the teapot clattering against the tray when she set it down. "Oh, bother. It is a wonder I have any china left at all. I am not so much in demand now that I am old and frail, but these hands were once strong. I was much sought after in those times. I never lost a lady in the birthing room. Not one." She sat taller, proudly. She had not answered his question—now that Richard thought about it, she had answered hardly any of his questions—but he did not feel it appropriate to press her either.

After a few minutes of lighter conversation, he thanked her and bid his farewells.

She tried to stand, but Richard begged her not to exert herself.

"Very well, young man. If you insist. I do hope I have been helpful to you."

Richard smiled at her. He had always had a soft spot for women of a certain age. "If you remember anything else—"

"I shall send for you. Then, I shall have the pleasure of your company again."

If only he found it as easy to please a lady of a more marriageable age. He pondered that detail along with the fastest route to Devonshire as he returned to his family's residence.

AMELIA FINCHLEY WATCHED Colonel Fitzwilliam leave from the curtains of her upstairs parlor. He would be trouble if she was not careful. She had known this moment might come in her lifetime, and she had been prepared. The lines she had rehearsed over and over had flowed over her tongue, too little to encourage further investigation and just enough to make her seem helpful and above reproach.

She gave him every reason to believe her nothing more than a forgetful woman well past her prime. If he only knew the truth…. Amelia's lips twisted and she rubbed her hands together. Peers of the realm paid her for her silence. She held them in the palm of her veined hands. Clenching her fists, her smile widened. She would give the colonel a few days, then she would pay him a call. Perhaps he would prove useful to her. One never knew when an opportunity presented itself, and Amelia was always ready.

THE PRISTINE PORTLAND stone of his family's home was always a welcome sight to Richard. As was Rouncewell when he pulled up beside him in a carriage a short distance from Matlock House. Handing his horse to the groom to take to the mews, Richard joined Rouncewell at his conveyance. His step faltered when he saw who sat across from his old friend.

"Colonel, I apologize for sneaking up on you like this, but the young lady insisted on speaking with you." He handed Miss Rothschild out of the carriage before the lady's footman reached the door. Her auburn hair glistened in the late summer sun. She wore a blue gown the color of the sky.

"Miss Rothschild, allow me to present Colonel Richard Fitzwilliam. Colonel, this is Miss Emily Rothschild." Rouncewell spoke hurriedly. That done, he nodded at them. "I apologize, but I cannot stay a moment longer. I have to track down a street sweeper who remembers seeing two sailors he had not seen before who nobody else seemed to know, and they have not been seen since. It is difficult to learn anything in that part of town. Loyalties run deep, but these two sailors were outsiders. One had an eye patch."

"Any word on Miss Bennet's disappearance?" Richard asked. If Rouncewell had any new information, Mr. Bennet and Mr. Gardiner would wish to know it.

"That is what I aim to find out from my informant.

It would be convenient if the same two sailors seen near the tavern where Mr. Darcy was taken were also responsible. I have no proof the cases are related, but the timing is suspect." He took a step away. "I will keep you informed. I must go."

Miss Rothschild spoke, her voice confident, her tone rich. "Mr. Rouncewell, my carriage shall take you wherever you need to go. It is at your disposal."

With a bow, Rouncewell said, "Thank you, Miss, but your fine conveyance would draw too much attention where I must go."

"Another time, then."

He nodded and was on his way.

Richard did not detain him. Turning to Miss Rothschild, he extended his arm. "Would you like to walk?"

She took his arm, and the exotic scent of jasmine filled his senses. "I remember seeing you at Bow Street with Mr. Rouncewell. He is a kind man," she said.

"We have been friends for many years." With such a handsome woman so near him, Richard was pleased he could speak in a complete sentence. It was a proud moment.

She nodded, peeking up at him and inspecting him under thick eyelashes. She had the kind of perceptive gaze that saw beneath the surface. "He said you are a trustworthy gentleman. I am inclined to believe him. I wonder what Rouncewell told you about me?"

Richard looked at her in astonishment.

The corner of her lips quirked. "Do not be so

surprised, Colonel. Men gossip every bit as much as women do, and men in possession of information are the worst of all. I know he must have said something."

Richard was grateful Rouncewell had said nothing untoward, or she would have known. "He said very little. Merely that he pitied your peculiar case."

He heard her exhale. "He does not hold out much hope, but he does not mock me as the others do."

Richard slowed his pace, watching her. "Surely, you must know that any crime—if indeed there was a crime committed—done so long ago would be difficult to prove. Clues will have disappeared; all leads long dead." All obstacles which might prevent him from revealing the truth about Darcy and Blackburne.

"I know it."

"And yet, you persist."

She glanced up at him. "For the same reason you do. A great wrong was done, and it is up to me to expose it. I do not know that the damage can be undone, but I shall try."

He wondered how much she knew about him. "What else did Rouncewell tell you about me?"

"Oh, he said nothing. However, I was at the office when Mr. Connell—you know him, of course ... the thief-taker—was informed that his prisoner was freed under the charge of the Earl of Matlock. He is your father, is he not?"

Richard nodded. "Why would Rouncewell connect your investigation with mine?"

"Mrs. Finchley is the common denominator. Were you aware that baby snatching has been a booming business over the years? And that several of the women she assisted had their children stolen after they were born? They were snatched from their wet nurse's room while she slept or from the exhausted mother's side. I think that Mrs. Finchley is the brains behind a baby snatching operation which has lasted almost three decades—as long as she has been a midwife to the upper classes. But nobody will listen to me. They think I am crazy."

Richard had difficulty believing her. Mrs. Finchley did not seem like a hardened criminal, and he had known several. But he would hear Miss Rothschild's proofs with an open mind before casting judgment. "What does that have to do with my family?"

"I am often at Bow Street. Lord Matlock caused quite a stir when he insisted upon the release of a prisoner. I am convinced that the Darcys were her first victims. That Nicholas Blackburne is, in fact, Mr. Darcy's twin, and that Mrs. Finchley arranged his kidnapping."

"You are forgetting the nurse in the room with her."

"Her accomplice … who was later found dead after delivering the stolen Darcy."

Richard tried to give her story credit, but it seemed too far-fetched.

"Where was the nurse found?" Miss Rothschild pressed.

"Outside Devonshire."

"Have you asked Mr. Blackburne where he is from?"

"Devonshire."

"I knew it!" she exclaimed triumphantly. Clutching his arm more firmly, she asked, "Do you believe in coincidences, Colonel?"

He had to own he did not.

"Then, we agree. It is possible that solving one case might resolve the other. I shall continue to pursue answers, and if I discover anything regarding Mr. Darcy or Miss Bennet, I shall inform you immediately."

"I could do no less for you."

She smiled at him fully. "Thank you. I admit I had hoped to secure your support." She pulled a calling card out of her reticule and handed it to him.

"Wimpole Street, Marylebone," he read under his breath.

"That is my address. Please, if you learn anything, send a message to my butler, Parrot."

How very proper. Richard could not rightly correspond to a young lady to whom he was not engaged, but there was nothing to prevent him from writing to her butler. Smart.

He saw her into the carriage and watched the conveyance until it disappeared down the wide street, doubting he would ever see her again but hoping that he might.

CHAPTER 21

"Is this right, Brother?" Georgiana leaned closer to Nick, holding up the ribbons he'd shown her how to braid and knot into the figure of a heart. Sailors often gave a Celtic knot as a keepsake for the loved ones they'd leave behind.

Nick wished he could be as relaxed in her company as she was in his. He was still adjusting to being a big brother to this wide-eyed maiden who looked at him as though he'd made the sun. He'd try his best not to disappoint her, but he was a black mark on the Darcy name. Nick knew it. Lord and Lady Matlock knew it.

Lady Matlock sat nearby with her two daughters, who peeked at him when they thought he didn't notice. Mrs. Annesley, Georgiana's governess, stuck to her side, her embroidery stitches miraculously neat and even, though her eyes darted between him, her charge, and the door where Mr. Bennet and Mr. Gardiner had

183

entered a quarter of an hour ago. Lord Matlock was with them ... leaving Nick guarded by a bunch of females. But they were kindly guards, and over the past hour he'd grown to rely on their calm encouragement, warning looks, and gentle nods.

"It's perfect. Ye're quick to learn." He prayed the blush his praise provoked on her cheeks was from pleasure and not embarrassment. Lady Matlock's warm look and gentle nod told him he hadn't said anything wrong. He exhaled in relief. One hour in their company was more exhausting than an entire morning pumping bilge water.

Looking at Georgiana's wrist, Nick calculated its circumference in comparison to the threads he'd braided, looking for the point where he needed to splice them together. He didn't know how it'd come about, him showing Georgiana how to braid and knot ribbons in lieu of ropes, but it'd been Mrs. Annesley's doing. Slicker than a wet plank, she was.

Tucking the last of the thread through, Nick broke off the extra length and handed the bracelet to Georgiana. "Here," he blurted gruffly, realizing that he should try to say something grander, but not knowing how to speak softly when everything about him was rough. Even his fingers were rough; his touch frizzed the silk threads.

What'd he been thinking? He shook his head at himself, feeling the fool. There was nothing he could give Georgiana that she didn't already have. She prob-

ably had dozens of bracelets of far superior materials—
gold and silver, inlaid with jewels.

"It is beautiful!" she exclaimed, rolling the pink,
yellow, and blue strands over her hand. "It fits perfectly." Cheeks pink and eyes bright, she pressed her wrist
close to her heart. "I shall wear it every day."

Nick didn't know how to react. "I'm honored," he
choked out, bobbing his head in what he hoped looked
like a gentlemanly bow.

Georgiana held the bracelet closer to Mrs. Annesley, who nodded her approval. "It is lovely," she said.
Then Georgiana turned to her aunt and cousins, who
praised Nick's artistry.

He wasn't the sort who easily blushed, but Nick felt
the heat rising to his face and a strange mixture of
satisfaction and mortification that made him both
happy and miserable.

When he heard the entrance door open and footsteps against the marble floor, Nick popped up to his
feet. He needed a reprieve. To escape before he made a
muddle of everything.

To his left, the colonel strode. And to his right,
coming down the stairs, was Lord Matlock, followed
by Mr. Bennet and Mr. Gardiner. Nick breathed a sigh
of relief. Georgiana followed him, but he was no longer
outnumbered. He could blend in with the men and
trust them to take charge of all the pleasantries that put
Nick on edge.

"Richard, see what Nick taught me to do?" She

showed the Celtic knot, then raised her wrist to be admired. "And he made me this bracelet."

Far from the oohs and aahs of the ladies, the men grunted approval. "Very nice," Richard said, looking to his father, who echoed the same sentiment. Mr. Gardiner agreed, and Mr. Bennet merely chuckled. After Georgiana had returned to the parlor, he commented, "You appear as comfortable surrounded by a bevy of females as Mr. Darcy."

Lord Matlock nudged the gentleman with his elbow. "Darcy is more likely to insult a young lady than to flatter her, poor devil."

Nick choked on his tongue.

"As my dear Lizzy can confirm," Mr. Bennet added with a snicker.

"Best they get all these misunderstandings out of the way now; then they shall have a lifetime to be happy together," Mr. Gardiner commented.

Mr. Bennet shook his head. "Now, do not speak of such things before it is time. I do not know what I shall do without my favorite daughter, and I refuse to anticipate an event which will surely lead to her departure."

Lord Matlock rested his hand on the father's shoulder, his voice grave. "Do not trouble yourself yet. We have yet to find them, and when we do, I know Darcy too well. It will take a great deal of persuasion to convince my bull-headed nephew that he has not ruined his chances beyond repair."

The colonel bunched his cheeks and nodded agreement. "Beyond redemption. Those were the words he used."

The same words Nick often used on himself. He had more in common with Darcy than he thought. He preferred determined and tenacious rather than bull-headed, but Nick supposed they had that in common, too.

Colonel Fitzwilliam asked, "Any promising leads regarding Miss Bennet?"

Mr. Bennet frowned. "We have inquired at every stable and post inn near the location of the abduction, and Gardiner has sent as many of his workers as he can spare to ask at the turnpikes." He took a deep breath and squared his shoulders. "But there are still a few more places left to ask, and I trust that, with Lord Matlock's assistance, we shall find her." He glanced at Mr. Gardiner. "We should go. If we leave now, we can stop at The Swan with Two Necks. There is the Wild Boar and the Royal Hawk at Arms—

He could have gone on longer, and that was when Nick took a closer look at the gentleman—at his sleep-lacking, red-rimmed eyes and his pale complexion. Mr. Gardiner interrupted Mr. Bennet, "Mrs. Gardiner expects us to return with news. You cannot continue without rest."

Mr. Bennet's forehead furrowed. "All my life, all I have done is seek peace, rest. I have had my fill and shall rest again when I lie in my grave. My Lizzy is missing, and I was standing right next to her." His shoulders slumped. "I was standing *right there*, and I did not know she was in danger until she was gone."

"We shall go to The Swan, and then I am taking you back to Gracechurch Street for a proper meal and a quick rest."

Witnessing the father's concern for his daughter, and seeing how he placed her welfare above his own need for rest and nourishment kindled a fire under Nick. Whoever had kidnapped Miss Bennet deserved a solid lashing.

Lord Matlock's tone was firm. "We shall find Miss Bennet. And my nephew. I have hired a small army to see them safely returned to us."

"Thank you, My Lord," Mr. Bennet responded, but there was no feeling in his words. "I am grateful for your assistance, but until Lizzy is returned, I simply cannot be reassured."

"I understand," Lord Matlock said, and they all agreed. Nick did not know Miss Bennet or Darcy, but he saw how their loss affected their families. It was strange that Miss Bennet should disappear so soon after Darcy. It made him wonder if the same person was responsible. He sensed that finding one would lead them directly to the other, but he had no proof beyond his own instinct and the suggestive timing of events.

Still, it was worth pursuing.

After overhearing the colonel and his father report on their findings of the morning—clues, clues, and more clues, but no Darcy or Miss Bennet—Nick determined it was time for him to try things his way. "There're places I can go, people I can talk to that're too dangerous for ye."

He heard a gasp behind him, and he turned to see Georgiana.

Nick felt wretched. Had he known she was standing there, he'd have waited until he, the colonel, and Lord Matlock were in the study, far away from listening ears. Smiling softly at her, he said, "I'll be with me own kind, love. They'll talk to me. I know how to make 'em talk." He looked away from Georgiana, cursing his blasted tongue.

"Only do not go to The Devil's Tavern." Lord Matlock leveled his steady gaze first at the colonel, then at Nick.

Nick felt his hackles rise. Grinding his teeth, he took a deep breath and reminded himself that he was a guest in His Lordship's house. This was *his* ship, Lord Matlock was the commander, and Nick would do well to remember that.

Still, it grated his every nerve to take orders from another man—even one he respected. With a curt nod, Nick acknowledged the command, though he took care not to agree with it or give his word to comply completely. The best chance they had of learning anything was in the same tavern where Darcy was last seen.

"If you were to appear, they would think you are Darcy, and anyone who had been involved in his capture would create more trouble," Lord Matlock explained.

Nick held in a snort. He was well aware of the danger, and it was of little concern to him. He could manage himself.

"My men and several others have made inquiries, and there is nothing there to be learned," he added.

Nick bit his tongue. The folks who frequented spots such as that had a nose for sniffing out the law and anyone associated with it. They would have closed ranks and protected their own, no matter the cost.

"Richard shall accompany you," Lord Matlock concluded.

Drat. It was a direct order, and Nick knew better than to complain. While he would defy His Lordship's wishes if it uncovered a path leading him to Darcy, he could not endanger the colonel or ask him to act against his own father.

Blast.

Struggling to contain the mutiny threatening to overpower him, Nick excused himself to change into clothing more appropriate for the occasion. He suggested the colonel do the same. They could not poke around the underbelly of the wharf looking like wealthy targets.

Hopkins looked on in dismay as Nick donned his old clothes. "Wishing ye'd burned 'em while ye had the chance?"

"Precisely, sir," was the valet's grim reply.

Deepening Hopkins' consternation, Nick tied the cravat securely around his ribs. He'd tuck a knife on each side, snug to his body, hidden between his shirt and coat.

"I need four knives," he said, adding when Hopkins did not hop to the task, "Two to hold at me side; and one to tuck in each boot."

"Is that really necessary, sir?"

Nick grinned. Truth be told, he itched for the opportunity to throw his knives. He preferred the sword, but taverns were too crowded for that.

He tousled his hair, and that proved to be too much for Hopkins to endure. Darcy's valet departed, mumbling under his breath as he disappeared down the hall.

Pretending he already had the shivs tied to his sides, Nick practiced pulling the blades out, adjusting the cravat around his middle until it was at the perfect angle to free the knives from their sheathes without disturbance. He missed the special vest Connell had taken from him. That had room for three blades: one at each side and another between his shoulder blades. He sighed. A man must make do.

The colonel rapped on the door and stepped inside. He wore simple garb, but it was still too fine. He handed Nick four sheathed knives. "I do not know what you want with so many weapons, but my father agreed on your promise that you shall not use them to harm another."

"Not even if it's to defend meself from attack?"

Richard shook his head. "You have already been spared from the noose, and he will not house a murderer."

Nick mumbled, "When ye put it that way..." But what other way was there to put it? He'd lived his entire life scrapping to survive. Life had become cheap, something his peers cast off like yesterday's linen. He'd felt the same until he'd found a reason to live to a good, ripe age.

Except she hadn't wanted to grow old with him.

He shook his head. Alex had made her choice, and he had to move on. He had a job to do and a family to repay for saving him from the gallows. They were good people. If finding Darcy meant he could serve them a good turn, then he'd look under every bridge and crawl through every hovel to find him.

# CHAPTER 22

*G*rabbing the knives, Nick hid them on his body and turned to the colonel. "Yer coat's too fine."

"It is the simplest I could find."

Nick grunted. It probably belonged to a servant. But even a servant's lot was better than that of the rough folks who made their living from the wharf.

Once they left the pristine west end of town, Nick asked the carriage to let them off. They were near Limehouse Reach. Drunks were plentiful, and he found one passed out against a wall. "Take off yer coat. The stench of his'll help us blend in where we're going."

The colonel did not protest. He stripped off his coat, then draped it over the man whose smelly garment Nick had quickly removed. "At least he shall stay warmer during the cold months to come."

Nick smiled at him. "Ye're a good man, Colonel."

193

"Call me Rich. That is what Darcy calls me."

"Rich," Nick repeated. "I'll not have ye calling me Blackburne anymore. It's Nick to ye from now on."

Nodding in the direction they needed to head, Rich said, "Narrow Street is this way."

Nick was grateful for his knowledge of London's streets. While he had a vague idea of the city's geography—sailors were a chatty bunch—that was the extent of his knowledge.

They continued forward, passing several narrow streets and dark alleyways. One look around told Nick it was inhabited by people who'd given up on having anything worth having long ago. The dirty streets and putrid air reeked of despair.

"I'll do the talking," Nick said. "Stick close and watch me back."

They stepped inside a tavern dimly lit with sooty lanterns. Dark shapes and shadows huddled over tables, speaking in low voices. Smugglers making deals, no doubt. The tavern's position on the bend of the Thames made it an ideal spot for such business.

Nick sauntered over to the bar and asked for a tankard of ale for him and the colonel. While the barkeep tapped the barrel, Nick asked, "Ye seen any fancy gents millin' about here lately—say, a week ago?"

The man's expression and posture remained unchanged. "We don't get many gents this way." He set their tankards on the counter and shouted over them. "Molly!"

A pretty lass with an empty tray in her hands walked toward them, a bounce in her step and a glint in her eye. When she set the tray down on the counter, Nick knew to keep an eye on her hands.

She leaned close to the colonel, fluttering her eyelashes and reaching over his chest to brush a piece of flint away.

Nick reached out to grab her hand, but Rich beat him to it. Holding the barmaid's forearm, he turned her closed palm to reveal his pocket watch.

The barkeep chuckled. "Sorry 'bout that, but enquiry agents and runners like to pass themselves off as one of us, and I can't blab to them without betraying one of my own. You seem like a decent sort, so I won't toss you out on your ears." To the barmaid, he added, "You're losing your touch, lass."

She scowled and slapped the watch into Richard's open hand. "Your coat stinks," she spat and made to leave.

Nick stepped in her path. "One moment. Ye're one to notice a gent. Have ye seen any about last Sunday?"

She shook her head, still pouting.

"None dressed simple like?"

Saucily, she replied, "A gent's a gent—even in rags." She sized up the colonel. "Like this one. I knew he was a gent the second he came inside." She turned her gaze to Nick, raking him over from toes to face. "You're no gent."

If Nick had ever dreamed he might improve himself

enough to deserve a family like Darcy's, her disinterested assessment squashed that hope.

"Come on, Nick. They cannot tell us what they do not know," Richard said.

Nick tried not to let the barmaid's comment bother him as they made inquiries at The Black Sail, then the Fighting Cock, then over to The Brazen Lass. By the time they left Bucket of Blood and alighted a hired carriage to convey them to their next destination, Nick could not think of anything else but the barmaid's comment. "Would Darcy be ashamed to have me for a brother?" he asked.

"Why would he be ashamed?"

Nick scoffed. "Ye can't be serious, Rich. He'll sure not go around boasting about me."

"Georgiana had no compunction accepting you as her brother."

Nick grimaced. She was so polite, acting interested as he showed her how to braid and knot her ribbons into figures. "I'm not fit company for her," he owned.

"A gentleman ought not to be judged by his looks and manners but by the values he displays."

"I've lived as a thief and blackguard all me life. The only thing I've valued is me own skin and the next prize." And Alex, blast the infernal woman!

"And yet, here you are, helping me find a man you have never met for a family of people who are all strangers to you."

"Ye'd give me proper motive when I have none."

"You are not as bad as you think you are, Nick. Remember that."

Nick heaved a sigh. If Richard only knew his mutinous thoughts, he wouldn't think Nick possessed a shred of honor. It was time to test the colonel's loyalties. "Ye won't speak so highly of me when I try to convince ye to accompany me to The Devil's Tavern."

"We gave our word—"

"Ye gave yer word," Nick interrupted. "I didn't. It's the best place to go, and ye know it. Nobody there'd speak to yer father's men, but they'll talk to me."

"They will think you are Darcy."

"Exactly. All we need to do is watch for reactions. Our man'll be mighty surprised to see me when they must think me kidnapped or dead."

The colonel sighed.

"Still think I'm a good man?" Nick teased, trying to make light of the pain in his heart.

Richard shifted his weight.

"If he asks, I'll tell him I forced ye to go against yer will," Nick offered.

That earned him a glare. "If you think I would allow you to take all the blame or lie to my father, then you severely underestimate my honor." He tapped the roof and told the coachman their new destination.

Nick had heard about The Devil's Tavern before. It was the kind of hovel sailors liked to brag about. But seeing the miniature noose and gallows hanging off the balcony still made Nick swallow the lump rising in his throat. Darcy was either foolhardy or as brave as Nick hoped he was to enter such a place.

The atmosphere was dark and boisterous. Men sat on beer barrels at the bar. Women sat on men's laps at the tables. Coins jingled, bills waved in the air, darts and daggers sailed through the air—men flaunting death and women drawn to danger.

Voices hushed and bodies stilled when they saw Nick.

His heart galloped. This was the right place. They knew something.

He stepped toward the barkeep, but a big man stepped in front of him, knocking Nick to the side with the force of his shoulder.

Richard whispered behind him. "We should leave."

"Not 'til they tell us what they know," Nick replied, giving the brawny man breathing on him his stoniest glare.

"They shall start a fight," Richard hissed into his ear.

Nick grinned. His eyes were still fixed on the brute. "Do I look like I'm afraid of a little fight?" He stepped back, getting a better look at his first opponent. Stocky, thick fingers, well-built, and about the colonel's height. There was a pistol tucked at his waist, but Nick saw no knife, though he knew the man must have at least one hidden on his person.

The ruffian leaned against a thick beam that ran up to the ceiling, protecting one side of his body. Smart man. Of course, he did not know how handy that beam would be for Nick.

Over his shoulder, Nick muttered to Richard, "Stick to the wall. Cover yer back."

"In for a penny, in for a pound," Richard mumbled under his breath, patting his pocket. Nick understood the motion. The colonel had a pistol.

Nick turned back to the brute.

"Who are you?" the man asked.

Nick weighed his options. He couldn't reveal his real identity. Word would spread, and young blades out to make a name for themselves would seek him out to challenge their skill against his, much like the muscled oaf sneering at him. Nick couldn't do that. Darcy would never be safe.

However, Nick couldn't rightly pretend to be Darcy either. He evidently looked and sounded like him, but that was where their similarities ended. He shrugged. He had to try. Imitating Richard's finer speech, he said, "Nobody of consequence."

The ruffian's glance darted over to the bar, and the barkeep shook his head. He was the one calling the shots, then.

"We don't want no trouble." The brute jutted his chin toward the door. "Out with ye."

Out of the corner of his eye, Nick watched the barkeep. He leaned against the bar, his fingers splayed against the polished wood. He was the one Nick needed to speak to. Nick took in a deep breath, steeling his nerves and steadying himself on the exhale. *In for a penny; in for a pound.*

Keeping one eye on the man behind the bar and the other on his bruiser, Nick placed himself between the two, praying the man with the beefy fists would shift his position against the beam.

People clambered out of the way, knowing what was going to happen.

Finally, the man turned to face Nick.

Perfect.

Taking another deep breath, Nick held it at the top.

Quicker than a viper strike, he crossed his arms and reached under his coat. Flinging the blades to his left side, he heard the metal thud into the wooden bar. He reached into his boots. Wasting no time to see if he had hit his targets, and knowing very well that he had (because he always did), Nick drew a shiv from his boot and flung.

The ruffian would have stumbled back had the post not been behind him. And he might have sunk to the floor had some of his hair not been pinned to the beam along with his hat.

Several gasps echoed through the room, and a few guffaws erupted when the henchman looked cross-eyed up at the dagger vibrating in the post above his head.

Nick took pride in his aim. Close enough to the man's scalp to pin his hair to the beam without parting his skin. Nick turned to the barkeep.

He did not feel so smug when he saw the barkeeper's bloodied knuckle. Barnacles. The other blade was clean, but there was no denying that he had nicked the man. Blast. Alex would not have missed. Of course, she might have pinned the man's fingers to the bar on purpose.

Pulling out his last knife from his other boot, Nick waved the sharp end at the crowd around him. "Anyone else?" he asked, imitating Richard's accent. Now that he'd given them a scare, he could continue with his plan. He'd pretend to be Darcy.

The tavern fell silent.

Richard walked over to the oaf and pulled the knife out of the beam, motioning with it for him to join Nick and the barkeep at the counter.

Leaning nonchalantly against the bar, Nick pulled the daggers out of the wood, saying, "I'll get straight to the point. I want to know everything you can tell me about the men who attacked me nearly a week ago just outside your door."

The two men exchanged a look and clamped their lips shut.

Nick trailed the tip of a blade along the bar, cutting a nice groove in the grain. The barkeep cringed. He must be the owner. He would have noticed Darcy.

Leaning in, Nick cut deeper.

The owner relented. "Tell 'em, Grimbly. I don't want no trouble. You gents talk to Grimbly, and you leave."

Grimbly narrowed his eyes at Nick. "Is that how you got away from those blokes? You did one of them fancy tricks with yer daggers?"

Nick nodded. Blokes. There had been more than one. "Something like that. The buggers got away from me though, and I mean to make them pay."

Grimbly looked at him askance. "You sound like the same gent what came here last week, but ye're different."

"I wasn't angry before." Nick flicked a chunk of wood off the edge of the bar.

Grimbly swallowed hard. "What d'you want to know?"

"Tell me everything you remember. What they looked like."

"One had an eye patch."

That described too many men. "Which eye?" Nick asked.

"The left."

Nick frowned. He knew several sailors who'd had a line snap in their face or a cannon blast debris into their eyes. Eye patches were not entirely unusual. "What else?" he pressed.

"They were English, but sometimes they spoke funny. A bit like you when you first came in."

Nick felt his frown deepen. An accent like his. He waved Grimbly to continue.

"The other one was bigger than me, solid and square. And he was missing the tip of his finger."

Nick went cold. He asked, "Which finger? Which hand?"

"Little finger, right hand."

*Blast the mizzenmast.*

Richard's brows furrowed at Nick for a moment before turning to Grimbly. "How is it you know all this?"

Grimbly grinned, his eyes as hard as flint. "The boss told me to keep an eye on the gent. Make sure he left the property ... unharmed, you see."

More likely that his employer sent Grimbly to swipe Darcy's purse and steal his boots. Nick headed to the door. He was done here. He knew who had Darcy.

At the door, he tossed back, "Ye follow us, I'll aim for yer neck."

Nick charged down the street, the colonel hurrying to keep up. When they reached a wider street, he hailed a carriage.

Only then did Richard speak. "You know who is responsible."

Nick pursed his lips, his nostrils flaring as he let out his breath. "Aye." He pounded his fist against the squabs.

He spent the rest of their journey across town attempting to convince himself he was wrong. He nearly succeeded, too.

Lord Matlock called them up to his study the moment they returned. "Mr. Bennet and Mr. Gardiner have departed for Hampshire. Two men were seen at

The Swan with Two Necks in the company of a young lady they claimed to be ill. The stable boy overheard them mention Southampton, so that is where they are headed."

"Two men? Did the boy give a description?" asked Nick.

"No. He only said that they 'talked funny.'"

It wasn't much to go on, but it was enough when his suspicions already pointed to that she-devil. "I'm gonna kill her."

CHAPTER 23

*E*lizabeth tried to recall a more entertaining—
and delicious—dinner than the current one,
but this one was simply too splendid to surpass. Not
only was the food worthy of the finest table, but
watching two equally strong-willed and determined
individuals accustomed to having their way was most
diverting.

Alexandra sliced her meat into tiny slices and
looked at Fitzwilliam, clearly expecting praise. He
glared daggers across the table at her. She made a face,
then resumed ignoring him, very much like a younger
sister who had tired of her strict brother.

Washing down her dainty bites with a gulp of wine,
Alexandra said, "Did ye know that Boone was an
ordained clergyman?" Her eyebrows furrowed.
"Ordainments don't expire, do they?"

A priest turned pirate? Elizabeth imagined there

was quite a story behind Boone's change of occupation, but the stormy look on Fitzwilliam's face told her that now was not the time to ask.

"Do you really think I can court Elizabeth knowing that I am the reason she is here? Knowing how her family would be frantic with worry about her welfare?"

Alexandra rubbed her finger against the base of her wine glass. "That must be nice."

"To cause her family concern?" Fitzwilliam scoffed.

Her gaze shot up to his. "To have people in yer life who concern themselves over yer welfare." She looked down at her plate and shrugged as though her thoughts had not taken a melancholy turn. "I imagine it'd be nice. That's all I meant."

While Elizabeth could never condone Alexandra's behavior—two kidnappings!—she began to understand how such a person might justify her actions. Elizabeth imagined what it would be like not to have her loved ones in her life. The loneliness the thought alone provoked was enough to steal Elizabeth's breath. She may never see eye to eye with Alexandra, but she could sympathize with her. "Do you not have any family aside from your brothers?"

A cold, empty laugh escaped Alexandra. "They'll not wish to claim me after what I did." She rubbed her finger against the edge of her knife.

Fitzwilliam opened his mouth, but Elizabeth shook her head at him. He would demand that Alexandra take them to shore, but Elizabeth sensed that Alexandra would only bristle under his command. She was a woman accustomed to being in charge, and if Elizabeth's suspicions were correct, Alexandra could be led to draw the correct conclusion on her own if they managed their conversation intelligently.

He pursed his lips, the muscles on the side of his jaw flinching as he seemed to grind his teeth ... and it struck Elizabeth that even though he was unaccustomed to yield to anyone, he was willing to yield to her. She felt the distinction of his deference as fully as she had felt the strength of his protection earlier.

Softly, staring at the dent the knife made in her skin, Alexandra murmured, "I can't go back. I made me choice."

"You can *always* return to your family," Elizabeth said.

Alexandra chuckled. "Ye don't know me brothers. They'd sooner blast me out of the water."

"Surely not! You must have at least one champion you can turn to."

"I only have Nick—or had, I mean."

Elizabeth shook her head. "Having only sisters, I cannot imagine what it must have been like for you to be raised with brothers, and in your ... profession. Your mother must have had her hands full with you. Was your father a seafaring man, too?"

Alexandra shrugged. "Never knew 'em. Jean and Pierre raised me as best as they could. Taught me everything I know. I was climbin' riggin' and tossin' knives before I lost me first tooth."

Again, Elizabeth engaged her imagination. Surrounded by the roughest men who roved the seas, it was no wonder Alexandra had no manners, no proper sense of right and wrong, and no regard for consequences. "Have you never known tenderness? Concern? Loyal friends who only want the best for you? Someone willing to share your burdens?"

Alexandra looked at her blankly. Scratching her head, she said, "Ye mean someone I trust to see me weak? I cried once in front of me brothers, and that's a mistake I'll never make again. Men won't back a weak captain."

"There is more to emotion than simply crying. The ability to understand not only yourself but others gives you invaluable insight and power."

"I have to be stronger than any man aboard me ship. If I don't react quickly and decisively, they'll think me inferior. Weak."

Which explained to Elizabeth why she was presently aboard the *Fancy*. Elizabeth chewed on her lip, pondering how best to use this information to benefit her and Fitzwilliam. Alexandra only thought of the moment. She was constantly under scrutiny and, therefore, always had a great deal to prove. That was a lot of pressure to live under every day. "But I thought you were the captain of this vessel?"

Alexandra puffed her chest and lifted her chin

proudly. "I've been voted captain for the last five years now."

"An amazing accomplishment, to be certain." Captaining a pirate ship would never make Miss Bingley's list of ladylike accomplishments (more was the pity). "Then I wonder why you would not prefer to be in control rather than always reacting to your crew's expectations?"

"I'm in control," Alexandra rebutted.

"Are you really?" Elizabeth pressed. "Do you mean to tell us that your decision to keelhaul Mr. Darcy was not a direct result of your anger and fear?"

"I'm not afraid of nothing."

"Oh? You were not afraid of your crew's lessened opinion?"

Alexandra did not reply.

Elizabeth continued, "Tell me how keelhauling Mr. Darcy affected the attitude of your crew toward you."

"They dare not defy me."

That was not the point, and Elizabeth would not allow her to believe it was. "No doubt, but how did your rash reaction affect your crew's view of Mr. Darcy?" Elizabeth leaned back in her chair, confident her reasoning was on sturdy ground. She had seen how Cotton, Bauer, and Jean-Christophe treated him.

"They respect him," Alexandra grumbled.

Feigning surprise, Elizabeth asked, "Really? Why is that, do you think?"

Crossing her arms and pursing her lips, Alexandra

said nothing. Either she did not want to own to her mistake or she really did not know.

Elizabeth supplied an answer. "You maintained their fear, but Mr. Darcy won their respect and loyalty. Why do you think that is?"

Still no reply.

"Could it be because he acted boldly in favor of another, selflessly putting their lives before his own?" She sought Fitzwilliam's gaze, smiling when his eyes met hers. "There is no greater proof of goodness than a person who rises in your defense at the risk of their own life." No greater proof of love. He had not said the words, but she felt them in the warmth of his contemplation.

Alexandra clapped her hands together, ruining their moment. With a grin, she said, "That's why I arranged for Darcy to fight me. I knew ye'd be impressed."

The old adage that one attracted more flies with honey than with vinegar popped into Elizabeth's mind. She must find praise where she could. Forcing a smile, she stated, "You learn quickly. However, Mr. Darcy is a gentleman. He does not need to prove himself because honor is part of his nature and influences everything he does." That, and her heart was his long before the dangerous display. Her cheeks warmed under Fitzwilliam's tender gaze.

Again, Alexandra interrupted their moment. "He's as fine a man as me Nick. Which is why ye're here. I need to learn to be more like ye."

Because Elizabeth kidnapped ladies and dragged them across the country to a pirate ship. She bit back her retort, saying instead, "What would Nick think of your course of action?"

Alexandra squirmed in her chair, grumbling, "He'd say what he always does."

Elizabeth raised her eyebrows. "What does he say?"

"That I ought to use me fool brain and think before I leap into the fray."

Fitzwilliam's lips quirked. "A wise man, this Nick. I would like to meet him."

Alexandra scowled and wrapped her arms around herself. "I've made a real mess of things, haven't I? Ye must think I'm a horrible, unredeemable wretch."

She looked so miserable, Elizabeth rested her hand on Alexandra's shoulder. "Do you want to know what I really think?"

"That I'm a selfish pirate who acts rashly and without a thought for anyone but meself?"

*Close, but not quite.* Elizabeth shot Fitzwilliam another silencing look, ending in a conspiratorial smile because his thoughts were undeniably the same as hers.

Teasing him and consoling Alexandra (without letting her completely off the hook), Elizabeth said, "A gentleman recently taught me that first impressions are not always the most accurate measure by which to judge a person's character. The proof of a person's goodness is seen in their actions and the way they treat others—especially those inferior to them."

Alexandra lowered her head to her hands. "If that's how it is, then I'm a lost cause. I believe in strikin' before I'm struck. I don't know if I can change that … or if I want to."

Elizabeth nodded. "Nobody is a lost cause. Are you willing to try to improve your character?"

"I have to if I'm to convince Nick that I'm worth havin.'"

"It will not be easy, but you stand to win a great deal —the respect of your crew, the admiration of the man you love, and perhaps some new friends to support you."

Alexandra looked lost and little. "Ye'd do that? For me? After what I've put ye through?" Looking at Darcy, she asked, "After keelhaulin' ye and cheatin' ye out of a win ye deserved?"

Begrudgingly, he answered, "If Elizabeth extends her friendship to you, then I shall too." He lowered his chin and narrowed his eyes, adding, "However, if you abuse her friendship in any way—if you put her in any more danger—I shall cut you off forever."

"I'd expect nothing less from ye," Alexandra said, looking as though she wished it were otherwise. Pounding her fist against the table, she groaned, "Blast the mizzenmast. Bothersome barnacles. How'm I supposed to learn how to be a lady Nick'll fall in love with when I have to let ye go?"

Calling Jaffa, who was always nearby, she ordered,

"Tell Nuñez to chart a course for Weymouth. We're goin' ashore."

She sounded so miserable, so hopeless and vulnerable, Elizabeth knew that her instinct to befriend Alexandra was the kindest course of action. "Your decision to take us ashore proves you are further along in your progress than you suppose."

They were going to shore. Their freedom was guaranteed.

Fitzwilliam shook his head at her, a lopsided grin spreading over his face and his eyes wide with wonder.

MRS. FINCHLEY ADMIRED the fine houses at Mayfair. Her own address, carefully selected so as not to draw attention to her wealth, was the price she paid to keep her activities hidden. Nobody questioned an old woman living in a rundown house. They pitied her. And she despised them behind a mask of benevolence.

The carriage stopped in front of the address on Colonel Fitzwilliam's card, and she took in the bay windows, swept pavement, and manicured rose bushes on either side of the door, the bitterness rising in her bosom making her hands shake on her cane. If Lady Anne had called for her services, she would not have died in childbirth bringing another brat into the world. It served her right.

Clambering out of the carriage, making certain to

JENNIFER JOY

lean against the footman and walk feebly, she walked to the door.

The butler saw her immediately into the parlor, where Lady Matlock sat like a queen with her princesses ... and—Who was that? Amelia's heart fluttered.

Colonel Fitzwilliam had been useful to her after all!

CHAPTER 24

*A*heavy fog settled over them, so dense Darcy could not see beyond his wrist when he stretched his arm out in front of him. Navigating without the help of the stars was impossible and slowed their progress to shore considerably. However, Alex did not waver in her decision, and by the end of the second day en route to Weymouth Harbor, Darcy's humor was completely restored. He even—miraculously—found himself feeling much more forgiving toward the captain.

Beckett and Nuñez assured Darcy they would gain the harbor the following morning. He could almost see the lantern lights along the wharves.

The men were in a merry mood. They had enough spices in the hold to pass for a merchant vessel, and along with the fresh food and water they would bring aboard, they would have their turn taking leave on land.

Darcy had helped roll up the last of the sails and clear the deck of loose lines, and most of the men, too excited for the morrow, gathered on the main deck with fifes, whistles, and even a fiddle.

The clouds had lifted enough to see their position and continue in their plotted course.

Darcy left the crew for the quarterdeck, where Alex stood at the helm. Elizabeth beside her, her long hair braided down her back, ruffled shirt billowing gently in the soft breeze. She smiled when he neared.

"Alex wishes to know how proper ladies and gents court when our interactions are limited. What do you say, Fitzwilliam? What do you recommend to encourage affection?"

He grinned, remembering one of their previous conversations. "Dancing," he quoted, "even if one's partner is barely tolerable."

She laughed as he had hoped she would.

"Beckett!" called Alex.

The wiry man appeared seconds later, quiet as a cat.

"I aim to join the men in their merriment," she announced, leaving the helm in his capable hands. Grabbing Darcy and Elizabeth's hands, she pulled them along. "Come with me. Ye can show me how proper folks dance."

The deck was a stage, with men performing a jig of motley origins, blending Irish footwork with the sweeping arms of the Scottish highlanders. With Elizabeth's twinkling eyes in his mind and the sound of her laughter in his ears, Darcy joined them, stomping and bounding and swooping to the encouraging cries of the crewmen.

A guitar strummed, and the deck cleared. Nuñez's fingers moved quickly over the strings, and several men stamped their feet and clapped their hands to his varying rhythm, at one moment flowing, then next a dry staccato. He played as well as any performer Darcy had ever heard.

Alex stood in the center, waving for Elizabeth to join her. She started slowly, showing Elizabeth how to sway her hips and stamp her feet to the music.

Darcy was mesmerized. Those who opposed the waltz as indecorous would have suffered apoplexy to witness such an openly seductive and powerful dance. Elizabeth was stunning, twirling and clapping. She learned quickly.

The fiddler began playing again, and the crew rushed forward to claim dances with the ladies. Darcy stepped forward to break up the pushy crowd, but Alex promptly flicked one man over her shoulder, sending him sprawling over the deck with a loud groan.

Elizabeth looked at her in awe. "Can you teach me how to do that?"

Darcy's heart leapt in his throat, a mix of panic and pride.

Alex, who now had several feet of empty space

around her, gestured to her crew. "Which of ye fine men'll volunteer?"

Nobody stepped forward. With a sigh, Darcy offered himself. "I will."

The shock on Elizabeth's face was reward enough for what was sure to come. He would volunteer himself a hundred times over just to see that expression again.

He arched his eyebrow, trying to control his smile. "Why should I not?" He took delight in ruffling her as thoroughly as she had effortlessly done so many times in the months of their acquaintance.

Her lips twitched. "Are you not afraid, Mr. Darcy?"

He was just a little afraid (he had seen what had happened to the last fellow, who only now was able to rise to his feet), but Darcy would never admit it.

Alex called Jaffa over, and Elizabeth paid rapt attention as the movement was described and again demonstrated. Jaffa, knowing what to expect, landed on his feet, unharmed.

"Now, ye do the same with Darcy. We'll start with a more common maneuver, and then I'll show ye how to flip a man twice yer size over yer head," Alex said. "Most'll go for yer wrists when they're tryin' to grab ye," she added, nodding at Jaffa to come at her.

He grabbed her wrist.

"If he tugs me forward, I'll fall right into him. But look at this when I turn to the side." Alex shifted her weight to the side and Jaffa tugged. She did not budge. "We're smaller, so we must use the weight of our body to advantage." She looked at Elizabeth pointedly, only continuing when her student nodded her understanding.

"Good. Now, ye try," Alex ordered.

Darcy reached for Elizabeth's wrist, and she promptly shifted her feet to the side. He tugged, but she did not move. So much for the embrace he had hoped for.

Next, Alex showed Elizabeth how to move in and raise her arm to free her wrist from her captor's grip.

Darcy did not believe the efficiency of the movement until Elizabeth pulled her wrist free of his firm hold with ease. He moved around her, testing her in growing amazement from different angles, and every time, Elizabeth gained her freedom within seconds. She was amazing.

"Now that ye've mastered that, let's move on to the more diverting maneuver." Alex rubbed her hands together. She talked Elizabeth through the motion, moving her into position under Alex's shoulder and using the angle as leverage. Seeing the move up close and in slow motion, Darcy's unease abated. The sailor Alex had flipped over was a topman, not much taller than she was. Given the disparity in their heights and size, Darcy grew confident as the danger to his person diminished.

He encouraged Elizabeth, for he would never discourage any lady from defending herself should it become necessary. If anything, he anticipated Elizabeth teaching Georgiana what she was learning. He would love nothing more than to see the Wickhams of the world thrown onto their backsides by the very ladies on whom they preyed. It would serve them right.

Darcy would play along. He would allow Elizabeth to believe herself the victor if it increased her courage … not that she needed Darcy's help for that. She was already the most courageous lady of his acquaintance.

Jaffa stood by Alex, and Darcy watched him intently with the aim of imitating how gracefully he flipped in the air to land on his feet.

Bowing to Elizabeth, Jaffa said, "You are ready for a larger opponent."

With his blessing, Elizabeth turned to Darcy, the wide smile of pleasure narrowing into a thin line of resolved concentration.

Darcy moved forward, and Elizabeth expertly whipped around under his shoulder. The heady whiff of lilacs in her hair was still in his nostrils when Darcy realized he was upside down, flying through the air. He landed inelegantly on his side on the ground, his breath effectively knocked out of him … in more ways than one.

Hoots and hollers pierced Darcy's consciousness as he tried to make sense of what had just happened. "Now, there be a fine lass!" a sailor shouted.

Elizabeth's knees bent before his eyes, and her face hovered before his. "Fitzwilliam! Did I hurt you? Are you well?"

A deep voice cackled bawdily. "Give 'em a kiss, lass! That'll put him to rights!"

Darcy finally caught his breath. Pulling himself up to his elbow, he said as loudly as he could, "A lady deserves better than to be kissed in front of you scurvy savages."

Elizabeth heaved a sigh and, to his initial consternation, she offered him a hand up. "Come on, Fitzwilliam. We are equal partners now." Her eyes brimmed with mischief, and he knew she would not hesitate to use the same maneuver on him again if he ever got out of line. The prospect was equally disturbing and thrilling. She had delivered a masterful blow to his manly pride, but he was too pleased with her accomplishment to dwell on his loss. She was right. They were equals. In mind, in birth, and in strength.

Choosing to elevate her esteem rather than insist on his own, Darcy accepted Elizabeth's hand and rose to his feet accompanied by the crew's whoops and wails.

CHAPTER 25

*N*ick helped Lord Matlock into the gig, widening his stance when the narrow boat wobbled. "At the front, Yer Lordship," he said, earning a grunt from the man who, since his arrival in his carriage earlier that same evening, had insisted that if Nick was not ready to claim him as his uncle, he could at least address him as a friend without the formalities. Nick couldn't explain why he hesitated. It just didn't feel right for him to take such a liberty … it probably never would.

Along with Richard, Nick had ridden ahead of Lord Matlock, passing Mr. Bennet and arranging for changes of horses and allowing the older men to travel in greater comfort.

His Lordship must have been exhausted—he, too, had overtaken Mr. Bennet, who did the best he could but did not have as sturdy of a constitution—but he did

222

not complain. Once Nick had learned from the local fishermen that the *Fancy*, with its scantily clad figure-head, moored ten miles off the coast, he had insisted on accompanying them out to the ship.

They took their seats. The gig rocked and bobbed on the water. It was built for speed, and with the oarsmen aboard (Nick included), they would sneak up noiselessly on the *Fancy*. It was the only way. Alex would shoot them out of the water if she suspected their threat.

He pursed his lips, his nostrils flaring as he exhaled and gripped the oar to plunge into the water. The familiar burn in his shoulders brought some comfort. At least that was the same. Unlike *her*.

He'd thought he knew Alex, but if that was true, then he'd need more answers from her. Why'd she moor ten miles off a busy port? Why'd she let him leave? Why had she betrayed him?

And the biggest one of all: Why was she here? He doubted she chased after him to apologize. Alex rarely suffered from a guilty conscience. So what was she up to?

Lord Matlock interrupted his thoughts, asking, "No doubt, you and Richard have discussed the matter at length, so my apologies for making you repeat yourself. However, while I see clearly how she mistook Darcy for you, I cannot comprehend what that has to do with Miss Bennet. As if one kidnapping is not enough!"

Nick answered honestly. "I'm not certain. Alex

doesn't change course. When something gets into that fool woman's head, she'll stop at nothing to see it done."

"Why do you suspect she is behind both disappearances?"

Nick dug into the water, his breath more forceful now. Whether that was Alex's fault or the exercise, he couldn't distinguish. "It's all in the timing. Darcy disappeared Sunday night and Miss Bennet only four days later." He shrugged. It had started out as a hunch and had gained strength with every clue they had discovered along the way.

Lord Matlock looked out over the water and shuffled his thumbs impatiently. "Your hunch led us to Lafitte's ship, so I am inclined to believe you are correct. I only pray that Darcy is still there … and unharmed … along with Miss Bennet."

Richard asked, "With the navy actively patrolling our waters, how has she managed to avoid discovery?"

Confound it if Nick knew. Her choice to moor off Weymouth Harbor was nonsensical … like everything else the backstabbing siren had done lately. Taking a deep breath to calm his ire, Nick explained, "The *Fancy*'s a fast little frigate, and Alex knows not to stay long in any one place. Her strength is in her speed. She can outrun any ship. And if one of the King's finest stops her, she has a hold of spices to convince 'em she's a merchant. If that doesn't work, she's got several letters of marque."

"From whom?" Richard asked, shocked.

"From whichever country's handy," Nick replied with a wry grin. The lawless had to take extra precautions when flaunting the laws of the land and, had the colonel asked, Nick could have elaborated half a dozen other means to escape notice.

Lord Matlock grunted. "How did you know she would sail this direction when it exposes her to danger?"

"Alex hates the cold," Nick shook his head at the weakness of his reasoning, but the truth was that once he had heard of Miss Bennet's disappearance and her attachment to Darcy, he had known. He had felt it in his bones. "I believe her plan, when she thought she had kidnapped me, was to go south, where she could pillage merchant ships and capture Spanish warships for the crown. When she learned her mistake, she could either return north—a foolhardy option sure to earn her unwanted attention—or head west with the rocks and islands to hide behind and bide her time until she formed a new plan."

Lord Matlock nodded. "Intuition can only carry you so far, Nick. How did you know to ask at Weymouth? The *Fancy* might have reached Falmouth by now."

One of the oarsmen scoffed. Looking around him uncomfortably, he looked down and mumbled, "Begging your pardon, Your Lordship."

"Enlighten me, good sir," Lord Matlock insisted.

"It's only that nobody be sailing anywhere in the fog we've had. No stars, no direction."

Nick agreed. He'd counted on the fog to hold her back. Not even Nuñez, as capable as he was, could navigate through that dense fog. No one could.

"You assume a great deal too much for my taste." Lord Matlock leveled his gaze at Nick.

Nick smiled. Richard had said the same over the past three days of riding. He responded to the father the same way he had to the son. "Men like me learn to live by our instincts and act quickly, or we get caught and hanged."

"As you have proved. However, we are creeping up on Miss Lafitte, who by your account has lived a life similar to yours. What can we expect from her? I do not assume she shall be pleased to receive us."

Nick's shoulders tensed, and between the strokes of his oar, he twisted his neck from side to side, his bones crunching and cracking. He looked forward to the altercation. Just wait until he boarded Alex's ship. Wouldn't that be the perfect revenge—taking the *Fancy* as his prize? He already knew her crew. Once he made them aware of what she'd done, they'd mutiny. They'd vote captain, and he'd throw her in the bilge with the rest of the rats. He'd lock the door himself and toss the key over the side.

Avoiding a direct answer, he whispered, "We're getting close."

As he'd expected, the ship was dark. What he hadn't

expected to hear was music and laughter. They drew closer, careful to paddle softly, and listened.

The crew silenced for a few seconds before they rose in a cheerful roar. Some game must be afoot. Good. A distraction.

Nick guided the gig to the starboard side, where a wooden ladder stretched up to the main deck. Making sure his weapons were ready, he crept up the ladder and slipped over the side, signaling for the others to follow when he went unnoticed.

Alex's sailors faced the center of the deck, fists pounding the air, their loud whoops piercing the night. Nick couldn't have asked for a better distraction. Even the lookout watched the deck when he ought to have spotted them approaching.

Curious, Nick used his height to peer over the crew. A man was flat on his back. A young lady knelt down at his side, then rising to her feet, she held a hand out to help him up.

That was when Nick heard Alex, saw her out of the corner of his eye, laughing and clapping.

The hairs on the back of Nick's neck rose on end and, before he thought better of it, he shoved through the crowd, pulling his loaded pistol out of his waistband.

Whispered exclamations—"There be two of 'em!" "If I didn't see it with my own eyes..." "Which be which?"—faded under his heartbeat drumming in his ears.

Alex, vixen that she was, smiled at Nick and stepped forward, closer to him and the pistol he pointed at her. "Nick!" she exclaimed, not in the least bit concerned. She didn't think he'd do it.

"Don't test me, woman. I'll shoot." He gritted his teeth and cocked the pistol.

Her smile wavered. She looked confused, but he wouldn't let the treacherous siren fool him again. She'd sooner lead him to the rocks and let him drown than let him leave to find whatever it was he'd thought he was out to find. Anger and the prospect of revenge had fueled him over the miserable weeks crossing the Atlantic to London, but now that she stood close enough for him to shoot…

Drat it all to the crushing depths, he couldn't do it.

Lord Matlock's voice broke the silence. "There shall be no bloodshed, Nick."

The man the lady had handed up earlier spun around. "Uncle?"

Nick felt his eyes bulge and his mouth drop. His hands shook, and he dropped them to his knees. There was no pistol there. When had someone plucked it from his grasp?

Richard and Lord Matlock brushed by him to the man. To Darcy. They embraced him and bowed to the young lady they called Miss Bennet. Their greetings were happy.

Nick thought he would be sick. He seemed to have a head cold, complete with a useless, stuffy nose and a swollen throat. His chest ached, and his eyes blurred. Definitely sick. He closed his eyes and filled his lungs.

A hand fell on his shoulder. Two boots stood before him. Taking another deep breath, Nick forced himself to stand straight. After twenty-eight years of searching for something he couldn't name, something which had always been just out of his reach, the truth crashed over him like a rogue wave he couldn't have foreseen or prepared for.

Darcy held him by the shoulders, steadying himself as much as he steadied Nick. In a low voice, he said, "You *are* my brother."

Sweet, warm release flooded through Nick like a double ration of rum. He had never been happier. His cheeks were wet, but he didn't care. He wasn't alone anymore. He had a family.

And then, he saw *her*.

# CHAPTER 26

*D*arcy saw the moment Nick noticed Alex. His eyes hardened, and his jaw clenched. It was a fearsome look to behold. It occurred to Darcy that he must look the same when he was in high dudgeon, but Nick's hand reaching to his side and the knife flying past Darcy's nose to plunge into the plank at Alex's boot tip prevented any further pondering on their likeness.

Alex jumped backward. "What'd ye do that for? These're me favorite boots!"

Another knife flew by her ear, close enough to make her eyes double in size ... then narrow as she reached for her boot.

Darcy moved in front of Nick. Jaffa appeared at his side, strengthening the barrier. "Get outta me way," Nick seethed between his teeth.

"No." Darcy blocked Nick's attempt to get past.

"You will have to kill me first, Cap'n Nick," Jaffa said.

Given the lethal gleam in his brother's eye, Darcy added, "I cannot allow you to injure a lady."

"Ye call her a lady? That conniving viper?" He raised his arm to shove Darcy out of his path, but while he was the same size and very strong, Darcy had a slight advantage in weight, and he used it. To protect Alex. Why on earth he would protect that woman when she had caused him and Elizabeth and their families so much trouble, Darcy could not say. But it was the right thing to do, God help him.

"Ye're one to talk, Nick. Lightin' off in the middle of the night like a thief, leavin' yer friends. Yer family."

"Ye're not me family, and ye never will be, ye faithless female." Another shove, another block. "Get outta me way!"

Elizabeth stepped in front of Alex, facing Nick. "Are you going to shout insults and threats at each other all night, or shall we discuss the matter like mature people?"

Nick's finger jabbed over Darcy's shoulder, pointing at Alex. "She's a traitor! I'll have her hang."

"Ye no-good deserter!"

"Does that answer your question, Miss Bennet?" Richard teased, walking between them with Uncle.

"I ain't no traitor!" Alex shouted over them.

Nick shoved his knife back into its sheath, and only then did Darcy let him step around him. "Then why'd ye tell the thief-taker me route? Ye were the only one I'd told me plan."

Alex took a step back, her fists balled up at her stomach. She sounded breathless when she spoke. "That's what ye think of me?"

"Ye don't deny it?"

"I swear on the stars and swells, it weren't me." Her voice shook, not in the rage Darcy had heard from Alex before, but with something he had never expected to hear from the hard-as-nails captain.

"Ye didn't come with me. What else was I supposed to think?" Nick's voice had lost its edge.

Elizabeth moved closer to Darcy, close enough for their elbows to touch. They exchanged a brief look, and Darcy understood that she did not intend to interrupt, nor would he. It was a time to clear misunderstandings. Richard and Uncle parted, allowing Nick to pass.

Alex flailed her arms wildly heavenward. "Ye came to me with this crazy, grand idea. I wanted to go with ye—I wanted to so bad—but ye asked me to leave everythin' I'd ever known and go with ye into the unknown. I weren't ready."

Nick widened his stance and crossed his arms, his voice decidedly more unsteady than his posture suggested. "Ye didn't rat on me?"

She shook her head.

"Then, who did?"

"I thought it was me brothers." Her face twisted.

"But I started to have doubts…" She stubbed the toe of her boot into the wood plank and blurted, "…as soon as I broadsided their favorite ship." She squeezed her eyes closed, her whole face twisted into a guilt-racked wince.

Darcy groaned. Never again would he complain of his or Elizabeth's family's faults. They tried his patience, yes, but they had never—not once— attempted to blow him up or evaporate his residence.

"Ye did what?" Nick boomed, the sides of his lips quirking upward. "What'd ye do? Take out a mast?"

Her scowl deepened. She mumbled, "I aimed five cannons at their hold."

"Five!" Nick's smile widened.

She dug her toe into the plank at her feet. "Blasted the *Sea Queen* to bits."

Nick's smile was a full grin now. "Ye sunk the *Queen*? For me?"

Alex shifted her weight, her eyes bright and her fists clenched. "I was angry!" She looked apologetically at Elizabeth. "Elizabeth here's been teachin' me to hold me temper and think 'fore I react. I'm tryin', Nick, but it's so blasted hard."

Darcy bit his lips together. He would not laugh at Alex's lady-like attempts when her effort was genuine. He would not. He sucked in his cheeks and held his breath for good measure.

Elizabeth was far more gracious than he was, though the glint in her eye was present. Addressing

Nick, she said, "Alexandra is an excellent student. She did not even reach for her cutlass when you threw your first knife at her."

Alex grinned like a child praised before her parents. "Ye're right! I only reached for me dagger after the second one whizzed past me ear! I *am* learnin'! Oh, Nick, it's so hard, but I'll keep tryin'. I'll get better, I swear. Just don't leave again. Ye took all the life out of me with ye; I had to find ye, and now that ye're here, I'm not gonna let ye out of me sight again..." Her words scattered like grapeshot until she looked down and clasped her hands together. "That is, if ye still want me."

There was a collective holding of breath now as the eavesdropping sailors watched the scene intently.

With a loud whoop, Nick wrapped his arms around Alex's waist, picking her up and twirling in circles while he peppered her face with kisses. "Call Boone! I'll marry ye here and now with the crew—and me brother —as our witnesses." He set her down, looking between Darcy, Richard, and Uncle Matlock. Pressing his hands together, he wrung his hands and bowed his head. "Perhaps ye'd agree to be me best men. If ye have no objection to me asking ye."

Richard's reply was swift. "I would be honored."

Darcy nodded, dumbfounded at how quickly the tide had turned.

Alex hopped at his side. "We can have a double weddin'!"

Darcy would be lying if he said the thought had not occurred to him. But Elizabeth's eyes were windows into her soul, and the conflict he so plainly saw was answer enough for him.

After their long conversations over the past few days, he knew she was not as indifferent as she had once claimed to be. Perhaps she even loved him.

But it was too soon for declarations, and Darcy would not damage the progress he had made inching his way to her heart by losing his patience now. "While I have family here to witness what shall surely be the most joyous day of my life, Elizabeth's family still thinks she is in danger."

She smiled at him, biting her bottom lip and nodding. He had guessed correctly. "Thank you," she whispered.

Darcy had felt his chest fill with pride on numerous occasions before, but those were nothing compared to the pride he felt that moment. He understood her, and she appreciated his understanding.

Uncle Matlock's commanding tone cut through Darcy's reverie. "Mr. Bennet and Mr. Gardiner are on their way. The gig is waiting for us to return, and it would be a kindness to be at the inn when the gentlemen arrive. We should leave immediately."

Several sighs were heard, some from the crew. Where Darcy had once considered jumping overboard and swimming to shore days before, he was now stunned to feel hesitation.

Uncle continued, "Under the circumstances, I think it would be best if Miss Bennet accompanied us to shore, where I shall secure a room and a maid to attend to her."

Darcy felt Elizabeth lean closer, and he tucked her hand in his arm. They both knew what needed to be done. Uncle was right. When Darcy looked up from her, his eyes met with Nick's. His brother's gaze darted between him and Alex, his brow furrowing at the choice he must make. The family he had chosen or the family he had only just found.

It was too soon to part ways. Darcy had a brother! A brother he wanted to know. There were so many questions he wished to ask Nick—twenty-eight years of catching up to do. "Will you consider staying with us for a while? Your family shall want to meet you ... and your wife."

Alex looked up at Nick with a smile. "The men'll be happy for some shore leave. They can sell the spices and see to the fresh water and food supply."

"But the press gangs—"

"They'll be careful and carry their letters. Won't ye?" she asked around, and received several eager nods and affirmations.

"But if ye're found out—"

She interrupted, "I'll use me new name. Nobody knows Alexandra Blackburne, and few have seen me likeness on this side of the Atlantic. So long as nobody calls me Lafitte, I'll be safe enough."

Richard, who had been quietly observing the proceedings, added, "We are near Devonshire. We might find some clues to what happened to separate you at birth." Looking between Nick and Darcy, he asked, "Would you not like to resolve that mystery?"

"Yes," they said in unison.

Uncle lifted his chin, his deep voice resonant, "Then it is decided. We stay together until we are satisfied justice has been served." He placed one hand on Nick's shoulder. "While you are a grown adult in command of your own life, as my nephew and one in need of the protection of my name, I would like to speak with this young lady before I extend my protection to her and give my blessing on your union."

Leave it to Uncle Matlock to take over command. Alex had sense enough to look nervous. For a second. Before her features twisted into a rebellious expression. She squirmed away from Nick and Uncle, crossing her arms over herself defensively … or, maybe it was defiantly. Jutting her chin toward Elizabeth, Alex asked, "What about her? Don't ye need to inspect her, too?"

Uncle turned to Elizabeth with a chuckle and took her free hand gently in his own. "I have not had the privilege of formally meeting Miss Bennet until this moment, but I have met her father as well as her aunt and uncle. They are upstanding people I shall be happy to call friends … and perhaps something more in the future. Besides that, I have heard of little else but her from my nephew and his sister over the past months." He cast a wry look at Darcy that made him blush. He kissed her hand—the old rascal—and turned back to Alex. "You, however, I have read about in the newspapers and broadsides. They sing songs about you in the lowest taverns."

Alexandra scowled. "Invented stories, the lot of 'em. Mostly. Well … some of 'em."

A shout from the watch overhead broke the stillness of the night. Men shuffled over the deck, all looking up to see where the danger came from.

*Boom!* Then a whistle, a high-pitched shriek getting louder.

Darcy wrapped his arms around Elizabeth, shouting, "Uncle, Rich, get back!" Cradling Elizabeth, he ran away from the noise.

"Man yer stations!" Alex shouted, already moving. "It's an attack!"

Darcy felt the crash, the jolt shaking the timbers under their feet, the deafening blast of cannon fire.

# CHAPTER 27

Splinters scattered through the moonlight. Smoke choked Elizabeth's throat and burned her eyes. She could not see Fitzwilliam, but she felt him behind her. While his touch was a comfort, it also meant his back protected hers, thus exposing him to peril. She reached behind her and latched on to the fabric of his shirt, tugging him along faster until they rounded a bulkhead.

The night was clearer away from the debris. Lord Matlock and Colonel Fitzwilliam wiped their faces with handkerchiefs. Nick and Alexandra had stayed behind. Elizabeth had known they would, but she had hoped they would flee for safety. She held her breath, trying to calm her racing heart as one realization led to another and sent her heart galloping anew. The gentlemen—Fitzwilliam—would join in the fray. Not for the excitement most men felt at the prospect of a fight or the glory they stood to gain when they boasted of their narrow escape, but because they would protect the people they loved. They would stop the fight.

Fitzwilliam's honor put him in danger, and there was nothing Elizabeth could do. She could not plead with him to change when it was his very character which had won her over.

He caught her hands in his and looked into her eyes. "Stay here."

Elizabeth had known it was coming, but her heart still leapt into her throat. She had to help stop the fight. But how? How could she—or anyone else, for that matter—stop a fight amongst men who lived for danger? Granted, the men aboard the *Fancy* had tempered their habits and speech in her presence, a fact of which she was grateful, but she had observed their struggle to do so. And the men who had assaulted them with cannons would not cease their attack merely because she politely demanded that they stop. They would sooner shoot Fitzwilliam and laugh than comply.

Elizabeth pinched her lips together and looked away. Would that the right words would come to her. She could not lie to him. Nor could she make a promise she had no intention of keeping.

Colonel Fitzwilliam and Lord Matlock were already gone. Only she and Fitzwilliam remained on the walkway behind the bulkhead.

His grip on her hands tightened.

She met his gaze, lips parting—

*Boom!*

Elizabeth screamed as the ship groaned and shook. She grasped onto the most solid thing nearby— Fitzwilliam. She clung to him, more terrified that he would come to harm than that he would leave her alone. If anything happened to him…

His palms rubbed against her cheeks, and she protested when the night air chilled her where his warm body had been. Before words came, he pulled her to him and pressed his lips against hers. She leaned into him, tracing a path up his chest and around his neck, tugging him closer by the curls at his neck.

She never wanted it to end, but it had to. Pulling away, she looked into his eyes—dark and so full of devotion, it would have taken her breath away had she any to spare. She pressed her fingertips to her mouth, determined never to forget the feel of his lips against hers, his breath caressing her cheek, the roughness of his whiskers against her skin.

"She's goin' down! To the pumps!" a sailor shouted from below.

"I must go." He dropped his hands from her and bolted away before she could stop him, the burning in his eyes haunting her. She had not liked Fitzwilliam's stares before she understood his motive in watching her, but what if that was to be the last one? What if that first kiss was also their last?

Elizabeth balled her fists and stiffened her arms.

She could not accept it. Saying a quick prayer begging that their lives be spared, she left the relative safety of the bulkhead.

The deck swarmed with men, swords glinting in the moonlight, pistols raised and ready.

She ran forward. She had no plan, but she knew she had to try something. A sail snapped above her in the wind, the rope holding it quivering in front of her. She stopped and looked up, calculating the trajectory of the sail if she cut it. The men could not fight if they could not see with the canvas covering them. It might work.

A dagger sailed past her head, burying itself in the mast. Heart thundering in her ears, she pried it loose. It was just the tool she needed to drop the sail.

"Halt! Halt, I say!" a voice bellowed through the smoke and fog. "I said we capture him alive, not blast him out of the water, you fools!"

Confused silence ensued. Elizabeth stepped out from behind the mast, knife in hand. The men were at a standstill, the line distinguishing the enemy parties widening.

Seeing her opportunity, Elizabeth weaved through the crew, twisting and shuffling around their drawn weapons, her eyes searching for Fitzwilliam.

He was at the front of the fray, too near their foes. He and Nick bent over a supine figure. They appeared unharmed—thank the Lord for that!—but Alexandra…

Jaffa held her bleeding head. Gently, he wrapped a

length of cloth around her wound, talking to her softly all the while.

Elizabeth dropped to her knees beside him, next to Fitzwilliam. "Is she alive?" she asked, looking for the rise and fall of breath and seeing nothing.

Her fingers trembled so much, the dagger fell with a clatter to the deck. Alexandra was many things (not all of them pleasant), but Elizabeth had imagined them becoming friends as their husbands closed the gap which had separated them since birth. She mourned the future she had looked forward to.

"If she has a pulse," Jaffa said, "it is very weak."

Elizabeth's heart ached to see Alexandra's happy ending, her promising new start, come to an abrupt, twisted halt. She did not want to believe it.

Nick pressed Alexandra's hand against his chest, as though his heart could beat for her. The guttural sound he made filled the night and demanded respectful silence.

When Alexandra did not respond, Elizabeth ached for him.

He leapt to his feet, roaring, "You!" He lunged at the man standing at the front of the boarding party, grabbing him by the collar and lifting him until the man's toes dangled helplessly above the boards.

Lord Matlock's shout reached them from a distance, growing louder as the gentleman came nearer. "If you kill Connell, I shall have no choice but to turn you over, Nick. He is not worth it."

If Nick retaliated, nothing would stop the ensuing fight. More lives would be needlessly lost. Elizabeth caressed Alexandra's cheek. If only she would wake. If only they knew for a certainty she was alive yet.

Elizabeth gasped as an idea struck her. Grabbing the dagger now nestled between her knees and Alexandra's shoulder, she held the blade in front of Alexandra's mouth and nostrils, angling the blade so that the moon reflected off the edge. Please, let it cloud. Please, let there be breath. Jaffa leaned closer, watching with her.

Nick roared, and Elizabeth imagined him shaking Connell as he spoke. "An eye for an eye. That's God's justice, not mine. I'll not defy the maker of the seas."

Elizabeth uttered another supplication … and she saw it. A hint of fog. She glanced up to see that Fitzwilliam had risen to his feet. "Look!" she called. "She is breathing!"

Nick lowered the man to his toes, but he still held him at the neck. His chest heaved violently.

Fitzwilliam stepped over Alexandra and placed his hand on his brother's arm.

Several gasps, followed by whispers, flowed through the newcomers as they saw the brothers standing beside each other, one the exact replica of the other.

Fitzwilliam ignored them. Softly, he said, "Let Connell go. He is not worth it. She is alive."

Nick dropped Connell, letting the man fall like a sack of coal to the deck.

"Lexi's alive?" Nick sank to his knees beside Alexandra.

Elizabeth held the knife in front of Alexandra's airways so he could see for himself.

Alexandra's chest inflated with a deep, visible breath.

Jaffa gently helped her rise onto her elbow, facing Nick. With a groan, she raised her fingers to the side of her head. "I'm bleedin' like a stuck pig!" She winced and blinked several times, looking past Nick, her eyes widening. She scrambled to push herself up from her elbow. "Arnold!" she shrieked, wincing again.

Nick spun around, and the men cleared away from the man called Arnold.

Forgetting her manners entirely, though Elizabeth could hardly blame her, given the duress they were under, Alexandra pointed at Arnold. "Ye betrayed Nick. It was ye! His own First Mate," she said a little softer and without a single wince or grimace.

# CHAPTER 28

*E*lizabeth, along with Jaffa, helped Alexandra to her feet, all the while watching the accused man. He was of a similar age as his captain, shorter and built like a man accustomed to hard labor. There was nothing in his looks to distinguish him from any other man crowding the deck, but the sneer on his face, the hatred in his eyes, was blatant.

Nick's voice was low. "Is it true? Did ye betray me to this thief-taker?" He motioned at Connell, who stood beside Arnold, rubbing his neck.

Alexandra twisted free of Elizabeth's hold on her arm. Without turning around, she made signals behind her back. Elizabeth did not know if she should be worried or not, but she knew not to draw attention to the gestures.

Arnold glared at Nick. There was no regret, no

shame. His lack of a reply was boldly rebellious, and it thickened the air surrounding them.

Elizabeth cast another glance at Fitzwilliam. He stood beside his brother and, while Elizabeth appreciated the loyal gesture, she could not help but wish he would take a few steps away.

"Why'd ye do it?" Nick asked, his tone sharp.

"Amnesty," Arnold replied mockingly.

"Ye turned me in to clear yer own name when ye knew I was leaving that wretched life?"

The man sneered. "And turn down the opportunity to take command of yer ship under the protection of the Crown? I could continue takin' ships with the blessin' of the Admiralty. I'd be rich. Be called a hero fer freein' the seas of The Blade." Arnold pounded his fist against his chest. "It'd be *my* name they sang about in the taverns."

He raised his other hand from his side, pointing a pistol at Nick, who now had a sword in his hand. Arnold cackled. "Yer no different from me. Look at ye. Yer fingers are itchin' to see if ye can run me through 'fore I shoot ye." He had the impudence (or, Elizabeth thought, the stupidity) to stretch his neck, offering a larger target. As though he wanted Nick to exact his revenge.

Fitzwilliam watched Nick as intently as Elizabeth did, willing him to act wisely.

Elizabeth had no air in her lungs, but a bit of breath

still whooshed over her lips when, with a flick of his wrist so fast she did not know what she had seen, he sent Arnold's pistol clattering to the floor. Nick's blade pointed steadily at Arnold's throat. Elizabeth had never seen anything like it. One thrust, and he had completely disarmed his enemy. Arnold's life was in Nick's hands.

Nick raised the sword into the air, beckoning everyone's attention. "I'll not give ye the easy way out. Let it be known ye're a lily-livered coward who betrayed his mate. That's the song they'll sing about ye." He stabbed his sword into the deck.

Out of the corner of her eye, Elizabeth saw Alexandra reach into her boot. Elizabeth grabbed her hand before she could extract her knife. Resenting how short-lived her relief a moment ago had been, Elizabeth whispered, "If you act in rage now, they shall retaliate. Arnold will shoot Nicholas." Or Fitzwilliam. "Your men would fight for you, and many of them would die."

Jutting her chin toward Connell and Arnold, Alexandra hissed, "Their kind don't deserve to live. One flick of me wrist, and I'll make sure the world's never plagued by their offspring."

Pirate justice was harsh, indeed. "I shall do my best to stay on your good side. God forbid I ever provoke your anger."

Alexandra moved her hand away from her boot, a tear trickling down her cheek. "They maimed me ship. Me lovely *Fancy*. They must pay."

"The *Fancy* can be repaired," Elizabeth reassured her, looking to Jaffa. He nodded in affirmation, and she continued, "You and Nicholas are alive. Do not waste your future on those men who mean nothing to you. Think beyond this moment."

Speaking of worthless men, Arnold spoke. "Ye'll regret crossin' me." He gestured at Fitzwilliam. "This is yer brother. He called the gent behind ye 'Uncle.' Ye takin' up with highborn folks now, eh? We'll see how good ye are with that blade when I picks 'em off one by one."

"That is enough from you, Mr. Arnold," Connell said, reaching behind him. A man slapped a pair of irons into his palm. "I am here to arrest Nicholas Blackburne on the charge of piracy. I have no bone to pick with anyone else here."

Fitzwilliam folded his arms over his chest beside his brother.

Elizabeth looked around her, but Alexandra had slipped away. She looked at Jaffa, but he put his finger over his lips.

Lord Matlock stepped forward, flanking Nick on the other side. Elizabeth instantly liked him. She saw where Fitzwilliam's unbending loyalty came from as well as his uncompromising determination. "The ship is sinking," Lord Matlock reported. "The men are pumping water as quickly as they can, and my son is helping them move the ballast to lift the injured side out of the water, but unless we wish to go down with her, we had better continue this discussion elsewhere."

This discussion. That was one way to put it. Elizabeth ought to have swooned as much as she had held her breath over the past quarter of an hour. Or five minutes. Or an hour. Elizabeth could not be sure, nor did she have the audacity to inquire about the time just then.

Connell stepped toward Nick. "I will not leave without my prisoner. I caught him, fair and square. He is my prize."

Lord Matlock said, "He was released under my custody, yet you dare defy my authority and that of the magistrate."

"I did not chase him over the Atlantic and back not to get my reward. He is a criminal—a plague on humankind. He deserves to hang. Surely you see that, Your Lordship."

"If he did not have such a large reward attached to his capture, you would not care so much about justice. If it is the money you desire, I am prepared to pay the amount to you myself."

Arnold jabbed Connell in the ribs. "He's tryin' to buy ye off, but ye stick it to him good. He knows ye can take his name to the papers. Tell how he housed and protected a known, feared pirate; how he attempted to bribe ye to save his criminal nephew."

Gaining courage in the turncoat's support, Connell

said, "How would your peers like to know about the black mark on your family name?"

Arnold cackled. "They won't be invitin' ye over fer tea no more!"

A shrill whistle pierced Elizabeth's eardrums. She lifted her shoulders to shield them.

Alexandra stepped forward, slipping her hand around Nick's arm. "While ye fools were busy gabbin' and breathin' threats, me men saw fit to take yer little clipper."

So that was what Alexandra had meant when she said she would make the men pay for injuring her *Fancy*. Elizabeth knew it was wicked of her to be impressed, but she was.

The men standing behind Arnold and Connell spun around to see dozens of pistols aimed at them, the crew that had been left behind bound and tied. Alexandra's crew saluted with their free hands. Impertinent lot. Much like their captain. Much, Elizabeth owned, like herself.

Another narrow boat, the one Nick must have arrived on, was beside it. None of the men looked harmed. That must have been how Alexandra's men had got over to the larger ship unseen. Brilliant! Elizabeth looked at her friend in ever-increasing admiration.

With a roguish grin at his betrothed, Nick pulled his sword out of the deck, and ordered, "Weapons down."

Pistols and blades of every shape and size clattered to the ground.

Pointing the tip of his sword to the men behind Arnold and Connell, Nick said, "Who of ye wish ye'd never heard of these two men and would separate yerself from their company given the chance?"

Not surprisingly, all the men volunteered. Some offered explanations, too. "'Tis only a hired job." "We had no idea…" "Anything to save my clipper."

Nick raised his hand. "Just remember who spared yer lives. Jaffa, Cotton, Bauer, stand guard over these men until we can get the boat to carry 'em all over to their vessel."

"Me vessel now," Alexandra corrected him. Not allowing for anyone to say otherwise, she turned to the two remaining men standing before them—Connell and Arnold. As casually as one ordered a meal at an inn, she said, "Time for ye to walk the plank. I want ye off me ship."

Nick grabbed a pistol from the deck, encouraging the men to walk to the front of the ship, where a plank had already been set up over the edge. Too far away from the other vessel for it to be of any help to the two condemned men.

Fitzwilliam stepped in front of Nick, caution in his face.

Lord Matlock said, "I cannot condone this kind of conduct."

Nick grinned. "I'll not bind their feet or hands.

They'll have as fair a chance of surviving as any with all the debris floating in the water from the blast. They'll just be mighty uncomfortable for a spell. Ten miles in the currents is a fair swim for any able-bodied man." His grin widened. "Give 'em time to think of their mistakes, like."

Elizabeth liked him. Judging from the twitch in Fitzwilliam's lips and how he stepped out of his path, she suspected he liked Nick, too. Lord Matlock uttered no more objections.

CHAPTER 29

*N*ick watched the wharf approach, his attention divided between the crippled *Fancy* dragging behind them and Darcy standing at the railing beside his young lady.

Miss Elizabeth was as fine a lass as a man could find. He'd never forget how she'd run to Lexi's side. She hadn't balked or swooned at the sight of blood, nor had she cringed at the back of the boat at the first sign of danger. This was a good woman. Nick was pleased for Darcy—for his brother.

Brother. How strange the word felt in his own mind when Nick had always been alone. Strange, but wonderful. Comforting.

He was close enough to the couple to hear Miss Elizabeth speak when she smiled up at Darcy. "After a great deal of consideration, I think it best to keep my letter to my family brief and to the point."

"Very discreet. If you refusing Mr. Collins was enough to give her the vapors, imagine how her poor nerves would suffer to learn you had been kidnapped by pirates."

Miss Elizabeth laughed. "Until she learned you were also on board, wherein she would pray for a compromise."

Darcy went solemn. "Elizabeth, I—"

She nudged him playfully on the arm. "No harm has been done. We are free to make our own choices for our happiness. Why should we not reflect on our adventures with anything but pleasure?"

Darcy's deepening frown piqued Nick's interest and warned him that he was now eavesdropping. Leaving the railing, Nick sought the rest of Alex's crew. He prayed Darcy and Miss Elizabeth would be safe and happy. He'd do what he could to make certain they were. It was the least he could do.

Nicholas stopped, his brief glimmer of happiness dampened with reality. Which was worse: to find his place only to know his existence meant danger to the people he yearned to call family, or to wander the world searching for another place to claim?

At least he had Alex. And he'd care for her the best he knew how.

Boone, Beckett, and Alex stood in a circle with Lord Matlock, their arms crossed over their chests and their expressions grim. Whatever they were discussing was unpleasant for all four of them.

Boone clenched his hands in front of him. "If I get me hands on Arnold—"

Lord Matlock opened his mouth to protest, but Beckett spoke before he did. "Just as you have yer laws on land, we must abide by a certain code of conduct we swear to uphold the moment we join a crew. If we don't respect our own code, then mutiny's born. Arnold broke the code, Yer Lordship. He must pay the consequences."

Alex nodded tersely. "I hope the sharks eat him, or I'll shoot the scurvy cur meself."

"Justice must be meted out. He'll not make it to shore. We honor the code," Boone agreed.

Lord Matlock raised his palm. "Tell me no more. He made his choice and shall suffer the consequences the same as any man"—he eyed Alexandra—"or woman." Looking at Boone and Beckett, he added, "See you serve your captain better than he served his."

Nick approached, addressing the Quartermaster and First Mate. "Take care of her ship, will ye? I'll see about hiring caulkers, sawyers, blockmakers, and whatever else the *Fancy* requires to put her to rights."

"If you meet with any trouble, you come to me," Lord Matlock said. "I doubt the prize Connell hoped to receive at my nephew's hanging shall exceed the damage he caused tonight."

Nick's head reeled. His Lordship was a man to be admired, and the ease with which he claimed Nick as his own nephew made Nick's heart soar and his stomach twist into knots. It wasn't right. He might've belonged to them once, but Arnold had been right to call Nick a black mark. He'd only tarnish their name and bring danger to their doorstep. He already had.

Alex leaned closer to him, oblivious to the direction of his thoughts. "Never mind that, men. No expense shall be spared repairin' the *Fancy* when we're comfortable on this clipper. She'll be yers to command, Beckett, once the *Fancy* is returned to me."

Lord Matlock's reaction was immediate. "This ship is not yours."

*Oh, Lord!*

Alex whipped her head around to face him, and Nick noted how Beckett and Boone disappeared down the deck. Smart men. "I took her fair and square!" Alex said.

"Had this ship belonged to Arnold or Connell, she would be yours to take. However, it was hired."

"They had to know what'd happen if they crossed me. It's fair pillage!" Alex looked to Nick for support, but he knew this was a losing battle. And in the long run, Lord Matlock was right.

Of course, Alex was not one to consider consequences before taking action, and Nick would only start a fight if he attempted to point out the flaw in her reaction.

A gangplank was lowered to the dock, and Nick used the excuse it offered him to usher Alex off the ship to the Gull and Anchor.

She balked at Lord Matlock's insistence that a surgeon see her injury, and Nick admired his relative's patient firmness with her. Finally, she agreed to allow da Silva to at least clean her wound.

After a bath and change of clothes, they all met up in the private parlor where such a spread as Nick had rarely taken part in was displayed across the tables. It was a beautiful sight.

Maids carried pitchers and teapots, plates and platters back and forth from the kitchen to their room, attentive to their every need and quick to return with whatever His Lordship requested. Darcy, too. The attention they commanded was tempered, not with the selfish entitlement Nick had observed too often with the rich of the upper echelons of society, but with sincerity, gratitude, and dignity. Servants were not invisible to them, but hard-working, self-respecting individuals worthy of their notice.

When the last maid had slipped through the curtain separating their room from the others, Richard leaned his arms against the table. He looked exhausted. Pumping water and moving cargo was back-breaking work. He asked, "You know where we are?"

Nick knew the path down which his cousin's thoughts had led him, and he thought it best not to reply. Parting would be painful enough as it was. Why make it harder by delaying the inevitable?

Richard continued, "We are a stone's throw from Devonshire. Let us put this mystery to rest."

Alex piped up. "I'm willin'." With a pointed glare at Lord Matlock, she added, "It's not as though I've a seaworthy ship right now, anyway."

Lord Matlock did not look the least bit repentant. Nick suppressed his grin. "Thanks to Lord Matlock, we're in the people's good graces in Weymouth. We've provided them with work that'll pay." Had Alex insisted on keeping the ship she'd taken, she'd be hard-pressed to hire anyone to help her fix the *Fancy*. And she knew it, judging by the scowl on her face (now directed at Nick).

"I already made inquiries, and the work shall begin in the morning," Lord Matlock said. "Your men shall be happy for the shore leave, no doubt."

Nick marveled at his family. Lord Matlock would make a marvelous captain with the way he assumed command and respect. People bent to him without a fight, and as powerful a skill as that was, Nick had yet to see him abuse it. He was starting to doubt he ever would.

Even Darcy, dressed as the gentleman he was, commanded respect. Nick noted with pride how Darcy graciously acknowledged the privilege granted him.

And then, there was Richard. He was a man of action, the best of men. He'd held his own at the seedy taverns, and he'd manned a pump to keep the *Fancy* afloat without being told or instructed on what to do.

Also, Miss Elizabeth. Nick couldn't help but admire her. With one look, she'd calmed Darcy and controlled

Alex's flaming temper. Nick would have to ask her how she did that. He needed all the help he could get.

Good people, the lot of them. Good people whose lives had taken vastly different paths, and yet, here they were, together.

Nick wished he could enjoy their company longer, but his heart was already trying to convince him to betray what his mind had already decided.

If he were to make his escape, he'd have to sneak away that same night.

# CHAPTER 30

*T*ry as he might, Darcy could not sleep. The *need* to know what had happened to separate him from his twin gnawed at him, just as his need to see Elizabeth safely home to her family tied his stomach in knots. He tossed the covers aside, turning and kicking his feet free of the sheets twisted around his legs.

He had to speak with Mr. Bennet the moment the gentleman arrived. Darcy had a great deal to explain, and even more for which to apologize. There was no excuse for the danger into which he had inadvertently embroiled Elizabeth. Darcy could not rightly ask for forgiveness. He could not explain how it had happened; he could not justify how Elizabeth occupied such a place in his dreams that he had uttered her name in his sleep. His face heated at the thought. Some excuse that was!

Never mind that Darcy had every intention of asking for Elizabeth's hand. Why should Mr. Bennet grant his heart's desire after witnessing Darcy's ungentlemanly manners at Hertfordshire? And there were more offenses—against Mr. Bennet's favorite daughter, no less! If Elizabeth were to tell her father the whole, he would be certain to refuse his consent. Darcy cringed at the memories, wishing with all his might that there were fewer of them to recall.

Sleep became impossible, for now that his demerits had a firm foundation, they piled taller and taller on top of each other.

Would Mr. Bennet allow Elizabeth to attach herself to a man with ties to piracy and thief catchers? Darcy scrubbed his hands through his hair. Compared to his own family, the Bennets were as tame as lambs.

Rising to his feet, Darcy pulled the curtains aside and peered outside at the foggy black through the window. He had tried to make amends—to arrange for Lydia's union with Wickham, to apologize to Bingley for imposing his own erroneous views—but was it too little done, too late? What if Mr. Bennet disapproved of him? What if Darcy was beyond redemption regarding the family he most wished to please, for Elizabeth's sake?

A gust of wind rattled the window at the same time he heard a creak out in the hall. Or had it come from the rafters? Senses alert, Darcy heard another noise— one not easily dismissed as the complaints of an aged, wind-battered inn. He held his breath and listened harder.

*Scratch-scratch.* Like fingernails scraping against a door.

Grabbing his breeches, Darcy tiptoed to the door, feeling foolish for his precaution. It was the darkest hour before dawn. He was unlikely to wake anyone at this ungodly hour. More likely, he would scare a maid who was merely trying to warm their rooms before their occupants stirred.

One peek. He would see the maid, then he would try … again … to go to sleep.

Quietly, so as not to scare the poor girl, he eased his door open a crack. Nothing. Widening the gap, he looked down the hall.

Nick stood in front of Alexandra's door. Jaffa sat in a chair beside it. His eyes met Darcy's. He nodded once, then looked up at Nick.

A stuffed canvas bag was slung over Nick's shoulder; his boots dangled from his hand. Was he trying to escape? Darcy did not want to believe it. Not after all his uncle had done to secure his brother's freedom. "Nicholas?"

His brother's shoulders deflated as he turned to face Darcy. His cheeks were bunched up like a child caught doing something for which he knew he would be punished. "I can't stay."

"You cannot leave." Darcy responded louder than he

should have. Looking up and down the hallway, he waved for Nick to come inside his room.

The embers still glowed in the fireplace, and Darcy coaxed them to life with the poker, adding more wood from the rack beside the hearth. *Poke-poke.* Why would Nick escape like a thief in the night? *Jab-jab.* Without so much as a farewell, nice to meet you? *Stab-stab.* Was he so heartless to leave so soon after finding his own family? How could he turn his back this quickly?

Nick sat in one of the chairs placed around the fire, his bag on the carpet at his feet. At least now, at this moment, he was here.

Darcy took a deep breath, cooling his blood and calming his thoughts. Had he learned nothing from his failed courtship? His assumptions had led him to all the wrong conclusions when one open conversation would have cleared the misunderstanding between him and Elizabeth. He could have made a more favorable impression had he not haughtily taken for granted that she would feel the honor of his attentions. What a fool he had been.

He would not be a fool now, making assumptions— none of which were flattering to his brother. Darcy turned to Nick. "Why can you not stay?"

Shoving his hands through his hair, Nick dropped his elbows to his knees. "I can't change what I've done; who I am—"

Darcy spun around to face him. "You are a Darcy."

A gasp that sounded painful, like it was wrenched

from Nick's chest, soothed Darcy's ire. "In face and form, yes, but ye know I could never belong."

Darcy shook his head. "It does not need to remain thus." He motioned toward the hall where his uncle and cousin slept. "We are your family." As he spoke the words, Darcy wondered how Nick had escaped without waking Richard. With Elizabeth's family soon to arrive and in need of a room, Richard and Nick had shared a room, as had Alex and Elizabeth.

Nick winced. "I put a pinch of da Silva's sleeping powder in Richard's drink, if that's what ye're wondering. Alex told me ye're familiar with the stuff." He paused, took a deep breath. "I ought to have put a pinch in yer drink, too."

"I am glad you refrained. Otherwise I would not have had the chance to convince you to stay."

"I see how ye are. How Lord Matlock and Richard run to yer aid as fast as Alex can fling a knife." He took a deep, shaky breath. "But I can never be a Darcy. Not truly."

Darcy put the poker down and sat. He imagined riding over the property with Nick, slowly introducing him to the rest of their family as his long-lost twin. He would save Aunt Catherine for last. They would get along like oil and water. There was nothing in the moment to smile about, but Darcy felt his lips quirk at the images in his head—the images of him and his brother.

"I shall show you." Darcy realized, as his heart

squeezed and his throat swelled, just how much he wanted his newfound brother to stay in his life. He would even endure Alex if it meant Nick would stay. Darcy swallowed hard, adding, "Please, stay."

"And repay yer uncle's kindness by endangering ye?" Nicholas squeezed his hands against his temples. Looking up, he met Darcy's gaze. "What about Georgie? She came to London to help find ye, ye know?"

Darcy leaned forward in his chair. "You met Georgie?" He had thought she was safe with Mrs. Annesley at Pemberley, far away from this mess.

"She's safe," Nick assured him, as though he sensed what Darcy needed most to hear. "I met her at Matlock House. She and her companion came when they heard ye'd disappeared."

While it pleased Darcy's heart that his little sister had been concerned enough about his welfare to make the three-day journey to London, he wished she had stayed away. Until he knew how best to proceed.

Nick leaned back in his chair, looking wistfully into the fire. "She's a fine young lady. I'd never forgive meself if her reputation suffered because of me. I'm a black mark on yer family. The farther away I go, the better."

Darcy opened his mouth to speak, but Nick continued, "Ye know it's true, Darcy. Don't deny it."

"You are as bossy as Richard."

"He's a good man. Wise beyond his years."

Scowling at his brother as he would have had it been Richard sitting across from him, Darcy felt the connection like a kick to the gut—merciless and undeniable. Nick fit. He and Darcy were too similar. If Darcy really wanted him to stay, he would have to reason with him as if he were reasoning with himself. "If Richard were here, he would tell you to stay. Uncle Matlock stretched his neck out for you. If you leave, he will have no choice but to hunt you down lest he be accused of enabling your escape."

Nick laughed mirthlessly. "And allow Connell to continue threatening ye?"

"We do not know if he is even alive."

"Beckett saw he made it safely to shore. We spared Connell's life, as yer uncle wished, but he'll be a plague to ye until I leave … or he carries me back to Newgate for trial."

"My uncle's authority exceeds his. So long as you stay with us, you are safe."

"And what of ye? Would ye risk another kidnapping?" Nick asked with a scoff.

"In all fairness, the kidnappings had nothing to do with you." Darcy bit his tongue. They had little to do with Nick, and everything to do with Alex. The woman who would be his sister once she and Nick married.

Nick waved his hands. "Me. Alex. It's all the same. Once a pirate, always a pirate. Nobody'll see me as anything different."

Darcy shook his head. "Nobody here knows you.

267

Nobody could testify to your likeness. They only know your name. That is what they fear. It is the same with Alex. If you truly wish to change, now is your chance. Let me help you."

Squeezing his eyes shut, Nick bowed his head. Was he frustrated? Was Darcy wearing his resolve down?

Praying he was making some progress, Darcy voiced his most powerful argument. "Do not make me hunt you. I could not do it." His voice was softer than he had intended, but the thought of chasing his brother down to spare his uncle's honor was too deplorable to exclaim.

Nick heaved a sigh. "What if it's too late? What if I'm beyond redemption?"

The air sucked out of Darcy's lungs. He knew exactly what his brother felt, having only recently worried the same about Elizabeth.

And yet, he would ask Mr. Bennet for her hand at the first opportunity. Darcy would fall to his knees and apologize and explain, and he would beg the man for his blessing. Darcy would do it because he loved her enough to take the risk of another (final and permanent) refusal.

He looked intently at his brother. Did he love Nick, a brother he had only recently met, enough to accept the risks an attachment to him would surely bring to his family?

Darcy knew without a shadow of doubt what Elizabeth would counsel. Her loyalty, her love for her family, would never allow her to forsake them—not even to spare herself society's censure. She would rise to their every challenge, eyes glinting with mischief as she upheld what she knew in her heart to be true and right and kind. Elizabeth had no time for those who would mock her, and she was clever enough to laugh at the faults and flaws of the people she loved so as to lessen the power of society's cuts. She was above their reach.

How could Darcy ask Elizabeth to spend the rest of her life with him unless he was willing to demonstrate that his loyalties were as strong as hers? Slowly, Darcy spoke. "I will not deny the risks, the scandal we stand to confront. However, if people will interfere and make accusations, let them do so to our faces, so that we may unite in opposing them. We are stronger together, and few would dare mock my uncle. Few would dare to mock me. They will soon learn better than to mock you."

"Ye'd endure that for me?" Nick asked, more in shock than incredulity. "Ye don't know me."

"I know enough. Or would you allow me to believe you had nothing to do with my and Elizabeth's recovery?"

"That was nothing." Nick batted the compliment away with a wave of his hand. "Ye'd already convinced Alex to bring ye to shore. She told me everything." He shook his head. "Yer lady is a worker of miracles. I've never seen Alex work so hard to be proper. She hasn't uttered one curse since I boarded the *Fancy*—and that was with yer uncle denying her the ship she'd captured. Like taking a bone from a hound is taking a prize from a pirate. The man has gall!" His eyes were wide with awe and respect.

Darcy accepted the change to a lighter topic, seizing the opportunity to learn more about his brother's life. "How did you end up at sea?"

"An old fisherman and his wife raised me, taught me how to make and mend fishing nets 'til I was old enough to apprentice on a merchant ship. We were captured near Charleston."

"The Lafittes?"

Nick nodded. "The captain didn't even put up a fight. Just let 'em board and take their cargo. The ones who fought got shot. I climbed up the rigging for a better look and to learn what the pirates meant to do with the rest of the crew—with me. They saw me dangling like a monkey from the lines over their heads and figured I was more useful to them alive than as crab feed at the bottom of the harbor."

Condensing twenty-eight lost years into the small hours of dawn was no trivial task, but Darcy did his best. And with every strum of the passing hour, his conviction strengthened. His brother was a good man.

CHAPTER 31

*E*lizabeth slept soundly. How could she not when Lord Matlock and Fitzwilliam were at one end of the hall, the colonel and Nick on the other, and Jaffa sat on a chair just outside her and Alexandra's door? Elizabeth was surrounded by protectors, and she finally felt safe.

The only cloud on her otherwise perfect morning was the knowledge of her imminent departure. She would rather stay with Fitzwilliam and Nicholas—her curiosity demanded satisfaction—but her father would wish for her to return to Longbourn. What would she tell him? What would Fitzwilliam tell him? Knowing what she did about Fitzwilliam, the way he took everything so seriously, responsible to a fault, she feared he would assume more blame than he deserved for the events of the past week.

Her father lived such a comfortable life…. How would he react? What would he say?

Elizabeth did not know how to make light of the situation, but she trusted she would think of how best to phrase what must be said to achieve the desired outcome along the journey. She had days to think.

True to her word, the innkeeper's wife had found two gowns for Elizabeth and Alexandra to wear. They were a simple design—one plain blue muslin, one a printed pink. Not nearly enough frills and lace to suit Alexandra, but Elizabeth selected the plain blue for herself in the hope that the floral print would appease Alexandra. She would get along famously with Mama and Lydia. A smile creeped up Elizabeth's lips as she thought of that trio, feeling wicked at the pleasant realization that, for once, her mother and sister would not be the most scandalous in a room whilst in Alexandra's company.

Tying the layers into place, dismayed at the stiff, scratchy muslin, Elizabeth went downstairs in search of some nourishment.

The taproom was full to the brim with the *Fancy*'s crew, many of whom nodded respectfully, mouths crammed with food, at Elizabeth. Boone rose to his feet, head bowed, hands clasped in front of him. "The gents are behind ye in the private parlor, Miss."

"Thank you, Boone." She felt like she should wave and say something posh like "carry on" so that the men would resume eating. They were a motley lot, and it struck Elizabeth as strange that she should feel as comfortable as she did in a taproom filled with rough sailors.

She walked past the curtain separating Lord Matlock's private parlor from the others, and stopped short when she saw Fitzwilliam sitting beside his brother at the table. A maid poured coffee into their cups, and Elizabeth watched with increasing interest as both brothers poured the same amount of cream, measured one spoonful of sugar into their cups, and stirred clockwise precisely three times before they harmoniously shook the spoon and balanced it along the edge at the top of their plates. Both were completely unaware of their synchronous behavior.

She joined them, taking the place Lord Matlock motioned for her beside him and the colonel at the table. He nodded at the empty chair on her other side when Alexandra walked into the parlor shortly afterward.

Alexandra was not wearing the gown, as Elizabeth had hoped she would. Lord Matlock's cheerful countenance briefly flickered with disapproval, but he replaced it with a smile, saying, "I am pleased we may partake of one more meal together before we must part ways. Richard and I shall continue to Devonshire with Nick. Darcy shall remain with you to receive Mr. Bennet and Mr. Gardiner." He checked his pocket watch. "I expect them shortly. Then he shall return with you to London where his sister waits, and you,

Miss Alexandra, may stay as a guest at Matlock House. My wife and daughters shall take good care of you."

Alexandra stiffened. "I'll stay with Nick."

Elizabeth pursed her lips. She was no more pleased than Alexandra, and she particularly hated being the reason Fitzwilliam would not stay with his brother.

Lord Matlock lowered his chin, meeting Alexandra's stare boldly. "You shall travel with Miss Elizabeth. Once we find the answers we seek, we shall join you in town. Unless you decide to accompany Miss Elizabeth to Hertfordshire, upon which we shall meet you there. That choice shall be yours to make, but this one is not. You go to London." His voice brooked no argument, but that did not discourage Alexandra.

"I ride as good as Nick. I don't need a carriage."

"You would be the only lady in our party."

"I don't need no special treatment. I can sleep by the fire just like any man. I won't be no trouble to ye."

Lord Matlock's gaze bore into her. "I doubt that, young lady."

Nick and the colonel laughed. Fitzwilliam clenched his jaw.

Anger flushed in Alexandra's cheeks, and her eyes darted to the knife on the butter dish.

Elizabeth rested her hand gently over Alexandra's. "Perhaps your arguments will be more effective if you test them out in your own mind before attempting to use them to persuade an equally strong-minded man."

Alexandra's hand clenched into a fist, but she

dropped her gaze away from the knife. "Nothin' I say'll change his mind."

"Throwing a butter knife at him will not help your cause either."

Alexandra grimaced. "I wasn't gonna hurt him. Just get his attention, like."

"And by getting his attention, you mean to intimidate him to change his mind?"

"Probably won't work, will it? I'd end up worse off than before."

Elizabeth smiled at her. "You catch on quickly."

"But I still don't have what I want." Alexandra scowled.

"Sometimes a bit of patience is all that is required. Your betrothed shall soon join you in London. In the meantime, I am certain my father, aunt, and uncle would be happy to meet you. Not to mention their children! They would love nothing more than to hear some of your stories … the tamer ones, mind. We could even arrange for you to have a few dresses made."

"Why do the gents get to wear leather and silk, and us ladies are stuck with scratchy cloth?"

So, she *had* tried the gown then.

"I don't know how ye're wearin' it, Elizabeth. It's awful. Ye couldn't pay me to put that against me skin. And there's the matter of the skirt. How do ye mount a horse or climb a hill? I swear I'd have to hold the skirts up to me knees to do anything at all. And me knives! Where would I hide 'em?"

Elizabeth imagined a trip to the modiste with Alexandra and tried not to giggle.

It was then, while her smile was wide, that her father and uncle Gardiner walked into the parlor.

Elizabeth jumped up from the table, leaving the chair toppling behind her, and into her father's arms. "Papa! You are here! I am so glad you have come!"

He wrapped his arms around her and kissed her hair, his breath shaky. He dabbed at his eyes when Elizabeth welcomed her uncle with a hearty embrace. Papa patted her arm, as though making certain she was not some apparition.

"What a relief to see you safe and well. You are well, Lizzy? That was a rough lot we passed in the taproom," he said, gesturing behind him.

She pressed his hand against her cheek. "I have never been better, Papa."

Lord Matlock invited them to the table, ordering more refreshments to be brought in and introducing Alexandra to them.

Alexandra was quick to reassure Papa. "That's me crew out there, mostly. They'd each one of 'em protect yer daughter with their life if I asked 'em to."

Father raised his eyebrows. "That has been the company you have kept these past six days?"

While Alexandra puffed up with pride at what she understood to be a compliment, Elizabeth saw the horror in her father's expression. She had hoped he would be more amused than upset.

Colonel Fitzwilliam intervened. "How was your journey? You traveled at a brisk clip and must be fatigued."

"At least we did not have to keep up with your breakneck pace, young man." Uncle Gardiner sat in an empty chair opposite Alexandra.

The conversation around the table stayed on superficial matters—their journey, the state of the roads, the weather along the way.

But when Papa pushed his plate away, Fitzwilliam asked if he might have a word with him and her uncle Gardiner.

Elizabeth held her breath, knowing that she would be the subject of their conversation and regretting how unprepared she felt for it. When they sat at the other side of the parlor, she was relieved that she could at least observe them.

Fitzwilliam explained. Uncle listened quietly. Her father interjected with questions. The longer they talked, the deeper became Papa's frown. When he started rubbing his chin, Elizabeth thought she would go mad with concern. She leaned closer to Alexandra. "This is not going well. My father is agitated, and Fitzwilliam looks penitent. It is just as I feared."

"Why should Darcy look guilty?"

Did she really not know? Elizabeth glared at Alexandra. "He is a gentleman in every sense of the word. He feels responsible for my welfare, and he will take the blame for my kidnapping."

"But that was me idea."

"My father apparently does not see it that way."

"Ye mean he might not give his consent for ye to marry the man who loves ye to distraction?"

"I do not think that is the subject of their discussion right now, but yes, that is exactly what it could mean." Elizabeth clenched her hands together to keep from wrapping them around Alexandra's shoulders and shaking some sensitivity into her.

Alexandra shrugged. "I'll ask Boone to marry ye. Or there's this place called Gretna Green..."

Elizabeth's blood stirred. "I have sisters to think of. They would suffer from my defiance, and I would lose my father's trust and friendship."

"Ye thought of all that just now?" Alexandra snapped her fingers. "As fast as that?"

"Yes."

"How? How d'ye do it?" Her jaw fell open.

Elizabeth sighed. It was impossible for her to stay angry at Alexandra when she looked at her with such boldfaced admiration. "It gets easier with practice."

"It'd be easier still if ye only had yerself to think of."

"True, but I could never ignore the interests of the people I love."

Alexandra twisted her mouth and wrinkled her nose. "Ye make me see how selfish I am."

What could Elizabeth say to that? She remained silent and tried to read her father's lips from across the room.

After several minutes of distinguishing only a few words out of their hushed whispers, Alexandra startled Elizabeth when she spoke again. "I'll make Nick love me as deeply as yer Darcy loves ye, and I'll be hanged if I allow him to take the blame when we all know I'm the one yer pa ought to be cross with."

Before Elizabeth could prevent it, Alexandra marched over to them, rudely interrupting their conversation when she stepped between them.

Elizabeth looked to Nick, and then at Lord Matlock, but neither of them seemed to know what to do any more than she did.

Alexandra would either be a helpful ally leading them to a brilliant victory or a perilous adversary inducing a disastrous defeat. Elizabeth moved closer to either witness her success or intervene if she failed.

# CHAPTER 32

*D*arcy looked up in horror as Alexandra walked up to Mr. Bennet and blurted, "No matter what Darcy says, he's not to blame for this. Not for any of it."

Mr. Bennet pinched the bridge of his nose. "Are you saying he has been lying to me, then?"

"It was me idea to kidnap yer daughter, Mr. Bennet. I'm a selfish wretch, not at all like Miss Elizabeth, ye see. When I learned how ardently Darcy loved her, I wanted to know what she'd done to him to win such deep affection."

Darcy felt his stomach plummet to the floor. If only they made muzzles for people like her. He felt Mr. Bennet's gaze on him, inspecting him, and it was all Darcy could do to meet his eyes when he wished the ground would swallow him whole.

"How could you possibly have learned such a

thing?" Mr. Bennet asked, his expression changing to one of immense shock. "He did not mention my daughter while he was on your ship, did he?"

It was the angriest Darcy was ever likely to see Mr. Bennet, and he could not blame the gentleman. Darcy blamed himself, too.

"Not at all, sir! I asked him in as many ways as I could think; tried to trick him, even. But Darcy isn't an easy one to trick. He's too clever. It weren't 'til I slipped a little sleepin' powder in his grog—"

"That is enough," Darcy warned.

"Ye weren't talkin'. So I helped ye along, knowin' how some men speak more freely in their stupor, sayin' things they'd never say when they're alert. It must've been a pleasant dream. Ye smiled through the whole—"

"Enough. That is quite enough." This was Darcy's worst nightmare come to reality. He covered his burning cheeks with his cold hands, hating how that woman could make him lose his composure where so many others had tried and failed.

"So you are the outstanding intellect behind both vanishings?" Mr. Bennet responded with his usual amusement, graciously turning his attention away from Darcy and toward Alex.

Unfortunately, Alex was relentless in her intent to clear Darcy from blame. "I wouldn't call meself outstandin' in anything polite and proper, but I can tell ye that Darcy'd never expose yer daughter to danger."

"Not knowingly perhaps, and yet that is what has

happened ... repeatedly, I might add. Sword fights, cannon balls, sinking ships, and pirates..."

"We aren't pirates no more, sir," Alexandra interrupted. "Nick's determined to be a proper privateer and help His Majesty's Navy take down the Frenchies."

Mr. Gardiner gave her an odd look. "Are you not a Lafitte?"

"Me father was French, but the origins of me mother aren't exactly known. I might be Portuguese ... or Spanish ... or—"

"Please stop," Darcy begged.

"Not 'til I'm done helpin' ye."

"Believe me, you have helped enough."

She rolled her eyes, then continued talking, ignoring his supplications completely.

"Look here, Mr. Bennet, yer daughter's been teachin' me how to be a lady, and while I've a way to go yet, I've learned enough to understand that a gentleman worth his salt always places the welfare of his lady above his own. That's what I want to tell ye. From the moment I brought Elizabeth aboard, Darcy did everything he could to return her safely to ye. He even agreed to fight me with the sword—nearly beat me, too. He'd have done ye proud."

Darcy dropped his head into his hand, massaging his temples. If Mr. Bennet and Mr. Gardiner did not think him a complete scoundrel, they would now. Fighting a woman ... and with swords, no less.

"Really? He almost bested ye?" Nick asked. At least *he* sounded impressed.

Alexandra continued. There was nothing Darcy could do short of clamping his hand over her mouth to shut her up. "The thing is, sir, I'm alive and the captain of me own ship because of me keen instincts. And while me instincts have always been selfish—puttin' Darcy and Elizabeth in danger and worryin' ye and yer family is proof enough of that—I've seen with me own eyes the firmness of Darcy's character. He's a gentleman through and through. He's defended and protected yer girl from the start. He'd give his last breath to make her happy. The danger to yer daughter was my doin', and for that, I … I…" She swallowed hard, speaking rapidly, "I'm sorry."

Nick started clapping. Only then did Darcy realize how quiet the room had been. Even his uncle must have been listening to their conversation. Darcy's mortification was complete. He squared his shoulders and raised his chin, ready for the blow. Ready for Mr. Bennet and Mr. Gardiner to tell him never to travel within five miles of Longbourn or Gracechurch Street.

Elizabeth poured more tea into her father's cup. "Are you up for an intellectual challenge such as you have never experienced, Papa? A real mystery to solve?"

He looked at her, intrigued. As did Darcy. How had he not considered that angle?

"We are near the first clue, the place Nicholas was deposited after being taken from the Darcys at

Pemberley. The delay to our return would be insignificant, and you would have a worthwhile riddle to ponder."

"What of the danger?" Uncle asked.

"You shall see for yourselves that the danger has passed. We are on land. What could happen now?"

Nick added, "We're not needed here. The *Fancy*'ll need several weeks before she's seaworthy, but it'd sure be a boon to have an astute mind like yers to help us puzzle out what happened."

Mr. Bennet's sharp eyes snapped to Nick. "I am astute now, am I? Since your observation cannot be the conclusion of previous study, I must assume your compliment to be influenced by my daughter's artful wording."

"What about Connell?" Alexandra asked.

Elizabeth shrugged. "He can follow us if he pleases. What can he do so long as Nicholas is surrounded by his influential family? Perhaps he will find a more worthy prize to pursue, then we may carry on in peace. Imagine that, Papa. A couple days, just a trifle delay, of peace."

"You call cramped, jostling carriages peaceful?"

She smiled, her eyes twinkling. "I never claimed that my argument was perfect."

Mr. Bennet chuckled, and Darcy knew she had won. He also knew he was doomed to lose most of their disagreements. While he was accustomed to always having his way, he did not find the prospect of losing to Elizabeth troubling in the least.

THE MAN MRS. FINCHLEY trusted with her dirtier tasks stood in front of her, twisting his hat in his hands and shuffling his weight, enduring her blackest stare.

"You let her get away?" she repeated through her clenched teeth.

"She must've climbed out the window at the dead of night."

"And you have no indication where she went?"

His head bowed lower. "No, ma'am. But I'll find her. You can count on it."

An excuse Amelia had heard many times in her life. One she did not accept lightly. Slowly, deliberately, she rang her bell. "Send another cup up. Mr. Smith must be parched," she ordered, motioning for him to take a seat.

He did so reluctantly.

"You can hardly be blamed. She is as slippery as a greased piglet. Like a bird, she flits away," she chuckled at her own joke.

"I appreciate your understanding, Mrs. Finchley."

She cooed, "How could I not extend you some leniency when you have been in my employ these twenty years? Not once have you given me cause for complaint until now. No, Mr. Smith, let us put this behind us. Find her, and bring her to me, and all is forgiven."

The maid returned with the teacup and saucer, and Amelia poured, fumbling the service just enough to tap some of the powder from her ring into Mr. Smith's cup.

"You have been a benevolent employer, Mrs. Finchley, and I thank you." He toasted her health and drank.

While he sang her praises, she planned her escape. She could not stay in London where they could find her. She must get away.

He lifted his cup again. "Thank you for the bit of refreshment, Mrs. Finchley. Now, I have a bird to catch, so I will take my leave."

Amelia smiled at him. She figured he had an hour left. Two tops.

Weak hearts were so unpredictable.

CHAPTER 33

*N*icholas had captured ships and fought opponents more skilled than himself. More than once, his wits and pure, unabashed luck had saved his skin. But he had never felt himself more in danger than he did at that moment: aboard a two-sail fishing boat, surrounded by family and people who were fast becoming friends.

They huddled together mid-deck, enjoying the clear skies and salty breeze.

Had he been wrong to listen to Darcy? What if Nick's past was better kept hidden? He could fend for himself, but what of Lord Matlock? He was a powerful man, but he wasn't young. Nick could see he was tired. He was the reason Nick had agreed to hire another boat rather than travel overland. Nick hadn't needed Nuñez to inform him that Lympstone was only thirty-seven nautical miles away to know travel by sea would

287

be much more comfortable for their party … with the exception of poor Mr. Gardiner, who was currently leaning over the side of the vessel.

It would not be much longer.

Alex stomped past, fists clutched in determination, chin lifted to add to her height, talking as she followed the captain. "If ye'd bear up and beat to windward…"

Nick shook his head and chuckled. The captain could not shake her, no matter how fast he walked or how busy he made himself appear. Alex would point out how ineffectively his sails were trimmed, his ill use of port tack on the weather side….

"We'd be there already if ye listened to me," she huffed.

"Leave the man be, Alex," Nick called after her.

She ignored him. She never was one to back down. It was one of the many things he loved about her. She'd never give up on him.

Jaffa sidled away from her to kneel beside where Nick stood, watching over his group.

Keeping his eyes on his charge, Jaffa said, "Big changes are coming, Cap'n Nick."

"That they are." It occurred to Nick that once he and Alex married, Jaffa would be at loose ends. He wouldn't wish to accompany them on their wedding tour any more than Nick wished for Jaffa's looming presence near his wife. "What'll ye do?" he asked.

Jaffa put his hand on Nick's shoulder, his grip as firm as the expression in his eyes. "I am not needed anymore. My purpose is complete. Cap'n Alex cannot have two men in her life."

Amen to that.

"Will you guard her with your life?" Jaffa continued. "Will you protect her as I have done?"

The loyalty Jaffa had displayed since Alex had freed him from the slaver when she was a sprite of a girl filled Nick's chest with awe. Placing his hand on top of Jaffa's, he met the man's gaze with an intensity of his own. "On the stars, I swear I will."

Jaffa nodded, dropping his hand. "Then, I will return with these men to the *Fancy*. It is the last thing I can do to serve my good cap'n."

"What'll ye do when the repairs are finished?"

Jaffa's face relaxed, and he looked off into the distance. "I will find my family. As you have found yours." He smiled, meeting Nick's gaze.

Nick cleared his throat and sniffed. "I wish ye well."

They both turned to see Alex trailing after the captain. "She'll miss ye," Nick stated.

"I will miss her, too. Which is why I must leave quickly, today."

Nick clapped him on the shoulder, wishing there was more he could do and knowing Jaffa would never accept it.

Mr. Bennet interrupted the moment with another question. "I have never been to this part of the country. What is Lympstone like, Mr. Blackburne?"

By the time Nick looked back over his shoulder,

Jaffa was gone. *Farewell, good friend. May you be repaid generously.* Alex would send word to Boone, guaranteeing that Jaffa got his share of the treasures hidden in the holds of the *Fancy*. He'd never want for anything. He'd return to his family a wealthy man.

Taking in a deep breath, Nick turned to the curious faces trained on him. So many people eager to listen to him, desirous of his conversation. Even Mr. Gardiner hobbled over to drop into a chair beside his brother-in-law and niece. Nick would do his best to take the gentleman's mind off the discomforts of sea travel.

"Lympstone's nestled along the eastern bank of the broad estuary of the River Exe, between cliffs of red breccia." Mr. Bennet smiled. He was the sort of gentleman who would take an interest in the geology of a site.

Nick continued, "It's a pretty townlet, a fishing station with a significant trade in ships. The fishermen from Exmouth bring oysters to fatten up on the beds of the estuary. When the tide goes out, maybe we can dig for some."

Mr. Bennet chuckled. "Only if I am not the one wielding the shovel. I have read about them."

"Those little buggers're quick. I'll dig for ye."

"Where shall we stay?" asked Lord Matlock, his focus on more practical matters.

"It's the off-season, so I reckon we'll have our pick of lodgings. I'd prefer The Swan. I remember the innkeeper being a kind man who kept up with the comings and goings in the village."

Richard folded his arms over his chest and stretched his legs in front of him languidly. An officer always on duty never loses an opportunity to relax when he can. "Was not John Nutt from Lympstone?"

Nick had been waiting for such a question. He couldn't avoid them, nor would he deny his audience satisfaction. It wasn't every day they could speak freely and openly with a pirate. A *former* pirate.

Mr. Bennet leaned forward, as did Elizabeth (though she was more discreet in displaying her curiosity). Darcy looked distressed, and Nick smiled reassuringly at him.

"John Nutt—now, there's a story to inspire. His was a happy ending, made all the happier by his brush with death. Ye see, back when the King was granting royal pardons, Nutt requested one from a Mr. John Eliot. He was the Vice Admiral of Devon at the time. After some negotiations, Eliot granted Nutt a full pardon in exchange for a five-hundred-pound bond—a hefty sum. But piracy'd been a rewarding venture for Nutt, and he was smart enough to know when to quit. Five hundred pounds for a fresh start and a new life as a free man with no price on his head—he must've figured it was a fair price." Nick would gladly pay double—nay, triple—to clear his conscience.

"Yes?" Mr. Bennet asked impatiently.

Nick paused a moment longer, adding to their

suspense. "Imagine Nutt's surprise when he finally returned to England only to be arrested once he set foot on her shores."

Elizabeth gasped, her pinched expression displaying how disagreeable she found the unjust treatment. Darcy, too, looked like a thundercloud. They would fight the world's injustices very well together. If Nick had the influence his brother did, he liked to think he'd do the same.

Returning to the story, Nick said, "Eliot was a sly one. He arrested Nutt as soon as he returned to England. Tried and convicted for piracy, Nutt was doomed to dangle at the gallows until an old friend who had risen to the office of Secretary of State intervened."

"Calvert," Lord Matlock said.

Nick nodded. "Precisely. Mr. George Calvert'd been an associate of Nutt, considered him a friend. He granted Nutt's pardon and tossed Eliot into prison for abusing his position. Had to pay one hundred pounds to Nutt in compensation for his betrayal."

Richard whistled. "Freed, pardoned, and a hundred pounds richer. Not bad."

"He fared better than his peers." Lord Matlock frowned, and Nick suspected he was thinking about another pirate whose ending had not been so favorable.

"Right! Captain Phillips! How could I forget when my own brother-in-law shares his same surname, though he is a law-abiding solicitor in Meryton, I assure you." Mr. Bennet looked at Nick. "I am certain Mr. Blackburne can relate the account much better than I can."

Nick took a deep breath, reminding himself that these stories were entertaining for most people—told to delight or, in this case, to shock.

Elizabeth touched her father's sleeve. "Perhaps this is a story best left untold."

The gentleman's disappointment overruled Nick's reluctance. He was a pirate no more. So long as he kept his hands clean and his name out of the papers, there was no reason to believe his nightmares would become reality. Little reason. Middling reason.

Nick shook his head, tossing his fears aside. A life lived in fear was a life half-lived, and he would live his to the full and enjoy this time with his family and friends … as long as it lasted.

# CHAPTER 34

*N*ick began, "Aye, his is a sorry tale. Phillips captured over thirty vessels in the year he turned from cod fishing to piracy. But his men turned on him. It was a bloody mutiny." He stopped, sparing his audience the gory details.

If only Alex had followed suit. Aboard a ship she did not command, after hours of her orders going unheeded, she was in a foul mood. Sinking to the deck and crossing her legs, she drew her dagger out to clean her nails, a sure sign she was agitated. Bitterly, she said, "Lost a leg, then had his skull crushed by his mutinous crew—"

"Alex," Nick warned.

She paid him no heed. "If that weren't bad enough, they lopped off his head the same way they did Blackbeard and hung it from the bowsprit, then—"

"Alex," he interrupted, louder.

She turned to him. "What? I didn't even get to the part where they sent his head to Boston in a pickle barrel."

Nick groaned. He saw Elizabeth wrap her arms around herself and shiver. Darcy openly glared at Alex. Nick didn't blame him. He hoped that Alex's lady lessons would teach her when to keep her mouth shut. Between Arnold and Connell, Nick could easily have ended the same.

Elizabeth recovered quickly. "That is enough gloom for today. Please, tell us something pleasant about the place where you grew up."

They were coming close to Darling Rock. It wasn't much of a needle anymore, but it had been once.

Nick pointed at the formation jutting out from the shore. "That there's called Darling Rock. It's said that a fishing fleet got lost in the fog on their way home. Anxious with worry, their wives ran out to the rock. They sang at the top of their lungs. One of the men heard and called out, 'Oh, my darling.' Those brave women sang their men to shelter, guiding them all the way into the harbor with the sound of their sweet voices."

Elizabeth smiled at him. "Now, that is lovely. A charming story for a charming village."

The main street ran parallel to the estuary. Nick remembered the buildings being taller, grander.

Richard asked, "Who should we talk to first?"

"We'll inquire at the inn and the rectory. The vicar lives just outside the village, along the main road."

Nick helped the sailors moor, tossing the lines over to the dock, wrapping them around the cleats to secure the boat until all the passengers had disembarked.

He'd hoped Alex wouldn't notice Jaffa didn't join them until they were at the inn, but, of course, she noticed.

"Jaffa!" she called out when the sailors released the ropes from the dock and it became clear that they meant to ride the retreating tide out of the estuary back out to sea.

Jaffa blew a kiss and waved, teeth white.

Alex bit her lips together, silent tears pouring down her cheeks. "I'm gonna miss him terrible, Nick."

He tucked her against his chest and ran his fingers through her long ebony hair. The tide had turned, and the boat couldn't stay. It amazed Nick how similar life was to the tides and currents with its twists and turns and constant movement.

With a sniff, she wiped her cheeks against her sleeve. "He's a free man, so I shouldn't expect him to stay. He looked happy." She twisted around to look up at him. "Didn't he look happy, Nick?"

"He did, Lexi. Ye did good letting him go without a fuss."

"It's that Elizabeth. I heard her voice in me head tellin' me not to be so blasted selfish. Jaffa was like a brother to me, but he's a real family to find." She sighed. "I hope he finds 'em. I hope the slavers didn't get 'em."

Nick pulled her away. "Let's join the others at The Swan."

He walked up the lane with Alex on his arm, nodding politely at the people they passed. He didn't realize he held certain expectations for his home-coming until nobody recognized him. Not one person called his name or waved a greeting. Instead, they gave him a wide berth, tucking their heads and quickening their pace until they walked past.

Maybe it was the clothes? He was dressed the same as Darcy and Richard.

He saw them speaking with the innkeeper, the man's manner respectful and acquiescent. However, that same man's eyes narrowed the moment Nick stepped through the door.

Would he ever be seen as an honest man? He nodded at the innkeeper. The years had grayed his hair and softened his middle, but it was the same man he remembered from his youth.

And he did not recognize Nick. Not one glimmer of remembrance until Darcy said Nick's name. And then, the man only saw a thievin' rascal whose stories would forever haunt Nick.

He readied himself to be tossed out on his ear. The Swan was a reputable establishment, and they did not knowingly lodge renown buccaneers.

Elizabeth tsked, looping her arm through Alex's and

tugging them forward to stand beside Darcy in front of the innkeeper. "This gentleman is not so gullible as to believe everything he reads in the papers, Mr. Blackburne. He is a well-informed innkeeper with too much sense to fall for those sordid tales. Surely, anyone who keeps company with the finest families in England, peers of the realm, is worthy of the same treatment as the Earl of Matlock, the Darcys of Derbyshire, the Gardiners of London, and the Bennets of Hertfordshire." Her eyes sparkled at the inclusion of her family with the upper echelons.

Her purpose was served. The innkeeper let Nick keep his room, and when Alex sashayed through the taproom in her breeches, he hardly batted an eyelash.

It was decided that the young men would walk to the rectory while the ladies and older gentlemen rested.

St. Mary's church was a fine structure boasting an embattled tower and five bells that peeled at the top of the hour. Nick had learned to read there, taught by Reverend Moorshead's wife. Mrs. Moorshead had taught the poorest children of the parish with all the tender attention of a woman who'd not been blessed with children of her own. Nick prayed she was still alive. Not that he held any hope that she'd remember him—nobody else did. But it was a tragedy to think of such a kind woman passing. That was the ultimate injustice. Kind people ought to live forever.

A white-haired woman wearing no bonnet leaned

over to pluck several blooms bordering the fence around her garden. She looked up when they approached, and Nick smiled at Mrs. Moorshead.

The blooms fell from her hands, and she lifted her palms to her cheeks.

Nick hurried forward. He hadn't meant to startle her.

"Nicolas Blackburne? Is that you? My, how you have grown!" she said.

Reaching over the fence, Nick took her outstretched hands. "I'm amazed ye remember me, Mrs. Moorshead."

"I never forget a face, especially a boy so clever and quick to learn as you were, Nicholas." She looked between him and Darcy. "But how is it that I see two of you?"

Nick introduced his brother and cousin. "We've come to see what we can find out about me history."

"Mr. Darcy of Pemberley in Derbyshire. I must say, I am not surprised our Nicholas proceeds from such fine origins. I am pleased to meet you, sir. And you, too, Colonel Fitzwilliam. Now," she wiped her hands against her apron, "how is it that three dashing young gentlemen have come to call on an old woman?" She grinned, arching a thin brow. "Could it be that you heard about my beautiful guest? She is so lovely, I had to pick a few flowers to place on the table beside her." She plucked the fallen blooms from the grass.

Nick rushed around the fence to help her while

Darcy and Richard apologized for interrupting her call, offering to return at a more convenient time.

Mrs. Moorshead chuckled. "My dear boys, at my age, I must seize every minute I am given. Please, come in. I insist. I do not often have the pleasure of new callers, and I wish to know what young Nicholas has been up to all of these years."

She must not keep up with the papers. Nick was relieved.

She led them through the garden, turning before they entered the house. "This is providential, you arriving while the young lady is still here. I have a sense for these things. Over fifty years as a vicar's wife will do that, you know." She led them into a parlor, chattering all the way. "The nurse is sitting with Mr. Moorshead. The doctors say he does not understand what I tell him, but I just know that he shall be interested in the news I shall be able to share with him today…"

She stepped inside a warm, tidy parlor that smelled of her garden and the slices of cake sitting on the table where a young lady with hair the color of a sunset sat.

Nick heard Richard suck in a breath behind him.

CHAPTER 35

"*M*iss Rothschild!" Richard said rather loudly. How charming she looked in that color of green with Mrs. Moorshead's flowers beside her on the table.

Richard felt his skin heat as everyone turned to him. The young lady's eyes brimmed with amusement. He prayed it was amusement of the favorable kind— that she was as pleased to see him as he was to stumble upon her. "What are you doing here?" he blurted, then bit his tongue before another forward exclamation burst from him.

"I am here to call on Mrs. Moorshead, the same as you it appears. I could ask what you are doing here!" she replied with enough sauce to provoke Richard's laughter and effectively break the ice.

Mrs. Moorshead clutched her hands at her chin. "A

reunion! How wonderful." Wagging her finger in the air, she added, "Providential."

After brief introductions and a clipped version of how they had met, Richard sat back in his chair and ceded the conversation to Nick. He stretched his legs out in front of him, crossing one foot over the other, hoping to appear as though he had not a concern in the world.

In reality, his feet bobbed and twitched with the effort to contain his unasked questions. Questions he would not voice even if it were appropriate to do so: Was she happy to see him? Had she thought of him as much as he had thought of her? He was not the handsomest man—of that, he was aware. However, he would be content to know she thought of him kindly maybe once or twice. Any more than that would be the height of presumption. She was a beautiful lady—an heiress—who could have her pick of gentlemen.

Still, he sat taller in his chair and tried to calm his fidgeting feet as she and Nick exchanged the little they knew of their stories.

Mrs. Moorshead pinched her chin as she listened.

Darcy asked her, "What do you remember of Nick's arrival?"

So, Nicholas was Nick now. Richard was glad to hear it.

With a sigh, Mrs. Moorshead said, "I am afraid there is precious little to tell. I woke early one morning to milk the cow and feed the chickens, and nearly tripped over a basket filled with blankets perched just outside the door. At first, I thought that someone had left the blankets there for the poor, but when I lifted the basket to put it inside, I noticed how heavy it was. Heavier than it ought to have been." She smiled at Nick, pressing her hands against her heart. "Imagine my surprise when I moved the blankets aside and saw a baby! He did not cry or make any noise at all. He simply looked up at me and glowered."

That sounded about right for a Darcy. Richard looked down at his boots and bit the insides of his cheeks.

Mrs. Moorshead chuckled. "I see your expression has not changed much, dear boy."

"A family trait." Darcy smiled at his brother. Richard was relieved to see his cousin's easy acceptance of the newcomer to his immediate circle when he tended to be cautious with new acquaintances.

"My husband was similar. I often wonder how he made any friends at all before I came into his life." Mrs. Moorshead looked up, in the direction of her husband's sickroom, Richard presumed, her eyes warm, her face soft. She took a deep breath and dabbed her eyes with a bit of lace tucked into her sleeve. "I hope you find young ladies who encourage you not to take yourselves so seriously."

Darcy and Nick smiled confidently, and something in Richard's chest tightened. Some day, he would be the one grinning as wide as his lovelorn cousins. Some day.

He knew the danger of getting caught, but he could not help a brief flicker of his gaze to Miss Rothschild. Not many young ladies in her position had the persistence or wherewithal to question what others would encourage her not to trouble herself over. If a wrong had been done, her appearance in Mrs. Moorshead's parlor was proof that she was determined to right it. Truth and justice above her own comfort as they ought to be.

Before Darcy or Nick could distract Mrs. Moorshead with stories of their betrothed (for what man or woman could avoid the indulgence of speaking of the person they most adored), Richard asked, "That must have been a shock. What did you do with Nick after you found him?"

"The Fleys had no children of their own, and they had been kind enough to keep on a milkmaid who had fallen into sin. She lost her baby—a sad business, even if it was the price of her sin. I took Nicholas to them directly, and they were happy to take him in."

"What became of the milkmaid?" he asked.

She frowned. "Some women do not learn. Nicholas must have been nearly three years old when she bore a child of her own. Happily, the man—a fisherman from Exeter—married her."

Nick rubbed his side whiskers. "I don't remember her. Did she ever ask about me … later?"

"I am afraid not, my dear." Mrs. Moorshead's voice

reflected her regret. "In any case, she knew nothing more of your origins than I do."

The milkmaid was a dead end, then. On to the next. "Does the name Currey mean anything to you?" Richard asked. He cast a glance at Miss Rothschild, but the mention of Mrs. Finchley's nurse did not alter her expression.

"Currey, Currey. Now, where have I heard that name? It is not too uncommon, you know," Mrs. Moorshead mumbled.

"A Mrs. Catherine Currey?" Richard added.

"Catherine Currey," Mrs. Moorshead repeated, pressing her eyes closed only to open them so suddenly, Richard's heart jumped and collective gasps echoed in the parlor.

"I remember now. It was the oddest thing, but as the rector, my husband's duties called on him to sit on the magistrate's bench besides seeing to the births and deaths within our parish. He was called to the magistrate, let me see … it must have been a week or so after Nicholas showed up in a basket. Our own Baby Moses, as I have fondly referred to him over the years, although my husband preferred to think of him as Jonah. He was a faithful prophet who suffered a moment of weakness…"

Richard hated to force the elderly woman's conversation to the topic when she clearly wished to reminisce, but if his cousins were to have any peace, they needed to get to the bottom of the unsettled affair.

"You said it was odd about the magistrate and Mrs. Currey?" he prompted her.

"Yes, the strangest thing. Mrs. Currey was the only traveler in the midday post coach. It was scheduled to be full—I remember, my husband checked that detail— but the other travelers never claimed their seats. She was traveling alone," she repeated, her voice softening the way it did when one must sharpen a memory. "Not too strange for a woman of her age and profession, but she carried no reticule. Had my husband not inquired at the ticket office, he never would have learned her name from the register. And, even then, he would not have known to pick that name from the other travelers who were supposed to be in the carriage. We never could find any of them to ask why they had changed their plans at the last minute. I supposed they were so relieved not to have been in the carriage when it tumbled down the embankment, they praised the Lord for saving their souls and lived better for it."

A carriage accident? With a lone traveler?

"It is strange your husband and the magistrate could not find even one person to speak to," Darcy commented, echoing Richard's sentiments.

"It made it more difficult to identify Mrs. Currey, that is certain. I only guessed that was her name because she had a CC stitched on the handkerchief in her pocket."

"That was clever of you," Miss Rothschild said.

"Not clever enough to find her family. I put an

advertisement in several papers, but after a week had passed, we had little choice but to bury her in the common graveyard." She looked down at her hands and sighed. "It pained me to lay her to rest without so much as one friend to grieve her loss. It was not until another week had passed that I received word from her employer. She was greatly agitated. Her nurse had disappeared, and she feared the worst. I showed her Mrs. Currey's handkerchief, shawl, and bonnet." She looked up sheepishly. "I had held on to them in the hopes of such a meeting. Really, the shawl was plain gray wool, nothing spectacular or else I would have buried it with her."

Richard nodded at her. "You do not need to explain yourself, Mrs. Moorshead, when you and your husband had done more for an unknown deceased than many do for their living relatives."

"A sad commentary on our society, but true, nonetheless, Colonel. I imagine you have seen more than your fair share of the darker side of humanity. As a rector's wife, I have learned that the best way to manage the injustice and disappointment is to actively look for the good. And in Mrs. Currey's case, I found it in her employer. She recognized the items I had saved immediately. She arranged for a proper, engraved headstone. There was no detail too small for her attention. You can see the gravestone yourself, if you wish. I prune the weeds away and put fresh flowers on the grave when I can. But I only have so many flowers, and there are so many neglected graves..." Her gaze settled on the flowers she had picked for Miss Rothschild, and Richard imagined she would pluck more beautiful blooms from her garden to take to the cemetery as soon as her guests had departed.

"Do you remember the employer's name?" he prodded, helping her along when her brow furrowed. "Perhaps a Mrs. Finchley?"

Miss Rothschild leaned forward at the mention of the midwife's name.

Mrs. Moorshead grinned. "Yes! That was her name. She was deeply aggrieved, them being old friends besides working together. You know, it is strange that you ask me about the two women. I have not thought about them these past twenty years ... yes, since the last time someone else asked me about them."

Richard practically felt his ears perk, but Nick beat him to the question. "Someone else asked about her? Who? When?"

"Well, like I said, it was about twenty years ago. She was a young woman with sharp features, pristine, very nice. She said she was a nurse, and she looked like one. You know, the sort who reminds you to straighten your apron and pat down your hair."

Miss Rothschild's posture had straightened even more. If she leaned forward any more, she would topple over like a stiff board. "What was her name?" she asked, the strain in her tone increasing the tension in the room.

Mrs. Moorshead twisted her hands. "Oh dear, I seem to have caused some upset."

Miss Rothschild forced a smile. "It is only that the woman you described sounds familiar to a description I heard recently. Do you remember her name?" She bit her lips together, and Richard had to bite his to keep from chuckling when he saw her knee bob up and down impatiently.

"Well, as it happens, I do," Mrs. Moorshead said. "I remember thinking that someone so clean and particular ought to be named Mrs. White, not Mrs. Brown."

Miss Rothschild leaned back in her chair, chin up, eyes flashing. "Mrs. Brown was Mrs. Finchley's nurse."

First, Mrs. Currey. Then, Mrs. Brown. "Have you spoken with Mrs. Brown?" Richard asked Miss Rothschild.

She scowled rather prettily. "She died five years ago. Of natural causes ... or so they say."

"You suspect she was ... helped along?" asked Darcy.

Perhaps someone in Mrs. Finchley's employ? Richard could not imagine the kindly woman harming anybody.

"I hardly know what to think. Mrs. Brown was of a sturdy constitution, never sick a day in her life, according to my other sources, and yet she supposedly died of a weak heart. The last lady I talked to mentioned you, Mrs. Moorshead, which is why I am here. She said that Mrs. Brown had traveled to Devon where she apparently concluded some business which allowed her to live more comfortably. I came here in the hope of learning more."

Mrs. Moorshead reached over the table to place her hand on top of Miss Rothschild's. "I am sorry I know nothing of any business she might have done here. I only spoke with her once. I have told you everything I know."

Miss Rothschild turned her palm, lifting the elderly woman's hand to her cheek and kissing it. "But it has been significant. Thanks to you, we have learned there is a connection between Mrs. Brown and Mrs. Currey of which we were previously unaware."

Richard wanted to ask what she meant, to see if she had the same suspicions he did, but the floor creaked outside the parlor and another woman appeared in the doorway. "The reverend is agitated, Madam."

Mrs. Moorshead rose to her feet and, with her, her company too. "I must tend to my Edmond. He is used to me reading to him at this hour. I do hope I have been helpful in some way."

Nick bent over and kissed her on the cheek.

She caressed his face. "I wish with all of my heart and I shall pray every day that you find what you are searching for." She turned to Miss Rothschild. "You too, love."

They walked out to the gate, lingering when they ought to have made haste to inform the rest of their party what they had found. Two nurses, both employed by Mrs. Finchley. Both dead. That was something to pursue.

Darcy and Nick distanced themselves by a few paces, leaving Richard with Miss Rothschild behind. He wished they would not have. What was he supposed to say to her? Normally, he had no trouble conversing with ladies, but when she turned to face him, he found himself tongue-tied and stupid.

"I wonder, Colonel…" she began, chewing on the corner of her bottom lip. "Perhaps you shall think me impertinent, but I shall regret not taking the risk…"

"I like impertinent ladies." He smiled, earning a confused expression from Miss Rothschild and several poorly masked guffaws from his cousins ahead of him. "That is to say, impertinence is too often a term men use to refer to ladies who are more clever than they are. I shall not hold such an estimable quality against you. Now, how may I be of service?" He bowed, grateful to have his usual charm restored to him.

She rewarded him with a smile. "Thank you, Colonel. What I wish to suggest is that we join forces. I know where Mrs. Brown was buried and, consequently, where we might find more about her activities with Mrs. Finchley."

Richard turned to his cousins, but Nick's line of vision was fixed to the side of a large building. Under a sign reading "Callaghan and Sons, Cider Merchants," Richard saw Connell doing his best to melt into the shadows.

"Where do you plan to go next?" Nick asked, without taking his gaze off his pursuer.

"Bath."

"Then, allow us to accompany you."

Just like that, their party multiplied and their journey continued.

CHAPTER 36

*E*lizabeth climbed into the carriage on their second day of travel, Miss Rothschild at her side, Papa and Alexandra sitting opposite.

No streaks had stained Alexandra's cheeks that morning, but Elizabeth knew she still felt Jaffa's departure keenly.

"He shall be happy to return to his family after all these years." Elizabeth tapped Alexandra's knee.

Leaning her forehead against the window glass, Alexandra sighed. "I trusted him more than anyone." With a sniff and an inelegant wipe of her nose against her sleeve, she added, "But I have Nick now."

Papa handed her his handkerchief. "Three is too crowded. Jaffa is both trustworthy and wise."

Miss Rothschild observed the scene quietly. She was a welcome addition to their party, though not for the reasons the gentlemen had presented two days before when they had made introductions. According to them, she had provided them with their next clue, which had set them on the road to Bath. With her help, they would succeed in discovering why Nick, and a slew of other babies all over the country, had been separated from their families. What Elizabeth saw was how Miss Rothschild's gaze fixed on the colonel ... and how he attempted to balance the attention he wished to show her with what he considered proper.

Lord Matlock was on to the pair. The evening before, he had met Elizabeth's gaze over the dinner table, his eyes glinting. She wondered what he planned. Lord Matlock's firm exterior housed a soft heart, especially where his son and nephews were concerned.

Alexandra regaled Papa with stories of her exploits. She was an accomplished storyteller with an inclination to exaggerate, but it made for a lively trip. Elizabeth wondered if Nick did the same with Fitzwilliam, the colonel, and Lord Matlock. She hoped so.

Rolling pastures led down to the River Avon. Elizabeth watched the scenery with interest, knowing they were coming upon Bath.

"Your mother shall never forgive me for going to Bath without her," sighed Papa.

"I shall not tell if you do not," Elizabeth said.

Uncle Gardiner had already promised he would keep the more exciting details out of his report. For his brother-in-law and niece's benefit, as well as the nerves of his wife and sister, he would make their jaunt across England sound as mundane as possible. Jane and Aunt would know otherwise, but Mama would be comforted to know her husband and daughter were safe and not enjoying themselves too much without her.

A string of ionic columns and white doors shaped in a crescent rolled by, and the pastures transformed to an extensive, manicured lawn as the carriage stopped.

"This must be Mr. Darcy's residence." Papa peeked through the window.

"Mr. Darcy's?" Elizabeth gasped. How many houses did he own?

Her father smiled impishly at her. "He is quite wealthy, Lizzy."

It had been easy to forget after seeing him in frayed trousers and borrowed boots.

The verdant lawns called to her, but Elizabeth pulled her attention away from the temptation to another, more handsome one. Fitzwilliam waited for them by the front door of his fine residence.

Having so little luggage, it did not take the group long to settle and refresh themselves. They reconvened in a parlor with large windows facing the park. High ceilings and elegant furniture clustered in perfect balance with the proportion of the large room added to the grandness of the house.

Fitzwilliam's knee bobbed up and down, and he hardly touched the generous repast spread over the table. Elizabeth had been hungry, but she felt his nerves as keenly as if they were her own, and she only managed a few bites before she gave up.

Finally, when Fitzwilliam looked about to burst, he rose and addressed Papa. "Would you like to see the library, Mr. Bennet?"

Elizabeth was eager to see the library herself. She pushed her chair away to join them.

Nick set his roll down on his plate. "I've never traveled to yer part of the country, Miss Elizabeth. What's it like growing up on an estate like…?"

"Longbourn," she supplied, settling back into her chair with resignation. Papa and Fitzwilliam had already disappeared down the hall.

He snapped his fingers. "That's it, Longbourn. What do ye do all day?"

"My mother, sisters, and I read edifying books, write letters, draw landscapes, embroider flowers on cushions, paint tables…"

Nick made a face. His interest dissipated the moment his brother and her father left the room, setting Elizabeth's suspicions on high alert. However, Nick gave such a gallant effort asking questions about something he knew nothing about, Elizabeth tried her best to make estate living sound as exciting as she could make it. Unannounced calls were more annoying than exciting, but still, she tried.

What did Fitzwilliam want with her father? What did they have to talk about for over a quarter of an hour?

Just as she was about to dismiss herself and ask the housekeeper to show her the way to the library, Fitzwilliam appeared in the doorway, pink-cheeked and smiling. He did not look nervous anymore. "Mr. Bennet declares the library satisfactory and has already informed me that we ought to dine without him this evening, as he has more pressing matters to attend to."

Lord Matlock rose with a chuckle. "And I shall retire early to my rooms. This old man requires more rest than you young ones."

Fitzwilliam's eyes met Elizabeth's, and the look in his eyes, the happiness she saw, made her impatient with curiosity.

"Would you care to accompany me for a stroll down to the river, Miss Elizabeth?"

She could have kissed him. "I would love nothing more."

Alexandra tossed her napkin onto her plate and shoved her chair back. "I'm in need of some activity, too."

Nick's eyes widened. "I'll walk with ye. Wouldn't ye rather peek inside the shops?"

She scowled. "What use'll ye be when neither of us has been to Bath before? Me bum is sore after so much travel, and I'd like Darcy to show us the sights."

Miss Rothschild said, "I hear the abbey is an impressive structure. We are not far. In fact, I believe I observed the bell tower on our way here."

Their party of two soon grew to six, and

Fitzwilliam's smile was now a decided scowl, aimed mostly at Alexandra. He could not have looked more like a cross older brother than he did at that moment. When the colonel gave him a teasing shove, Elizabeth observed the struggle with which Fitzwilliam restrained himself from shoving back.

Elizabeth's humor rose, and she laughed. "The more, the merrier."

Fitzwilliam did not agree, but his scowl lightened. By the time they reached King's Circus, his manners had improved from tempestuous to only slightly blustering.

A perfect circle of houses surrounded them. Several groups of ladies and gentlemen picnicked on the grass, and passersby stumbled over the uneven ground, too enraptured with the new architecture to pay heed to their feet. Clusters of young men and soldiers laughed and talked loudly.

Fitzwilliam offered his arm. "There is a spot in the center of this circle where everything echoes."

She tilted her chin and arched an eyebrow. "Is that why you chose to live at the Crescent? To avoid the cacophony?"

He laughed. "That is precisely why. Too many people clap their hands just to hear the echo."

"I should think most people would enjoy being surrounded by constant applause." She grinned. "Shall we give it a try?"

He tugged her forward, then came to a stop at a

particular spot. Raising his hands, he clapped ... and received an ovation in return.

Elizabeth clapped, delighted. Her laughter echoed back to her, accented with the claps of her hands.

Fitzwilliam turned to her, his eyes dark and deep and brimming with mischief. It was a look she had not seen before, and she determined right then it was a look she would provoke as often as she could. Standing off to the side, she teased, "Clapping is too easy. When one comes to a place like this, they must share their wisdom with the world."

"Or they could remain silent," Fitzwilliam teased.

"Oh, no, that I cannot allow."

"Very well. Tell me what you wish to hear, and I shall take pleasure in saying it."

"You ought to know that I expect much more of you by now. Or have you not yet discovered something that shall amaze the public and be handed down to posterity with all the éclat of a proverb?"

All seriousness, he replied, "I have."

Elizabeth's heart tripped. "Really? Then, by all means, amaze us."

Raising her fingers to his lips, he bowed over her hand and said, "I love you, Elizabeth Bennet."

"I love you, Eliza—I love you, Eliza—I love you, Elizabeth Bennet—Elizabeth Bennet—Bennet." Everywhere Elizabeth turned, she was surrounded by Fitzwilliam's declaration.

Dozens of witnesses looked at them, nodding and

whispering, but he did not seem to notice them. Silent, taciturn Fitzwilliam Darcy stood in front of her, his heart wide open for all to see. The uncertainty in his eyes, the quickness of his breath, told her this was not the proposal of a man assured of a positive reply. She could not bear to see his doubt. Raising his hands to her face, she ran her lips over his gloves.

"Oy, Darcy! It *is* you!" a loud voice, an unwelcome voice, an odious voice ruined the moment as surely as a bucket of cold water dropped over one's head.

Elizabeth turned to see Mr. Wickham, grinning like a drunk fool, a half dozen of his cronies staggering behind him.

"Where is your wife?" she asked. That was as close as she could get to dashing him with frigid water, and the effect was satisfying.

His smile disappeared. "Probably spending all of my money." His tone was bitter. Wickham's friends hooted and howled behind him.

Elizabeth imagined her sister and her new husband foolishly squandering all of their money on gloves and boots and bonnets that would be scuffed and in tatters within the year living a champagne life on a budget more suited to ale.

"Speaking of money," Wickham clamped one hand on Fitzwilliam's shoulder, steadying himself. "Allow me to offer my heartfelt congratulations. Now that we are to be brothers—"

"You shall get nothing from me. And the lady has yet to answer."

Elizabeth felt fumes course through her veins. How dare Wickham ruin what was building up to be a promising, charming proposal. She could throttle him.

"Tut tut," Wickham cackled. "We both know that a lady such as Miss Elizabeth would never refuse a gentleman of fortune and consequence."

Through clenched teeth, Fitzwilliam asked, "Why are you with these … men … when you ought to be with your bride?"

Wickham shrugged, too foxed to heed the underlying threat in Fitzwilliam's tone. "Why bother? She'll move into Pemberley with you, and everyone's happy." He flailed his free arm in the air.

Elizabeth was shocked he could think such a thing. Did he not understand Fitzwilliam's character at all? He would never be welcome at Pemberley, nor anyone attached to him—

The full extent of Fitzwilliam's declaration hit her with a force that knocked the breath out of her lungs. A union with her would forever attach Fitzwilliam to Wickham, and yet he was willing to endure the connection. Because of her.

Until that moment, Elizabeth had not truly understood the depth of his love. Breathless, she looked up at him, her heart brimming in her eyes. To think that Fitzwilliam loved her so ardently, so thoroughly. And, oh, how she loved him! With every inch of her being, every thought, and every heartbeat, she loved Fitzwilliam Darcy.

Wickham belched and tightened his grip on Fitzwilliam's shoulder.

Elizabeth's anger boiled over. If Fitzwilliam was willing to endure a connection to his worst nightmare, then she would ensure Wickham knew how little they desired his company. "I love my sister, but I cannot shield her from the consequences of her actions. Nor do I feel obliged to spare you the results of your choices. I do, however, expect you to at least pretend to be an attentive husband to Lydia."

He scoffed.

Elizabeth's restraint snapped. "Or do you limit your attentions only to gullible maidens?"

Out of the corner of her eyes, she saw Alexandra draw a dagger from her hair. "This rascal givin' ye trouble, Lizzy?"

Nick stood beside Alexandra, his fists raised and ready. The colonel, too. Miss Rothschild had no dagger, nor did she raise her clenched fists, but the imperious glare she cast at Wickham would have melted a better man.

Wickham's friends were quiet now.

He turned to her, placing his hand on her shoulder. "I would never harm you. You know that. I am your brother now."

His familiarity put Elizabeth's teeth on edge. "Kindly remove your hand, sir," she warned.

"Ye know what to do," Alexandra said with a double wink.

Darcy stepped in and would have made short work of Wickham, but Elizabeth shook her head. She wanted to discourage Wickham from ever discounting the admonition of one he considered weaker than himself.

She knew precisely how to handle this rascal.

Grabbing his hand, she spun around and wedged her shoulder under his.

# CHAPTER 37

*D*arcy dove out of the trajectory of Wickham's boots just in time. Had he looked as ridiculous as Wickham did, flying through the air, limp and stunned?

With a loud huff, Wickham landed on his back on the grass.

Elizabeth looked every bit as triumphant—more so —and charming as she had their last night on the *Fancy*. Darcy's chest inflated. She did not suffer fools. Wickham would never place his hand on her again. In fact, he would likely think twice before approaching her at all. Now *that* was a pleasant thought.

The group of drunken soldiers watched nearby, cackling and hooting. "Overthrown by a miss!" "Toppled by a lady!" "Hefted over like a sack of rubbish!" They smacked their thighs and guffawed.

Wickham sputtered and tried to stand, but Elizabeth had knocked the wind out of his sails thoroughly, and Darcy knew from experience that it would take a moment to gain his breath. So, Wickham squirmed and stammered, his face as red as his coat, providing a ridiculous spectacle at which his so-called friends laughed freely.

Darcy leaned over him and Nick followed suit, both of them watching over his prostrate figure and neither of them offering a hand up. "Who's this ninnyhammer?" Nick asked.

Wickham blinked several times, gasping, "My eyes! Something's wrong with my eyes." He tried to crawl back, and Darcy pitied the batman who would have to scrub the grass stains out of the posterior of Wickham's breeches.

Alex wedged herself between Darcy and Nick. "Who's this dunderhead who'd lay a hand on me best friend?" Quicker than a flash, she flicked her hand up to her hair, removing a thin dagger.

Nick grabbed her hand. Darcy saw her flinch with her other hand, and he clasped it before she could reach for another hidden weapon. There were too many folds and creases of lace in her gown to trust. "Not here," Darcy warned in a low tone. "There are too many witnesses."

Wickham's eyes doubled in size and, had Richard and Miss Rothschild not been blocking his way, he might have continued crawling away on his elbows and heels.

Alex pouted. "I saw an alley over yonder that'll do." Her hands restrained, she jutted her chin in the direction from which they had come. "Ye three strong men could drag him over there, and I'll guarantee he never lays a hand on anyone ever again."

"Alex," Nick warned.

"Come on, Nick! It's only a hand."

Wickham tucked his hands under his back.

Deepening her pout and blinking up at Nick, Alex pleaded, "Please, Nick? He'll be perfectly fine without one."

Darcy hoped she was teasing or merely trying to scare Wickham with fright. But Nick's grip around her hand showed no sign of loosening, so Darcy followed his lead and tightened his hold on Alex's other wrist.

Wickham's friends were no longer laughing. They watched from a safer distance, too cowardly to assist their brother-in-arms but too curious to leave.

Elizabeth plucked the knife from Alex's hand and flipped it over in her palm to grip the handle. What other tricks had she learned from Alex? He watched the woman he loved flip the blade in her palm, then from one hand to the other like an expert. He was mesmerized, as was Wickham, who stared at the blade with his jaw open and a drained complexion.

"I would love nothing more than to practice my new skills on a man whose welfare means nothing to me." *Toss-toss-flick.* "However, he is my sister's husband,

and for that reason—and that reason alone—we must spare him."

Alex made to argue, but Elizabeth cut her off. "If he has any regard for his own self, he shall remember this moment. Every time he throws the dice or holds his cards or grips a tankard or pinches a barmaid … he shall recall how my sister—his wife—is the reason why he yet possesses his hand. And he shall behave more decently toward her out of sheer gratitude for what she spared him, for it is certainly not due to any goodwill or mercy on my part."

Wickham sat stupidly, wordlessly, at their feet. Darcy waited for the moment when Wickham's senses would catch up with his breath and he would try to wiggle his way out of the predicament he was in.

But Elizabeth's patience was worn thin. Pinching the blade, she squinted her eyes and took aim. "My aim is not as good as my friend's, but I shall be happy for the practice."

"You would not dare!" Wickham scampered back until he bumped into Richard's legs.

Elizabeth smiled slowly, impishly, until a flicker of doubt entered Darcy's consciousness and he wondered about the danger of their constant association with Alex.

"You are not certain I shall not do it, are you? After all, you are still sitting on the ground where I put you..." Elizabeth adjusted her trajectory, her tongue peeking between her lips as she calculated.

Darcy was making calculations of his own. Could he prevent her from doing something she was certain to regret without loosening his hold on Alex, who would not hesitate to maim a man merely because Elizabeth had made known her disdain for him?

Relaxing her pose and her expression, Elizabeth held the knife in front of Alex's outstretched hand. "Very well, if you are unwilling to promise to be a better husband to Lydia, then maybe, I shall give this dagger back to my friend."

"Who is she that I should fear her?" Wickham scoffed. He always had been rather stupid.

Nick mumbled, "Steady, woman."

Alex strained against their hold. "I'll tell ye exactly who I am, ye thick-headed numbskull. I'm Cap'n Alexandra Lafitte, and I'll make ye wish ye'd never crossed me mates."

"Lafitte? La Femme Lafitte?" Wickham choked, his skin ash white.

Darcy groaned. So did Nick.

The soldiers' backs retreated down Gay Street as quickly as their polished boots could carry them. Wickham, too, looked ready to bolt.

Elizabeth repeated, "You shall not leave here without a promise." The last time Darcy had seen that degree of determination fixed on her expression was when she had refused his offer of marriage.

Wickham relented. "I swear I shall be a good husband to Lydia."

"If I hear of you being unfaithful or preying on another unsuspecting maiden or appealing to any of us to spare you from the consequences of your choices, then—"

"I'll take great pleasure in carvin' out yer heart," interrupted Alex, "and eatin' it for breakfast."

*Dear Lord.*

A hard swallow, and Darcy could see it took a great deal of effort for Wickham to stand on his shaking legs. "I swear, I swear," he groveled, backing around Richard and continuing until he turned and ran.

Elizabeth turned to Alex. "That was unnecessarily dramatic. I was going to say that we would refuse to cover his debts and allow him to fend for himself lest he end up in prison." She blushed, turning to Darcy and adding, "That is, assuming you agree, of course."

Darcy shrugged. Any threat he or anyone else could have made would pale in comparison to Alex's. "I have already assured Wickham he shall not see another penny from me. My dealings with him are done."

She deflated. "Oh. Well then, maybe Alexandra's threat was just the thing."

Alex puffed up until she noticed Elizabeth's continued agitation. "D'ye think he'll keep his promise?" she asked.

"For my sister's sake, I hope so."

Darcy gave him a week, though he prayed he was wrong.

Elizabeth sighed. "He is too lazy to hurt Lydia—

thankfully—but I fear he is already bored with her. Indifference is just another form of cruelty." She blinked several times, and Darcy knew she thought of her own father and mother.

Miss Rothschild, who had every right to be offended at the shocking company she kept, finally spoke. "People forget promises, and words are often fickle. But that young man shall not likely forget the terror you two ladies inspired within him. You did what you could; the rest is up to him." She brushed her hands as though to rid them of dust. "Now, I was wondering if perhaps you could teach me to do that trick? It seems to be a useful skill for a lady to know."

Richard grinned from ear to ear.

Miss Rothschild seemed to mistake his display of pride for humor. Her eyes flashed, and her skin darkened. "It is not reasonable to expect a young lady to always rely on gentlemen—some of whom are more treacherous than the worst ruffians—for our welfare and protection. We must learn to be more self-sufficient."

"I could not agree with you more." Turning to Alex, Richard added, "I hope you will teach my sisters, and Georgie, as well."

"I'd be honored to show ye a few things," Alex agreed with a grin.

The abbey bells rang.

Elizabeth sidled closer to Darcy's side. "I have heard

that the stained glass and stonework of the abbey are second to none."

Ready to pick up where he had left off before Wickham's interruption, Darcy held out his arm. "Shall we see?"

Doubts soon encroached on his bravery. Every step made Darcy increasingly aware that he had yet to ask, and knowing that she was aware of it only increased his nerves. What if he bumbled the whole thing again? What if he did not meet her expectations?

By the time they reached the abbey, he was more nervous than when he had spoken with Mr. Bennet earlier. He had used his library as a buffer, knowing that the well-stocked shelves and original printings guaranteed a more favorable conversation. Darcy was not above using the manipulative arts when it came to his future with Elizabeth. He needed every advantage.

He had Mr. Bennet's approval and blessing, but by the time they had admired the windows and the bell tower, Darcy had received no strike of romantic inspiration.

But he had to say it. He could not go another day holding in his heartfelt desire.

Miss Rothschild suggested a walk through Guildhall Market, and Darcy seized the opportunity to part from their company in favor of the River Avon. They would meet at Pulteney Bridge.

The bridge offered a beautiful backdrop of the river with its crescent-shaped weirs forming rings into the running water. As loud as the rushing river was, Darcy's heartbeat was louder.

He had survived kidnapping, keelhauling, sword fights, and cannon blasts, but all of these combined paled in significance compared to the task before him. He would propose—again—to Elizabeth Bennet.

Pulling the bit of rope from his pocket, wishing it was his mother's sapphire and diamond ring, he dropped to his knee before he lost his nerve. Clearing his throat, he said the words he had been practicing since Elizabeth had given him the first glimpse of hope that starry night on the foretop. "Will you marry me, Elizabeth?"

That was it. His throat dried, and he looked up, unable to speak another word. He shoved the rope he had woven into a ring in front of him.

He felt her hands on his cheeks, pulling him up. "You made this for me?" she asked, sliding her slender finger into the circle, then wrapping her arm back around his neck. "It fits perfectly."

She was kind to praise his simple ring, but as he looked at the roughness of the rope against her soft skin, his embarrassment grew. "As soon as we return to London, I shall replace it with one more worthy—"

She covered his lips with her fingers. "This is my favorite ring, and no fancy jewels you can give me shall convince me otherwise."

Darcy let out his breath. He ought to have known she would not demand fineries. Not his Elizabeth. He tightened his arms around her waist, pulling her closer. More confidently, he asked, "Will you please marry me?"

"Aye," she answered, rising to her toes and keeping his lips too busy for any more speech.

CHAPTER 38

*B*right colors competed with vendors, all clamoring for their attention. Nick lingered behind with Richard while the ladies flitted from one stall to the next. He wondered if Richard had seen Connell yet. The thief-taker stood, partially hidden, behind a length of cashmere.

Richard jabbed Nick with his elbow. "He is not subtle, is he?" he observed, nodding at the cashmere.

Nick twisted his lips. He ought to have known that a trained soldier would be as alert to danger as he was. "He's been following us since we left the house. I thought for certain he'd arrest me when Elizabeth tossed that ne'er-do-well over her shoulder."

"Had you been the one to put Wickham in his place, I have no doubt Connell would have found his excuse to take you back to Newgate." Worry etched Richard's brow.

Nick was worried, too. Any little mistake, and Connell would close in on him. Had he overheard Alex's foolish blunder? If he knew he could bag not only one, but *two*, renowned pirates, Connell would jump at the opportunity. Nick was grateful for Lord Matlock's protection, but he could not presume that his relatives would extend their protection to Alex, too. They'd already done so much.

And what could he do for them in return? How could he possibly repay them?

Concern weighed heavily on Nick. He'd do what he could to lighten the load on his family, but it'd never be enough. Turning so his back was to Connell, Nick grinned. "We'll give Connell a mad tour of England before we're done with him."

Richard seemed to understand his need for levity. With a nod, he smiled, and they continued walking until they joined the ladies.

Alex held up a gold earring, and Nick provoked her agitation when he paid for the earrings without any attempt to barter. He'd pay twice the sum just to see her happy … once he unburied one of his caches. What was money to him when his ill-got gains could be used to help the family selling their wares? At least *they* earned an honest living. Everything Nick possessed had been taken at some point.

Leaning into him, the smell of jasmine in her hair swirling Nick's senses, Alex asked, "Has Connell given up yet? Or is he still followin' us like a gull eyein' a picnic?"

Nick scowled at her. He'd almost forgotten about Connell. Now he had to start all over again. "Ye saw him, eh?"

"Since we left Darcy's house."

"If ye knew he was watching us, then why on earth did ye say yer name where he could hear it?" Nick snapped. "Fool woman, yer infamy'll be the death of me."

She faced him square, fists on hips. "If ye'd let Boone marry us, I'd've had a different name to give."

Nick leaned down, looking her in the eyes. "Would that really have stopped ye from using yer surname against him? Yer only thought was in terrifying that scoundrel."

She crossed her arms over her chest. "If Lizzy felt threatened by him, then he's an enemy to me."

"Ah, it's Lizzy now, is it?"

"That's what Mr. Bennet calls her. It suits her."

Nick gritted his teeth. Alex was loyal to a fault. He couldn't stay agitated at her for that. He didn't realize Richard and Miss Rothschild stood nearby until Alex addressed the colonel. "What'd that awful knave do, anyway?"

Richard took a deep breath. "Wickham grew up with Darcy at Pemberley, the son of the land steward and godson to Darcy's father. He was given a gentleman's education, and all the advantages that came with an attachment to an established, respected family. He became accustomed to living beyond his means and of always being provided for."

Nick had no respect for men of that sort. Always with their hand out, and ungrateful, besides.

"Mr. Darcy provided a living for him in his will," Richard continued, "but Wickham was not interested in the church or the stability the living represented. He sold it for a healthy sum, which Darcy generously paid."

Alex made a noise. "He spent it all, didn't he?"

"He appealed to Darcy for more money and, when Darcy refused, he disappeared for a while. Long enough for us to believe ourselves rid of him." Richard took another deep breath, seeming to weigh his words. "The easiest way for a man such as him to gain a fortune is to marry into one, and he set his sights on Georgiana."

Nick's body tensed; fire burned through his veins.

"Darcy's little sister?" Alex gasped.

Nick ground his teeth. Georgiana was barely out of the schoolroom. The idea of that rakehell trying to taint her innocence made his rage boil over. "Had I known, I'd have run him through."

"And have you hang over it?" Richard, too, spoke through his clenched jaw. "Wickham is not worth ruining your life. It is a fact I have had to repeat to myself many times."

"I could make it look like an accident," Alex offered.

She glanced up at Nick. "We could make him disappear easy. Tie a rock to his middle and dump him in shark-infested waters. Nobody'd ever find him."

Nick kissed her forehead. It was a lovely thought and he was sorely tempted, but it'd mean returning to the life he had worked so hard and suffered so much to leave. Richard was right. Wickham wasn't worth ruining his reputation with his family—almost, but not quite. "Tempting, but me days of revenge are through."

Miss Rothschild asked, "Is not your ship called *The Revenge?*"

Nick, Alex, and Richard turned to her, mouths agape.

"What?" she shrugged. "Is a lady not allowed to read anything entertaining?"

Richard tried to hide his smile, but Nick knew he was pleased with Miss Rothschild's spiritedness.

In his mind's eye, Nick saw his beautiful ship, his glory, his haven. "Aye, she was." He looked at Alex. "I hope yer brothers have her. Maybe they'll forgive ye for blasting the side out of their fastest ship if they gained *The Revenge.*"

Alex wiggled her fingers between his and squeezed his hand. "We'll get her back, Nick. I promise."

He shook his head. It was dangerous to entertain such thoughts. "I'm done plundering and pillaging."

"Ye'd only be reclaimin' what's rightfully yers. Surely, there's nothin' wrong with that."

He pressed her hand against his chest. "So long as

ye're with me, I'm happy. I was never more miserable than when I thought ye were lost to me forever."

She grinned. "Is that why ye threatened to kill me?"

He returned her grin. "Ye get under me skin like nobody else."

Behind her, he saw Connell move to another stall. Like a wet blanket over a fire, Nick's contentment dampened, yielding once again to anxiety. If anything happened to him, he could bear it. But if Connell realized what other prize dangled in front of him, Nick'd never forgive himself for endangering Alex. "Let's get back. Mr. Bennet and Lord Matlock'll worry if we don't return before dark."

"You can call him Uncle," Richard said.

Nick could not presume that intimacy yet. He couldn't explain why, so he just nodded and walked out to the river.

Darcy was where he said he would be with Elizabeth. The two held each other, and Nick praised the Heavens that his brother had found happiness. Elizabeth was a capable lady with a witty tongue and a kind heart. She'd always be a comfort to Darcy.

Nick walked up to them, teasing, "Ye'll have to marry her now, Darcy."

His brother had a wider smile than Nick had seen him show before this. "I intend to. Perhaps we ought to apply for licenses and make it a double wedding."

Alex clapped her hands, but Nick was too stunned

to react. Darcy had not known Nick for a fortnight, and he would share his wedding day with him?

Darcy dropped his voice, and Nick understood his words were meant only for him. "I would like my brother to be a part of the most important day of my life."

Nick shook his head, speechless. He didn't deserve Darcy's unrestrained acceptance.

Alex jerked on his arm. "All this plannin' makes me hungry."

"Have you ever enjoyed a Bath bun?" Miss Rothschild asked.

"I'll warn ye, Emily—Can I call ye that? Miss Rothschild's such a mouthful."

Miss Rothschild graciously smiled. "Of course, you may. If Miss Elizabeth agrees to address me the same."

"I am Elizabeth, or Lizzy, to you." Elizabeth arched an eyebrow, her gaze flickering to Richard ever so briefly. So, Nick wasn't the only one who thought they'd make a winning match. Nick's admiration grew. It was easy to like people who agreed with you.

"What did you wish to warn me about, Alex?" Miss Rothschild asked.

"I've been spoiled most of me life with a French chef. I'm not easy to satisfy at the table."

Miss Rothschild was not discouraged. "Then you must have a Sally Lunn bun. They are teacakes. I have only ever managed to eat half—they are massive—but I think you shall like them."

They squeezed into a carriage and returned to the Royal Crescent before nightfall with a basket of buns too light to have much substance.

Nick devoured the top half. It was smothered with butter and cinnamon. To the bottom portion, he added the cheeses and cold cuts Darcy's housekeeper provided on a large tray. Had the bun not been so delicious, he might've been tempted to save a portion for Jean-Christophe. Maybe he could secure a few more for their trip.

Mr. Bennet was delighted with the idea. And Lord Matlock declared the recipe unchanged since the last time he'd eaten a Bath bun in his youth.

Lord Matlock dabbed his mouth and spread his hands over his middle. "We must rest for the morrow. It promises to be a busy day."

"Do we have no other name or residence? No clue besides the cemetery?" Darcy asked.

Miss Rothschild sipped her tea. She'd only eaten through half of the top of her bun. "My detectives have found no living relatives. Mrs. Brown was raised in an orphan asylum until she ran away. All of the institution's records were destroyed in a flood. As far as they learned, she did not maintain any friendships after she left."

"We ought to make inquiries anyway," Mr. Bennet suggested.

Darcy frowned. "Mrs. Currey had no family either."

Elizabeth had nearly managed to clear half of her

bun. "Do you think Mrs. Finchley selected nurses without family or close friends on purpose?"

"We cannot discount any possibility," Darcy answered, "but we must not hasten to believe the worst of her before we have all the facts."

Elizabeth blushed. "You will never forget how I misjudged your character, will you?"

Mr. Bennet raised the last of his bun in the air. "Not if he is as intelligent as we know him to be. We gentlemen must use every advantage to maintain a level field, my dear."

"Papa! You would compare our relationship to a battlefield?"

"Love *is* a battlefield," he declared, popping the last bite into his mouth and closing his eyes as he chewed. There was a man who enjoyed a teacake.

What Darcy said stuck with Nick, who tried not to eye the ladies' as-yet unfinished buns. "It's true, though. Closed minds're blind. The truth could be right in front of our noses, and we wouldn't see it."

Alex, who had started out eating as slowly as the other ladies at the table but had given up all pretension of delicacy after three bites, pushed her empty plate away. "Remember how ye told us about the rector's wife, how she takes care of all of them graves? I wonder if Mrs. Brown has someone like that."

Lord Matlock shrugged. "It would take no time at all to have a look."

"The cemetery might tell us something," Miss Rothschild said. "My detectives learned nothing at the asylum, though I should like to make inquiries myself." If she did not attend to her bun soon, Nick was tempted to offer to help her with it. Would that be considered rude in his present company? Probably.

"It is as good a place as any to start," Lord Matlock agreed.

Nick thought they had too little to go on. Then again, this mystery—if, indeed, there had been a crime committed—had been kept silent for nearly thirty years. They couldn't expect the clues to be loud.

# CHAPTER 39

*E*lizabeth ran her finger over the strands of her ring, her attention arrested by the token Fitzwilliam had made her over the scenery her father constantly pointed out to her, Alexandra, and Emily through the carriage glass.

"It takes a lot of effort to make something as fine as that. Braidin' and splicin' twine with blistered, calloused fingers be no simple task," Alexandra commented.

Emily turned away from the rolling pastures to admire Elizabeth's ring. "I think it is romantic."

Papa chuckled and rolled his eyes at the simpering females surrounding him. "I am pleased to know my daughter is engaged to a thoughtful gentleman. You know, I tried being thoughtful once with your mother?"

Elizabeth guffawed. "Only once?"

He wiggled his bushy eyebrows. "Perhaps I should give it another go?"

All three ladies replied in unison, "Yes!"

Alexandra, who was less inhibited than her two friends, asked, "What'd ye do for yer missus?"

"I gave her a handful of wildflowers," Papa answered proudly, as he ought to. Elizabeth was rather partial to wildflowers.

"That is lovely," Emily said with a sigh.

"I am relieved to know it. All these years, I thought my gesture insufficient," Papa said, his tone sad. Summoning greater sarcasm, he added with a sardonic smile, "Mrs. Bennet told me she prefers hothouse flowers. They are more exotic. More costly."

Emily furrowed her brow, looking uncomfortably at Elizabeth. "Perhaps your wife equates your willingness to spend money on her with love."

Papa chuckled in earnest. "How unfortunate for my purse. I do believe you are right, young lady, and I shall advise you to have pity on your poor future husband by appreciating the small gestures as well as the grand ones."

She shook her head firmly. "Forgive me for speaking so plainly on the subject, but I have a great deal of money, and while it undeniably makes my life more comfortable, it has never made me happy. True happiness, I have come to believe, comes from the friendships we make and the people we are generous to. I could never attach myself to a gentleman who did not feel the same." She closed her mouth and looked down at her clasped hands, her cheeks in high color.

Elizabeth leaned forward and rested her hand on top of Emily's. She had spoken with so much passion, her voice shook, and Elizabeth wondered how long Emily had held her admission inside her without anyone in whom to confide.

Alexandra wrapped her arm around Emily's and rested her head against her shoulder. "I think it's more about knowin' that a gentleman was thinkin' of his lady than the flowers." She sighed, her eyes staring off into the distance. "When I'm away from land for ages, I love the sight of flowers. They're one of the few things I miss. Nick, too. He's partial to roses."

Emily unclenched her hands and relaxed into Alexandra's side in the same way Elizabeth did with her sisters. "My French maid has been teaching me the language of flowers. Did you know that every flower has a meaning ascribed to it?"

Papa groaned. "You ladies have too many secret languages as it is. Handkerchiefs, fans, parasols … now flowers! Mrs. Bennet tried to teach me the language of the fan, but I never caught on. When she signaled me to flirt or ask her to dance, I thought she wished for me to send for the carriage."

"If yer missus knows these Frenchie languages, ye might've offended her with yer choice of blooms."

"What flowers did you give her?" Elizabeth asked.

"Daffodils and daisies. It was spring."

Alexandra turned to face Emily. "What's their meanin'?"

"They are both excellent choices. Daffodils symbolize regard and unequaled love."

Elizabeth poked her father's arm. "Not bad, Papa."

"And daisies are associated with innocence and loyal love." Emily twisted her lips to the side. "Were you to make another attempt at thoughtfulness, perhaps she would prefer roses. Red or pink blossoms. Or any color really—with the exception of yellow. That implies jealousy or infidelity."

The carriage jolted to a halt, and they piled out of the conveyance, their minds full of flowers and hidden meanings. Lord Matlock, Fitzwilliam, Richard, and Nick waited nearby.

"This is Mrs. Brown's final resting place?" Lord Matlock asked.

Emily nodded. "According to my detective, it is."

"Then, let us go inside and see what we find," he said.

With a wink, Papa left Elizabeth at Fitzwilliam's side to join the earl at the head of their retinue.

Ahead of Elizabeth and Darcy walked Nick and Alexandra, and behind them, the colonel and Emily. The latter made a handsome couple, in Elizabeth's estimation.

She squeezed closer to Fitzwilliam, tugging his arm so he would lean down for her whisper. "Far be it from me to interfere, but if the colonel wishes to please

Emily, I have it on good authority that she likes flowers and thoughtful gestures. She is also aware of the language of flowers, so he ought to take care which bloom he presents to her."

Fitzwilliam's eyes twinkled. "You wish for me to relay this information to Richard? Without interfering?"

Elizabeth laughed. "I trust you to find a way."

He straightened to his full height with a cackle. "You trust me more than I do myself."

"Ah, but you are not too proud to fix your mistakes or to overlook mine. A beneficial trait to have in a marriage, do you not agree?" she teased.

"So long as you continue to minimize my errors with your humor, I shall continue to humble myself."

Lord Matlock stopped beside two men digging a grave. They pointed down a tidy row of grave markers, and Elizabeth's mood grew more somber as they walked deeper inside the cemetery's grounds.

They came to a stop, and their group circled around the grave at a respectful distance. *Martha Brown* read the stone. There were flowers covering the dates of her existence. Richard moved them aside, confirming they had the correct Mrs. Brown.

After their conversation in the carriage, Elizabeth could not help but fix on the blue violets and pink carnations. They were wilted and dry, several days old. Looking at Emily, Elizabeth asked, "What do those mean?"

"Blue violets represent faithfulness." Softer, Emily added, "I shall never forget you. That is the meaning of the pink carnation." Her gaze met Elizabeth's. It was a clue. A significant one if the giver knew the significance of his choice.

"A relative?" Elizabeth wondered aloud.

"More likely, a lover," Alexandra suggested. "Yer detectives uncovered nobody significant in Mrs. Brown's life?"

Emily's brows furrowed. "She had no family, and though she was called Mrs. Brown, she was never married." Such a disparity in address was common enough. Many spinsters preferred to allow others to believe them widowed than unwanted. One would be hard pressed to find a companion or governess who did not claim to be a missus rather than a miss.

"Somebody cared enough about her to tend to her grave," Fitzwilliam observed, taking off down the row until he joined the two gravediggers. Clever man. If anyone could tell them anything about the flowers, it was them.

One of the men took off his cap, and Elizabeth was close enough to hear his reply by the time she caught up. "I'm happy to see the flowers again."

"Again?" Fitzwilliam prompted.

"Aye." The man scratched his head, saying, "I thought the man had fallen ill or gone traveling. It must be two, maybe three months he didn't show when it was his custom to leave a new bunch every Sunday."

Sunday. That was tomorrow.

His companion added, "'Tis sorrowful work, ours is. It's nice to have something pretty to look at in this place."

"I imagine so," Fitzwilliam acknowledged with a bow of his head. Elizabeth loved how he sympathized with the gravediggers.

"Every Sunday, you say?" Lord Matlock asked.

The man wiped his cap over his brow. "Like a clock. He shows up between ten in the morning and a quarter after the hour."

They thanked the men and walked a short distance to confer in privacy. It was a quick counsel, as they all agreed to return at the appointed hour the following day to meet the man who maintained Mrs. Brown's grave.

They spent the rest of the day together, easy in each other's company, sharing stories and laughing. Elizabeth felt so comfortable with Fitzwilliam and his family, Emily, and Alexandra, she wondered how it was possible that they had not known each other all of their lives. She held every minute close to her heart, cherishing it along with her favorite memories.

But with her happiness, a trickle of melancholy crept in. Today they were together, united in their purpose. But what about when they discovered the truth? Elizabeth did not allow herself to doubt they would reveal who was behind Fitzwilliam and Nick's separation, as well as Emily's. Would they continue to be friends? Would it ever be safe for Nick and Alexandra in England? If Fitzwilliam had to choose between his family and the status into which he was raised, would he prove as steady as Elizabeth had always witnessed him to be? Furthermore, how could he be loyal to one without forsaking the other?

It was not a decision she wished him to ever have to make.

CHAPTER 40

*D*arcy tried not to resent the size of their party; he tried not to feel guilty about his resentment when that same party consisted mostly of his relatives and Elizabeth's. But when it meant that he could not sit beside his betrothed in the same carriage, he felt a degree of resentment appropriate.

Looking across from him, he suspected Nick's thoughts ran along a similar vein. He either sighed or scowled ... much like Darcy.

Uncle clucked his tongue at them and chuckled knowingly—irritatingly. "I have been married to the woman I adore for thirty-two years, and you lads are reminding me of my youth, how every minute without her was agony. I pray you are always impatient for your loves."

Now Darcy felt wretched. He had been so intent on his own misery, he had not considered how Uncle must miss Aunt, who was taking care of their daughters and niece back in London, no doubt worried and impatient herself to hear the news and know that her husband and nephews were unharmed.

Nick smiled, then turned his gaze to Richard. "Speaking of loves, I've seen how ye look at that fiery-haired lass. She's got a level head on her shoulders and a strong mind. Good qualities."

Richard smiled, a sad twitch of his lips that died before it reached his eyes. "Miss Rothschild is an heiress. I could not rightly pursue her without feeling like a fortune hunter. She deserves better than that."

Nick looked at him askance. "Are ye a fortune hunter?"

"No. But it is no secret that I would do well to marry into a fortune."

"So, ye won't pursue yer suit because she has exactly what ye need?" Nick scratched his head.

"I respect her too much."

"Ye like her—could love her even—but ye won't tell her because she happens to be an heiress in possession of a fortune?" Nick shook his head. "Sounds a bit backwards if ye ask me."

"It is more complicated than that. I would never want her to doubt that my affection stemmed from a sincere heart."

"Ye're an honest man. Just tell her. She'll believe ye," Nick said with a shrug.

Richard looked to his father and Darcy for support,

but Nick's reasoning was too simple and sound to refute. If Miss Rothschild trusted him to speak the truth, then why should Richard not allow her the opportunity to form her own opinion? She did not seem like the kind of woman to be easily swayed by public opinion or give credence to society's gossip. Not a woman unafraid to take on the Bow Street Runners and hire detectives when everyone told her that her efforts were futile and a waste of time.

"Give the lady more credit, Richard. She knows her own mind better than you ever shall," Uncle urged.

Darcy stifled a snort. Had he heeded his uncle's advice, he never would have presumed to do or say half of the things he now regretted regarding Elizabeth and her family.

"But what about her friends and family? Surely they would advise her to avoid gentlemen of my sort," Richard said.

"That is pride, and it has no place in a happy home. People talk no matter what you do, but you are constant and therefore have nothing to fear. You shall love the woman you marry more with every passing year. Let them talk about that."

Where had Uncle and his advice been before Darcy traveled to Hertfordshire? Of course, Darcy had to own, he would have been too proud to pay his uncle any heed.

But that was no longer the case. He had learned his lesson, and Darcy now knew that he would always be learning. Elizabeth was a charming teacher, but she had high expectations. And he would do his best to rise to them.

Nick laced his fingers together and leaned back against the cushions with his eyes closed. He had no expectations, nor had he—not even once—used his newfound connections to his own advantage. And just as Darcy hoped Richard would overcome the obstacles holding him back from a young lady who could be the making of him, Darcy was determined not to allow anyone or anything to separate him from Nick. They were brothers. Darcys.

They arrived at the cemetery before the man with the flowers, but they did not have to wait long. At ten after the hour, he appeared, one hand carrying a bunch of violets.

Piling out of the carriage, the ladies and Mr. Bennet holding back a few paces so as not to overwhelm or frighten the poor man, Darcy waited for his uncle to approach, standing near enough to hear but not too close to crowd.

The man nodded, and Uncle gestured for their party to join them by Mrs. Brown's grave, introducing them as they trickled in.

"This is Mr. Allan," Uncle said. Lowering his tone, he added, "Please allow me to express my condolences for your loss. You must miss her dearly."

Mr. Allan removed the dried flowers, replacing them with the fresh violets. He took a deep breath when he straightened, as though tending to the grave brought him immense satisfaction. "I was away for two months, and it broke my heart to know nobody tended to Martha. But my mother needed me."

"Is she ill?" Alex asked, adding a hastily, "I'm sorry to hear it."

Mr. Allan took off his cap. "Thank you, Miss. She lived a good life and will need me no more, though I will miss her just as I miss my dear Martha. They leave, and I remain."

They stood together in respectful silence until Mr. Allan replaced his cap and spoke. "Now, how may I help you? Your Lordship mentioned you had some questions?"

Miss Rothschild spoke softly. "Did your beloved have any friends or family, aside from you?"

"Not that I know of. She was a quiet person who kept to herself." He sighed, saying more to himself than to anybody, "She saw a great deal too much and kept many secrets."

Drawing closer to him, her eyes intent on Mr. Allan, Miss Rothschild said, "It is one of those secrets which led us here to you."

He nodded, eyes downcast. "You one of 'em?" he asked.

Darcy swallowed his gasp.

"One of the stolen children? Yes, I believe I am," she answered.

Another nod. "I suggested to Martha that she keep a list of the babes as well as the families they went to."

"Does such a list exist?" Richard asked, eyes bright.

"Not by Martha's hand. She resented them, you see." He looked up, eyes pleading, "How could she not when she was denied everything they took for granted? She had no parents, no kin willing to claim her and give her a home. Everything she gained, she had to fight for tooth and nail."

Elizabeth's voice was gentle. "We are not here to defame her character. We only wish to know the truth and restore the stolen children to their rightful places."

He finally looked up, inspecting their faces one by one. After several minutes, he said, "I worked at the orphanage. My family couldn't afford to keep me, and I took on any work I could find nearby. The orphanage was a horrible place, but that was where I met Martha. She had all the plans. I had none. She dreamed of escaping and making her own way, certain of her success. I'd still be working at the orphanage if it weren't for her. I almost wish she hadn't left. 'Twas her ambition what killed her."

"She did not die of natural causes?" Uncle asked.

"My Martha was as fit as a fiddle."

"What do you think happened?" prodded Miss Rothschild.

Mr. Allan hesitated. Whatever his thoughts were, they were contradictory and difficult. Crossing his arms over his chest, he looked levelly at Uncle. "Do I have your word as a peer that you will not make known what I will tell you?"

"That is not a promise I can give lightly."

"All the same, I will have it, or I will remain silent."

Uncle tucked his chin into his chest and exhaled.

Mr. Allan added, "Martha's sins were forgiven at her death. There is no reason for her memory to be maligned when there are precious few who remember her."

"None of us are interested in smearing the name of the departed, but we do seek answers. If these crimes are continuing and your information assists us in bringing the criminals to justice, then I am prepared to give proper credit to you for sharing what you choose." Uncle paused, securing Mr. Allan's full attention before he pulled a pouch of coins from his pocket. "And proper remuneration, of course."

Mr. Allan pocketed the purse eagerly. "I see you are a fair gentleman. I will tell you what I know." He looked at Darcy, then at Nick. "It started at Pemberley —your family's estate, I presume?"

Darcy nodded, too breathless to speak.

"Martha wasn't there, but she was a clever one who put two and two together. She heard of a midwife who required a young, fit nurse to assist her. Mrs. Finchley was recommended among the first circles; she had a reputation for never losing a lady." He added softly, "They ought to have been more concerned with the babes."

Darcy held his breath, as though his doing so would make Mr. Allan speak faster.

"She had another nurse at the time—Martha would never have agreed with the scheme, though she contrived to profit from it once it was done—a Mrs. Currey. In her business, it is not uncommon for child-less families of a certain class to offer exorbitant sums for an heir. I don't know the details, but something went wrong, and the deal went sour. They disposed of the child as they saw fit, and nobody except Mrs. Currey was the wiser. But it bothered her conscience. She threatened to reveal what Mrs. Finchley had done to the Darcys. Knowing where the child was, she went to fetch him." He rubbed his hands over his forearms.

"But Mrs. Currey never made it, did she?" Miss Rothschild prompted.

He shook his head. "Carriage accident. Mrs. Finchley lost no time replacing her nurse, a position Martha was eager to take, what with the woman's reputation of assisting fine ladies. But she was a curious sort, and she soon suspected that not all was right when Mrs. Finchley hired her only after assuring herself that Martha had no family or close friends. She even warned her against courting, but my work as a messenger never suited me for settling down. It was just as easy for me to meet Martha wherever she was than for us to make a home. She only went by Mrs. Brown at her employer's insistence—made her sound more mature and capable."

Elizabeth had been right. Darcy saw no satisfaction on her face, though—just voracious curiosity.

"Martha stole away for a couple of days. She learned about the first nurse and the accident, heard about the basket of blankets concealing a baby. When she met with me, she was more excited than I had ever seen her. She had a plan what would make our dreams a reality. No more riding at all hours in the rain and sleet for me; no more sleepless nights and agonizing days for her." He looked up sheepishly. "She made a deal with Mrs. Finchley: her silence for a healthy allowance every month."

Blackmail. As long as Mrs. Brown was in Mrs. Finchley's employ, that would have added up to a heavy sum ... and a firm motive. Years she had known, and she had said nothing. Years where his brother might have been restored to him, would never have been taken by pirates, would not have a price on his head or worry that his life would end at the end of a rope. Wrapping his arms over his chest, Darcy tried to tamper the bitterness rising within him. What Mrs. Brown had done was unconscionable.

Elizabeth's words were sharp. "She blackmailed Mrs. Finchley until the midwife grew tired of paying? You suspect murder?"

"I do. I don't know how, but I'm certain Mrs. Finchley is the reason Martha died."

"What of the other snatched babies?" Miss Rothschild asked, her tone urgent, desperate.

Mr. Allan shook his head firmly. "Martha only knew of the one instance. She never would have gotten mixed up in that."

Darcy was not so certain. And judging by the looks of everyone except Mr. Allan, they were not convinced of Mrs. Brown's innocence either.

Elizabeth looked like she would spit daggers. Alex twirled her fingers in the ringlets nearest the knife hidden in her hair. Miss Rothschild's cheeks were as red as her hair.

It was time to depart.

Mr. Bennet, who had been quietly observing the conversation, said, "You have been helpful, sir, and we thank you. Do you have any other observations or suspicions which might assist us regarding the other stolen children?"

"I do not, but I imagine the nurse Mrs. Finchley hired after Martha's death is either a hard-hearted accomplice in her employer's evil ways or is eager to be out from under her influence. You find her, you might get enough proof to send that murderer to—"Mr. Allan cleared his throat—"that place where people like her belong."

"Do you know her name?" Uncle asked.

"Mrs. Bird."

Mr. Bennet, being the only one whose voice was not choked with rage, bid their farewells and expressed what gratitude he could.

Another nurse?

On their way back to the carriages, Darcy asked Richard, "Did Mrs. Finchley not mention a third nurse?"

"She had no cause to, but the timing is right. Mrs. Brown died five years ago, and Mrs. Finchley only recently retired. As old as she is, she would require someone young and strong to help her."

"We must return to London. We do not know where Mrs. Bird might be found, but it is time we paid a call on Mrs. Finchley," said Uncle, his voice menacing.

# CHAPTER 41

*A*fter two days of hurried travel, the sight of Gracechurch Street was a comfort to Elizabeth and her weary travel companions. Her father bore it well, but Elizabeth had noticed how much stiffer he walked with every change of the horses—and especially since Newberry.

Alexandra detested being cooped up, but she did not complain. Instead she sat silently stewing like a simmering pot ready to boil over.

Emily, who was kind enough to allow them the use of her well-cushioned, newly springed carriage, did her best to put everyone at ease, but she was tired, too.

Elizabeth did not wait for the footman to hand her out. Stretching her legs, she ran down the path and up the steps to her aunt and uncle's waiting arms.

"Please, come inside and take some refreshment," Aunt insisted.

"You must be exhausted and hungry, and we are anxious to hear your news," Uncle added.

Aunt turned to Alexandra. "Edward said your ship will be inhabitable for some time. We hope you will consider staying here as our guest. The children are eager to meet you."

Emily said, "You are welcome to stay with me as well."

Alexandra smiled for the first time that day. "I've never had so many people willin' to show me hospitality." Taking Emily's hands, she said, "I thank ye for yer offer, but I feel I ought to stay with Lizzy."

Uncle motioned for them to sit, then took his place in the center of the grouping of chairs and sofas. "Then that is settled." The tea trays were brought in. "We are expecting Mr. Bingley for dinner, so I apologize that this repast is perhaps a bit lighter than you might have hoped. You are, of course, invited to dine with us." Looking at Papa, he added, "We knew to expect you after receiving your message from Bath."

Papa raised his eyebrows. "Mr. Bingley?"

Uncle chuckled. "He has been hanging around like a lost puppy. The only place he would rather be is at Longbourn near Jane, but knowing you were soon to return, I could not rightly give my consent for him to marry Jane when you could meet with him yourself." He leaned back, lacing his fingers over his stomach. "After hearing his story, I felt a little penitence would serve the young man well. Strengthen his determination not to make the same mistake of doubting Jane or allow himself to be so easily influenced again."

Elizabeth approved fully. She wanted only the best for her dearest sister, and while she was inclined to like Mr. Bingley very much, he lacked the strength of character she wished her sister's husband to possess.

Papa said, "That suits me well. Perhaps I shall suggest he accompany me to Longbourn on the morrow."

"So soon? It took me several days to recover from our jaunt through the country. I admire your stamina, Bennet," Uncle remarked.

Shaking his head, Papa declared, "I fear that if I stop to rest now, I shall not be able to get going again. You know your sister, Edward. Fanny will be beside herself without news, and I cannot permit dear Jane and Mary to bear the burden of her excessive nerves. Kitty is too senseless to be of any comfort."

He shrugged, but his furrowed brow told Elizabeth he had not completely dismissed the matter from his mind. She was glad of it. She loved her father dearly, but his ability to ignore the consequences of his indolence had contributed more to their current predicament than he would ever have previously owned.

They described the events of the past few days to Aunt and Uncle between sips of tea and nibbles of sandwiches.

Papa stirred his drink absently until a break in the conversation revealed his turn of thought. "You did well, Gardiner, and I thank you. Mr. Bingley and I have a great deal to discuss, for I shall not allow Jane to marry a young man any less steady and reliable than Mr. Darcy"—he looked from Elizabeth to Alexandra —"or his brother."

Alexandra grinned. "Yer unlikely to find any gent their equal. But I hope for yer daughter's sake that this Bingley fellah comes close."

Elizabeth was proud her father thought so highly of Fitzwilliam. Theirs had not been an easy courtship. However, for Jane's sake, she could not allow Mr. Bingley to seem as fickle as he must sound to her companions. "Mr. Bingley is everything affable, much like Jane."

As she spoke, it occurred to her that the colonel was the perfect combination of affability and dependability. She looked at Emily, but she said nothing. The struggle to contain her unbidden opinion helped her appreciate how natural it must have been for Fitzwilliam to offer his own opinion at Mr. Bingley's request.

Papa reached for a sandwich. "I intend to depart on the morrow, but I know Lizzy shall wish to stay."

Uncle did not hesitate. "Of course, she must stay until this business is resolved. We already have the guest room ready, and she and Miss Alexandra shall be as comfortable as we can make them. I daresay His Lordship will continue tirelessly in his endeavors on behalf of his nephews and shall soon have news to impart."

"Have you received word from Matlock House in our absence?" Elizabeth asked. Miss Darcy must have been beside herself with worry over her brothers.

Aunt replied, "No, but I did not expect any while Edward was gone, as I have not yet met His Lordship or the countess, nor did I feel it appropriate for me to call before we have been introduced. One simply does not show up on the doorstep of an earl's residence and expect to be admitted."

Elizabeth could have described how wrong her aunt was, but she would find out for herself soon enough. Lord Matlock used his position to his advantage, but he was not haughty or above humbler company.

Emily set her teacup and saucer on the table. "If I am to call with the gentlemen on Mrs. Finchley on the morrow, I had better get some rest."

"Do you think they will allow you to join them?" Elizabeth asked, knowing the answer as well as Emily must.

"No, but they cannot prevent it. They know very well that if they do not allow me to accompany them, I am determined enough to go alone … and they will never allow that."

"What if she does not receive you?"

"The colonel has already called on her, and surely she cannot refuse His Lordship. I will take those odds."

"Then I wish you success in the use of your persuasive arts." Elizabeth was only half teasing.

They said their farewells and made plans to meet again on the morrow after their call on Mrs. Finchley.

While Elizabeth had no reason to be present for the meeting, she could not deny how much she wished she could be there. The colonel's descriptions of the sweet elderly lady conflicted so much with the evidence they had heard against her, Elizabeth was curious to meet her … from a distance, surrounded by several gentlemen capable of protecting her.

Elizabeth turned to the stairs, eager to wash, change out of her travel-worn gown, and rest before dinner.

The knocker on the door stopped her before she reached the second step. *Rap-rap-rap!* The rapid staccato communicated an urgency which set all her nerves on point and made her think, What now?

It was a message from Matlock House addressed to Uncle. He read it, saying aloud as his gaze reread the page, "Mrs. Annesley is missing. She has been gone for a full week."

Aunt asked, "She is Miss Darcy's companion, is she not?"

Elizabeth sank to sit on the step. "Why would she disappear?"

Papa handed the message back to Uncle. "Evidently, she left a note begging them not to attempt to find her. Lady Helen wisely entrusted the matter to her husband's man of business, but she feared doing anything more until Lord Matlock's return lest Mrs. Annesley come to some harm." He looked at Elizabeth.

"Miss Darcy is greatly distressed, as you can imagine. Matlock requests that you call on the morrow. He prays they shall have some news to impart by then."

"Of course, I shall go to her." The poor dear! First her brothers, and now her trusted companion.

Papa crossed the room, stopping short in front of Alexandra. "I cannot delay my return to Longbourn any longer than I already have, especially when my presence is not necessary in this matter. However, I shall secure your promise that you will not endanger my daughter or allow Elizabeth to put herself in the way of further peril."

Alexandra puffed up to her full height, lips pinching into a thin line, but something happened at the height of her offense to calm her expression. "That's fair enough—after all the trouble I've caused ye. I swear I'll be as meek as a lamb, Mr. Bennet. I swear on the North Star."

Papa leveled his gaze at her. "I trust you to honor your word." Then he turned that same severe gaze at Elizabeth. "I shall also require your promise not to become involved in this business with Mrs. Finchley and Mrs. Annesley. Leave Lord Matlock, Mr. Darcy, and Mr. Blackburne to handle their own affairs as efficiently and thoroughly as we know them capable of doing."

Elizabeth could not see what she could possibly do to find Mrs. Annesley, and she had already begrudgingly accepted that she would not get to meet Mrs.

Finchley. She would comfort Miss Darcy from the safety of Matlock House as best as she could and allow the gentlemen to bring Mrs. Finchley's sins to light without her interference.

"I swear on every book in your library, I shall not interfere or knowingly put myself in any danger." It was an easy promise to make, even easier to keep.

# CHAPTER 42

*D*arcy woke early after a night of fitful dozing. Georgiana and Aunt Helen had searched Mrs. Annesley's room, but there had not been much to see. She appeared to have left in haste, taking little more than a change of clothing with her.

There had been a locked box behind the gowns in her armoire. Nick wanted to open it. But even under the circumstances, it seemed wrong to open Mrs. Annesley's personal cache. The likelihood that they would find anything inside pertaining to her disappearance seemed minimal.

And yet the slight possibility had robbed Darcy of sleep. He had dreamed of smashing the box to pieces—in one variation finding a relevant clue that solved everything from Nick's kidnapping and Mrs. Finchley's role to Mrs. Annesley's location, and in the next, finding nothing at all.

Elizabeth called early with Alexandra and the Gardiners. Darcy was grateful. He did not know how to comfort Georgiana when he felt at odds and ends himself.

They all convened around the table in the morning parlor, ignoring the generously apportioned sideboard when they could take comfort in each other's company.

Uncle took the coffee Aunt poured, explaining, "Helen sent a message the moment they discovered Mrs. Annesley's disappearance, but we had already departed for Bath and, while I informed her in a letter of our plans, I do not recall making mention of it to the innkeeper. It must have been enough of a delay to prevent the messenger from delivering his message to us at Bath."

Aunt added, "Georgiana and I searched Mrs. Annesley's room and interviewed every member of the household. They offered to make inquiries amongst their friends and relatives, but so far we have learned nothing."

Both Elizabeth and Alex leaned closer to Georgie. She had not touched her tea.

Uncle related, "Darcy hired another detective, aside from my man." He looked intently at Georgie. "We shall find her."

Elizabeth asked, "Should we send for Miss Rothschild?"

Richard said, "As far as we know, Mrs. Annesley's disappearance has nothing to do with her."

Alex contended, "Seems like she should be here. She's clever."

Aunt rang for paper and her writing utensils. "I shall send for Miss Rothschild at once." Before Uncle had finished relating the rest of their efforts to find Georgie's companion, she had sent a footman off with her note.

Next began a discussion of Mrs. Annesley herself. Did she have any family? Close friends? What about her references? How had she come to be in Darcy's employ? What did they know of the woman?

Darcy was ashamed at how little he really knew. She had no family. Few friends. Her references had been impeccable, but when it came down to it, he had been so anxious to secure a safe companion for Georgiana after the debacle with Wickham, he could not quite recall the details of how Mrs. Annesley had come into their lives. He supposed they had been introduced by a mutual friend, and that she had been recommended by the same.

What he clearly remembered was how cautious he had been—following his mistaken judgment in Mrs. Younge, he had to have been. Then why could he not recall the particulars?

Miss Rothschild arrived at the peak of Darcy's frustration. But it was not until Nick brought up the box in the armoire that Darcy's guilt ceased flagellating his conscience.

"A hidden box? Let's see it!" Alex leapt to her feet like a pirate in possession of a treasure map.

Nick looked at him, his expression asking if Darcy had changed his mind. What was the greater wrong: searching through a lady's personal property or failing to pursue a clue which might reveal her whereabouts? Was it even a clue? Probably not ... but it might be. Darcy nodded, quick to commit to a decision that had taken him all night to ponder.

Uncle rubbed his chin. "I lost a great deal of sleep over that box last night. It seems unlikely it should help us find Mrs. Annesley when, in all likelihood, it holds the usual trinkets and trifles a lady's memory box contains. But as long as there is a possibility—no matter how slim it might be—that it conceals a clue as to her whereabouts, I believe that for the lady's welfare, we ought to look." He rested his palm over his wife's hand on top of the table. "Helen, you are abreast of recent events, and you were here when she slipped away. As the lady of the house, you can preserve a measure of Mrs. Annesley's privacy by searching through the items in the box. I trust your discretion."

Aunt nodded. "Very well. If I find anything pertaining to our search, then I shall share it. If there is nothing, Mrs. Annesley's secrets are safe with me."

They filed up the stairs to the guest chambers, where Mrs. Annesley's room joined Georgiana's.

Aunt Helen removed the box from the armoire,

twisting the square from side to side. "Did you, perhaps, find a key?"

Alex reached out. "I'll help with that."

Aunt raised her eyebrows, but she handed it over.

Plucking a pin out of her hair, Alex turned the box around so that the hinges faced her, shoved the pins through their fastenings, and opened it in a matter of seconds.

Aunt took the box to a chair set in the corner, and Darcy held his breath as he heard her shuffle and poke through the items inside. Then the rustle of pages … and silence.

When Aunt Helen turned, her face was ashen white. Her hand trembled as she handed the papers to Uncle.

He took one glance, his hand raising to his throat, then out to steady himself against the armoire.

A clue.

Darcy could contain himself no longer. "What? What is it?"

Uncle held the papers out to him, speechless.

Richard and Elizabeth closed in on his sides; Nick read over his shoulder.

The first name at the top of the list. *Darcy—sold.* Only the word *sold* had been crossed out, and beside it was written *disposed.*

He shuffled through the pages. There were half a dozen of them, crammed with names and words such as *fostered, adopted, sold,* and *disposed.*

So intent was he on his name, the first in the

hundreds of surnames listed, Darcy handed the rest of the pages to Richard without looking up. He heard Richard's rough finger run down the parchment, heard his gasp, and his pained, "Rothschild is on the list. *Rothschild, adopted.*"

Miss Rothschild was at his side in a flash, leaning over him as she read and tried to blink away her tears. "I knew it," she whispered.

A swishing sound at the door alerted them to a visitor, and Darcy looked up to see Mrs. Annesley standing beside the butler in the hall. She stumbled forward, hand clutching her throat. "Did you find it? Oh, I had hoped you would. This saves us valuable time. I dared not appear until you had returned." She hastened over to the curtains, drawing them closed. "She has men watching the house."

"Who? Mrs. Finchley?" Darcy asked.

"She has dozens in her employ. Her resources are limitless. She will know I am here with you. We must take this evidence to the authorities immediately before she escapes."

Miss Rothschild crumpled the handkerchief in her hand. "Wait, who are you? How did you get this list?"

Alex looped her arm through Miss Rothschild's, her eyes narrow. "Why should we trust you?"

Georgiana clung to Aunt Helen. "If you knew about Mrs. Finchley's dealings, why have you not spoken up before?"

Mrs. Annesley wrung her hands, her voice desperate. "Every minute lost is a minute to her advantage."

"First, we must have some answers," Uncle demanded. "What is your role in this atrocity?"

All eyes turned to Mrs. Annesley. Darcy felt Elizabeth's hand near his, and he reached for her, needing to hold her. Needing her support.

# CHAPTER 43

*M*rs. Annesley bowed her head. Taking a deep breath, she began, speaking rapidly. "My real name is Mrs. Bird. My husband died two years after our marriage. Consumption. We were not blessed with children of our own and, being an only child, I had always wanted a large family. My mother was a midwife, and after I had married, she taught me her trade. The fever took her, and I was truly alone. Widowed and of meager means, I sought employment. I remember the day I first met Mrs. Finchley." She pinched her eyes closed and took a deep breath.

Darcy leaned forward, willing her to return to her narrative. Elizabeth wrapped her fingers around his, and Darcy pulled her closer.

"She had the reputation of never losing a lady," Mrs. Annesley continued, her voice edgy and bitter. "She was so knowledgeable and kind. How I wish I had never crossed paths with her. She is a monster." Mrs. Annesley's chest heaved.

After a few calming breaths, she resumed her story. "After assisting her with a birth, during which she observed my skills, she asked me to work as her nurse. She offered me a higher wage than my mother ever made. I ought to have known, I ought to have been suspicious, but her clientele was of a higher status than I was accustomed to. I dismissed my doubts and took the position. When she swore me to secrecy and indebted me to her by securing me a more presentable wardrobe along with new instruments, I assumed she was only being kind, only protecting the reputations of the ladies she assisted—not all of them being wed, mind you. Midwives must be discreet above all else if our services are to be sought after."

A nauseating twist turned Darcy's stomach. He looked at Georgiana, who looked as ill as he felt.

"Are you willing for Miss Darcy to hear the rest?" Mrs. Annesley asked.

Aunt Helen wrapped her arm around Georgiana. "Keep the details to a minimum. But she has a right to know what happened to her brother."

"Very well." Mrs. Annesley took another deep breath and resumed, "Mrs. Finchley is a skilled midwife, but that pales in comparison to her role as a procurer."

"Please explain," Uncle said.

"She procures children for families willing to pay to adopt or foster. For a greater sum, she procures a child for barren couples in need of an heir. She procures young ladies from privileged families for her lying-in houses. For a fee, she sees the lady through her confinement and disposes of her inconvenient child, thus preserving the family's dignity and the lady's reputation."

Elizabeth raised her hand to her mouth, gasping between her fingers. "Disposes? You cannot mean … she murders babies?"

Darcy felt acid burning in his throat. All those names, all the times *disposed* was written beside them.

"There is no delicate way to put it. Quiet death, natal death … they are all the same. The babe is starved to death after its birth, making it look as though it was stillborn or died during birth. It is impossible for the doctors to know the difference, and by the time he arrives, the young lady is removed as though nothing has happened."

"What of the children who survived?" Darcy asked. Like Nick. *Sold*, then *disposed*.

"They were sold. Some as slaves, the more fortunate to prominent families. Others were adopted, such as in Miss Rothschild's case." Mrs. Annesley bowed her head, her voice soft. "I am so sorry you have lived with doubt all your life when I might have eased your mind. Had I met you earlier, I would like to think I would have found a way to tell you the truth."

"You know my story? You knew my real mother? My father?" Miss Rothschild's voice choked.

"Mr. Rothschild's sister suffered the consequences of her indiscretion. She was only fifteen and innocent in the ways of the world, as is too often the case with young ladies of the gentle class. The family sent her to one of Mrs. Finchley's lying-in houses, a discreet cottage in the country the villagers know not to ask questions about. She bore a healthy child—a girl with flaming red hair. Just like her mother, I was told."

"Me?" Miss Rothschild's legs buckled, and Richard wrapped his arm around her waist before she dropped.

"Miss Rothschild, apparently your mother refused to give up her child. She wrote to her brother expressing her wishes. But she died of a fever not one month later. He paid Mrs. Finchley for her silence, and he adopted you as his own."

"He really was my family after all?" Miss Rothschild whispered. "And my father? Do you know who he is?"

"I am sorry, I do not know. There were so many children. I only know of your case because it was one of the first I came across after accepting my position as Mrs. Brown's replacement. She started this list. A maid in a lying-in house slipped it to me."

"Why did you not come forth? Why the silence until now?" Miss Rothschild whimpered.

"There are no laws against what she was doing. What Mrs. Finchley was doing was respectable … on the surface. She was providing a safe haven for ladies in a terrible situation, and she was procuring homes for some of the infants. It would have been her word against mine, and I had no basis other than this list left behind by Mrs. Brown to make any accusations. Once I realized what happened to the children deemed 'inconvenient,' I started adding to this list, collecting my own proof. I befriended the other midwives and nurses she trained. They knew I had Mrs. Finchley's confidence, so I was able to gather a good deal of names and stories. Most of them appreciated the opportunity to admit the truth to someone who would not turn them in. We were all indebted to Mrs. Finchley, you see. She made certain of that. And anyone who got too greedy or had a change of conscience ended up dead. Like Mrs. Currey. And Mrs. Brown."

Richard held up the pages. "This is a great deal of evidence."

"I thought that if I could secure enough to thoroughly accuse her of her crimes, she might be stopped. Her influence is strong. One word from her, and some of the most influential families in England would be embroiled in scandal. These are people who will do anything to cover over their indiscretions."

As much as Darcy wanted to argue, Mrs. Annesley was right. If it became known that an heir of an established family in the first circles was adopted or otherwise procured, their privilege and status would be endangered. The scandal would be unbearable.

Mrs. Annesley continued, "But I asked too many

questions. Some of the nurses grew suspicious of me, and I was found out. Mrs. Finchley threatened me. She told me how easily she had disposed of her first two nurses. One suffered from a sensitive conscience and would have destroyed the operation before she had a chance to fully establish her planned business. The other had blackmailed her for years and got too greedy for her own good. She would have killed me had her pistol not misfired. I ran. With the list and the money I always sewed into my gown, I made my way to Ramsgate." She met Darcy's eyes. "And that was where I recognized your surname from the list. Her first victim."

"Why did she do it?" Darcy asked.

"A family of the aristocracy had approached Mrs. Finchley some time before. They were willing to pay an exorbitant sum for an heir, and while she had no idea how to provide them with what they wanted, she recognized the opportunity your mother presented to her. An heir and a spare."

Richard gasped. "When I spoke with Mrs. Finchley, she told me she always took advantage of opportunities that fell into her lap." He rubbed his hand over his face. "Had I only known how literally she spoke."

Darcy tucked Elizabeth's hand in his arm, close to his chest. "How did my mother not know? Was nobody else in the room?"

"Evidently, the birth had exhausted Lady Anne so greatly, she was too weak to even notice what

383

happened. When the second twin came, Mrs. Finchley told her it was the afterbirth. Her Ladyship was none the wiser. It was her first child, and she trusted the highly recommended midwife. The nurse snuck the baby out of Pemberley in a basket of blankets she said she was taking to the wash."

Nick crossed his arms. "I didn't end up with no fine family."

Mrs. Annesley bunched her cheeks. "The family you were supposed to go to—I do not know their names, so you may save your breath—they had intended to live on the continent. The arrangement suited Mrs. Finchley perfectly. After all, she could not allow you to meet each other or risk a mutual acquaintance associating you together. But the gentleman's father died suddenly, and he had to assume the responsibilities of his inheritance immediately. It was a real problem. She could not sell you to the family as she had intended, nor could she return you to the Darcys."

Alex huffed, "So she dumped me Nick off at an old fisherman's hut?"

"Just so."

Darcy felt Elizabeth's fingers pinch his arm. "Why did you continue in this deception? Did you not have enough evidence to take to the authorities? That list is impressive in its length."

Mrs. Annesley shook her head. "The prosecution would have fallen squarely on my shoulders. Mrs. Finchley would have discredited me before I could even present my proofs. She would have the complete support of the families intent on keeping their secrets safe." She turned to Uncle. "Had I told you that your own nephew had a secret twin, would you have believed me?"

"I see your point," he admitted.

She turned to Darcy, her eyes pleading for a reply.

He had to own to the truth. "I would not have believed you until I saw Nick with my own eyes."

Her shoulders relaxed. "I would have exposed myself and secured nothing more than my own death sentence. All those children, all those families who have no idea what really happens at her lying-in houses … they would continue in their ignorance while those innocent babies are slaughtered right under their noses —their own kin. When I saw Miss Darcy, saw that she was of an age to require a companion, I made myself available. What safer place could I find than with the Darcys—a family Mrs. Finchley avoided for the failure and danger they represented to her?"

Darcy straightened. "Your references were impeccable. I checked them myself."

Clasping her hands together and looking down, she said, "Forgive me, sir, but after years surrounded by criminals, it was not very hard to fake my references. A few coins here and a few well-placed mentions at the right places there … I know it was wrong to deceive you, and my guilt has increased with every kindness you and Miss Darcy have extended to me. I accept full responsibility for my deception. I lied to you to secure my position. I kept silent when I might have spoken. I know you to be a gentleman of strict values and unbending honor, but I hope your sense of justice will encourage you to trust me now."

Strict and unbending. Months before, Darcy would have taken Mrs. Annesley's assessment of his character as a compliment. Today, they felt like blows. Swallowing his tattered pride, he asked, "Why did you flee?"

"Mrs. Finchley called here, at Matlock House. She recognized me. I knew she would come after me, and I feared Miss Darcy might come to harm should she attempt to protect me. Fleeing was the only way I could keep Georgiana away from that monster until you returned and I could throw myself on your mercy and beg you to help me put an end to this devastating business." Pressing her hands together in supplication, she pleaded, "Please, let us help those ladies and children in her clutches, and then you may do with me what you feel is best. I shall not run from you."

Nick leaned closer to Darcy. "We've tarried long enough. Why waste time on this fish when there be a bigger shark in the waters?"

Darcy nodded. Nick was right. He addressed Mrs. Annesley. "We must go after Mrs. Finchley immediately. How you act henceforth shall determine how we deal with you later."

"Thank you, sir," she answered gratefully.

Georgiana went to her, wrapping her arms around

her shoulders. "My brothers are fair. You can trust them."

"They have already been more understanding with me than I had dared to hope. I will not abuse their kindness."

Uncle cleared his throat, commanding attention. "Darcy, Nick, you shall accompany me to Mrs. Finchley's residence. We shall ensure she is in and keep guard to ensure she does not attempt to escape until the authorities arrive. Richard, you shall accompany Mrs. Annesley and Miss Rothschild to Bow Street. Summon Mr. Rouncewell and as many constables as you can to meet us."

Mr. Gardiner prepared to take his leave. "We shall return to Gracechurch Street. If I may be of any service, please do not hesitate to send for me. However, right now I believe my wife and I shall feel better once we have seen our children are safe with their nurse."

"Of course. I shall keep you informed of any further developments," Uncle offered.

Alex tugged on Elizabeth's hand, pulling Darcy with her. "Then we'll return to Gracechurch Street with ye. I'll go mad not knowin' what's happenin', but I promised Mr. Bennet I'd keep her safe."

With a parting squeeze, Elizabeth let go of Darcy. It took all of his resolve not to pull her back into his arms. She smiled at him, and her parting image haunted him across town as his sense of loss deepened.

## CHAPTER 44

"*D*o you trust this Mr. Rouncewell explicitly?" Mrs. Annesley asked. Even knowing her surname was an assumed one, Richard could not bring himself to think of her as Mrs. Bird. There had been enough upheaval for one day without adding another complication.

"Yes. He is a good man—a man without a price."

Mrs. Annesley clasped her hands together and looked out of the carriage window. "Such men are rare, Colonel."

Unfortunately, she was right. Otherwise an operation such as Mrs. Finchley's could never have succeeded. Life should be precious, priceless. But there were too many who would not hesitate to trade life for a fortune without a second thought.

Turning away from the window, Mrs. Annesley relayed, "Too many runners and even a couple of the magistrates are under Mrs. Finchley's thumb. They have relatives who have benefited from her services."

Richard understood her concern. "I shall speak only with Rouncewell. Once he sees your list, he will know whom to avoid and whom to approach."

Mrs. Annesley handed the papers to him. "Here, you keep them."

They saw Rouncewell leaving the office just as their carriage clattered to a stop. "I must catch him!" Clutching the list in his hand, Richard jumped onto the pavement and chased after his friend.

Rouncewell must have heard his hasty approach, for he spun around, fists raised. He dropped them to his side immediately once he recognized Richard. "You gave me a fright, Colonel." His expression turned grave. "What has happened?"

Richard shoved the list at his friend. "We have enough evidence to prove that Mrs. Finchley is the head of an extensive operation trafficking children, from newborns sold to wealthy families to older children taken for ransom or sold into slavery. The inconvenient births are"—the word tasted bitter and awful crossing his tongue—"murdered."

Rouncewell clutched his stomach and grimaced as his eyes read down the page. "I have only recently heard of the practice. 'Baby farming' they're calling it. Monsters, the lot."

"If we can charge Mrs. Finchley with the crimes she has committed, then we might be able to discourage the practice. My father is watching her residence with Darcy and Nick to ensure she does not attempt to escape, but we dare not apprehend her without the involvement of the law."

"I will summon a couple more constables."

Richard grabbed his arm. "Only men you trust. She is a slippery one; her reach is far."

With a nod, Rouncewell bounded back inside the office.

Mrs. Annesley and Miss Rothschild paced on the pavement near the entrance with the colonel standing between them and the street. Their carriage had to continue around the square or risk the angry shouts and jeers from all the conveyances it obstructed. Richard prayed Rouncewell would have his men ready by their carriage's return. They were so close, any delay was unbearable, as was their risk of exposure.

A flower girl with chapped cheeks, a shift too light for the coming winter, and shoes that clapped against the sidewalk as she scurried over to them pressed a posy of daisies she had probably plucked from nearby Hyde Park against Richard's hand. She was no taller than his elbow. Following her was an older girl, better dressed, with bunches of flowers in a handbasket. "Two bundles a penny, primroses! Sweet violets, penny a bunch!" she called out.

The little girl scowled and pressed, looking up at Richard with a fierce determination that undid his resolve not to part with a coin. "These is the finest daisies to be found in town, sir! Halfpenny a bunch!"

"Those weeds? I saw you pick them at the park." The girl with the basket held up a posy of vibrant violets. "These come from a flower shop and will not wilt before you give them to your lady."

The little girl slid her grip up the stalks of her drooping daisies, holding them upright. She nudged her wilted daisies against his hand, as though to remind him of her continued presence.

Stooping over and dropping his voice so as not to be overheard, Richard pulled a few pennies out of his pocket—enough for her to eat that day. The girl's eyes widened, and she licked her lips. "I only have the one little bunch, sir."

"And I shall give you these coins for your daisies so long as you promise me you will go directly to the baker and buy yourself some bread."

"I could get a meat pie!" Quick as a flip of the whip, she shoved the flowers into his hand, grabbed the coins, and ran.

Richard watched her, content that her belly would soon be full. It was a small consolation when he knew she would only wake hungry on the morrow.

He held up the flowers, inspecting them. The daisies around the edge were wilted from the heat of her little hand, but the three or four daisies in the middle were in fine shape. Tossing the worst into the street, he joined the ladies.

Mrs. Annesley tapped her foot and watched the entrance of the Bow Street office intently. She gave no indication she had even seen or heard the flower girls. Miss Rothschild, on the other hand, smiled wider the closer he drew to her. Her sunny reception warmed Richard from top to bottom.

"You paid too much for those flowers," she observed.

Richard's face warmed with something other than pleasure. He had not intended to be overheard, to show her how easily he was manipulated by a small child with ill-gotten flowers. He tried to think of something clever to say, but the warmth in Miss Rothschild's eyes melted him inside, and he found no words at all. Certainly not clever ones.

Dumbly, he held the daisies out to her, wishing they were roses or lilies or something more elegant.

He had not thought it possible for her smile to brighten, but Miss Rothschild's emerald eyes sparkled as she reached out to take the flowers, her fingers brushing lightly over his and nearly knocking him over with the force of her touch. He widened his stance to avoid falling and making a worse fool of himself.

"How did you know that daisies are my favorite flower?" She took the largest bloom and tucked it into the buttonhole of her redingote. The others, she pressed into a book she pulled out from her reticule, beaming at Richard all the while and making him feel like he had truly done something grand and heroic.

Before Richard could compose an adequate reply—or any reply at all, for that matter—his father's carriage stopped along the pavement, and Rouncewell joined them with two other constables. "You lead the way, Colonel, and we'll follow," he said, hopping into a hackney behind them.

Right. Back to Mrs. Finchley. Richard handed the ladies into their conveyance, and by the time they reached Bloomsbury, he had convinced himself that Miss Rothschild's smile had not been as brilliant as he had imagined.

Father handed the ladies out of the carriage while Darcy paid the constables' fare. "Three carriages arriving in a string," Father grumbled. "We will have drawn some attention."

"You have not seen anything out of place?" Richard asked.

"No, but I am concerned. Nick approached a maid seen leaving Mrs. Finchley's residence, and when he asked if her mistress was in, the maid scurried away. He is afraid he spoke too forcefully or that his presence scared her, but I fear it is something else."

Their corps crossed the street, Father taking the lead with Richard beside him.

The first sign that something was amiss was at the door. The knocker had been removed.

Then the butler opened the door before Father's knuckles touched against the painted wood. "I regret to inform you that Mrs. Finchley is not in." His stuffy voice belied sharp eyes that took in every detail of his mistress' callers.

Prepared for such a reply, Father handed the butler his card, which only served to make the man stand stiffer. Smoothly, Father asked, "When do you expect her back?"

"I cannot say, Your Lordship. She gave no instructions."

Nick nudged himself between them. "Not in, me eye! Stand aside, mister, unless ye want me to stomp over ye."

The butler shifted his weight ever so slightly behind the door but otherwise held his ground.

Darcy spoke. "You can have no doubt why we are here, and who these men are." He motioned to the constables behind him. "If you are protecting your employer, you shall be held in contempt of the law."

The butler swallowed hard. With a sniff, he straightened his shoulders, though Richard noted how he managed to take one more step behind the protection of the door in the process. Nick saw his opportunity and stepped into the opening, half in and half out, and thoroughly confounding the butler by preventing him from closing the door.

"Sh-she departed," he gasped. "I do not know where or when she plans to return, and that is the truth."

Rouncewell disappeared around the back of the house. He would check the butler's story with the other servants.

Richard leveled his glare at the man, using his most authoritative tone, the one he spared for those insubordinates in danger of stepping out of line. "When precisely did she depart?"

"Th-three"—the butler cleared his throat—"days ago."

"Three days!" Miss Rothschild gasped. "She could be anywhere by now."

Richard turned back to the butler. He knew more, and Richard would ensure he learned what that was. Tossing a look at Nick, who seemed to grow in the doorway, towering and glowering at the shrinking butler, Richard asked, "Where do you think she went?"

Another half step behind the door. "I-I cannot be entirely sure. B-but it is my belief, she may be on h-her way to-to Ireland. More than that, I really cannot say."

Rouncewell returned. "The cook and the groom report that the lady of the house departed three days ago, leaving no instructions for her return."

It matched what the butler said.

Drat. Richard clenched his teeth.

"Lord Matlock—" began Nick.

"For the final time, I am your uncle," Father snapped.

Nick made to object, but Father raised his hand. "You once lamented that you were in my debt. Well, I have settled on a satisfactory recompense. You address me properly as a nephew ought to, and I shall consider your debt erased. Now, what were you going to say, Nephew?"

Richard tugged his hair. Father and Nick's bickering would not produce Mrs. Finchley. Where would she go? If they split up, they could ask at the port towns, but she might have already left England.

"Our jurisdiction is London. If she has fled from the country, there is little we can do to capture her," Rouncewell admitted. "I am sorry, but there are few men willing to chase a criminal so far without guarantee of a reward. Most are thieves themselves."

That was it! It was such a simple solution, Richard wondered why he had not thought of it sooner. "I know such a man."

CHAPTER 45

$\mathcal{U}$ncle placed one hand on Nick's shoulder, another on Darcy's. Nick's chest tightened to be the recipient of such care from a man he respected and admired. His uncle.

"Your betrothed shall need to be informed of this development." Uncle lowered his hands. "Go to them. I will see where Mr. Rouncewell's questionings lead us with Richard and Miss Rothschild, and I shall secure Connell's services in tracking her down." He looked over their shoulders, his gaze darting back and forth. "If I know Connell, he is nearby."

A stiff west breeze brushed past them. An ill wind that sent a shiver down Nick's spine.

Uncle felt it too. "Go," he urged.

They ran to the carriage, Darcy calling "To Gracechurch Street!" in a manner that left the coachman in no doubt of their need for haste.

Darcy wedged his knees against the cushion, and Nick was grateful he imitated his brother's posture when the carriage jolted and turned abruptly. "He used to race curricles before he came to work for me," Darcy explained.

Nick chuckled. "Ye know how to pick a fine crew."

"My estate is only as sound as the people in my employ."

"Just like me ship."

"It is not so different. We are both masters in our own domains."

"'Cept yer quarters're far more extensive than me frigate. Over one hundred men occupying one hundred thirty-five feet from bow to stern gets crowded."

"You shall love Pemberley. High ceilings and large rooms indoors, rolling green hills and forests as far as you can see out of doors."

The shelter he'd never known. The place he'd have played with his brother and cousins instead of mending nets with raw fingers in a damp hut. Where he'd have been loved by a mother and father instead of working to pay his way until he was old enough to apprentice on a ship with nothing but the shirt on his back and a pair of castoff shoes that didn't fit. Not that Nick carried any resentment toward the old man who'd taken him in. He'd fed him, taught him a trade, let him learn to read, and never raised his hand against Nick. He'd even given him his name. After knowing what his fate was supposed to have been, Nick was grateful for his life.

He rubbed his chest. "Sounds lovely, Darcy." So lovely, he didn't want to see it until he'd learned to control his resentment. He'd make peace with the past, then he'd embrace his future with no reserves. His family deserved as much, and so did he.

The carriage slowed. They were close.

Darcy peeked through the glass, leaning forward abruptly. "What is that blackguard doing here?"

Nick snapped to attention. The door to the Gardiners' house was open, and Wickham stood in the entrance with his arms crossed, a smirk on his mug. Nick clenched his fists at the sight. He'd love to draw that man's cork. The slimy eel wouldn't think himself so charming with blood running out of his nose and staining his starched shirt.

Darcy descended from the carriage and charged across the street. Nick tried to catch up with him to prevent him from doing what he would do for the both of them.

But he was too late.

The fool lifted his chin haughtily. "Not so high and mighty now, are you, Darcy?"

Leaping up the steps, fist raised, Darcy landed a solid shot right where Nick had imagined punching only moments ago.

Wickham's reaction was most satisfying. Shriveling

into himself, covering his face, he sputtered and moaned.

Darcy was too dignified to gloat or exchange a word with the rogue. He breezed past Wickham, where the Gardiners' man attempted to suppress a smile. "They are in the parlor, sir," he announced.

"Thank you, Perrot," Darcy answered coolly, as though nothing had transpired. He was so smooth and composed, and Nick could not be prouder. *That* was his brother.

Reaching into his pocket, he pulled out a handkerchief and tossed it to Wickham before continuing into the parlor. He could be smooth, too.

Connell stood when they entered. The satisfaction on his face stopped Nick short.

"My uncle was looking for you," Darcy said.

Mr. Gardiner rubbed his temples. His wife stood behind him, clutching the back of his chair. Elizabeth's jaw clenched, and Alex cast him a look that tensed every muscle in Nick's body.

Connell stood. Gesturing at the Gardiners, he stated, "This family is harboring a known criminal."

"His Lordship, the Earl of Matlock—"

Connell raised his hand, stopping Darcy short. "Not *that* criminal." His smile widened and he pointed at Alex. "That one. *She* is wanted for crimes against the Crown."

Alex's nostrils flared. "I am not!" She attempted to

stand, but Elizabeth reached for her arm to prevent it. Less confidently, she added, "I don't think."

Nick could reach into his boot and rid them of Connell with one flick of his dagger. He dismissed the idea the instant it reared its ugly head in Nick's mind. Aye, they'd be free of Connell, but he'd have murdered a man in cold blood in front of people who believed him changed. He couldn't betray their trust like that.

There had to be another way. He met Alex's gaze, and was relieved to see her fingers relax at his warning look.

Darcy stepped closer, his shoulders brushing against Nick's. When Nick looked at him, Darcy winked. Twice.

Nick tensed again. Whenever Alex winked like that, disaster was soon to follow.

Standing taller, Darcy nodded at Nick. Understanding that he must be on his best behavior, Nick lowered his shoulders and lifted his chin. At least, Darcy appeared to have a plan ... which was more than Nick had. When Wickham slithered through the doorway behind them, Nick expanded his chest as Darcy did. Wickham scurried behind Connell like a scared cur.

Darcy spoke again. "Ye don't wish to cross Lord Matlock. He—"

Nick's eyes widened. What was Darcy doing?

"His Lordship is not here." Connell failed to notice what so completely unnerved Nick. Could the man not tell them apart? "And even if he were, he can't protect her."

Cold fear gripped Nick by the throat. If they took Alex, he'd never get her back. It wouldn't matter that she'd changed. She'd pay not only for her previous crimes but for her brothers'. Their infamy was too grand. The Admiralty would make a show of her hanging, using her to send a warning to those who raised their glasses in her name and sang the poems revering her exploits ... just as they'd have done to him. They'd exact their revenge on her all the more cruelly because they'd still be sore from being forced to let him go.

Connell jabbed his thumb over his shoulder. "This gentleman said you assaulted him at Bath ... and it would seem you have done it again."

Handkerchief stuffed up his nose, Wickham grumbled, "Once a pirate, always a pirate."

Darcy opened his mouth to defend him, but Nick shook his head. It didn't matter what he said. People would always assume the worst of Nick, and he wouldn't allow his brother to lose face before a man like Connell. He'd only accuse Nick of being a corrupting influence, and Darcy would be in danger. Nick would not allow it.

Taking courage, Connell added, "Furthermore, the Gardiners can be accused as accomplices. They knew they were housing a renowned criminal."

That, Nick could not allow either. He spoke in his most dignified tone, trying to imitate the authority with which his brother exercised his influence. "I asked them to. They're only doing so as a favor to me. They trusted my word and had no inclination of their guest's former activities."

Connell looked between him and Darcy, confusion marking his brow.

Out of the corner of his eye, Nick saw Darcy wink at him again. Dear Neptune, what was he up to? Nick watched Darcy closely, trying to figure out his plan, but Darcy didn't reveal anything. Drat the pest.

With a parting raise of his eyebrow that filled Nick with dread, Darcy offered, "Leave the Gardiners be, and I'll come with ye."

If Darcy was trying to confuse Connell, he'd be the one to end up behind bars, and Nick refused to go along with it. Crossing his arms over his chest, praying his imitation was as sound as Darcy's had been, he asserted, "I will come with you. I am the man you want."

Darcy, the stubborn blighter, jabbed his thumb at his chest. "'Tis a lie. I'm the man ye want."

If lives weren't at stake, Nick would have laughed at the sight of Connell scratching his head.

"If ye want to arrest Nicholas Blackburne, ye'll have to pick yer man." Darcy grinned, his eyes pleading with Nick to go along with the farce. Under his breath, he added, "Think of Alex."

In that exchange, Nick understood. His brother was willing to go to prison to save Alex. Uncle might not be able to secure Nick's release again, but he could for Darcy. He'd show up with irrefutable proof of his true identity, leaving Connell humiliated before the very men he sought to impress to earn his reward. He'd have no choice but to drop the matter and chase after Mrs. Finchley, grateful for the guaranteed payment Nick himself would contribute to. In a flash, he saw it.

But the risk was overwhelming.

His brother was willing to go to prison ... for him. Choking down his emotion, Nick matched Darcy's grin and taunted Connell. "Choose yer man, sir." He held his wrists in front of him, praying Connell would choose him. "Is it me?"

"Or me?" Darcy—curse him!—held his wrists up, too.

Alex and Elizabeth clung to each other, eyes as wide as the bores of a cannon.

Swaggering around Connell, Wickham stood before them. The man had a great too much bravado for his own good when he was a coward at heart. Nick had seen many like him. They were the sort that talked of their bravery, their skill, and their composure in the heat of battle. But when the first shot was fired, they could be found shaking in their boots in a dark corner calling for their mamas and making empty promises to God to spare their miserable hides. Nick despised them.

But Wickham had laid his hand on Elizabeth, and

he'd attempted to weasel his way into Georgiana's heart for his own selfish gain. Nick hated him.

"I know Darcy better than anyone," Wickham bragged. "We grew up together at Pemberley, as close as brothers. His father loved me as his own son."

Nick narrowed his eyes. So he knew Darcy, did he? He would flaunt the place that had rightfully belonged to Nick as his own? He tightened his arms over his chest lest he forget himself. A glance out of the side of his eyes confirmed that Darcy's stance mirrored his own.

"Darcy despises me, but he is a gentleman through and through. He would never do me bodily harm," Wickham stood directly in front of Darcy, as smug as a thief making off with a lady's necklace, "unlike his roguish, lawless, pirate brother."

Darcy looked past him to Connell. "Are ye certain ye trust this scoundrel?"

Wickham spun on his heel, pointing his finger at Darcy. "He is the man you want. He is Blackburne. I would swear my life on it."

Again, Darcy asked Connell, "Are ye certain?"

Connell hesitated. He wasn't a fool. He knew the risk to himself if he chose the wrong brother. But he was determined, and he was too near his goal to back down. He held up the irons and clapped them over Darcy's wrists.

Nick thought he could hold his composure, but when Connell clicked the lock into place and the chains clanged between his brother's hands, he simply couldn't go through with it. "Wait!"

Darcy turned and grinned like the rogue he pretended to be. "Ye'll not be rid of me so easy." Another wink wink.

Connell pushed him forward and, with Wickham following triumphantly, they escorted him out to the barred carriage.

Alex and Elizabeth ran forward, flanking Nick. Alex asked, "Why'd he do that?"

Nick breathed, but there was not enough air in his lungs to reply.

Elizabeth's voice trembled. "It was the only way."

Mr. Gardiner joined them, speaking softly as they watched Connell shove Darcy into the back of the conveyance, "If Connell took Nick, there would have been nothing we could do. So long as they can prove Connell arrested the wrong man, they can protect Nick and free Mr. Darcy. It shall be a mistake Connell shall rue making." He stepped in front of Alex, blocking Connell and Wickham's view. "You should return inside. They made no guarantee they would not arrest you."

As though they had overheard Mr. Gardiner, the two men returned to the house with another pair of irons. "Alexandra Lafitte," called Connell, "you shall come with us."

She reached up to twist a curl, her fingers twitching

toward the hairpiece that hid the long, thin weapon hidden in her thick tresses.

Connell snapped his fingers, holding out his palm. "Your weapons, madam."

With a scowl, Alex pulled the dagger free of her hair and laid it across his palm.

"That is a promising start, but we all know you have more," Connell said, shoving her dagger into his pocket.

Another deeper scowl and she pulled the dagger from a pocket Nick had never noticed before.

When she placed the weapon on Connell's palm and he patiently waited for more, she grumbled as she fished under her skirt for her third knife.

"Is that all of them?" Connell asked.

She nodded, looking vulnerable without her knives.

"I'll come for y-you," Nick remembered his assumed accent just in time.

She winked at him. "Ye'd better." With that, she marched down to the carriage and hopped in beside Darcy, as proud as if she were walking to the helm.

As they watched the carriage pull away, worry settled in Nick's stomach. He already felt he'd given his family a great deal more trouble than he was worth … and now this?

Someone always had to pay, this Nick knew. He couldn't let it be Alex.

"Fitzwilliam will not allow Alexandra to come to harm." Elizabeth stood beside him, her eyes still trained on the lane down which the carriage had disappeared. "I am glad he popped Wickham a fair jab. A man as crooked as he is ought to sport a crooked nose."

"He makes me wish I hadn't changed me ways quite yet. If Darcy's hurt, or Alex, because of him…" Nick couldn't finish his sentence.

Elizabeth snapped, "It shall not come to that. Come, Nick, we must find your uncle and cousin. Wherever they may be, we shall chase them down. This is more urgent than Mrs. Finchley." She sounded like a general, confident and two steps ahead of the enemy. And when her uncle insisted on helping, sending messages for his workers to assist them in finding Lord Matlock, Nick was fairly overwhelmed at their unified display of loyalty.

He might've lost his ship, his crew, and his whole life purpose, but what he'd gained was worth more than all the gold in the world.

"$\mathcal{A}$re you certain I am Nicholas Blackburne?" Darcy asked for the third time, assuming his own accent. Connell had been too easily swayed by Wickham, too easily deceived, and Darcy's sense of fairness demanded that he give the man an opportunity to amend his choice before it was too late.

"Of course, you are. Darcy would rather glare at our backs than protest as you do," Wickham scoffed.

The weasel had insisted on accompanying Connell to the prison, no doubt to secure his portion of the reward. Wickham never did anything unless it was of some advantage to himself.

Clearly content at his expected profit, Wickham continued, "I cannot wait to take the story of the great Fitzwilliam Darcy's criminal connection to the papers. Watch him struggle to keep his composure while his privileged name is dragged through the gossip sheets and whispered derisively about in drawing rooms." He turned to Connell. "Thanks to me, you have not one, but two criminals. I shall expect a larger portion of the prize."

"You will get what we agreed upon. Not a farthing more," Connell snapped.

Wickham did not like that answer. He would try again later, Darcy knew.

"Lizzy's sister's married to *that*?" Alex said, her voice dripping with scorn.

Darcy scowled. Would that Lydia had made better choices, she might have been happier. It pained him to know that Wickham would never love her more than he loved himself. Her immaturity would drive him to loathe the sight of her before long if it had not already. Elizabeth would always worry about her youngest sister, and Darcy would always feel guilty he had not saved Lydia before she let Wickham ruin her.

"Where is Mrs. Wickham?" he asked.

Wickham shrugged. "Probably at the mantua maker getting fitted for her new gown. Spending money I do not yet have." He raised a finger into the air, his tone bitey. "At least we shall arrive at my new post in the north in style."

Darcy was surprised Wickham was willing to part with money not intended to feed his vices. A new gown was promising. "Why are you not with your regiment?"

"I volunteered to ride as a messenger, leaving me

free to roam." His lips quirked insolently. "I cannot help it if people are not where they are supposed to be all the time."

Richard would love to hear that. He would take great pleasure writing Wickham's superior to put him on a humbler duty.

Rather than continue down that trail, which was certain to lead to more disillusionment (for while Darcy had long ago withdrawn his friendship, he did not know how to stop hoping that Wickham would change), he asked the question that had troubled him since Elizabeth had received word of Wickham running off with Lydia. "Why her?"

Wickham did not reply immediately. "Why who?" He knew very well who Darcy referred to.

More pointedly, Darcy asked, "Why Lydia Bennet? She has no fortune, no connections." Nothing to tempt Wickham to stay once he had his way with her.

Alex jabbed him in the ribs. "Lizzy told us all about her … and yer scurvy self."

Darcy rubbed his side, wincing at his blunder. If Wickham caught on that he was Darcy, not Nick, he would be useless to protect Alex.

Wickham shrugged. "It just happened."

"Do you not realize that your actions always come with consequences? She's little more than a child." The same as Wickham, who was content to live off the generosity of others and benefit from their lenience.

Of the two, who would grow up first? Would they ever?

"You sound like a Darcy," Wickham spat, his eyes narrowing as he turned to face Darcy fully. "If I did not know better, I would think we had the wrong brother."

Darcy's pulse pounded in his ears. He should have held his tongue.

Connell cast him a worried look. "He had better be Blackburne. If he's not—"

"He's Blackburne, all right. Darcy is too far above my company. He would never condescend to talk to me as much as Blackburne has."

Alex gave Wickham a dirty look. "Ye really are scum."

"And yet, here we are. I shall get a fat prize, and you shall hang." Wickham turned to face forward.

Alex leaned closer to Darcy, whispering into his ear, "Ye must love Lizzy a great deal to endure him as a brother."

His lips turned up and his heart softened. "I do."

"Ye must love Nick a great deal to endure me as a sister."

Darcy bit back a laugh. Truer words had never been spoken. But as he looked at Alex sitting beside him on the hard bench, looking as repentant as he had ever seen her, he could not equate her with Wickham. As contentious as Alex was, as many problems as she had caused him and Elizabeth, her often misguided and frequently impetuous heart was loyal to the friends in her circle. He nudged her with his shoulder, dropping his voice, "You and Nick shall always be welcome in my home."

Her chin shook. "I'm sorry for … everything. I know I don't deserve yer kindness when I've been nothin' but a plague to ye."

An apology? Darcy did not have to wonder how difficult it was for Alex to admit to her wrongs. She looked positively miserable. Much like he had felt when he had barged into her cabin to find Elizabeth on the *Fancy*. "I could do nothing less for my sister."

Her eyes shot up to him, and a smile spread over her teeth. Shaking her head, she said, "Yer very loyal, Darcy. For Nick's sake, I'm glad. He's always longed for a place where he truly belonged." She looked down. "I'm relieved—and proud—ye've sense enough to treat him like the good man he is. He never had it in him to be a pirate. He built up his skills with the sword to scare off ne'er-do-wells and stop fights before they started."

Darcy teased, "Then how did he fall for you? You would sooner run to an altercation than avoid it."

"He always said I add spice to his life. Yer Lizzy, she's the same. Though she's much more discreet about it."

Spice. Darcy liked that.

Connell smacked the handle of his whip against the bars separating them from the box he sat on. "Stop

413

whispering back there. There shall be no escape for you this time."

Darcy doubted that. He did not yet know how, but he and Alex would walk out of Newgate before nightfall.

CHAPTER 47

*E*lizabeth had never been afraid to tell Fitzwilliam precisely what she thought, and it was with boundless ease she did the same with his twin brother. Hands clenched, arms crossed, and chin up, she repeated, "You are not going to Newgate without me."

She understood his arguments, the inappropriateness of her going near the prison—much less inside—but she simply could not accept that she must stay secreted away when Fitzwilliam and Alexandra were in grave danger. She must be allowed to help, and she could not do that from the confines of her uncle's house on Gracechurch Street.

Aunt Gardiner clutched her fichu. "My dear, I hardly think Edward would have left you here if he understood your intentions."

Elizabeth shot her aunt a look she hoped appeared

415

more shocked than piqued. Aunt could be counted on to voice reason, but on this occasion, Elizabeth would not budge. She must go to Fitzwilliam. She must make certain Alexandra did not suffer the fate they all feared. Nick would be crushed, and Fitzwilliam would blame himself for being unable to prevent it.

Tears burned and pricked her eyes, and it was through a tight throat she uttered another plea, "I cannot stay." Her voice warbled. "It's Fitzwilliam, Nick. And Alexandra. If anything happened to either of them, and I did not try to do anything to prevent it, I would never forgive myself."

Nick sighed deeply, and Elizabeth knew she had advanced her cause.

"Ye're aware of the risks."

"I am responsible for my own choices, not you," she reassured him.

He rolled his eyes. "Darcy'll skin me alive when he finds out. And he *will* find out."

"Let me tell him. He knows how determined I can be once my mind is decided."

Another sigh.

"Would you be able to keep Alexandra from accompanying you if she were standing here instead of me?"

A scowl. They both knew nobody could prevent Alexandra from doing whatever she pleased.

Elizabeth had gained precious ground, but it was still shaky. What else could she say to convince him? She grasped at one last straw. "You must consider how dangerous the streets are for an experienced sailor in this time of war. The press gangs are on the prowl, and you are walking into their territory without the protection of a letter of apprenticeship. Who shall speak for you? Your only hope of escaping their notice is to have me on your arm. They shall think twice before depriving a young lady of her escort in that part of town."

He grimaced. She had won.

Aunt tapped her finger against her chin. "I do not like it one bit, but you are right, Lizzy. Only take care. There is a current of discontent stirring the population, and you are heading into the heart of it."

Taking a deep breath, Nick nodded and looked squarely at Aunt. "I'll protect Elizabeth with me life."

"I do not doubt you, young man. And I know my niece will not reconsider. Therefore, I shall remain behind to stew and fret until you return, God willing, unscathed."

Elizabeth embraced her aunt, kissing her cheek. Then, before either she or Nick could reconsider, she wrapped a shawl over her shoulders and grabbed her bonnet from the hatstand by the door, tying the bow as she descended the stairs out to the street.

They hailed a hackney, their first hint of impending trouble being when the driver refused to take them in that direction. "There be trouble brewin' near Newgate. Saw the press gang tryin' to impress a young lad, and I got out when I saw a mob formin'."

Nick offered him double the sum to take them, and to do it quickly.

The driver hesitated, but he snapped his whip over his horses' backs, and they set off down the cobbled road.

People milled about, eyes alert, darting. Mothers held their children close, pushing them down the street with frequent glances over their shoulders. Several groups of men clustered on corners, noses red from drink, shouting and blustering every time someone hastened past them.

It did not escape Elizabeth's notice that the direction everyone hastened away from was the very place they were rushing to. Her aunt had been wise to warn them, but what other choice did they have? Fitzwilliam risked his life for her, for Nick, for Alexandra…. For Elizabeth to do anything less was unacceptable. She loved him too much to place her life above his.

Crowds thickened and their carriage slowed.

"We're gettin' close," Nick murmured.

Progressing at an agonizing crawl, Elizabeth heard the sounds of smashing glass and rebellious shouts over the clamber of the wheels. She smelled smoke.

The carriage stopped, and the coachman turned. "This is as far as I go."

Nick handed the driver his fare and held his arm out to Elizabeth. A man walking too closely jostled against them.

Elizabeth clutched Nick's arm, and when the crowd

merged into one, sweeping mass, he moved in front of her, pushing his way through. "Hold on, Elizabeth."

She grabbed onto his coat and held fast.

Like a powerful wave carrying them to the prison gate, Elizabeth rode the current until they passed Newgate's formidable walls.

Darcy paced the cell. He was grateful Connell had arranged for him and Alex to share a condemned cell rather than separate them into their corresponding sections. But the sounds on the other side of the prison walls were loud enough to reach them in the belly of Newgate.

Through the small squares of the metal door, he saw guards running by, keys clanging, swords and pistols drawn.

Alex stood in the far corner, rubbing her hands together and stretching her limbs. "Save yer strength, Darcy. Ye'll need it if their fight reaches us."

He was too anxious to still. Rioters had burned the prison once before. Would they do it again? How could they escape?

He examined the doors again, checking for weakness.

"Set in stone." She pulled a hair pin out of her coiffure and scowled at the implement. "And this'll do me no good when the lock's on the other side and the holes are too small to fit me hand through." Alex threw the pin to the ground. "We'll not get out unless someone lets us out." Darcy ought to have known she was already a few steps ahead of him. She was an artist of capture and escape.

Anticipating his question, she answered, "We wait. Nick'll come. He'll find a way, ye'll see."

Darcy did not doubt it, but the whole reason he had taken Nick's place was to keep his brother far away from this dreadful place.

Standing by the door, he watched and listened.

A voice he recognized reached him from down the dark halls. "Until I receive my payment in full, I shall be your constant companion, Connell. That you may trust."

Wickham. The lout. The Judas Iscariot, selling Darcy to the enemy for thirty pieces of silver. Disgust burned Darcy's chest but did not deepen to hatred. Pity, perhaps. Wickham was destined to be miserable the remainder of his days, while Darcy would get out of this predicament and spend the rest of his life happy with Elizabeth.

"You fool! Half of the prisoners here know me— have relatives and friends I have helped imprison. They will kill me given the chance. We must leave now. While we can. If we can."

Darcy called out, "Connell! Wickham," but they passed in a blur.

He pounded his fist against the iron door, the boom echoing in the cell and through the halls.

Connell feared the prisoners. The sounds Darcy had heard were from an attack on the prison. They had to get out.

He pounded again. Pounded until his hand ached and the irons around his hands rubbed his skin raw.

A deafening rumble, then the shouts grew louder, more violent. Acrid smoke pierced his senses. Feet scuffled by, weapons clanging.

Darcy pounded and shouted, kindled by desperation and the smell of smoke and the crack of shots and the screams.

*Clunk-clunk-clunk* shove. Darcy jumped back as a dark figure wielding a scimitar in one hand and keys in the other pushed the door open.

"Jaffa!" Alex squealed, leaping into his arms. "Why're ye here?"

"Some men at the docks spoke of Connell's latest prize. I had to make certain you were safe."

She squeezed tighter then released her hold. "I'm glad ye did!"

Jaffa grinned. "Where there is trouble, I find my cap'n."

"How'd ye get in here?"

"The gates were open."

Darcy's gut plummeted to the floor. It was the Gordon Riots all over again. Murderers and thieves running rampant, plaguing the innocent. So many lives lost senselessly.

Grabbing Alex's hand, Jaffa led them down the dark corridors, down the grimy stairs, jumping over dead guards stripped of their weapons. Alex paused at each one, collecting what she could.

Darcy urged her on, more concerned that they depart from that evil place.

"Ye should arm yerself, Darcy. We don't know what's on the other side of these walls."

He grabbed a sword, praying he would not have to put it to use.

Finally, they reached the courtyard, and Darcy went numb. It was a gauntlet of starved, diseased prisoners made desperate from the whiff of freedom the open gate advertised. Impassioned protesters fueled the chaos with their clamors of injustice as rioters fed the flames surrounding the gates. Soldiers and officers gathered, protecting the entrance, but there were too few of them presently to control the riled mob. Clinging to the wall, Darcy pulled Alex close and surged forward.

He sensed Elizabeth the second before she nearly tumbled him over. Elizabeth wrapped her arms around his middle, and Darcy had never known such horror and pleasure.

"You are alive!" She kissed his chin. "We got pushed in by the rioters. Please do not be cross with Nick. I made him agree to let me come. I could not stay behind. Surely, you had to know I must come. I had to see you."

Between her kisses and her plea, Darcy had difficulty remaining cross. Now was not the time for explanations. Pulling Elizabeth closer, he placed her between the thick, stone wall and himself.

Alex exclaimed behind him.

Over Elizabeth's head, Darcy saw Nick, sword drawn, standing off the rabid prisoners alongside the soldiers.

"Outta me way, ye scurvy knaves!" Alex cried, pushing against them as a skirmish broke out behind them.

Darcy turned to see Wickham scramble away from a prisoner in fetters. Even with chains on his wrists and ankles, the criminal fared better than Wickham. The man raised his hands to tighten the chain and ran toward Wickham, who tripped over his own feet in his haste to escape.

"Go, Mr. Darcy! I will protect Miss Elizabeth," Jaffa said, spinning his scimitar and whipping it through the air, effectively discouraging their nearest attackers. Elizabeth deftly tossed a dagger between her hands, proving herself far better at defending herself than Wickham was.

With a groan, Darcy let go of Elizabeth to stop the chained man before he strangled his brother-in-law with his shackles.

With a mighty shove, Darcy pushed the man aside.

"Get up," he growled to Wickham. "If you cannot help your brothers in arms, then get out."

Over Wickham's shoulder Connell stood, defending himself against two men intent on vengeance. Out of the corner of his eye, a third rushed toward Connell, a knife in his hand and murder in his bloodshot eyes.

Nick roared, "Darcy, duck!"

Grabbing Wickham, Darcy dropped.

## CHAPTER 48

*N*ick had fended off at least a dozen men with his blade, leaving a trail of injured men gripping their arms for the soldiers swarming through the melted gate to deal with. Those people held nothing against him other than his unfortunate position between them and their freedom. The man rushing at Connell with a dagger in his hand was different. There was hatred in his eye. He would rather murder Connell than seize his own liberty, and he would callously run through anyone who got in his way.

Connell had been a bur in Nick's side, but it wasn't right to watch him die. Not when Nick could prevent it.

Quick to react, Darcy tackled Wickham to the ground, leaving a clear path to the degenerate aiming his dagger at Connell.

Reaching into his boot, Nick flipped the dagger in his hand and sent it sailing, handle first, over Darcy's head.

The man dropped like a stone, his knife clattering to the ground beside Darcy.

Jumping to his feet, Darcy grabbed Nick's shoulder. "It is safer inside."

It was the last place Nick wished to go, but his brother was right. If anything happened to Alex, Elizabeth, or Darcy, Nick would rather rot inside a prison, for he would have no one for which to live.

Motioning for Jaffa, Nick waved toward the door. "Get Elizabeth inside." That done, he grabbed Alex around the waist and carried her, kicking and cursing, over to the condemned building.

"Let me down! Let me fight, ye lily-liver'd coward."

Nick held her tighter and kept running.

They ran inside and up the stairs to the cell he had occupied his first day back on British soil.

Setting Alex down, he held her arms at her side. She stomped on his foot. "Ye eel-skinned cheat!"

He ought to have seen that coming. Jumping out of her way when she brought her heel down again, he seethed, "Ye'll stay here and outta harm's way if I have to tie ye."

Wickham and Connell darted inside the cell.

Barnacles! Just what they needed. Another arrest.

"I came to offer my protection to the ladies," Wickham claimed, his back against the cell wall.

Connell gaped at Nick open-mouthed. "You saved me. I imprisoned the wrong brother, but you came for him. And you saved me—the man who would let you hang for a price."

Nick shrugged. "I wouldn't leave me own brother here."

"He could have hanged for you."

Nick shivered. Well he knew it.

"That was a risk we had to take." Darcy looked at Nick sheepishly. "I only regret the timing of this riot. It would have been far less complicated for our uncle to prove my true identity and insist on our release without you having to return to this wretched place."

A warmth Nick had felt many times over the past few days spread through him. He knew what it was now, and his heart was too full to breathe or speak.

Before Nick could mumble anything embarrassing ("I love ye, too, Brother," was too tender and senti-mental for a grizzled pirate to utter), Wickham pointed his finger at Darcy. "You bent my nose!" His voice reverberated off the walls.

"Sh!" he was unanimously reproved.

"That was you," he added, softer.

Darcy hissed at him, "And I saved your life. All the years I have covered over your indiscretions and debts out of loyalty to my father's wishes, but not once did you attempt to live up to his generosity. You did not deserve his loyalty, and you do not deserve mine. You would have let me hang and profited by spreading scandal about my family, even though we have treated you with nothing but consideration." He stepped forward, towering over Wickham, who seemed to shrink against the wall. "That ends now. This is not a debt I cannot overlook and which you cannot hope to ever repay."

Nick tried to control the twitching of his lips, but the shock on Wickham's face was comical. He blustered, "I shall not need you any more once I get my share of the reward."

Connell scoffed, a beautiful sound in Nick's ears. "You think me capable of sending the man who spared my life to the gallows?"

"B—but wh-what of the woman? She's a Lafitte!"

Connell shook his head. "I could not live with myself if I betrayed his betrothed."

"But—all my work—all the time I invested—" Wickham bit his tongue when Connell rolled his eyes.

"You dare compare the hours you lost to the months I spent chasing my prize all over the Atlantic, then all over England? You ungrateful cur. Do you truly believe yourself deserving of a reward you did nothing but point a finger to earn? You shall get nothing from me."

"And nothing from me," Darcy added.

Wickham swallowed hard, eyes wide with fear as he saw Darcy in a new light. It was about time.

Alex broke their silence. "There're few fates worse

than watchin' a reward ye've been chasin' slip through yer fingers. I'll not have it."

Nick grinned. Had she read his mind, or drawn the same conclusion? He wanted to credit Alex with brilliance, for by sending Connell after Mrs. Finchley, she was securing their freedom. No more hiding. No more chasing. "Once we've helped to calm the riot here, me and me uncle means to hire ye to track down a murderess, the evil woman who created this whole mess."

Alex added, "We already know ye're a tenacious man. Ye'll need all yer wits about ye if ye're to find Mrs. Finchley. She's a slippery one."

"I shall give you an advance on the reward my family is willing to offer for her capture." Darcy added an additional incentive. He was brilliant, too.

Wickham scrambled closer to Connell. "I can be of invaluable assistance—"

Connell cut him off. "If I ever see your face again once we leave this cursed place, I will draw your cork so thoroughly, your poor wife will not recognize you."

Wickham covered his nose and cowered in a corner.

Motioning for the door, Nick urged, "Come, gents! We've a riot to halt."

Alex pouted. "I fight as good as those men."

"Nobody said ye don't, but I need ye to stay here to protect Elizabeth … and the other ladies." He looked past her to Wickham.

She kicked Wickham's foot. "He's useless, isn't he?"

Elizabeth wrapped her arm around Alex's shoulders. "Not completely. You could show me more tricks with your knife." She flicked the blade over in her free hand, her smile growing as the blood drained from Wickham's face. "If he holds himself very still, I think I can manage well enough," she added with an impish gleam.

Darcy shoved Nick forward. "Come on. He is in good hands. Jaffa will make sure he does not give the ladies any trouble."

Jaffa nodded, scimitar drawn and ready, and stepped into the doorway of the cell.

Nick traded his sword with another, better balanced blade, then grabbed another from a fallen guard for good measure.

Poking and shoving their way to the front, Nick, Darcy, and Connell joined the guard at the gate.

"Nick! Darcy! I have never been so happy to see you two rascals," shouted Richard. He disarmed the prisoner he fought, turning to the next in a fluid motion.

Nick fell in beside him, Darcy on his other side. Twirling the blades through the air, Nick forced the prisoners back without shedding a drop of blood. When a few intrepid souls braved the sharp edges, he warded them off until they were too exhausted to try anymore. He used every trick he had ever learned or created, glorying in the fire burning in his muscles and the sweat stinging his eyes as, one by one, the enemy tired and retreated.

With a wide grin, Nick fought side-by-side with his cousin and his brother to the cheers of the men behind them. He was a part of something bigger, something that made him whole. They were his friends. His family. He loved them.

## CHAPTER 49

*R*ichard tilted his chin upward, giving his batman easier access to his cravat, and counted as he took a deep breath. The ceremony was not his, but he was as nervous as a groom at the prospect of seeing Miss Rothschild after weeks of absence. Four weeks and four days to be precise.

Every day, he schemed excuses to call. And every day, he reminded himself that the timing was wrong, that he would be an imposition to her, that he did not deserve the attention of such a fine lady ... no matter how badly his heart protested.

Had she hoped he would call? Had he disappointed her? Or had she forgotten him already? He had tried to forget her—a pointless enterprise which he had failed fabulously.

A knock sounded at his door, and Richard heard the heavy footfall of his father enter the room. Twisting his neck as much as he dared without undermining the exertions of his batman, Richard saw Father set a wooden box down on the nearest table with a loud thud.

Mother followed behind, glanced at Father flexing and rubbing his hands together, and made her way over to Richard's side. "You look very handsome." She brushed her fingers over Richard's cheeks and smoothed an imaginary stray hair.

Richard was accustomed to her motherly attentions, but her comment brought a heated blush to his entire person. He had taken a little extra care, knowing he would stand beside Darcy and Nick as their witness that morning. Knowing that Miss Rothschild would see him.

Father tapped the top of the box. "Whatever is inside is remarkably heavy."

Richard nodded at the box. "What is that?"

"In Nick's words, it is 'just a triflin' gift.' He apologized that he could not stay to give it to you himself."

"At this hour? On his wedding day?" Alex would string him by his thumbs from the yardarm if he was late to their wedding.

Father rubbed his whiskers. "Makes a man wonder what could be so important to Nick that he could not entrust it to a servant to deliver. He would not hand it to the butler."

Richard stood helpless, motionless while the batman put the finishing touches on his cravat. He had asked for him to take special care and could not rightly growl at him to hurry now that he was curious to see what the box contained.

Finally, the folds perfected, the batman declared Richard ready and discreetly departed.

The box was weathered but sound, rectangular, about the size of a saddlebag. A sturdy clasp held the lid shut, but there was no lock.

Slowly, Richard lifted the lid to the tune of groaning hinges.

He gasped, steadying himself against the table, his head spinning.

Father burst into laughter.

Mother mumbled between her fingers, "Dear heavens."

Nick hastened away from Matlock House. He couldn't risk Richard chasing after him, and he certainly wouldn't risk being late for his wedding. Alex would skin him alive.

Darcy House was in view, and he slowed his pace enough to catch his breath and dry the sweat slicked over his skin. Hopkins would be displeased, but one bath was enough for any man on any given day. At least he had not yet donned his tailored weeds or the new boots Darcy had insisted on purchasing for him. Hopkins had spent at least an hour polishing them into a mirror-like sheen. If Nick hurried, he could change and run down to the garden just in time. No need to alert Alex that anything was amiss.

Connell stopped him three houses away from Darcy House. Nick had been too preoccupied to see him standing on the pavement.

"Nick! Have you seen Wickham around by any chance?"

Of all the things Connell could've said, inquiring about Wickham was the last Nick would've considered. "I'm pleased to say I haven't … though I expect we'll have to endure his company at the wedding feast." It was a pity one could not choose one's family as easily as one chose his friends.

Connell scratched his chin. "No matter. Certainly nothing to concern yourself with. I meant to attend your wedding—thank you for including me among your guests … Lord knows, you did not have to—but one of my informants has a promising lead I can waste no time pursuing. I gave Darcy my regards and apologies, and now I give them to you."

Nick grinned. "Another family to put right?"

Connell nodded. "You could say that, although this family would be better off if my search resulted in naught."

If Nick had more time, he would have asked what he meant.

"It is not a story I wish to burden you with on this special day," Connell added. "Suffice it to say that I am so accustomed to people recoiling at my presence, it is nice to be made to feel welcome."

"Now, that, I can understand."

"I believe you do. I pray your transition from pirate to privateer goes as smoothly as mine from thief-taker to enquiry agent."

They were not so different when it came down to it, him and Connell. "Same work with a kinder name."

With a frown, Connell looked over his shoulder, past Nick, then over his other shoulder. "You ought not to be out unaccompanied. While there are few who would dare touch you after the riot, until you get amnesty from the Admiralty, there will be others like me seeking you and Miss Lafitte out."

Well did Nick know it. Six weeks had passed since the *Fancy* was maimed. Six weeks he'd been on land, at risk every day of being captured were it not for the influence of his family. Four weeks since he had walked out of Newgate with Alex, grateful for their lives and another chance at redemption. "We'll sail outta port once we're wed."

"That is for the best."

Nick's only regret was that he couldn't yet accept Darcy's insistent invitations for him to see Pemberley —his rightful home, as his brother often repeated.

But Nick was relieved he had a solid excuse to delay the visit. He'd been too long on land, and until he felt comfortable in his new law-abiding life with Alex, he couldn't think about Pemberley without sadness overwhelming him. All those years lost. He couldn't stand before his parents' portraits as he was now, with little to make them proud. It was a nonsensical thought, but he wanted to be a man they'd wish to claim as a son. A man who could gaze upon them honestly, with dignity.

Connell's hand clamped down on his shoulder. "I know you are done with taking ships, but allow me a word of advice: if you were to take an enemy warship, your chance of invoking the favor of the Admiralty would increase dramatically. They would be more inclined to overlook your former ... activities ... to grant you a legitimate Letter of Marque along with the protections that come with a naval auxiliary vessel— things that are beyond the influence of even Lord Matlock to arrange."

The idea stirred Nick's blood in a way that terrified him. Was he still a pirate at heart? Or was it the prospect of freedom—freedom on his terms, honestly earned—that appealed to him?

The news about his relation to the Darcys and Matlocks had appeared in all of the papers, but thanks to his flashy swordsmanship at the prison gates, they made him out to be a hero. The papers had romanticized his life, casting his former activities in a favorable light. Connell's account of Nick's actions inside the prison had helped. As had his brother's staunch support.

Nick was grateful for Darcy and Georgiana's sake. Darcy was an honorable man through and through, and Nick would rather disappear from his life than allow him to feel shame every time his name was mentioned.

"Will you consider the matter?" Connell asked.

Nick nodded. Even after his little gift to the colonel, he had the bond money—one thousand five hundred pounds—the surety of good behavior the Admiralty required of privateer applicants. "I will," he promised, extending his hand to the man who had once been a great enemy and was now an ally. A friend.

They parted ways, and Nick ran inside Darcy House, darting up the stairs and into his bedchamber where Darcy and Hopkins paced. "Where have you been?" they demanded in unison.

Shrugging out of his coat, Nick started undoing buttons as quickly as his calloused fingers allowed.

Darcy grimaced at the sight of his hair but dutifully reached for a comb.

The valet's hands deftly stripped and buttoned and smoothed.

They worked quietly, quickly, united in their effort to make Nick presentable in record time.

ELIZABETH WATCHED the double doors leading into the ballroom where the feast was spread over long tables. Jean-Christophe's cake, a towering creation he had painstakingly made, sat in the middle. Beautifully arranged flowers, the last of the summer blooms and the first of autumn, led a path out to the gazebo where the clergyman stood waiting.

Their guests stirred, eyeing the tables of food from the garden.

Mrs. Annesley conversed with Mary and Kitty by a stand of lilies. She would return to Longbourn with them for a few months. After hiding for so long at Pemberley, Mrs. Annesley was eager to live her life free of the fear of Mrs. Finchley (may her soul rot in the grave).

"He's not here. Thunder n' surf, is it too much for a woman to ask that her groom bother to make an appearance on his wedding day?" Alexandra seethed.

Georgiana looked near tears, distressed that anyone —even Nick's intended—should say anything against her dear brother. "Nick would never abandon you. He is incapable of such deceit."

Emily spoke calmly. "Calm yourself, Alexandra. There is time. The Matlocks only arrived a few minutes ago." Her gaze sought them out, settling on Colonel Fitzwilliam. She smiled, looking as happy as she had the day she received a letter from the Hales thanking her for helping them find their long-lost child.

Elizabeth was not a betting woman, but given the warmth in her friend's eyes, the blush in her cheeks, and the way Richard's gaze had lingered on Emily from the moment he had set foot inside the ballroom, she would bet her favorite book that they would be the next couple to exchange vows. Given the smile gracing Georgiana's face, she was of a similar opinion.

There was something different in the colonel's manners. The usual reserve in his expression had disappeared. Something had happened to bring on this welcome change, and while Elizabeth loved a good puzzle to solve, she had an impatient bride to calm.

Elizabeth caressed Alexandra's arm. "He shall come. You shall see."

Forcing her shoulders down, Alexandra said, "Yer right. Nick loves me. He wouldn't leave me standin' alone at the altar. I trust him." She narrowed her eyes. "He better show his face soon."

Emily and Elizabeth wrapped their arms around her, recognizing her struggle and insecurity. She had thought that Nick had left her once before; her fear was understandable, though Elizabeth did not doubt Fitzwilliam for one moment. There was a good reason for their delay, she was certain, for Fitzwilliam was as constant as the sunrise.

"Lizzy," Mama snapped and clucked her tongue. "You will crush your gown."

Biting her lips together, Elizabeth pulled away from Alexandra and smoothed her skirts, daring not to look at her mother lest she lose her composure and burst into laughter.

Mama kept one wary eye on the crowd assembled when she was not looking at Alexandra's excessive flounces and ruffles of lace. The wedding company was a motley crew, to say the least, with Alexandra's men on shore leave from the recently repaired *Fancy*. Jaffa, dressed in a beaded vest of bright colors and with gold necklaces covering his bare skin, was an especially appalling sight ... and one Mama peeked at often from behind her fan.

Oh, if only Lady Catherine could see them now! Elizabeth would delight in introducing the great lady to her new relations. Maybe then she would not complain so much about Elizabeth's family, she thought with evil humor.

Jane and Lydia slipped into the ballroom and out to the garden, followed by Aunt and Uncle Gardiner. Jane met Elizabeth's eye and gave a barely perceptible shake of her head. Elizabeth's humor rushed out of her in a disappointed exhale. Still no sign of Wickham, then.

The evening before, Lydia had shown up at Gracechurch Street donning her newest gown and holding a valise. Wickham had not returned to the inn for two days, and she had grown tired of waiting for him. That she had not attempted to find him before then was telling, no matter how Mama attempted to explain his absence away with glorified imaginings of secret army missions and clandestine assignments.

Still, Wickham's disappearance had been sudden and unwarranted, and Uncle had sent for Mr. Connell immediately. Elizabeth had not yet told Fitzwilliam, and she would wait to do so until after the wedding feast to spare Georgiana from so much as hearing his name.

"She is so beautiful," Mama mumbled after Jane, chasing after her with her fan open to slap the hand of any sailor who attempted to speak with Jane or looked at her too long.

Jane radiated contentedness. Mr. Bingley had returned to Netherfield Park to court her openly. He was already among their guests, and Jane wasted no time finding him. They would wed at Longbourn parish the following week.

Mama waved her fan at Cotton and Bauer, looking like a mother hen with her feathers ruffled. To their credit, the two men cowered under the threat of her snapping fan.

Alexandra chuckled. "I see yer ma's fan is as fearsome a weapon as me threats of keelhaulin'. I made me men swear they'd be on their best behavior."

So that was why the champagne had not been opened and the men were simply eyeing the food longingly but did not partake.

Elizabeth rubbed the braided strands around her finger. She had not taken it off since Fitzwilliam had given it to her, and she was loath to do so that day. No amount of diamonds and jewels could replace the sentiment the ring he had made for her represented.

Papa strolled languidly over to them from the entrance hall. "It is time for me to take you to the parlor so you may make your grand entrance." He held his arm out to Elizabeth. Jaffa joined them, holding his arm out to Alexandra.

"Nick's here?" she asked.

"He had a small matter to attend to, but it is done," Papa said, leading them out to the hall and into the parlor. Leaving the door open a crack to wait for their signal to come out, he turned to face Alexandra. "Pray do not punish him too severely. All is well that ends well."

"Mr. Bennet, you were supposed to wait until after the wedding." Jaffa looked nervously at Alexandra.

The fiery captain's fists clenched. "And what's *that* supposed to mean? What's he done now?"

Papa took her hand between his own, patting it. "That is not for me to say, but I am of a mind that you will eventually agree that Nicholas acted out of good faith and generosity."

Alexandra shot Elizabeth a scowl, but Elizabeth could only shrug. She had no idea what her father hinted at, nor what Nick had done.

"The gentlemen are in place, and the clergyman is ready," the butler signaled.

"I'm gonna kill him," Alexandra hissed under her breath.

Elizabeth looped her arm through Alexandra's and marched her forward. "Not until after the wedding, dear."

# CHAPTER 50

*D*arcy stood in his favorite place in any ballroom, in a corner against the wall where he could better observe the guests. He was not being anti-social, and nobody could accuse him of being reticent, surrounded as he was by Georgiana, Uncle, and Richard.

He watched Elizabeth, his heart swelling with awe that she returned his love. That she meant every word of her vows. The depth of emotion he heard in her voice when she said, "I do," would forever echo in his memory.

She was truly a marvel. She conversed with the sailors—who Darcy was pleased had shown proper regard for the occasion by arriving washed, shaved, and with their hair cut and smoothed into place—as easily as she did with his aunt and the few other guests Darcy counted among his most intimate friends in society.

Bingley laughed with Cotton and Bauer. He looked happier than normal—which was significant for a gentleman given to merriment. He would marry Jane the next week and ought to look very pleased, indeed.

Not far from them sat Mrs. Annesley with Miss Kitty and Miss Mary, sipping tea and nibbling on cake. Mrs. Annesley had agreed to stay with the Bennets for an undetermined time. Darcy credited her edifying influence as well as he did Alex's crew, from whom the Bennet ladies had no desire to draw attention and were therefore pleasantly more subdued than normal. Even Lydia sat quietly, enjoying her plate of food.

Uncle nudged Darcy with his elbow. "I wish your mother were here to see you today. Annie would love to know you exchanged vows with a lady you love as much as she adored her George."

Darcy's heart squeezed at the way his uncle still referred to Mother like the little sister she was to him. She would have loved to see the garden she cared for so carefully, her rose bushes which Darcy had maintained as she liked, used as his and Elizabeth's wedding venue. "She would have loved Elizabeth like a daughter."

Georgiana added, "As would Papa." After a pause, she continued, "He would have approved of your other guests, too."

Richard swallowed the last of his champagne. "He would be shocked to see evidence that his unbending son finally paid him heed." He raised an eyebrow at

Darcy in that annoying way older relatives did, the one they used when they made a point at your expense.

But Darcy did not mind today. Uncle could chuckle all he wanted, and Georgiana could save her worried glances for another occasion. He nodded, acknowledging Richard's jab and accepting its truth.

Darcy's father had always encouraged him to widen his circle. He had considered his father to be too lenient—Wickham was not a good candidate for his generosity—but now Darcy understood him better. Father would have approved of Darcy's new friends. Of Nick … and, yes, even of Alex.

As if they knew his thoughts had turned in their direction, Nick and Alex left their party to join him at his post against the wall. Elizabeth, too, departed from Jane, leaving her sister in Bingley's capable, eager company, her eyes fixed on Darcy's as she closed the distance between them.

Darcy's post improved significantly when she wrapped her arm around his and stood close enough for the smell of her hair to intoxicate his senses.

"Thank you for the gift you sent, Nick," Richard said seriously.

As content as Darcy was enveloped in the aroma of Elizabeth's rosewater, his cousin's appreciation expressed as it was—in front of Alex—was as sobering as getting caught in the rain. A storm was fast approaching.

Nick looked down at his polished boots, avoiding

Alex's stare. Carefully, without looking up, he replied, "So ye never doubt yer worth in yer lady's heart."

Richard, too thick to take a hint (for all that he was the superior, wiser, older one of the bunch), cackled. "And I need a trunk full of Spanish doubloons for that?"

"A trunk!" Alex exclaimed, her eyes shooting daggers between Nick and Richard (who now had the good grace to look sheepish).

"A small trunk. A box, really," Richard clarified.

Nick shrugged and glanced toward the doors. "It's blazing hot in here."

Darcy tried to help. "Stifling. Do you care for a turn —" he began, and was promptly interrupted by his new sister.

"Where'd ye get a trunk—"

Richard raised his finger. "Small—very small—box."

Alex rolled her eyes. "Where'd ye get a"—she glanced at the colonel with both of her eyebrows raised —"very small box of treasure? Ye've no ship. No cache I'm aware of in Europe." Her glare narrowed on Nick.

"I've no cache of treasure here. Or on the continent. Nor in the North of Africa," Nick added when Alex's glare showed no sign of softening. "In fact, I've written a letter to be sent to yer brothers indicating where a portion of the earnings I set aside during me years in their employ is stashed. It's sealed and on the corner of the writing desk in me bedchamber."

"Ye mean to send me brothers a treasure map?"

Darcy imagined it took a great deal to shock Alex, and he struggled to keep the twitch in his lips from deepening to a chuckle. Elizabeth, too, struggled. Her shoulders shook against his.

Nick grinned. "I couldn't let 'em stay angry with me bride when it's in me reach to recover some of their favor after yer little misunderstanding."

"I wouldn't've misunderstood if ye'd've told me yer plans."

Placing one hand over his heart, Nick said solemnly, "A mistake I promise not to repeat."

"Do ye mean it?" Alex eyed him askance.

"From now on, I'll confide everything in ye."

"Everything?"

Darcy sensed trouble. Given Nick's hard swallow, he knew he'd stepped one foot inside a noose, too.

"Aye. I'll not go back on me word," he answered bravely, despite the figurative rope closing around his ankle, ready to tug him off his feet.

Alex grinned, showing most of her teeth. "Good. Then ye won't mind tellin' me where ye hid yer doubloons."

Darcy hid his smile behind his hand. Alex would keep Nick on his toes as much as Elizabeth kept Darcy on his.

Nick groaned half-heartedly. "Ye promise not to lose yer temper in front of our guests? In me brother's fine house?"

Her brows furrowed, and she stepped away from

Nick. "I've learnt a great deal from Lizzy 'bout how to be a lady." Folding her arms over her chest and lifting her chin, she said in a supremely offended tone, "A lady never loses her temper."

Elizabeth's whole body shook, but not a peep of laughter escaped her control. Darcy admired her all the more for it when she said in a voice which passed as joyful and proud, "You are my most exemplary student."

Darcy nearly lost his composure. Alex was Elizabeth's only student. But it served them well not to remind Alex of that fact. At least, not now, when Nick's fate hung in the balance.

"Then again," Alex added, "I still have a great deal more to learn about ladyhood. I promise to wait 'til we're alone to make me real feelins' on the subject known."

Richard jabbed Nick with his elbow. "Take care not to be alone with her anytime soon."

Uncle leaned closer to Nick, his voice low enough only to be heard by Darcy, Nick, and their wives. "This does not bode well for your wedding night, son."

Nick blushed. To be sure, it took all of Darcy's composure not to blush with him.

Clearing his throat, Nick addressed Alex. "I hid enough doubloons on the *Fancy* to set me up properly in case I was caught. Not everyone on me crew was happy to change professions … as yer refusal to join me and Arnold's mutiny both proved."

Alex chewed on her lips, and Nick bowed his head and looked at the floor to await her verdict.

Finally, she spoke. "Ye hid a fortune on *me* boat? With *me* crew?"

"None of 'em knew."

"But they might've found it."

"*You* might've found it."

"Would ye let me keep it if I had?"

"Ye know I would."

Alex leaned into him, a smile spreading up to her eyes. "Today, ye vowed to trust me with yer heart, and now I get proof ye trust me with yer fortune? That's the most romantic thing ye've ever done, Nick."

Nick's head snapped up. "I'm not in trouble?"

"Hardly." Alex wrapped her arms around his waist and buried her face against his chest. "I love ye more than a million gold pieces."

Elizabeth's grip around Darcy's tightened. He rested his hand over hers and leaned down to whisper, "And I love you more than a million sparkling stars." Perhaps he ought to have said "more than my pride," but there was nothing romantic in that, and Darcy refused to allow Alex to best him.

"And I," Elizabeth said with a mischievous twinkle in her eye, "love you more than a million libraries. More than Pemberley's library, which I am assured is splendidly grand."

She had him there. "Do you know I love you more with every witty retort?"

Elizabeth's cheeks glowed pink, and Darcy had the gratifying sensation of knowing he had finally said the right thing at precisely the correct moment. It was a heady feeling.

He had rather forgotten they were surrounded by family until their party fell silent. Darcy looked up to see Cotton and Bauer shuffling their feet and clearing their throats.

"Speak up," Alex ordered, every inch their captain.

Bauer held a handful of clippings toward Darcy. "Me and Cotton be wonderin' if Mr. Darcy wouldn't mind writin' his name on these … as a keepsake."

Cotton nodded eagerly. "A token of friendship if ye like."

Darcy sent for a pen and ink well while the two sailors beamed.

"Ye and The Blade and The Cap'n"—Cotton nodded at Richard—"be a more excitin' story than the prison riots."

Bauer nodded. "Twas a pity the riot stole yer thunder. Ye should've been on the front pages fer weeks."

Darcy, for one, was grateful his name had not been plastered all over the broadsides or shouted in the streets by publishers hocking their papers … not for long, anyway. "Thank you, gentlemen, but I will gladly cede any fame our story might have provoked."

"And that evil woman what stole all those defense-less babes, murderin' the castoffs in cold blood," Cotton said with a bite.

Bauer shook his head. "If Connell hadn't found her dead at the inn, I'd have helped him string her up meself … old woman or not."

That had been a fortunate turn of affairs. Connell had traced Mrs. Finchley to Ramsgate. He had found her, cold and stiff, in her room, an empty teacup beside her bed. The doctor at the inquest had determined that she had died of a weak heart. Nobody at the inn had noticed, as she had paid for a full week, until her ship was set to sail, and had slipped the innkeeper a few extra coins to keep the maids away and secure her privacy.

Piece by piece over the past weeks, Connell had picked apart her operation with the help of Mrs. Annesley and her list and the indefatigable assistance of Miss Rothschild. They had a great deal more work ahead of them, but Connell was well on his way to becoming a wealthy man in high demand in his new role as a respectable enquiry agent.

Society was abuzz with news of the families exposed for buying heirs or eliminating the undesirables—all services Mrs. Finchley provided. Their hypocrisy soured Darcy's stomach. Too many of them had known what had happened behind closed doors, but nobody admitted to it and the same people proclaimed their innocence of this barbaric, inhuman sin, zealously condemning Mrs. Finchley.

But Darcy's secret twin brother, former pirate and Lafitte protege, had been spared further exposure. For that, Darcy would forgive society's folly. Their fickleness and craving for sensational gossip quickly moved on to the newest, most exciting morsel to be discussed in drawing rooms and spread at dinner parties. Nick held his head higher now that the danger had passed.

Hours later, the last bottle of champagne drained and the last slice of Jean-Christophe's confection consumed, the crew of the *Fancy* grew restless. Alex looked up at Nick, and Darcy knew they would leave.

It was time. But he was not ready.

He had to have one more word. "Can I not convince you to join us at Pemberley? It is your home as well as mine, your rightful place."

Nick's smile held a trace of sadness. "I don't need a grand house to know me place, Brother."

"You are always welcome."

"I know it. And I promise I'll show up when I'm ready." Nick turned and walked away.

Darcy made himself stay put and let Nick go, but fear needled his heart that he would never see his brother again. That was the only sad thought Darcy had on an otherwise perfect day.

# EPILOGUE

PEMBERLEY

3 MONTHS LATER...

*D*arcy found Elizabeth curled up in his favorite velvet chair in the library.

She closed her book when she noticed him, her smile brightening when she saw the letters in his hand. "Any worthwhile news?" she asked, biting her lips and lowering her eyebrows.

Darcy did not know why she tried to contain her curiosity when her inquisitive nature was one of the qualities he loved most about her. "There is no news of Wickham other than what we already know. His ship is not expected to return soon." He handed her the envelope from Connell.

She grabbed the letter, her lips pursing as she scanned over the page. "If he had stayed with Lydia instead of going out drinking and gambling, he would not have been press ganged."

Wickham had not been in uniform, not wanting to be recognized and forced to return to Lydia. What had he expected, in disguise, in *that* part of London where seafaring men were known to seek gin and companionship during their short leaves? Wickham had been too drunk to protest effectively, and by the following afternoon when he was sober enough to tell them he had an army commission, it was too late. The *HMS Lydia* had already set sail. "His wife would be a kinder mistress than the ship he must toil on," Darcy noted dryly.

Elizabeth set the letter down and rang for another cup to be brought in for him. "Mrs. Annesley has been a good influence on her."

With all the stories the midwife had discreetly shared of her profession—and which Elizabeth's sisters later recounted to her in their letters—they had learned the advantages of decorum. Lydia, relieved and with a renewed appreciation that she had been spared the pangs of motherhood, had calmed considerably.

Tapping her chin, Elizabeth smiled. "I noticed that Connell mentioned Mrs. Annesley more than once in his letter."

"They have been working closely," Darcy acknowledged.

"He finds many excuses to travel through Hertfordshire."

Darcy's suspicions had reached the same conclusion. "You think Connell has developed a particular interest in Mrs. Annesley?"

Elizabeth huffed and jabbed her finger against his letter. "Since when is Longbourn on the way to Kent from London? He has a copy of Mrs. Annesley's list. There is no need for him to seek her out."

Darcy settled in the chair beside hers. "And is that so wrong?"

Her smile sparkled in her eyes. "Not at all. I have it on good authority—Jane's—that Mrs. Annesley is not indifferent to his attentions."

Saving the best for last, Darcy handed Elizabeth the other letter he had received. It had taken him several minutes to cipher Nick's handwriting, but it was the first letter he had received from his brother since he and Alex had left Darcy House in London.

Elizabeth squinted her eyes, then turned the page one way, then the other. Handing it back to Darcy, she said, "It must have been storming when he wrote this. What does it say?"

Darcy loved how easily she excused Nick's poor penmanship. "They captured a Spanish warship off the coast of Portugal. Snuck right up on it in the dark of night, boarding her before the watchman had a chance to cry out. It was a risky move, as they had to weave around several British naval vessels, but they promptly turned their prize over to the closest ship. Alex is still mad at Nick for not pilfering the firearms and gold bars in the hold."

Elizabeth gasped. "A prize ship! Did the Admiralty grant them amnesty and a privateering license?"

"They could do no less," Darcy answered, relief coursing through his body. His brother could return to England now. The question only remained: when?

"After handing over such a fat prize, I should hope not!" Elizabeth untucked her feet from under her and leaned forward to pour the tea the maid set on the table.

"We shall read about it in the papers soon, I should think. Nick claims it shall be his last ship, but he knows better than to speak for Alex. Still, he hopes that when their first child is born, she might change her mind."

"She is with child! Oh, how lovely!" Elizabeth rubbed her stomach. "Would it not be wonderful if our children were born at the same time?"

Like him and Nick. Darcy slid forward, until his knees were on the floor and he could kiss Elizabeth's stomach. Her hands twined through his hair, pulling him closer.

Rubbing his cheek against her, he whispered, "I have not seen you, but I already love you more than anyone." He felt Elizabeth tug on his hair.

With a laugh, he raised his head and brushed his lips over hers. "Except for you, my love."

"That is more like it. We must be a team before our children are old enough to conspire mischief against us, or where would we be?" The way she twirled her fingers through the hair at the nape of his neck sent shivers down to Darcy's fingers and toes. And the sweetness of her lips, the softness of her skin, the silk of her hair ... Darcy could ignore the world and remain in her embrace for days.

"Did he say when they might return to England?" she asked, stroking his cheeks.

Darcy leaned back, still on his knees but feeling the need to stay close to her. "Not exactly. He said he would wait until the war is over and it is safer for them to cross. He wants to see Uncle Matlock—"

"He called him that? He called him Uncle?"

With a nod, Darcy added, "Nick wants his children to see the portraits of their grandparents. He said to tell you that he is as much a man of promise as I am." He eyed Elizabeth. "What did you make him promise?"

She sighed contentedly. "I knew he would remember. You and he are alike in so many ways."

Darcy waited for her to expound on the subject, aching to hear more. To know when he might see his brother again. Nick said he wanted his children to see their grandparents' portraits, but surely, he wanted to know his parents, too ... Darcy hoped.

Tickling her fingers over his cheek, caressing his

face, Elizabeth said, "I saw how sad you were when Nick left. You tried to hide it, but I knew. I thought you were worried you might not see him once he departed. So I hurried out to your carriage before it could take them to the dock. I made him promise, with Alexandra as a witness, that he would return as soon as the war was over or within the next five years. Whichever came first."

"You gave him an ultimatum?"

She shrugged. "A time limit sounds nicer. Alexandra heard everything, and she concurred. We agreed that he could return, purchase an estate near Pemberley, and open up a fencing school."

Darcy wrapped his arms around Elizabeth, his heart brimming with gratitude for her gift, already planning which rooms to make ready for his family and the places he wanted them to see, the stories and portraits he would share...

"What else did Nick say in his letter?" Elizabeth pressed, recalling Darcy to the present.

Pulling the chair closer, he sat and took the tea she had prepared for him just the way he liked it, with a little bit of sugar and a little more cream.

"They plan to purchase a property on the Mediterranean large enough for us to visit, as well as Richard and Emily, Aunt and Uncle, Georgiana, Jaffa..."

"They shall need their own Pemberley," Elizabeth snorted. "What of their crew?"

"Boone shall take over as captain with Beckett as his

quartermaster. Cotton and Bauer have requested places in the household. Alex figures they shall make decent nurses."

"A more protected infant would be hard to find." Elizabeth laughed.

They dreamed of Nick and Alex's return, of their own child (whose birth they would entrust with Mrs. Annesley), and the end of the war when they could all be together again.


TWO YEARS LATER...

The house had not been packed with guests for months, and for the first time, Darcy was free to finally see to the business he had already been putting off for far too long ... and Elizabeth would not hear of him departing for town.

Not that Darcy wished to go. He never wished to leave his dear wife, little Anne, or baby Thomas.

He had invited Elizabeth and the children to join him, but she had refuted his every suggestion. She simply, stubbornly would not budge. Nor would she allow him to leave Pemberley.

To make matters worse, it was a brilliant day—clear, azure skies with puffy clouds in changing figures and blooming flowers in the gardens. And instead of arranging a picnic at the top of the hill with a view of the wildflower-speckled fields and the river, she had been obstinate about spreading the picnic near the house with a view, not of the river or the fields or the woods or the flowers, but of the drive leading to the house.

Trying not to act as cross as he felt, Darcy lifted little Annie and twirled her until he grew dizzy and she giggled uncontrollably. Elizabeth rocked Thomas, who drooled all over his mother's shoulder, his toothless grin fixed on his squealing sister.

It was difficult to remain in an ill-humor, but Darcy did his best. He really must away to London. He had neglected his business too long.

Carefully setting Anne down, he was about to tell Elizabeth as much—again—when out of the corner of his eye, he saw a carriage approaching. An imperious monstrosity with gaudy carvings embellished in gold leaf. It did not belong to the Bennets, nor would his uncle be seen in such a horrendous conveyance. Richard's carriage was sleek and elegant. Bingley and Jane had only recently departed and were not expected for several more months.

"Are you expecting callers?" He glanced over his shoulder at his wife.

Casting him the same saucy look that had won his heart ages ago, Elizabeth winked. Twice.

And he knew.

All was forgiven. Kissing the woman he adored, Darcy lifted Anne into his arms, and with Elizabeth holding Thomas, they walked the blessedly short distance to the drive.

Nick leaped out of the carriage, and Darcy thanked all the stars in the heavens that he had such a clever woman for a wife.

Alex jumped down, a baby in her arms and a toddler wrapped around her leg. "Blimey, Darcy, when ye said ye're wealthy, ye weren't exaggeratin'."

Embraces were exchanged, Darcy showed Nick the portraits of their family, and they watched their children playing together. Darcy's life was rich enough, but that day he felt like the richest man alive. He had his family and as much happiness as a heart could hold. He was, truly, a fortunate man. A man of fortune.

**Can't get enough of Darcy and Elizabeth? Read on to find your next book!**

Follow Fitzwilliam Darcy as he overcomes various challenging roles on his path to love.
**Read all the standalone books in the Dimensions of Darcy series!**

Can curiosity and crimes lead a young lady to the altar? Join Elizabeth Bennet as she finds out!
**Read all the standalone books in the Mysteries & Matrimony series!**

Darcy and Elizabeth form a formidable investigative team as they work together to bring enemies to justice

and forge unbreakable bonds with their newfound family.
**Enjoy the complete Meryton Mystery series!**

A hidden letter that rocks the Darcy cousins' world. Will it ultimately lead them to their own happily-ever-afters?
**Enjoy the complete Darcy Cousins series!**

# THANK YOU!

Thank you for reading *Fitzwilliam Darcy, Man of Fortune*! Your support and feedback make the creation of these stories possible. I'd love to know what you thought of it, so please leave a review. I read all of them!

First and foremost, I have to thank my kids, Jonah and Rebekah. Their "pirate phase" last summer largely inspired this story.

A special thank you goes out to Debbie Brown for giving every word a thorough polish. You rock, lady!

And thank you, Jeanne Garrett. Without you, this book would have taken so much longer to get to readers.

**Want to know when my next book is available? You can:**

THANK YOU!

* Sign-up for my newsletter
* Follow my Author page on Amazon

# ABOUT THE AUTHOR

When Jennifer isn't busy dreaming up new adventures for her favorite characters, she is learning Sign language, reading, baking (Cake is her one weakness!), or chasing her twins around the park (because … cake).

She believes in happy endings, sweet romance, and plenty of mystery. She also believes there's enough angst on the news, so she keeps her stories light-hearted and full of hope.

While she claims Oregon as her home, she currently lives high in the Andes Mountains of Ecuador with her husband and two kids.

Made in the USA
Middletown, DE
20 July 2023